LAST CHANCE CHICAGO

DIANA DIGANGI

Bywater BOOKS

2022

Print ISBN: 978-1-61294-251-3

Bywater Books First Edition: December 2022

Printed in the United States of America on acid-free paper.

Cover designer: Ann McMan, TreeHouse Studio

Bywater Books
PO Box 3671
Ann Arbor MI 48106-3671

www.bywaterbooks.com

To my parents, for all of their support and guidance.

CHAPTER 1

NEW YORK, 2017

Sam didn't talk about her ex-wife in Cocaine Anonymous.

She liked to go to 12-steps at churches, that was her problem. The smell of a New York church basement brought her back to hypnotic afternoons spent in Sunday school, which made the boring parts go by that much faster.

Church meetings were mostly hosted by liberal Presbyterians, not the Catholics Sam grew up with. Sometimes when she hurried through the narthex with her head down, she would see a few female clergy going by in their robes. But even the most liberal church was still a house of God, and in God's house she couldn't say the words *my wife*.

"My ex-wife" was something she still wasn't saying to herself, months out from their divorce.

She could have gone to the other neighborhood Cocaine Anonymous meeting (Cokeheads Anonymous, she called it, when she was trying to be funny) but that one was at an LGBT community center.

Most people at an LGBT 12-step had lived hard lives. She couldn't look them in the eye and say, "I used to make almost three hundred thousand dollars a year. I used to help giant companies settle out of court after they lied, cheated, stole, and poisoned the water. I used to look out my office window over the Chicago River and do lines off my case binders."

It wasn't enough that she was gay. She was still a world away from them. And in meetings, she'd rather be able to talk openly about her career than about Amy.

She could talk about being a lawyer in the church meetings because those were the ones the Wall Street boys went to. Wall Street boys understood her—coke was almost always their undoing. Some of them were fired disgraces like Sam, the ones who had already lost their livelihoods and their marriages to their addiction, but some of them were still hanging on. Those guys came to meetings in nice suits and never talked, never looked at anybody.

The fired disgraces didn't envy the suits. If anything, it was the reverse. The suits were cloaked in panicky resentment, especially toward the guys who had already lost everything and then stayed clean for decades.

Sam didn't have to feel guilty when there were Wall Street boys around, and she wasn't scared like they were, either. She had brought trouble into her life and paid for it with everything, so the worst part had to be over.

The morning that trouble found Sam again, she was running late because of the subway.

She missed the C train by seconds. That meant taking the A and walking a few blocks down Greenwich Street, along the river, which wasn't ideal on a soupy fall day.

By then Sam was living in Chelsea and working a stone's throw away in Tribeca. When everything had gone really bad last year, her old college roommate Jess had called her up and lured her back to her hometown. Sam had been staring into the cold steel of the Chicago River like she was about to jump, gripping her phone, while in her ear Jess chirped: "Hey, why don't you go to rehab in New York? You can see your family, and maybe you can work with me at Byers for a little while! I swear Amy's gonna get past all this, she just needs time, okay? Just give it time, everything's so crazy right now for you guys. We could use you, we need another lawyer here."

Byers was the Tribeca crisis communications firm that Jess had left Chicago to work at six months after Sam and Amy got married. Sam didn't know the first thing about PR, but she was freshly fired and already broke from a bad shopping habit and a $200-a-day coke addiction before a judge slapped her with probation, a big fine, and $70,000 worth of court-mandated sobriety lessons. So a job was a job.

Sam and Jess had had a steady morning routine for about five months. They went to a coffee cart near work, complained about work while they waited in line, then walked to the office. The first few months Sam was at Byers, she didn't care enough to complain. The entire situation still felt temporary, like what had happened was a little squall on a summer day and not a hurricane that had left her for dead.

This delusion wasn't entirely her fault. While Sam was in rehab, she and Amy still talked on the phone all the time. They had started fumbling their way toward reconciliation more than once, only for Amy to spook like a horse every time Sam pushed for a decisive answer about their future.

"I can't, I can't," she'd say, angry and weepy. "I can't trust you. How can I trust you? You had this entire secret life, you lied to me every single day, and then you ran away to New York the second I asked for some space."

Sam begged for leniency, again and again. That person wasn't her—she was addicted. She had been sick. She was getting over it, like it was strep throat. She thought space was a literal concept.

Their calls dwindled, and in the end her protests came to nothing. Two years of marriage ended two weeks after she left her rehab center in Long Island City, on a sunny day in January when a bike messenger stopped her outside of her apartment.

"Are you Samantha DiCiccio?" said the messenger, who was only a kid, with cystic acne on his cheeks.

"Yeah."

He handed her a manila envelope containing divorce papers.

Sam held onto the envelope for a long time before she opened it. Just sat on the stoop and clutched it in her sweaty palms, trembling, until the sun started to sink below the Hudson. She already knew what was inside.

That night, she wised up: things were not returning to normal. Her wife was not coming back. No law firms were knocking down the door of the undoubtedly talented but notoriously mouthy attorney who had been busted for possession, to wit, of cocaine during a traffic stop and had her mugshot splashed on the front of the *Tribune*'s website the next day. Even their Chicago high-society friends, who had kept in touch when it still seemed like Sam and Amy were a united front against the scandal, began to drop away.

Jess stayed loyal, though. Jess kept calling.

"You're late," Jess called to her, shielding her eyes with her hand while she watched Sam hustle across the street.

Sam squinted at her through the bright morning haze. Jess was toward the front of the line, and when Sam sidled up next to her, the guy behind them sighed. Sam ignored him. If she were in a worse mood, she would advise him to kiss her ass, but it was Friday.

She turned to Jess. "Why are you doing *this*," she said, mimicking Jess's hand over her eyes, "when you've got sunglasses on?"

Jess felt for them where they were perched on her head. "Oh, no, these are to keep my hair from blowing around," she explained.

Sam let this go without comment. "I had to take the A," she said, in response to Jess's original greeting.

"Who are we blaming today?"

Sam gave it a few seconds of thought, then: "De Blasio."

Jess let her mouth fall open in mock offense. "No! My boy?"

"Your boy, sorry."

"Well, don't blame me. I didn't actually vote for him."

"Really?"

"I couldn't get away from work that day. But he's still my boy."

"Let's blame Cuomo, then," Sam suggested. "Send this thing all the way to the top, where it belongs."

"Good, I don't think I voted in that one either."

Sam laughed. "Jess, we were in college in Chicago when Cuomo got in."

"Oh, then I definitely didn't."

They moved up in line. Sam pulled a fresh pack of cigarettes out of her pocket and started hitting it against her palm to pack them.

"I forgot to tell you, we have a new client," Jess said, squinting up at her.

"Yeah?"

"Yeah, they're sending in a few execs today to lay out an action plan with Larry. I think he'll want you in the meeting. They're Chicago-based, actually. But I keep forgetting what he said they do."

Sam nodded. She had only processed about half of that. She found it nearly impossible to do small talk lately—it was like her head was bundled in swaths of cotton. Luckily, Jess kept talking no matter how monosyllabic she was.

The building they worked in was ancient, but had been overhauled recently into a gleaming, glass triumph of modern architecture that overlooked the Hudson. Once, Sam's cousin Bobbi had picked her up from work so they could go to midnight Mass with their grandmother, and exclaimed from the window of her GTO, "What is this, the fucking Javits Center?"

Byers Broadwell Inc. was on the fourth floor. They were a small team of nine fixers overseen by founder and CEO Larry Ochsner. Larry was a friendly, nonthreatening guy in his upper fifties who reminded Sam of the soccer coaches she'd had as a teenager. "Come on, team!" he was always saying, and when they did something that pleased him: "That's what I'm talking about!"

Sam tweaked him sometimes, out of fondness. "Good hustle," she had said the other week, when Jess got off the phone after bullying Page Six into pulling a nasty but true piece of gossip about one of their clients. Larry repeated this, grinning with pride.

It was obvious to Sam what Larry liked to hear. She had aced her interview with him—this in spite of the fact that she was only three weeks out of rehab and looked like it. But Larry almost seemed to respect what a disaster she was. It was the first thing he asked her about.

"So what brings a successful Chicago lawyer to a New York PR firm?" was how he'd phrased it.

Sam had given him a fake, toothy smile. She wasn't sure how much Jess had already told him, so best not to lie.

"I had to leave my job," she said. "And professionally, I'm a little bit of a pariah in Chicago right now."

Larry nodded. His office was all windows (as the entire building was one big window) and he was lit from behind by the noon winter sun, which turned him into a shadow-faced specter and made him look far more intimidating than he was. "Tell me more."

Sam inhaled, shifting in her seat. "I was, ah . . . I kind of got railroaded."

"Samantha," Larry said kindly.

"Sam."

"Sam. I work every day with people who've been railroaded.

Tell me the whole story so I can understand where you're at right now, and if this works out, what I can do as your boss to help you get back on track."

"Okay." She nodded. "I was on the partner track at my firm. My wife worked at a hedge fund. She was a vice president. We were looking at buying a house in Lake Forest, so I was working a lot. Sixty, seventy hours a week."

"I wouldn't expect you to do that for me, by the way," Larry said, and she laughed, then rubbed at her eyes with the back of her hand.

"I got addicted to coke," Sam said. She had gotten better at saying it out loud. It wasn't like she could hide it, after all; it was the first thing that came up when you Googled her.

Lawyer suspended after cocaine possession charge *Chicago Tribune*—3 months ago *DiCiccio was suspended from practicing in the Northern District of Illinois for 90 days after she was arrested for cocaine possession during a traffic stop . . .*

She continued. "It leveled me out, it let me work those eleven-hour days without getting burned out."

"And it was—" She bounced her leg. "It was part of the culture. We all did it. I'm not saying that to shift responsibility, I'm just saying, like, it's what lawyers at that level do. And I'm clean now, by the way. I'm sober."

Larry nodded. "Go on."

"I can pee in a cup, whatever."

He laughed. "We'll get to that later."

Sam looked down at her clasped hands. "I got pulled over during a traffic stop. I was driving erratically, 'cause I was tired. I wasn't drunk, I wasn't high. The cop said, why you weaving if you're sober? And I told him I'd just worked a ninety-hour week. He looked at me—I'm in a suit, with case binders in the passenger seat, and he says, oh, what d'you do? I could tell he already knew . . . I said I was a defense attorney. So he smiles, goes to his car and gets the K-9 out. And as it happens, I had a small amount of coke in the glove box."

"He did that just because you were an attorney?" Larry asked her.

"Yeah. I mean, that's Cook County cops for you," Sam said.

Amy had bailed her out after she spent three of the most miserable hours of her life cooling her heels in a chilly cell, waiting. The drunk who was in there with her had a nasty smoker's cough that rang out with upsetting regularity, like an alarm on snooze. Sam had sat there with her head in her hands, twitching every time that woman coughed, rehearsing what she was going to say to her wife.

She shouldn't have bothered. Amy didn't talk to her at all on the drive home. Sam tried, but she wasn't having it.

When they got back to the penthouse, Amy pointed at the couch, which was made up with blankets and pillows, then turned the kitchen light off and went up to their bedroom alone. Sam lay awake the whole night crying. The next day, Amy's face was puffy like she had been, too.

Over the next month, her life came apart like a ball of yarn picking up speed. An hour after her mugshot had begun to circulate with the local media, Bob Keating emailed her: *Sammy, I think you should come in so we can discuss your future here at the firm,* which meant she no longer had one. And after she had laid bare to her wife the full extent of her addiction, plus the ways in which she had lied to and manipulated her over the last year to hide it, Amy was silent for a long time before she said to Sam, "I think we need to take some time apart while I process this."

Sam gave Larry a condensed and unemotional recounting of these events, omitting Amy entirely. Larry had inhaled and said, "Well, I appreciate your candor."

Sam shrugged. "I didn't think I was going to get away with sugarcoating it."

"I didn't want you to. So you weren't disbarred, right?"

"Nah, I got off with probation, rehab and a suspension."

"Well, great." Larry spread his hands. "Look, every month I have more and more prospective clients coming from Chicago. I have a New York lawyer here, Alan, he's fantastic, but his experience is mostly in litigation. I need somebody who knows Illinois law, and corporate law. And to be honest, I'd love to have somebody around who understands what it's like to be . . . you know, pilloried. I think clients would relate to you, and open up."

Sam was surprised by this line of reasoning—that the mess she was in could be in any way considered a plus. "I totally agree with that," she said, lying her ass off.

"Great," Larry said, and hired her.

Now that she had worked at Byers for nearly a year, Sam had come to like Larry. He was more intense and sincere than she was used to, but he told the truth, and this transparency inspired great loyalty in his employees. She had forgotten that a boss could be like that, having been so long under the employ of Hughes, Roper, and the Keatings, who smiled at everyone they passed in the hallway but fired young associates often and with great pleasure. Larry always told everyone exactly what was going on, paid them well, and insisted that nobody work on the weekends.

So they all liked him, and for the most part they all liked each other, when they weren't jockeying for Larry's favor, since he had ultimate say in client assignments.

Depending on the case, Sam usually tried to sway him one way or the other with a pastry offering from her morning bagel run with Jess, but on that particular day she didn't bother. Executives from a Chicago business? She was going to get put on that account whether she wanted to be or not.

"Ladies," Larry greeted them when they poked their heads into the conference room for the morning meeting. "You're late."

"It's Sam's fault," Jess said, pointing behind her as she hurried into the room.

Sam spread her arms. "I had to take the A!"

"Because she missed her train."

"That was MTA's fault," Sam countered.

"Come on," said Trina. She was the prototypical PR agent—leggy, blonde and dish-faced. "Take some personal responsibility."

Sam laughed and sat at the far end of the table, with Jess at her right. This was how they always sat, even back in college when she would pore over her law books with Jess next to her, laughing like a hyena at BuzzFeed roundups of Tumblr posts.

Larry, at the head of the table, clicked a pen to get their attention. "Okay. So let's introduce our most recent client, because they'll be in around . . ." He glanced at his watch. "An hour, at the latest."

"They flying in this morning?" Sam said.

"They got in last night," said Larry. "I put two of them up at the Roxy."

"Why don't you let the clients get their own hotels, Larry, and keep the extra money for Christmas bonuses?" said Sean. Sean was an amoral twenty-five-year-old who had been poached from the staff of the *New York Post*, and he still acted like he was making *Post* money.

"Clients have to feel special," Larry demurred. "First rule of sales—make them feel good."

Trina laughed. "I thought the first rule is coffee is for closers."

"No, coffee is for everybody," Larry said cheerfully. "Anyway . . ."

He clicked a small remote in his hand, and the monitor behind him lit up with a PowerPoint.

"Our new client," he said, "is a Chicago-based mutual fund—excuse me." He coughed and cleared his throat. "I think it's a hedge fund, actually?"

Tingles began to trickle down Sam's spine, like her brain

was wringing itself out. She sat up straighter and focused on the screen.

"According to a report in Barron's, there are some securities fraud charges pending against them, which is making things difficult for them *vis-à-vis* investor retainment and recruitment. The fund is called . . ." Larry glanced down at his phone. "Atlantic Capital Management LP."

When it came to fight versus flight, Sam's body liked to pick a fight. The few times she'd been truly scared, like when she got mugged in college, her instinct had been to start swinging. But there was nobody to fight in the conference room. Larry continued to talk, his voice sounding tinny in her ears.

"Isn't that—" Jess sounded like she was a few steps behind, and then all at once she caught up. "Oh! Oh my God."

Their coworkers all looked over at her in curiosity. Sam tried to make her face into less of a desperate rictus.

"Everything okay?" Larry said. Behind him, his PowerPoint automatically transitioned to the next slide.

Sam nodded. "Um," she said. "Who—who all from Atlantic Capital is coming?"

"Well," Larry said. "Two senior VPs, Don and Dan. And then an assistant VP."

Normally Sam would say, "ha-ha, Don and Dan." But not right now. "Who's the assistant VP?"

"Her name is Amy, I think."

She dug her nails into her palms. "Amy Igarashi?"

Larry tilted his head. "Correct. Wait, you know her?"

"Yeah," Sam said. "Yeah, that's my ex-wife."

Everyone started paying a lot more attention then. Christiana, who'd been tapping away at her phone, looked up with interest.

"I didn't know you were married," she said to Sam. Obviously what she meant was, "I didn't know you were gay." It was in the shape of her eyes when she said it.

"Yeah," Sam said, and inhaled. The room had grown sharp and bright in the center of her vision, but blurry around the edges. "Our divorce went through in January."

"I remember this all being kind of amicable?" Larry wheedled her. "Right?"

Sam wasn't eager to hash it out in front of her coworkers, but she leaned her elbows on the glass table and did her best. The cream cheese that lingered in her mouth tasted like it was curdling. "No," she said. "I wouldn't use the word amicable. I mean, it wasn't a big blowup, necessarily. But we're estranged, we've been estranged. We don't talk."

Larry nodded, slowly. "Well, do you think you'll be able to work with her? I really need you on this."

"In a limited capacity, yeah, I don't see why not," Sam said, not quite believing it as she said it. She couldn't imagine even seeing Amy in person. What else was she going to tell her boss, though?

"Okay," Larry said, agreeable as ever. "We'll work around this as best we can, and see what we can do to make sure everyone's comfortable. Thanks for the heads-up. So, getting back to what we're going to try to do for Atlantic . . ."

Sam sat back in her chair, tilting her chin up and setting her jaw like she always did when she was on the back foot. No one was looking at her, except Alan, who was himself divorced and gave her a sympathetically grim smile. Larry's voice sounded garbled, like she was hearing him over a police scanner.

Jess scooted closer, looking stricken. "She knows I work here," she whispered. "I recommended us to her once, a long time ago, before you guys broke up. But she didn't say anything to me, like, even a Facebook message: 'Hey girl, it's been a while. I'm bringing my company to your freaking firm!'"

"She doesn't know I'm here now?"

"No, of course not," Jess said. "They wouldn't have come all the way out here if she did . . . Right?"

"Right," Sam murmured. For a few seconds she had entertained a wild fantasy where this was Amy's way of coming back into her life. It was nauseating what a short emotional leash she was still on. Even hearing Amy's name a few times had caused her heart to start throbbing in her chest.

Larry was still talking. She waited until he paused to clean his glasses, then asked him, "Why'd they come to Manhattan?"

He put them back on and peered at her. "Well," he said, "I think—I mean, first of all, we're one of the few elite crisis communication firms that counts most of its clients in the finance industry, as opposed to, say, politicians and conglomerates."

It was almost funny: Sam had only stayed in New York because she associated every inch of Chicago with everything she'd lost, and now the most important loss was a few blocks away, eating a continental breakfast. Or, more likely, drinking a milky coffee. Amy didn't usually do breakfast.

Chicago was a huge city. She probably could have stayed there and never run into Amy. In running, she had planted herself firmly in her ex-wife's path.

"And second of all, the company they're accused of colluding on insider trading with, it's here," Larry said. "A pharmaceutical company here in New York. I spoke with Atlantic's director, and he said DOJ is still determining where the charges will come down."

"Wait, so we don't even know where the trial's gonna be?" Sean said. "Because I don't have any pull with the press in Chicago."

"Can't they just tell us where they did it?" added Trina.

Alan laughed and rubbed at his cheeks. He was one of those guys who always had a five o'clock shadow even when he'd just shaved. "Yeah, that's a good legal strategy. Confess to your PR firm."

"Hey, we're not here to get involved with this case," Larry said, and clicked out of the PowerPoint as if to punctuate this.

"They have an excellent legal team, who I've been in touch with. We're here to rehabilitate their image, so let's don't get too deeply involved in this, any of you. We have other clients."

Sam said nothing. She was already too deeply involved.

CHAPTER 2

CHICAGO, 2012

Sam and Amy had been a setup, but they never said it like that when people asked how they met.

"At a party," is what they always said.

They had been introduced on a summer night in 2012. Tom Hardy's Bane was in theaters, and Mitt Romney's face was everywhere else. Sam had gone over early to Amanda's place to help cut up fruit for the punch, and to sneak more alcohol into it every time Amanda turned her back.

Out of everyone in their Class of '06, University of Chicago crew of friends, Amanda Deshaies was Most Likely to Play Hostess. At twenty-eight, she already had a gorgeous South Loop loft, with wide picture windows overlooking the park; this was because her parents were old money, something she was contrite about around their leftist college friends. For the most part they were all now employed in some selfless capacity: Erica taught at a charter school on the South Side, and Shane was a reporter at the *Tribune*. So, Amanda tended toward sheepish concealment when it came to her financial situation.

She spoke freely about money in front of Sam, though, because Sam loved money. Unlike Amanda, she'd grown up middle-class in Queens, but was already making six figures as an associate at Hughes, Roper, Keating & Keating.

Sam never felt right apologizing about money anyway. She hadn't gone to a top ten law school and taken all her internships at corporate defense firms so she could be a public defender, no offense.

"So this girl I texted you about," Amanda called to her from the living room, pink in the face as she fought to pull a stuffed lamb free from the jaws of her bichon frise.

Sam was cutting limes for the punch in the lofted kitchen. She stopped to take a break, resting her elbows on the marble island. "You said her name was Amy?"

Amanda looked up, her dark bob flopping around her face. She jerked her hand one final time and raised the freed lamb in the air like a trophy.

"Yeah," she said, then came back over to the punch bowl to stir it again. "We got into an accident," she added. "On I-90."

"Oh, this is the girl you smashed into?" Sam said. "You didn't tell me that part."

"I didn't *smash* into her ..."

"Yeah, yeah."

"And I did tell you that," Amanda said, with prim amusement. "You have selective hearing. That's why I invited her tonight, to apologize."

Sam nudged her. The sun was setting over the city by then, flooding the apartment with orange. Jess would be here soon, and then the rest of their friends would trickle in. "Alright, tell me more."

Amanda shrugged. "She seems nice. She wasn't mad that I hit her. She wanted to make sure I was okay. She's pretty."

"Job?"

"She mentioned it, but I forget. Something fancy. She drives a Beemer and she had on, you know, a pretty expensive suit."

"And you're sure she dates women," Sam pressed her.

16

"Yes! I told you. I was like, let me take you to lunch while they work on your car. We went to get poké. She mentioned an ex-girlfriend. I said, oh, I know, it's so hard being single in the city. And she said, yeah, I forgot how hard. She's on OkCupid, or something, but she says everyone on there's a weirdo. And I said, you know, not to be *that* person, but I've got a lesbian friend who's single and cool and you should meet her sometime."

"You show her a picture of me?"

"Ooh. Yeah, that didn't occur to me."

"What year is it again, Amanda?"

"I was shaken up, okay? I'd been in a car accident."

"Alright, alright."

"I like her for you, though," Amanda said. After a moment more of deliberation over the punch bowl, she poured a can of LaCroix in. "She has a certain classiness to her."

"Good," Sam said. "Opposites attract."

Jess arrived later than expected. Jess was always late, and always in a hurry. She had almost been kicked out of her sorority three separate times for tardiness to meetings, but each time had cried her way out of it.

She looked even younger than she was, and she was already so young that Sam hadn't actually met her in college. Sam had just finished undergrad and was a 1L at the University of Chicago Law School when she posted a request for a roommate in one of the Facebook groups, and a freshman PR major named Jessica Galvert popped into her inbox.

Sam knew Jess had arrived as soon as she buzzed up, because she always and unnecessarily buzzed three times. "That's Jess," she said, getting to her feet on the third buzz.

"Oh, good," Erica exclaimed. Her boyfriend lifted his craft beer in the air like he was toasting the idea of people arriving to things.

Everyone was pregaming, playing quarters. Sam had opted out, so as not to become sloppy. "I might go let her up and then go to the bodega," she said, feeling her back pocket for her wallet. "Anybody want anything?"

"No," several of them chorused.

"She's nervous about her date," Shane said, as if Sam weren't in the room. He jerked his chin to Amanda, who smiled. "She's gonna go buy cigarettes."

"I am not," said Sam, who in fact was. "Fuck off."

She went downstairs to let up Jess (who was encumbered with a case of beer, paddles for beer pong, an umbrella and a raincoat, and who needed help getting onto the elevator) then headed around the corner for smokes.

"Hey, is it raining bad?" she shouted as the elevator doors closed.

"Pouring!" Jess yelled back. "Hailing, probably, I don't know—"

"Great," Sam said unhappily.

It was summer, late July. Years later, Sam would still think of Amy every time it rained on a thick, hot summer night. The sun hadn't quite set yet, and the golden city felt fully alive with echoing honks and people running down the sidewalk, ducking under awnings, newspapers over their heads. Jess's reports of hail were exaggerated.

Sam took shelter under the overhang outside the corner store so she could light up. Traffic crawled to a stop in front of her. An older guy sat in his Buick a few feet away, his radio cranked up. She recognized the song he was blasting.

It sounded like Eric Clapton, but it wasn't. She gave it a few more beats, taking deep drags and letting the nicotine work on her nerves. No, Elton John.

"*My dad told me Amy's your name*," sang Elton, his voice pouring out the car window, and Sam laughed out loud.

The guy in the Buick glanced over at her, smiling. She smiled back at him.

Amy was late to the party, which Sam did not yet know was very unlike her.

"If this girl blows me off," she said to Jess, when the party was in full swing and they had both retreated to the kitchen area to pilfer from the hidden stash of Stellas in the crisper. "I kind of want to text Melissa to come by. She's in town. She snapped me from O'Hare yesterday."

"Please do not text Melissa," Jess begged her. She was bent over the fridge, looking around for snacks. Amanda wasn't the type to keep snacks. "You guys were so toxic."

"It's just I got ready, and I'm, like, feeling it tonight," Sam said. "I don't want to waste a good mood."

She didn't add that she had been painfully lonely lately, although she had been. It was getting hard to work seventy-hour weeks and come home bleary-eyed to nothing and no one. She went out with the other associates a lot after work, and she would often drink too much just so she would fall asleep faster that night and not dwell on her thoughts as she did, not lie awake in her big empty bed, listening to Chicago's sirens moan out her window.

Jess stood up and studied Sam. She was a finely built ceramic bobblehead of a person, and alcohol affected her almost immediately. Her round cheeks were pink and her fine chestnut hair was askew.

"Well, don't call Melissa," Jess said. "I don't like her."

"I know, but I don't think you got the right picture of her. I blew her off a lot, I was so busy at work last winter . . ."

Jess sighed at her. Sam was stubborn, and twenty-eight years in, people had been sighing at her for her whole life: her parents, her teachers, her friends, her girlfriends, professors, now judges, now bosses. And yet she continued to get her way. At some point it had started to feel like the sigh was just an admission of defeat.

"Alright, alright," Sam said. Jess was one of the few people she hated to argue with. "I won't."

"Good!"

Sam wandered away from her, back to the party, bringing the beer to her lips. Amanda's view was even better at night, its daytime panorama of the park and skyline turned into a glittering dark sea of shapes and pinprick yellow lights. The loft was filled with people by then, laughing and trying not to spill their drinks.

Amy got off work late as usual.

She left the office at 10:10 and doubled back to leave a series of four Post-it notes on the desk of her administrative assistant. Amy loved Post-its. She loved the constraints of the small squares, and the satisfaction of ripping one off, then firmly sticking it to a glass door or a desk phone or a piece of paper.

PLEASE CALL BILL DEMECK, she scrawled. Despite the fact that she was deeply type A, her handwriting was chicken scratch at best. Luckily her assistant Kelly was a pro at deciphering it. Sometimes Amy's coworkers would peel her Post-its off their office doors and bring them to Kelly, asking with a chuckle, "Sorry, what the fuck does this say?"

Amy stuck it to Kelly's desk.

HE IS WORRIED ABT INVST. IN CBL&A

Stick.

NEED MTG. W/ HIM THIS WEEK TO REASSURE

Stick.

CHECK MY SCHL. & LMK, THX!

Stick. She hurried out of the office, black umbrella in tow.

There weren't any cabs, so she called an Uber. She didn't like to ride the L this late at night. Amy was a worrier and a New York girl, so if she was going to get mugged to death on a train, that train would be underground, thanks.

In the back of the Uber she scrolled through Instagram. It was Saturday, and everybody else had been off, brunching or having picnics by the river.

"What are you up to tonight?" said the driver. He had a pleasant voice.

Amy put her phone down with some difficulty. "Just a party."

"Ahh."

"Has tonight been good for you?"

"Oh, yeah," he said. "Busy."

Amy glanced down at the app. His name was Maurice. "That's good." She kept saying the word *good*. She didn't know how to talk to Uber drivers, or hairdressers, or anybody like that. Her dad drove cabs for years and, as far as she knew, never chitchatted with his passengers. He was always worried about his accent.

"Is this a side gig for you?" she said. "Uber?"

He nodded and made eye contact with her in the rearview as they slowed to a stop in traffic. Amy squinted against the rain-pattered reflection of the high beams from the car behind them.

"I play trumpet in a jazz band most nights," Maurice said, then smiled at her, pantomiming fingering the keys with his right hand.

"Oh, cool," exclaimed Amy, who loved jazz. She leaned forward so he'd go on.

It wasn't love at first sight, but familiarity. Game recognized game.

Amy saw Sam first.

Amanda met her at the door, exclaiming in delight that she was there, taking her wet raincoat from her. Amy checked her watch, because she was one of those oddballs who still wore one and kept it accurate. Ten-forty.

"I'm so glad you could make it," Amanda said after a hug. "Did they manage to smooth your bumper out? God, I still feel so shitty."

"They did their best," Amy said, smiling at her. "Honestly, it's fine. It's not like I look at my bumper much."

Of course it did bother her, as a perfectionist, to have that one small dent in the otherwise flawless surface of her BMW. But being dicky to Amanda wouldn't fix it.

She saw Sam, then, over Amanda's shoulder. She was walking by. No—strutting, like a boxer. Amy liked that.

Sam seemed to feel eyes on her, because as she took the step up into the elevated kitchen, she swiveled a bit on her heel and flicked her gaze toward the entryway. They studied each other.

Sam didn't exactly smile, but her eyes danced with curiosity. She was attractive with strong features—sandy hair, hooded eyes set deep under thick brows, an aquiline nose. The rest of her face was delicate. She wore a little makeup, but less than she could have, as if she were trying to minimize the delicacy.

Amanda noticed they were looking at each other. "Sam," she called over to the kitchen. It was hard to get someone's attention in a loft like this because the air was cluttered with a half-dozen other conversations, but Sam heard and inclined her head. "This is who I wanted you to meet."

"Amy," Sam called back.

"Yeah," Amy replied, swiftly cutting out the middleman.

Sam smiled then, in a way that made Amy's palms prickle with sweat. "You drink beer?" she said.

The din rose. People in the living room were cackling about something. Amy nodded instead of trying to talk over it.

Sam held out a Stella and beckoned her. She went over, leaving her coat with Amanda.

Amy sidled up to the marble counter, leaning her elbow on it while Sam opened their beers. The loft was a picture of artful discomfort—exposed brick, clashing patterns, furniture that looked more like sculpture. The kitchen was lit by a hanging overhead strip of lights, a black wrought-iron bar that hung ominously low. This allowed Amy to see that Sam had dark under-eye circles and one or two premature gray hairs. It made her more attractive, not less.

"A little presumptuous," Amy told her.

Sam freed the second cap with a little pop and handed her the beer with a smile. "Huh?"

There was a coarseness to her voice that Amy liked. She sounded like she was from New York, and her voice seemed to come from deep in her gut, not up in her head.

"You asked me if I drink beer," Amy said. "You didn't ask me what kind."

Sam's smile widened. "What, you're too good for Stella?"

Amy laughed.

"Look how fancy the bottle is!" Sam said. "It has foil on it and everything."

"I'm kind of a beer snob," Amy admitted.

Sam took a sip from her own beer. "You don't look it," she said.

"No?"

"No, 'cause you look employed. When I think female beer snob, I think . . ." Sam took a moment to collect this image in her head, squinting at the ceiling. "Tattoos, definitely."

"A topless mermaid."

"Exactly. Or a pinup. Either way, topless."

"I don't have any tattoos," Amy admitted.

"And you're obviously corporate," Sam said, with a twinkle in her eye. "Since you're coming from work, and you're dressed like . . ." She gestured. "That."

"Is corporate a bad thing?"

"No, I'm extremely corporate."

"Okay, then I'll cop to that," Amy said. "So I guess I have to drink piss."

"Guess you do."

Amy gamely chugged half the bottle. It was mostly tasteless, and made her nostrils sting. Sam watched her.

"I want some of that punch, though," she added, wiping foam from her lips.

"Long day?" Sam said.

"Very," Amy said. "But it was self-inflicted." She was what guys in finance called a *hardo*.

"Oh, that's relatable."

They went out onto the balcony to talk more, because for all the surely very interesting conversations going on inside, the only people they really wanted to talk to were each other. Plus, the rain had stopped.

The air was thick with lakefront humidity, but they had a nice view of Dearborn Park. Sam guided Amy out, opening the door for her and then touching her lightly but confidently on the lower back as they stepped out into the muggy air.

"Okay, hit me with the headlines," Sam said. They both went for the railing and rested their elbows on it, then looked at each other. "Who are you? Besides a victim of Amanda's driving?"

"Sorry," Amy said. "Before we get into this whole thing—you're single, and you date women, correct?"

Sam laughed at this and turned her head to look out over Chicago, which felt like a bad sign, but then she said, "Yeah. Yeah to both."

Amy knew she was coming off tightly wound, so she said, "I

don't like to waste time, is all."

"Hey, me neither." Sam studied her. "Did you come to this party just to meet me?"

Amy gave a frazzled laugh. She was having a hard time being smooth. "Yeah. I did. I mean, Amanda seems nice, but she's the only person I even know here . . ."

"You're not missing much. You wouldn't have a lot in common with them," Sam said.

"You sound confident about that."

"Yeah, well, you're too together. They're not. I love my friends, but they're not. They're very much still figuring it out."

"You seem to think you know a lot about me."

"I'm good at reading people," Sam replied.

"I think that's for other people to say, not you," Amy teased her.

Her eyes twinkled. "Alright, then you tell me."

"You thought I didn't drink beer."

"You're right, I fucked up that one. But I'm not wrong that you're together."

Then, without warning, she took Amy's wrist in her hand. Amy's skin got hot where her fingers landed. Sam eyed her, then brought Amy's watch up close for inspection.

"I knew it," she said, dropping her hand. "Wound to the minute."

Amy ran her tongue over her teeth, trying again not to smile. "Why wear a watch otherwise?"

"See?" Sam crowed.

"Okay, headlines," Amy interrupted her. "I work in finance."

"Cool."

"Please, it's not cool, I know it's not."

"It is cool! I love money," Sam said, like she truly didn't give a shit. Looking at her, Amy could almost believe she didn't.

Below, a siren wailed. They both peered over the railing as an ambulance went by, its flashing lights catching rain puddles and making them glow red.

"Well, what do *you* do?"

"I'm a corporate defense attorney at one of the firms downtown," Sam said.

This phrase was clearly unwieldy in her mouth. Amy wondered if she usually said either "corporate lawyer" or "defense attorney" and had smashed these together to sound more villainous, just to make Amy feel better. It wasn't like corporations hired prosecutors.

"Okay," she said, nodding. "Okay. So you've got it together, too."

"Thanks, I like to think so. What do you do in finance?"

"Um, I help manage a hedge fund. I'm an associate."

"Oh, shit." Sam whistled, which was charmingly old-fashioned of her. "I bet that's not fun to admit to these days."

"Are you kidding? I usually don't even tell people, literally."

Sam laughed in appreciation.

"So, other than that . . . BA from Northwestern, MBA from Harvard," Amy concluded.

"Thanks for being upfront about that."

"Oh, trust me, I can't stand the 'I went to college in Boston' thing. I like baseball, craft beer, good food. I like jazz."

"What about family?" Sam felt the breast pocket of her button-down, then pulled out a lighter and a pack of Marlboros from her jeans. "You care if I smoke?"

"I don't love it, but go ahead." Sam smiled crookedly and went ahead. "I have an older sister. My parents moved us here from Japan when I was . . . one? Maybe a little older?"

"To Chicago?"

"No, New York."

"No shit?" Sam said in delight, her voice muffled by the cigarette. It waggled between her lips as she spoke; she was trying to light it despite the breeze. "I'm from Queens."

"Oh, I thought you might be," Amy said.

"Yeah?"

"Yeah, it's the accent. You talk slow."

Sam blew a little smoke at her. "Watch it," she threatened with a smile.

"What neighborhood?"

"Forest Hills. What about you?"

"I grew up in the Heights. My family's still there."

"Oh, a real New York girl, I like it. Mets or Yankees?"

"Oh, Mets, definitely."

"Good. Pets?"

"Nope. No time."

"Same here," Sam said wistfully. "I want a dog so bad. But lately I've been putting in a lot of seventy-hour weeks."

"Seventy? Are you partner track?"

Sam shook her head. "Trying to get there."

Amy finished the last sip of her punch and found that between that and half a beer, she was lightheaded and getting warm in the cheeks and chest. She leaned forward into Sam's space, which made Sam's eyes twinkle again. She liked it when they did.

"Are you a nice lawyer?" she said.

"A nice lawyer," Sam repeated huskily. She smoked some more, and looked contemplative. "What's a nice lawyer?"

"Are your clients innocent?"

"Sometimes," Sam said.

"Yeah? Can you always tell?"

She smiled. "I don't think about it."

"How can you not think about it?" Amy said in curiosity. "That's all I'd be able to think about."

"You don't think you could defend somebody you thought was guilty?"

"I don't know. I guess I'd want to know for sure first."

Sam laughed. "Even if it made your job harder?"

"I like honesty," Amy said.

27

"I mean, I massage the truth for a living."

"Well, that's work. This isn't."

"No?" Sam said, finishing her cigarette. "Because I'm working pretty hard here."

Amy laughed and looked out over the skyline again, her face growing a little warm.

They never went back to the party. The attraction was there, and it went past the chemistry of a good conversation. It was electrical impulses in their lips and hands and muscles.

Sam was a great kisser, despite tasting sour like cheap beer. She made the hairs on Amy's arms stand up, and her legs go weak, neither of which had ever happened before. That was mostly why Amy went home with her that night.

"I never do this," she whispered in the back of the Uber. It had started raining again, and her voice barely carried over the swish of the wipers. "And I'm not just saying that. I know everyone says that."

Sam smiled at her. Her teeth gleamed in the dark. "I know you're not."

"How do you know?"

She said nothing. She just kept smiling.

Years later, what Amy would think about when she looked back on that night was just how many times Sam had admitted she was a liar the very first time they met.

CHAPTER 3

THE SEC, PART I

Money had always been the linchpin of Sam and Amy's life together.

They both loved it and the more they made, the more they made. In the summer of 2015, Atlantic had a management shakeup, and Amy snagged a senior assistant VP spot. The hierarchy of the hedge fund didn't seem to have the internal logic of a law firm: besides the CS guys, it was an even split of analysts and traders, and the analysts were all ascended traders, but beyond that, seniority was barely a factor. Paul made analysts into VPs at will, like he was firing a T-shirt cannon. He kept the team balanced by firing just as indiscriminately.

Amy worked almost exclusively with overworked dicks and blowhards, so the fact that she never walked into Paul's office coked up and screaming obscenities at him eventually paid off for her. He created the position of senior assistant VP for her, which put her above the VPs but below the senior VPs, like mayonnaise between two slices of bread. She got a huge office that overlooked the river (Sam's office did too, and they used to call each other on their desk phones and talk dirty while they looked out at the same water) along with a salary package of $550K.

Sam had found that suspicious. Amy was only thirty at the time, and bonuses aside, it didn't make sense for a hedge fund to be so liquid in 2015 that it could pay the overblown salaries that Paul was handing out like gumdrops. But she wasn't going to dwell on the *hows* of it all when the two of them were bringing home close to $800,000 a year.

That was outrageous money for someone from her part of Queens, and she started dressing like a complete idiot. Amy stayed chic, but Sam bought crazy Gucci belts and ostentatious jackets. She used to fly home for Christmas and get a Porsche 911 from the Hertz Rent-A-Car at JFK just to drive achingly slow through her old neighborhood, so everyone she grew up with could watch her out their windows and die of jealousy. Bobbi once opened the front door just to scream, "SUCK MY DICK," at her as she went by. Sam blew her a kiss.

Sam saved barely anything. Amy was far more frugal and had a wide portfolio of investments, but as a couple they spent like sailors. (Sam had been informed by a stern rehab therapist that her charisma made her a chaotic influence on otherwise reasonable people.) They spoiled their parents, moved into a lavish penthouse, went on vacations that cost a fortune, and paid for bottle service at clubs. Their ritzy wedding at The Langham Hotel alone cost upwards of $100K, on top of the $25K that Sam had spent on Amy's engagement ring.

As far as they were concerned, the good life was never going to end. For Sam, that illusion had fallen apart almost overnight. Now she had to wonder if the same thing was happening to Amy.

Fifteen minutes before Don, Dan and Amy were due to arrive at Byers, the Keurig shit itself and died.

Sam had put a pod in and turned around to get her half-and-half out of the communal break room fridge when the Keurig let out a long, spastic *KKKRRRR* noise and then began to violently expel soupy coffee grounds all over itself and the floor.

"Jesus Christ," she said, and unplugged it.

Alan came in behind her and jabbed her companionably on the hips, then reached past her to grab a plastic fork out of a box of them on the counter. "What'd you do?"

"I didn't do anything," she protested. "I just put a pod in."

Alan stirred his tea with a fork. Sam watched this, unnerved by it. "Is there an error code?" he said.

"I dunno. I unplugged it."

Alan nodded and plugged it back in. He was stocky and handy. Due to the generally fussy nature of their PR-bred coworkers, he and Sam ended up doing most of the dirty work around the firm. They were "legal consultants" by title, but their clients only needed so much lawyering, so their fine legal minds were mostly put to the work of figuring out how much pressure they could put on a reporter or a client's wayward employee without breaking the law. Threateningly open-ended phone calls, ominous visits to people, filing endless cease and desists, picking out obscure lines of NDAs and interpreting them at will: all of these were within their purview.

Alan was about fifteen years older than her, and had worked as a civil litigator at a Brooklyn firm for most of his career before being laid off. He never went back to the law after that. Sam had asked him once why not. She missed practicing like crazy, and couldn't imagine having given it up if she hadn't been blackballed.

"Sammy," he said, smiling wryly. "It's not a real life. You know that, right?"

But Sam did not know that.

Alan was now typing the Keurig's error code into Google. He eyed the results and shook his head. "Yeah, I have no idea. I don't like this thing, anyway. Nobody has the time to brew a pot of coffee?"

Sam folded her arms tight and leaned against the counter. "I just needed some quick, before Amy gets here."

Alan nodded. "I'll make you a cup of instant."

This calmed Sam somewhat. Her dad always made her instant.

"I don't want to see her," she said, without having meant to say anything. It just jumped out of her, and stung her sinuses as it did.

Alan looked up at her. "Hey," he said, "it'll only hurt for as long as it's happening."

Sam took in a long breath. "Yeah."

"I had to sit across from my wife in mediation and listen to her attorney explain why I shouldn't get weekends with my own kids," he continued. "All because she wanted to move them to Seattle. It was hell. I had the shits for a week leading up to it, I had nightmares where all my teeth fell out. But then—" he snapped his fingers. "It was over. I walk down the courthouse steps, it's a beautiful sunny day, and it was over."

Sam nodded slowly.

"Look," Alan said, "most cases like this, they'll come in today and give us their sob story, and then head back to Chicago. Maybe we'll fly Trina out there or something, but when's the last time we had a client from another state hanging around here?"

"What if charges come down in New York?"

"But Amy's not the one getting charged, is she?"

"We don't know that." Sam said this without thinking, and then the full meaning of it struck her. She hadn't even considered that Amy could be complicit. Insider trading just wasn't her— she was a rule-follower who had always feared running afoul of the SEC.

"Look, you're probably the last person she wants to see, too. Once she finds out you work here, she'll want to get back to Chicago in a hurry."

"You're right," Sam said, and nodded. "Hey, I'm sorry about your wife."

Alan handed her the cup of instant. A little spilled onto his palms, and he brushed his hands off on his pants. "Don't be. She was a piece of work. I'm sorry about yours."

With that, he left her to her thoughts.

"Guys?"

Amy looked up from her BlackBerry. She'd been neurotically scrolling through her email, even though she had an away message: *I am out of the office until Friday, October 13. Please contact kellynunes@atlanticcapital.com if you need immediate assistance.*

A man was standing there in the lobby, hands in his pockets, shadowed by the noon glare coming in through the windows. She'd only spoken to him over the phone, but she figured he must be Larry. She said his name aloud, as a question, and he smiled and came over to shake all their hands.

"Hi, Larry, I'm Don—nice to meet you—"

"Don, hi there, great to see you guys—"

"Larry—Dan, nice to meet you—"

"Hey, Dan, thanks for coming all the way out—"

Amy had not done her usual amount of homework on this place, and she was relieved to see that the building was gorgeous and Larry was well dressed. Her boss, Paul, Atlantic's chief investment officer, had come into her office exactly a week ago and thrown a stapled-together stack of bad press on her desk. "Find us a fixer," he'd barked, and in a panicked rush she dug out the business card Jess had handed her several years ago. She got Larry on the phone, and he soothed her well enough that she hired him that same hour. Jess's presence at the firm was an afterthought.

He extended his hand finally, and gave hers a good solid

pump. "Amy, right? Great to meet you."

"Hi, yeah, you too."

Amy was vibrating with anxiety. She had been trying to remain in denial ever since the SEC probe started being reported on last month. Then she'd be skimming the *Tribune*'s front page on her phone, or get a worried call from an investor, and she'd find her hands were clammy and all the blood was leaving her head. "Hey, it's Andy Dikowitz. I'm just calling because I'm kind of concerned about this stuff I'm hearing, this whole thing with the *SECURITIES FRAUD*?"

It always felt like that, like it had been screamed at her. Even though much to the contrary, clients usually whispered it as if they thought Atlantic's phones might be tapped, which they probably were. "The, ahh, the *securities fraud?*" When she scanned the newspaper for coverage on them, those words leapt off the page, making her head seem to float like a runaway balloon and sweat pool in her armpits. The *SECURITIES FRAUD!* She always felt, abruptly, like she was being watched by a hundred eyeballs, like she was reading the *Chicago Tribune* in front of a grand jury.

Charges were coming down soon. They knew that much. That's part of why Paul had put her on this—he got a call from his friend in the DOJ. "Get your ducks in a row," the guy had said, *"fast."*

Amy had no idea what that meant. Jeffrey was the one who told her—he was a senior VP, but she had no respect for him because he was an overgrown frat boy who slept in his office with the door open, snoring. "'Get our ducks in a row'?" she had repeated. "What the fuck? Like, start destroying evidence?"

"*Shh,*" hissed Jeffrey. He was convinced that every inch of their office suites was bugged. When he first said this to her, with a dead serious look on his face, she had gone on the analyst team Slack channel and said, "Jeffrey is a fucking paranoid schizophrenic, a paranoiac," which everyone had thought was very funny. It wasn't quite as funny now.

Their entire office loved the Scaramucci rant and quoted it to each other all the time. It often made her think of her ex-wife with a pang; it was so quintessentially New York Italian. When the article first dropped, she had wanted badly to call Sam up, or at least text her, *Did you see this Scaramucci thing?* If they had still been together, it would be an inside joke of theirs, like how they were always quoting the coffee scene from *Glengarry Glen Ross*, or *Wolf of Wall Street*. She could imagine it so clearly.

Presumably, someone higher up than she was, was getting Atlantic's ducks in a row. Amy had passed the chairman of the board in the hall more times in the last week than she had in six years of working at the fund. It made her lightheaded each time she did.

Despite this, she kept telling herself that she wouldn't be called to testify. She had been on the account, yes; she'd written most of the pitchbook for it, been involved in both the purchase and the sale, but she had only had the most limited communication with Zilpah Drugs. Why would they call her up? There were nine people in the hierarchy above her. They wouldn't call her up.

"We're on the fourth floor," Larry said, jarring her from her ruminations. Amy nodded. As they walked, she lagged behind him and Don and Dan, who were both senior VPs. Her heels clicked on the marble and echoed in the lobby: the sound of being the only woman in a pack.

The elevator took a while to get down to them. It looked to be the only thing in this building that hadn't been recently overhauled. Inside, Amy leaned against the back wall and inhaled, briefly closing her eyes. She could never seem to draw a deep enough breath these days.

Sam saw Amy first.

She had an involuntary reaction, like anaphylaxis. Her throat closed and her vision swam.

Amy was as lovely as ever, though thinner, and her dark eyes darted around as she followed Larry through their suite of offices to his own toward the back. She had two men on her heels (Don and Dan? Dan and Don?) and a wool coat folded over her arm, dangling. Too hot here for that. It must have been a colder October in Chicago.

Sam noticed all of this in the instant Amy spent wafting gracefully by. But Amy, preoccupied as she likely was, didn't once glance through the glass walls and see her ex-wife sitting behind a desk, staring at her.

Jess, who shared an office with Sam, glanced up in time to see one of the Atlantic guys walking by. "Oh, shit," she exclaimed. "They're here?"

"They're he-ere," Sam said under her breath.

"You okay?"

Sam went over to the window, shouldered it open and put a somewhat crumpled Marlboro 27 in her mouth, then lit it. "Don't worry about me," she said, the cigarette wagging.

"I wish you wouldn't smoke," Jess said, and gave her a doleful look.

Sam thought of how Amy came to hate her smoking after they'd been together a while. She used to hide Sam's cigarettes, or use a red Sharpie to circle the surgeon general's warning on them and add perfect little exclamation points. She had always worried about Sam so much. It hurt to recall.

"Sorry," she said, and leaned her arm out the window to ash. "If I ever needed to smoke in the office, now's the time."

She looked out at the sparkling Hudson, which was reflecting the bright sunshine back into her eyes like steak knives.

Sam had never let Jess in on how badly in love with Amy she still was. Jess had never asked outright, and Sam had never volunteered the information. She suspected Jess could tell, regardless.

"She's going to smell the smoke and then she'll know you're nervous," Jess said. "You're giving up your home turf advantage."

Sam laughed appreciatively. She blew out a lungful of smoke and turned back to Jess. "I think she's gonna know I'm nervous when I walk in there shaking. How do I look?"

She messed up her hair. Amy had always liked it when her hair was mussed, although usually only when it was by Amy's own hand. When Sam did it herself, Amy laughed the pleasant, tinkly laugh she reserved for when Sam did things she found cute, then fixed it.

Jess studied her. "Like yourself?"

Sam groaned.

"I don't know." Jess pursed her lips and gave her another once-over. "I think you look better than you did a year ago. You don't look so sad anymore. I mean you still look *sad*, but it's like, in a less mopey way I guess."

"Brooding," Sam said, and smoked some more.

"Yeah."

"There's worse things to be."

"Yeah!" Jess repeated, with more energy. She sounded like the sorority girl she was when Sam met her.

They went back into the break room, followed by Sean, who darted out of his own office when he saw them walk by. He went over to the Keurig, only to have Alan slap his hand away.

"Don't touch," he said. "You want a cup, I'll make you one."

"Why?" said Sean. "Are you in a Keurig union?"

"Sam broke it," Alan said, pointing at her with the butter knife in his hand, which he appeared to have been using to dig around in the machine's innards. "I got it working again, sort of.

It'll stay working if no one touches it."

Sean eyed the scene, considered the "sort of," and made a face. "I'll have a Red Bull," he said, opening the fridge. "Hey Sam, your ex is *really* hot. Holy shit."

"Careful," Sam warned him.

"That's a compliment!"

"She's very pretty," Jess agreed. She had always mooned over Amy, who was put together and did tasteful things like pair an all-gray outfit with canary yellow accents. Meanwhile, Jess still sometimes shopped at Forever 21.

"Yeah, be grateful," Alan said. "That was downright gentlemanly. When I got divorced, Sean pulled up her Facebook and congratulated me."

"Hey, hey, that was about the fact that she was fucking around," Sean said.

"You said '*woof woof*?'"

Sean flapped his hand and turned from the fridge where he'd been rummaging. He hadn't found any Red Bull, but he did have a handful of those canned Frappuccino Doubleshots, which he offered to everyone.

Sam shook her head vehemently, but Jess took one. "We used to mix these with Burnett's in college," she said. "It tasted exactly like Bailey's."

"Okay, I doubt that," Sam said.

"Try it!"

"Well, anybody got alcohol in their desk?" Sam said. "I have to go into the conference room . . ." She checked her watch, and her heart lurched. "Like, now."

Sean raised his hand. "I do."

"Maybe only go in there smelling like alcohol or cigarettes, not both," Jess said.

"I'm kidding. You know I don't drink anymore, anyway."

Larry appeared in the doorway, clapping his hands to the sides of it and giving Sam a guilty smile. "So."

Sam sighed and wiped her sweaty palms on her pants. "Yeah?"

"I'd like for you and Alan to come join us."

"Just them?" Jess said.

Larry nodded. "The rest of you guys focus on your own clients today."

Jess reached out and squeezed Sam's arm. "Good luck," she said.

Sam smiled at her; then she and Alan followed Larry down the hall. The sun was still pouring in the windows relentlessly, making Sam squint. Each step she took made her feel an inch shorter. She fell behind as they entered the conference room, coming in last, folding her arms and leaning against the wall next to the door.

Amy was right there, seated, only feet away. Her sleek dark hair pooled where it was tucked over one shoulder. A muscle in her jaw was tense, and she didn't look up at Sam entering. She must have received prior warning.

"Don, Dan, Amy," Larry said, "I'd like you to meet Alan and Samantha, our in-house legal counsel via New York and Illinois, respectively. Obviously, Amy, you and Sam are acquainted."

Sam caught and squashed a laugh in her throat. *Acquainted.* Larry, shut the fuck up.

Amy met his eyes. Even though the look wasn't directed at her, Sam felt it like a glass of ice water in her lap.

"Obviously," she repeated, her voice thin.

"And I'm so sorry about this," he went on. "I had no idea—until Sam told me this morning, I didn't—I mean, what a crazy coincidence."

"Amy hired us because Jess recommended the firm to her years ago, when she first came onboard," Sam said, and paused, surprised to find herself speaking. She wet her lips. "It's not the craziest coincidence ever."

"Maybe an inconvenient one," Larry said graciously.

Amy nodded with an oddly robotic jerk of her head. Her lips had all but vanished, tucked into her mouth. She was staring at a fixed point on the wall.

Sam felt magnitudes better than she had in the hallway. Dread was killer, and confrontation was something she found she still lived for. Beneath the grief, she was grimly giddy. She wanted Amy to look at her so badly.

Larry was glancing between them with growing unease, like he'd just let a bunch of snakes loose in the room.

"Well," he said, and clapped his hands. "Let's get down to business."

"Yes please," chorused Don and Dan.

Alan snapped to attention and pulled out a chair for Sam—at the head of the table, so she wouldn't face Amy directly—before sitting beside her.

Larry took his own seat next to Dan, patting him on the arm. "So, guys," he said. "Tell us all about your troubles."

Don and Dan both looked to Amy then. Don steepled his fingers beneath his chin, and Dan tucked his lips into his mouth. Despite, or maybe because of their seniority, they seemed to be inviting her to do all the talking.

Amy cleared her throat. "Zilpah Drugs is a pharmaceutical company here in Manhattan. They were in development on a new type of opioid. They had claimed to us, as well as their other investors, that it would only be half as addictive as Oxycontin, but just as effective a painkiller."

"Huh," Larry said. "Sounds like a great investment."

"It did," Amy said. She was so tense that her arms and shoulders didn't move as she spoke. "It sounded too good to be true, but they showed us results from clinical trials that backed up that claim."

"These trials were done on people?"

"Yes. People and lab mice."

Larry clicked his pen. "And they weren't real?"

"They were fraudulent, correct. Everything started to unravel for us after the FDA told the SEC to start investigating Zilpah, and the SEC's attention turned to us."

"Right. Atlantic had invested how much in Zilpah?"

"We purchased fifty million dollars' worth of shares," Amy said.

Sam was just barely able to stop herself from sucking air in through her teeth.

"In a company whose shares are now selling at a fraction of their previous value," Larry said.

"Right," Amy said.

"But you sold your shares for . . ."

"About forty-five million, all said and done," Amy said.

"So obviously you guys managed to avoid falling off that cliff with them," Larry said, and clicked his pen again. He was usually masterful at saying accusatory things like that without putting the client on the defensive, but Sam could tell Amy was getting her back up anyway. "And the feds think that sale wasn't on the level?"

"Yes. According to a DOJ source we have, the SEC found evidence of, um, what they believe to be—they believe that we had insider knowledge of Zilpah, that there was someone in the C-suite who we were in communication with who told us that they had rushed through their clinical trials and manipulated the data, and that the FDA wasn't going to approve the drug. Basically, they think we found out we had bad stock on our hands and got a tip-off so we could dump it."

Sam looked over at Larry, who was nodding as he processed this.

"And you deny that totally," he said.

"Yes, we do," Amy said, but her voice wasn't strong when she said it. "We can provide evidence that our decision to sell was motivated by independent factors, we even wrote up a cost-benefit analysis—"

Larry put his hand up. "Don't get into the legal side with me," he said. "That's Sam and Alan's job."

What he actually meant by that was that he didn't want to know if they were guilty or not, but Sam didn't either. It wasn't her job to know. However, that made it hard to tell how serious their exposure was. Atlantic had either clipped a bumper or crashed into an iceberg, and Amy's face wasn't betraying anything.

"I just want to know what your public stance has been so far," Larry said.

"We haven't really had one," Amy said. "Obviously we're in a very bad place. We've been staying quiet."

"How fast did the stock drop in value?" Larry said.

"Over the course of one day, the valuation went from more than two hundred dollars down to fifteen dollars a share," she said.

"And you sold it soon before that?"

Amy was quiet for a moment, staring at the table. "We sold the stock at open that same morning."

Alan cackled at this. "Holy shit," he said. "Uh, okay."

Sam opened her mouth, then closed it, then opened it again. "It'd be in your best interest to settle up with the SEC as quickly as possible," she said. "Legally, you have an uphill battle here. You might be able to stop the bleeding if you can settle for paying a penalty fee."

Amy looked at her for the first time then, and Sam's heart dropped. Amy's eyes blazed, and her mouth was a tight line, but she wasn't without vulnerability. As soon as Sam looked away, she became aware of how hard her heart was pounding.

As if to break the tension, Alan said, "Who supervised the stock sale?"

"A lot of us had a hand in this investment," Amy said. "I worked on the pitchbook. I wrote the investment thesis. Don and Dan have both communicated with Zilpah . . ."

Don and Dan nodded in confirmation. They didn't seem to

have anything to contribute besides nods.

"Paul Weller, our chief investment officer, he probably had the most contact," Amy said. "And he authorizes any large purchases or sales. He authorized both when it came to Zilpah."

Sam eyed Amy. She was holding back information, Sam could tell, but what information might that be?

Alan looked over at Sam. "Looks to me like charges would come down in Chicago," he said.

"No, we don't know that," Sam said, then turned to Don, Dan and Amy, looking between them fast enough that she could avoid direct eye contact with her ex-wife. "How often is Paul between New York and Chicago? Did he fly out for personal meetings with Zilpah, or was his correspondence with them over the phone or email?"

"Dude," Don said, like she was straining his mental capacities with these two simple questions. "We don't know. You'd have to ask him."

Now that Sam was getting a good look at him, she recognized the telltale signs of cokeheadery. He was thin in the face, and he kept sniffing, plus there was a familiar teeth-grinding agitation to him. He was probably dying to squirrel away to the bathroom for a hit.

"Paul took several meetings in New York," Amy offered.

Sam dared to make eye contact with her again. Amy was staring her down with quiet desperation. She was rattled, and Sam recognized the look on her face. Not from being married to her, but from court. She had the wide rabbit's eyes of a witness under duress. It made Sam's sweaty palms prickle and the back of her neck itch.

"So is the DOJ coming after Weller in both states?" Sam said, to her and no one else.

"Samantha," Larry interjected. "I'd like to get away from the legal details for a moment, if we could—"

Ignoring him, Amy said to Sam, "We don't know. We don't

know that Paul is the one being charged."

"Okay," Sam said.

Getting these details out of her felt like towing a car along by a length of rope that tore at her palms as she tugged on it. Amy had never liked facing painful facts directly. Sam felt a brief, vindictive thrill over how miserable and frightened she was, but then it was gone, and all that was left behind was a desire to protect her. Like both a lawyer and a wife, she didn't care what Amy had done. It wasn't her job to care.

Amy looked down at the table. She was wringing her hands in her lap, Sam could tell. She had nothing else to say; her lawyer brain was busy digesting what it had heard. She inclined her head toward Larry, giving him permission to go ahead with his PR machinations. Larry smiled at her and mouthed *thank you*.

Sam stood up. Everyone looked at her.

"I have to do some research on where you guys might be vulnerable," she said. "Research" as in pulling up her old .epub of *Criminal Procedure: Second Edition* on Amazon and poring through every chapter she'd been too hungover to do more than skim as a 1L. "I'll loop you all in on an email when I know more."

"Sounds good," Larry said, and launched into his standard first client meeting speech about creating a new narrative.

Amy turned her gaze to him, and once again it was as if Sam weren't in the room.

CHAPTER 4

TOM AND PAUL

Jess came over with her boyfriend that night—uninvited. Sam didn't even have the chain on the door undone before Jess was yelling through the crack at her, "You should recuse yourself!"

"I should what?" Sam said, and let them in. They were carrying bags of Chinese food from her second-least-favorite place in the neighborhood, which they dumped on her tiny kitchen table, on top of the printouts and textbooks she had lying out.

"We were talking about this in the car," Trent said, by way of explanation.

He was only carrying one bag, because he still had a sling on his right arm. He was the star pitcher for the Binghamton Rumble Ponies upstate, but was on the IR list while he recovered from Tommy John surgery. That's where he had met Jess: at physical therapy. Jess had sprained her ankle stepping out of an Uber back in July. Sam had watched her do it and still had no idea how something that slapstick could happen in real life.

"Talking about what?" Sam said. Jess went behind her into

the crappy, cramped kitchen and started banging around in her cabinets. "I got paper plates," she yelled to her without turning around.

Sam didn't worry about bothering her elderly roommate, Edgar, because he was never home. He was dating a woman who worked for the comptroller, and he practically lived over at her place now. The only unfortunate thing about this was that the two of them had made it halfway through Ken Burns' *Jazz* together, and Sam didn't want to finish it without him, but she did want to finish it.

"No, you have to eat like a human being," Jess said in her best kindergarten teacher voice. "And be nice to the environment."

"I don't have a dishwasher."

"I'll wash the dishes."

"Oh, c'mon, you're a guest, I don't want you washing the dishes."

"We were talking about this problem you got," Trent said. "With your ex?"

"But what do you mean, recuse myself?" Sam looked at Trent, who was unloading the bags of Chinese food onto her table. "No offense, but you guys aren't lawyers, so do you even know what that means?"

"Um," Jess said, and returned with plates and flatware. "It's like, you have a conflict of interest, so you take a step back. You *excuse* yourself. You excuse-slash-remove yourself."

"Alright, yeah, but recusal's for judges, not lawyers. By the way, you guys didn't have to bring me all this food ... thank you, though."

"You can Venmo me, like, eleven bucks," Trent said, with an air of generosity. Then he sat down, dumped nearly an entire container of lo mein onto his plate, picked up a fork and started twirling it into his mouth. Trent Rizzo: he was the kind of Italian boy her mom would have wanted her to date, if she were straight. Her mom had always liked Amy, though.

"No bev, Trent?" Sam said to him. He shrugged.

"Jeff Sessions recused himself from the Russia thing," Jess said, sitting down next to Trent and taking the mouse's share of lo mein. "He's not a judge."

Jess was a lot smarter than she came off, which Sam had always liked about her. You couldn't be an idiot from a middle-class Wisconsin family and get into U of C. She had a way of poking right at the tender reality of a situation; they weren't talking about Jeff Sessions, they were talking about how much Sam still loved Amy.

"Prosecutors, I meant," Sam amended. "And I'm not actually representing anyone in court, here, so what are you really trying to tell me?"

Jess flicked her gaze up at Sam, her glittery eyeshadow sparkling in the low light. "Alan said you were staring at her in your meeting," she said. "Looking at her like, you know . . . not in a very lawyerly way."

Trent paused with a forkful of lo mein in the air and glanced between them. "Oh shit?" he said as a question.

Sam ignored him. "I was married to her," she said. "I can't look at her like I've never met her before."

"He said you looked at her like there wasn't even anyone else there."

Sam flushed in her face and chest, stiffening. "Alan's getting old. He's losing it."

"I'm just saying," Jess said. "I don't want you to get too involved. I don't want you to get hurt by her again, okay? I think you should tell Larry to take you off this."

"If they're facing charges in Illinois or from the feds, they're gonna need me."

"Why can't they use Alan? Is the law that different between states?"

"It can be, depending. Federal law's mad different. There's different judges, different precedent, different courts . . ."

"But they *have* a legal team," Jess said. "They came to us for fixers."

Sam finally took a seat then, and opened a container of fried rice. It looked lousy, but she took some anyway. She'd forgotten to eat all day. "They need my knowledge on libel and stuff," she said. "In Illinois, specifically. Their lawyers are gonna be busy defending them in court. They're not gonna have time to hit back against *ABC7* and the *Trib*."

Jess reached out for a fortune cookie. "Okay," she said, with reluctance. "I guess."

"Hey," Trent said, "the cookies are for after."

She flapped her hand at him. "I wanna know my fortune."

Sam watched as she crinkled open the packaging and cracked open the cookie, then unfurled the piece of paper. "What's it say?"

Jess's brow knit. "'It's a good thing that life is not as serious as it seems to the waiter,'" she read aloud. "What do you guys think that means?"

"Whoever wrote that doesn't like waiters," Trent said with his mouth full.

When the two of them had gone, Sam went up to the roof to smoke and call her sponsor.

Her phone screen had cracks spiderwebbing across the glass, which was common among addicts, although Sam had cracked her screen when she was two months sober. For a while she had what she called the depression fumbles, where objects just leapt out of her hands.

She could get a new phone if she wanted. Despite her credit card bill, she was making decent money, and she still had plenty of stuff she could pawn for extra cash—a mink coat, Rolexes, half her clothes and all her jewelry—but that stuff was all she had now. It was the only reminder that she had once lived a fabulous life, and she kept it to shield her from the full weight of her mistakes. Sam never cared about fashion; she just wanted real leather on her feet, a nice watch on her wrist, and gold on her neck. It was about what you were saying to the world.

When she'd been out at bars with the other associates until 3 a.m. on a weeknight, drinking like a maniac and then jolting herself out of her slobbering stupor with a few lines of coke in the bathroom, it was Theory and Ralph Lauren and Gucci that protected her from suspicion. Bouncers, cops, eagle-eyed bartenders: they all managed to ignore the well-dressed white woman stumbling, babbling, vomiting, her pupils huge. It was Tom Ford perfume that Amy smelled when Sam crawled into bed, sloppily apologizing for her lateness, assuring her that they'd just been celebrating a big win.

Her phone was different. Sam was the only one who was looking at it all day, and she didn't think she deserved better than cracks. Besides, she'd probably just drop the new one anyway. She was fumbly again today after seeing Amy.

Her sponsor had been sober for eighteen years, which was like several thousand in sobriety time. Jackie had the solid, fleshy face and upper body of a fisherman, plus a Roman nose and fierce amber eyes that made her resemble a hawk. She was also kind of mean. The whole effect was sexy, which made Sam glad Jackie was straight, because she'd heard all that stuff about the thirteenth step and to watch out for your sponsor.

"Hello," Jackie barked when she picked up.

"Hey," Sam said. "Any meetings tonight?"

"Not those coke ones you like, no. But if you want to come to NA, there's one in an hour down St. Francis."

"Aww, I don't like NA," Sam said. "Everybody there looks at me like I'm a stuck-up bitch."

"That's bull and you know it," Jackie said. "You just don't like being around active addicts."

"Can you blame me?"

"Yes. You think you're better than them?"

It was getting cold up here. Sam lit another cigarette, chaining it off her old one, and sat down on the roof ledge. "Nah, not at all."

It was true they looked at her like she was a bitch, but that wasn't why she didn't want to go. It was more, that whole opioid thing gave her the willies. She wasn't exactly miles away from them: uppers needed a downer, if you wanted to sleep or eat at some point. Her downer of choice was just usually alcohol or Xanax.

"There's an AA at Saint Peter's, but it's starting right now," Jackie said.

AA wasn't bad. There were usually more people there who were where she was—about a year sober and starting to feel the drag of inertia. Sam was about to ask her which Saint Peters she meant when she got a text message.

"Um," she said to stall for time, taking her phone from her ear, putting Jackie on speaker and swiping downward.

It was from an unknown number.

Hi. It's Amy.

Sam got light-headed. She scooted off the ledge and sat down against it, smoking furiously for a few moments, then continued to read.

I know this is incredibly inappropriate, but can I talk to you in person? I need legal advice, and I need attorney-client privilege. You can bill me.

It was like a punch to the mouth, so impersonal as to be an obscenity. You can *bill* me?

"Fuck you," Sam said out of reflex.

"Excuse me?" Jackie demanded.

She had totally forgotten she was on the phone. "Jesus, no, not you," she said. "I, uh. I just got a text from my ex-wife."

"Whoa," Jackie said, sympathetic for the first time all phone

50

call. "You need me to come over?"

"Nah, it's cool, I'm good," Sam said. Her heart was racing, and all she wanted was to be left alone to agonize privately. "I'll, uh. I might go to AA. I dunno. I'll text you."

"Okay," Jackie said, sounding disbelieving. "I'm here if you need me."

"Bye."

Sam hung up and flung her lit cigarette off the roof in a fit of pique. Whatever, man. What-the-fuck-ever. It was beginning to feel like there would never be an end to the indignities of life.

She would go, though. Of course she would. No doubts about the prudence of going to see her ex-wife, alone, could possibly penetrate her thick skull.

From the roof she watched as the sun went down. The whole world was lit in pretty gold; even the dumpsters got to be gold at this time of day. From up here, she could see the river, and the lights of little boats twinkling as they tugged along on it.

Amy had rejected Larry's offer of a room at the mid-rate Roxy and was instead putting herself up at an expensed $550 a night in a leafy and dimly lit boutique hotel owned by Robert De Niro. Truth be told, she resented the fact that Dan and Don were along in the first place. They were only there to be white men inside of suits; they knew nothing about what was going on and couldn't be counted on for the most basic insights or analysis. In fact, Amy suspected that they had been sent along just to keep an eye on her.

She would have rather had Jeffrey with her, because at least he was as nervous about this entire thing as she was, but that was part of the problem. When she had asked him to come, his face went a bloodless white, and he said he had to work on the 2018 Strategy Outlook all week.

The fact that both Dan and Don were senior to her was insulting. Neither of them had even gone to a target school—Dan went to *Duke*. *Puke*, Sam used to call it, but she admitted she was just jealous because Chicago's basketball program was so lousy.

Amy kept thinking about Sam as she waited for her. How could she not? Like a caged tiger, she paced her lavish and fragrant suite. This place was designed to relax you by any means necessary, but it felt like an expensive jail cell. No, no, better not to let her thoughts go there.

Sam had texted her back, miraculously, and with enough of her usual dry humor that Amy felt reassured. *Lol you don't actually need to pay me up-front to establish privilege . . . but I would not say no to a pack of smokes. Where are you staying?*

The Greenwich, room 622, she said, then typed fifteen different versions of "thanks" before settling on a simple, *Thank you.*

Np, Sam said back, like a teenage boy. That indicated that she was probably feeling passive aggressive. Well, fine. Amy could deal with a little chilliness from Sam if it meant staying out of federal prison.

While she waited, she lay down on the bed and agonized there in the sheets. Her anxiety was constant these days: her heart had seemingly expanded to fill her rib cage, stifling her breaths and making her pulse into a metronomic ache; she sweated constantly; she had the runs all the time. She was sweating right now actually, so much so that she pulled the blanket over herself because her room was a cool sixty-nine degrees and she was clammy.

Sam always knocked rudely. BAM BAM BAM! The moment you realized she was there, you were already feeling guilty for not getting to the door sooner.

Amy scrambled out of bed and slipped back into her heels, which she'd discarded by the balcony door. She didn't want to face Sam one-on-one without full armor. She looked at herself in the mirror as she went by the bureau, and was satisfied to see that she was still sort of gaunt. It was impressive to be gaunt, as long as your clothes weren't hanging off you and you didn't yet have knife elbows and a zombie face. No one had to know that her weight loss was accidental.

She turned off the Kamasi Washington she'd been blasting, dragged in a breath and opened the door.

Sam was a half step back from the doorway. She was in more disarray than she had been earlier in the day. Her dress shirt was untucked, collar wrinkled, her sandy hair messy. Sam seemed to be subject to a more violent entropy than anyone else on Earth. Even at the funerals Amy had accompanied her to, big and somber Catholic ones for distant relatives, Sam would slowly become undone over the course of the day. No amount of hairspray and sitting still in church could restrain her baby hairs or keep her shoes unscuffed.

Sam smiled at Amy with far more tenderness than Amy thought she deserved. She didn't seem chilly at all.

Amy smiled back, her face tight. "Come on in. Sorry about the mess."

She stepped hugely back so Sam could enter, and Sam lazed her way down the little hallway, inspecting everything as she went.

"This is a mess?" she said. "What, your robe's on the floor?"

"Well, and the iron is out," Amy said.

"Oh my God," Sam deadpanned. "Didn't see that. Disgusting."

Amy sighed, because she wasn't in the mood for sarcasm, but Sam turned back to her and shot her another smile.

"Here," Amy said, handing her a little CVS bag. "As requested."

Sam took it and peered at the contents. It was a pack of 27s. She seemed sort of sad to see this, for reasons Amy couldn't guess at.

She said "Thanks," though, and pocketed it.

"Come in," Amy said, walking her deeper into the suite. There was a dark wood breakfast table in a nook by the window, still littered with empty half-and-half containers from her coffee that morning. "Sit."

They sat. Sam had a look on her face like she wanted to light a cigarette, but was restraining herself. "So you need a lawyer, huh?"

"I need legal advice." Amy stared at the tabletop. She hated making eye contact with anyone lately, let alone her ex-wife. "I'm going to present a hypothetical situation to you, and then I'd like it if you could, um, tell me what someone should do in that particular situation."

"Ames . . . look, did you do something illegal, or not?"

Her fluttering heart grew sickeningly bigger, taking up even more room, encroaching into her throat. "I don't know."

"Alright, hold on, stop talking," Sam said, sounding harried and standing up as she said it. Amy was afraid that she was going to turn and leave, but all she said was, "Give me your phone and your laptop and whatever else."

"Give—what, you think I'm bugged? Like on *The Sopranos?*"

"That shit doesn't only happen on *The Sopranos.*"

"You really think they'd bug me?"

"I have no-o idea, because I don't know what you did," Sam whispered, "but erring on the side of you are, let's turn everything off and go in the bathroom."

Amy thought this was paranoia, but she gathered up all of her electronics, feeling fumblingly awkward under the watchful eye of Sam as she supervised. She handed over her phone, laptop, and her Apple Watch Series 3 ("I don't need *that,*" Sam said with a laugh, but took it anyway), and Sam turned them off and then tossed them on the un-slept-on side of the bed—the left side, her own side when they were married.

In the bathroom, Sam got the water running then turned the shower on. "Okay," she said, sliding the glass door shut and stepping back toward to Amy. In the close quarters there were only about ten inches between them, which made Amy hug her arms to her chest. "I think that's as good as it's gonna get."

"Would a bug even be admissible in court?"

Sam did that infuriating thing lawyers often did, which was to nod slowly and begin, "So . . ."

"Just a yes or no answer, please."

"Okay, well, depending on the bug, and the limits of their warrant, most likely no. And I think I could easily get one thrown out, if I were, uh—I mean, I'm not representing you—"

"I didn't ask you to," Amy reminded her.

"Okay, good, don't," Sam said. "I don't want to."

"I didn't ask!"

"If I *was* representing you, I'd get it thrown out, but the worry isn't so much that they use it in court as it is that they use it to inform their investigation. You know?" Sam cocked her head. "Like, they hear you tell me something incriminating—then they know where to look to find evidence you did something incriminating."

Amy sank down onto the edge of the tub, the cool glass against her back. Sam sort of comically took a seat on the closed toilet lid, her elbow on her knee and her fist pressed to her mouth. Amy's mom once said that the way Sam always hid her mouth was the sign of a habitual liar. Amy told her Sam wasn't a liar, she was just arch. It turned out they were both right.

"I didn't do anything," Amy said.

"Okay."

"It's about what I didn't do, really."

"Okay," Sam said, raising her eyebrows.

"Hypothetically, what would you advise me to do if I was pretty sure that Paul Weller were guilty of insider trading?" Amy said very softly, to her feet.

Saying it out loud cast a film of unreality over her vision, and everything within the field of it started to look absurd: toes,

Louboutins, Carrara marble tiles.

In her periphery she could see Sam's feet, too; she had on scuffed and dirty Chelsea boots. As she noticed this, Amy's breath was stolen by a stab of affection for her familiarity.

Sam was quiet for a while, then whispered: "I know I can't smoke, but can I hit my vape?"

Amy laughed. "Yes."

Sam took a slim object out of her breast pocket. "So you lied in our meeting? Hypothetically."

"Of course I lied, hypothetically. It wasn't like I could speak freely in that room."

Sam smart-mouthed, "But what about your cost-benefit analysis?"

"Don't be a dick," Amy pleaded.

"Sorry." Sam hit the vape, then exhaled sweet, pungent vapor into the air, which was already getting thick and humid from the shower running. "This could be really bad for you, Amy."

"I know."

"How long have you known?"

"How long have I known it's bad for me?" Amy joked.

Sam, to her relief, laughed.

"First, can we abandon the fake hypothetical? Either you're in this with me or not. It's okay if you're not."

Sam appeared to consider this for half a second, then hit her vape again and said, "I'm in it."

"You don't have to be," Amy said, making eye contact with her. "You can leave right now. I'd totally understand."

"Too-oo late," Sam sang. "Keep talking."

"Okay, if you're sure," Amy said. "Um, he back-channeled me on communications with Zilpah, because I was so involved in the investment. He was the one who brought the idea to me, but I wrote all the literature."

"Right, you said."

"Early in the year, when they were still wooing us as

investors, I went out to lunch with the COO. That was the last time I directly spoke to anyone there. Then at some point in May, Paul came to my office early, before the market opened. He'd gotten back from meeting with Zilpah in New York the night before. He told me we were going to dump that stock at open. I said whoa, no, they're down twenty points from when we bought in. That's nuts."

She stopped to gather her thoughts, and let out a small exhale.

"At what point in May?" Sam urged her.

"Oh, I don't know. Late May? Paul said, 'Amy, I'm making the executive decision—we are dumping this stock.' I told him that we were sitting on a gold mine if they had really made the product they said they had. I remember clearly that that's what I said, because after I did, he looked me right in the face and said, 'I don't care. I need you to dump the stock.'"

"Did you take it he was implying the gold mine wasn't actually there?"

"No," Amy said. "I thought he had a hunch. He has these incredible hunches—he's a genius investor—so my first thought wasn't insider trading."

"Even though he'd had that meeting?"

"Well, that was what I asked him. I said, Paul, did something happen in New York, did the meeting go badly? Does Zilpah look like a shitshow behind the scenes? He didn't respond to that. He just started telling me the details of the trade, and that we would have to lower the stop loss. That was urgent stuff, so I didn't ask any more questions."

"All of that didn't seem weird to you?"

"It did," Amy said. "It did. But I thought there could have been any number of explanations." She bent over her knees, wrapping her arms around them, a curtain of hair tickling her calves. "The stock tanked the next day. We barely sold in time. It went into a death spiral, and I started hearing rumors about the

SEC investigating Zilpah."

Sam sucked in air. "Okay. I mean, that's purely circumstantial. I don't know what kind of case the feds have already built against Paul—"

"That's not all. He brought the COO out to dinner a few months later."

"The same one you went to lunch with?"

"Yeah, Tom Naftalis. He's close friends with Paul actually— they were in the same final club at Harvard. It was me, Paul, and Tom ... Paul got drunk, and he kept, like, clapping Tom on the shoulder, going, my boy saved our asses! Tom was laughing and shushing him."

"You didn't ask him what he meant by that?"

Amy shook her head. "I was too afraid. I wanted to just assume the best. I wanted to think we just got lucky ... but the more this SEC noose tightens, the less I'm able to think that. At this point, it's pretty obvious to me that there was active malfeasance."

Sam sat there on the toilet, vaping, her face drawn in concentration. "Okay," she said after a moment. "Okay. Look, if you weren't in the position you're in, with having overseen this sale, I'd say fuck it. Don't tell the feds anything. Because then you're a whistleblower the rest of your life, and for what?"

"Right, of course," Amy said. "That's exactly why I haven't come forward. If Paul found out I was testifying against him, he would ruin me to discredit my testimony. And you don't even understand how wealthy and well-connected he is."

"No, I get it. But the facts being the way they are, I think you have to volunteer this information to save your own ass."

Amy's gut clenched. "Is that a sure thing?"

"Yeah. Look, from what I've heard, someone at Atlantic is going down for this. Pretty obviously it should be Paul, but you need to make sure it isn't you. Did you execute the sale yourself?"

"No, I'm not a broker, you know that. I provide analysis."

"But did you order a broker to short the stock?"

"We didn't short it. You're thinking of a different thing. I just relayed Paul's order to sell, and I set the stop loss. It was his decision. I cc'd like ten different people on it, like—if I thought I was committing a crime, would I cc ten people? Would I cc fucking anybody? Would I send an *email?*"

"You'd be surprised."

"Come on."

"I get it," said Sam. "I do. But this is why you need to go to the feds. You want to cut a deal before they subpoena you."

Amy nodded, still staring at the floor as the shower roared behind her and the room kept filling with steam. "Is there a way to do that without my name getting out? Without anyone finding out it was me?"

"I don't know," Sam said. "I've never handled anything like this. Terra incognita. I wish I could tell you more, but I don't want to talk out of school."

"No, I understand," Amy murmured. "I never knew you to have whistleblower clients at your old job."

Sam laughed. "Yeah, whistleblowers were nothing but a pain in my ass back then."

"So, um . . . could the feds subpoena you too, now?"

"About this conversation, if they knew about it? Yeah."

"What about attorney-client privilege?"

"Doesn't apply here, hon."

Amy was comforted by the "hon" and also disquieted by it. "Shit," she said. "I don't want to get you in trouble."

"Hey, I'm only in trouble if you told me about this," Sam said in a teasing tone. "But I don't think you did, did you? I think I came up here to drop off some paperwork from Larry, and then I went to an AA meeting."

"Right," Amy said, remembering who she was talking to. Sam had never been afraid to bend the rules. "That's what happened."

"Oh, and this goes without saying, but you need to get a lawyer."

"Right."

"And not one who's representing Atlantic. You need someone to advocate for you specifically."

Amy nodded some more.

"Why did you come out here, anyway?" Sam said. "I thought you always said Paul was the public face of the fund. He's the one who goes on Charlie Rose and shit."

"He's having me do more of that work lately," Amy said. "He's reduced his public role by a lot."

"That's suspicious."

"I agree."

Sam didn't go to AA. Fuck those drunks, and fuck their alibi. She went home to Forest Hills, with the mindlessness she'd had as a kid coming home to this same stop.

It was a good thing, too, that she'd done this trip so many times, because she didn't look up once the whole time. Her vision stayed fixed on a point three feet in the distance, unseeing, as her brain lurched sickeningly between hope and paranoia. *She wants me back in her life.* SHE'S USING YOU. *She texted me. Me. No one else.* SHE NEEDS A LAWYER, SHE'S A CON ARTIST, SHE KNOWS SHE'S SCREWED AND SHE'S USING YOU. *She smiled at me.* SHE DUMPED YOU WITH A SUBPOENA. *Yeah, but she smiled at me, though. She laughed at my jokes.*

She couldn't tell Jess what she was thinking because Jess would have an episode about it. And everything she'd say would be right, which would just be so obnoxious. She'd validate the miserable paranoiac, instead of stuffing the hopeful idiot with more hope. Did Sam have any friends who would validate the idiot? She didn't really have that many friends anymore. She'd ditched all her college friends for high society snob friends when she married Amy, and then the high society snob friends had ditched her when she fell from grace.

She still had parents, though, and at the very least they probably had pasta fazool.

Sam came up above ground around 10 p.m., blinking against the streetlights. The grand facade of Ridgewood Savings Bank stood resolute as always across the street, welcoming her home. She hadn't been back in a while.

She was ten blocks from her parents' little postwar house, and she walked them sweatily, shaded somewhat by the rows of leafy trees that lined every street in this neighborhood. Her mind continued to jitter as she walked. She looked for familiar neighbors on their porches, but anyone old enough to be porch-sitting in the evening had gone to bed by now.

Her dad, Sal, who she'd texted warning of her arrival, greeted her at the door and hugged her like she'd been away fighting in World War One. "Mel," he called to her mother. "You gonna put Candy Crush down? Your daughter's home."

"I'm not playing—hush!" Mel yelled back from somewhere, likely the kitchen. "You want a drink, honey?"

"I'm not drinking, Ma!" Sam called back as Sal led her through the entryway and into the living room, where New York 1 was on their large TV at volume 52. The ticker scrolled: *Hurricane Sandy, five years later . . . Search for motive continues in Las Vegas mass shooting . . . White House plans to withdraw from Obama's Clean Power Plan . . .*

Sal let out a scoff as Trump's face came up on the screen, then changed the channel to *Hogan's Heroes*. He'd disliked Trump for decades, though for his own esoteric reason: he felt betrayed that Trump had forsaken his Queens roots to grovel for approval from the Manhattan elites.

"I mean like a water or something!" Mel clarified.

Sal took a seat in his usual recliner, and Sam sat on the leather couch, which had seen much better days. "Yeah, water's good, thanks," she shouted.

Mel came in with ice water in a chipped coffee mug, handed it to Sam, then perched next to her on the couch. The mug said *Shuh Duh Fuh Cup* on it.

"What brings you out our way this late?" she said, reaching up to stroke Sam's head. "Your hair's a mess."

"Ma, come on." She sipped the water. "I just walked, like, twenty blocks."

Sal peered at her over his glasses. "What's up? You look weird."

That was all she was hearing today: reports about how weird she looked. Apparently Amy's presence in New York was visible on her face.

Sam, who was generally truthful with her dad, said, "Amy's company's in trouble, they're getting killed in the local news and the trades, and they came to Byers for help. So I saw her today. Twice."

"Ohhhhh my fuckin' God," Sal exclaimed to nobody while Mel crossed herself, like they were Silvio Dante and Paulie Walnuts getting screwed out of a truckload of dishwashers.

"Guys, it's fine," Sam said, putting up a hand. "It's cool. I just talked to her, actually. I went to see her—"

Sal put his finger up, pointing fiercely. "You stay away from that snake," he said. "She humiliated you, she abandoned you, she's stuck-up, Upper West Side trash. You decided you have to marry girls, fine, but you marry a nice girl from the neighborhood, you fucking gagootz. Let a woman with some values take care of you."

"You know, Steph Raccone's daughter Lucia, I think she's like you. I just saw her, and her hair's an inch long," Mel said, squeezing Sam on the shoulder. "She went to Rutgers—very smart."

"I'm not trying to get back together with Amy," Sam exclaimed. "She needed legal advice, that's all."

"Don't you give her any legal advice," Sal said, turning his attention back to the television. "Jesus God, you are hopeless, you. Finally you're starting to get your life back in order, here, and you let a snake in your house. You know, I'm not surprised to hear she's in trouble."

"I counseled her briefly and told her she needed to hire a lawyer who wasn't me. It's not her fault. She didn't do anything wrong. Don't *worry*, Dad."

"She tell you anything that could get you in trouble?" Sal said, getting up and walking down the hall into their little galley kitchen, slipping out of view but making plenty of noise rattling around in the drawers.

"No," Sam called back, "not really . . . but if anyone asks later on, I've been with you guys since eight tonight, okay?"

There were a few beats of silence, and then he went "*Agh!*" like she was killing him.

"Just in case!"

"Hon," Mel said, her dark eyes wide and searching Sam's face. "We worry about you, we do. You've been doing so well lately."

"I'm doing great," Sam assured her. "I'm fine, I swear. Job's good. I've been going on dates. I have my friends."

It was half a lie—she was dating, and her job and friends were fine, though she was not—but she had to lie to them. She was an only child of two Italians, which in itself was a goof, but they had had some fertility issue that they only ever vaguely alluded to. Sam was their miracle: she had all of their hopes pinned on her; she always had. She was both son and daughter, jock and brain, joy and pride, success and caretaker. Her mom's biggest grief about her coming out had been the loss of grandchildren, even though Sam assured her she'd find a way to have kids anyway.

63

She hadn't even wanted to move so far for college, but Chicago was the best school she got into, and her dad insisted that she go. "Go west, young man," he said. "Seek your fortune." And then she ended up falling in love and getting the big job and staying. In her gut, she'd always intended to come back to her family in Queens. She had wanted to buy one of the big Victorians here and fix it up, raise a couple kids there with Amy, and that way Amy could be near her own family, too. Sam's world was here: her mom and dad, her grandma, her aunt and uncles and her cousins: Bobbi, Sticky, Tony, Ed, Marissa, and Chrissy. Hector at the deli on Queens Boulevard, who called her Sammy Sosa, was here. Even Jess had ended up in New York. Sam could have had it all.

The money was never supposed to be the thing. The penthouse and the Rolexes, that wasn't the endgame. None of that shit had saved her when the earth fell out from under her. Every time she thought about the ninety-hour weeks and the push for partner, the reasons why slipped through her fingers like water. Why? Why did she want more and more and more, right up until it destroyed her?

Sal came back in with something in his hands. He came over and pressed it into her waiting palm. It was a cornicello keychain, the kind you kept on you to ward off the evil eye.

"Ah, Dad," Sam said with a sigh. She closed her hand around it protectively, but she knew it wasn't the evil eye that was dogging her. It was her own mania.

"Take it," Sal said. "You never know."

"At least give it to Amy," Mel suggested. Sal cut her a look, and she shrugged. "It sounds like she's not doing too well, that's all."

"Trouble finds you when you look for it," Sal said. "Just ask your daughter over here."

Mel made an *nnn* sound. "Sammy needs God," she said. "She needs spiritual guidance."

"I go to church with Grandma," Sam protested. "Me and Bobbi and Grandma, you know that."

"You go," Mel agreed, "but do you listen? Or do you go just to make your grandmother happy?"

This was a low blow. Mel knew how conflicted Sam was about the church, and how much she resented the things it said about her life and marriage. Still, she had an unusually supportive family, who thought her odd for being gay but not morally deformed by it, and Catholicism was in her blood.

"They don't say anything in church that they don't say at the 12-steps, Mom," Sam said. "It's all the same thing."

"Maybe it's not steps you need, then," Mel said. "Maybe it's just God."

CHAPTER 5

THE SEC, PART II

The coffee cart wasn't always on its usual corner, depending on weather or holidays or just, presumably, the whims of the coffee cart guy. Whenever it wasn't, Sam and Jess went to the Starbucks across the street from Byers.

This always felt awkward to Sam, because that was where Dani worked. Dani had been seeing Sam nonexclusively since late August. She was a twenty-six-year-old with the social life of a college student, and traveled with a pack of a dozen friends plus three roommates, who all thought Sam was very cool and wise. She didn't have the heart to tell them that sober addicts often sounded both cool and wise to people who had either never been addicts or never been truly sober. She wasn't cool, she was just thirty-three and had ruined her life.

Dani was a cool anti-drama millennial who didn't want more from her and didn't seem to be catching feelings, which was great. It was just awkward to see her when she was in barista mode, because it made Sam feel like a class traitor to ask a woman she was sleeping with to fetch her coffee. If she saw Dani behind the counter, she usually would give her a wave and then make Jess order for them both while she grabbed them a table.

Sure enough, Dani was at the register today, fielding a long line of business-casual drones and looking stressed about it. Her dark hair was tucked into a messy ponytail that waterfalled out the back of her black Starbucks cap, and her face had the telltale signs of an extremely late night, so Sam decided to not even bother with the complexities of a wave and instead leaned down to mutter to Jess, "Tall latte and croissant? I'm gonna get us a table."

"You are such a baby," Jess said. "You know she'd be happy to see you."

"It's just weird," Sam said. "She's got the apron on. I can't do it." She scanned the cramped restaurant for an empty table, then spotted one. "I'll be in the corner, alright?"

She had barely sat down—in fact, she was still fighting with her umbrella, her ass hovering above the seat—when her phone rang in her pocket. Usually these days it was a robocall, but she fished it out anyway, in case her grandma had fallen down or something.

No, it was an unfamiliar number. But unlike robocalls, it came with a *Maybe*. The *Maybe* was Metropolitan Correctional Center.

"What the fuck?" Sam said aloud, her heart skipping a beat and then beginning to pound. She picked up. "Hello?"

"Sam," Amy said breathlessly in her ear. "Hey. I don't know what's going on—"

"Ames, where are you calling from?"

"This detention center, MCC something? I think it's on Park Row."

"The MCC? Little Gitmo?"

"I'm *where*? Did you just say Gitmo?"

"Never mind. Did you get arrested?"

A guy at the table next to her glanced up briefly from his newspaper to side-eye Sam when she said this. She shot a look back at him like, *this is New York, mind your own business.*

"Yeah, they grabbed me this morning, the FBI came to my hotel room—"

"Stop," Sam barked. "Don't say another word. I'm coming."

"No, no, you don't have to come, I just need the number for a lawyer. I don't know any lawyers in New York."

"You can hire someone else later, but I'm gonna come down now and figure out what's going on first."

"Okay," Amy said in a small voice. "Okay."

"I'll be there in ten," Sam said wildly. She didn't even know why she said that. She had no idea how long it would take to get down there; it just felt like the thing to say. "Amy? Don't tell them anything. Nothing."

"I haven't, I haven't. I mean I gave them my address and stuff, but they were trying to ask me more, and I just kept saying 'I want an attorney.' They didn't let me call you until now."

Sam made a mental note of this. "Do something for me, alright? Let them know I'm your lawyer? Give them my name, tell them I'm barred in Illinois. Where are you right now?"

"I'm in an interrogation room. They brought a phone in for me."

"Fuck. Okay. I'm on my way."

There was a soft sound like Amy's breath had caught, then an inhale. "Sam, thank you," she said. "I know it's, um . . . this isn't appropriate, it isn't fair to you—"

"It's fine," Sam cut her off. "Forget about it. Alright? I'm on my way."

"Thank you."

Sam hung up the phone, high out of her mind on adrenaline. She got to her feet, picking her still-damp umbrella up from where she'd hung it on the back of the chair and mincing her way through the crowd of hovering Starbucks customers to find Jess at the end of the counter, waiting for their drinks.

"Hey," Sam said to her. "I gotta go."

Bafflement made Jess's cute face comical. She looked like

Thumper the rabbit. "Go where? We have work in twenty minutes."

"I—"

Dani was on her way over, smiling. She'd clearly spotted Sam. She stopped in front of the machine nearest to them, dispensing something into a cup. "Hi there," she said to Sam, flicking her gaze up at her. She was very pretty, in a kind of busty, obvious way that made Sam wonder why she bothered keeping an aging and exhausted lesbian on her sexual payroll.

"Hey," Sam said, trying not to look jittery. She didn't want to say anything about Amy in front of Dani, because she knew from experience that ex-wife shit would definitely count as "drama" in her book.

She didn't have to. On the TV next to the menu advertising Starbucks' fall specialties, CNBC was on, and there was a shot up of Amy being escorted out of The Greenwich Hotel by FBI agents in her pajamas.

TOP VP AT CHICAGO HEDGE FUND ARRESTED IN NEW YORK FOR INSIDER TRADING, the chyron read.

Jess looked up at Sam, then followed her gaze to the TV. "Oh my God!" she said, her hand jumping to her mouth. "*What?*"

Dani looked up from pulling espresso shots or whatever she was doing, her eyebrows arching.

"Just realized we're late for a big meeting," Sam said, while Jess continued staring up in horror.

"Oh, shit," Dani said amiably. She turned to her coworker, a curly-haired guy who did not seem to be mentally or emotionally present. "Trevor, do you have that latte and PSL for me?"

"Yeah," Trevor muttered, and swiveled limply to hand off the drinks, which Dani delivered to them.

"Thanks," Sam said, flashing her a smile. "I'll text you?"

"Yeah, let me know about tonight," she said.

"Will do."

Sam had to escort Jess and carry both their drinks, because she was so busy opening Safari and frantically Googling AMT IGARASSI ARRWSTES, AMY UGARSAGHE ARREST, then AMY ATLANTIC CAPITAL INSIDER TRADINH ARREST???, all to no avail. Sam watched all of this over her shoulder with a smile.

Outside, they huddled under the awning to shiver together as rain poured off it and passing cars splashed the sidewalk. Jess took her PSL from Sam and exclaimed, "What the fuck is going on?"

"Amy just called me from jail, like, literally a minute ago, but I didn't want her to get into the details over the phone," Sam said. "I need to go obviously. I need to see her and figure out what the fuck. Can you tell Larry I'm taking the morning off?"

"Sure, yeah . . ." Jess's blue eyes were roundly massive. She took a fast sip, then grimaced as if she'd burned her mouth. "Is Amy okay, though?"

"She sounded okay," Sam said. "I don't know much. I'll text you, don't worry."

"Does she want you to represent her? Like, what's going on? Does she need money for bail?"

Sam pulled up the Uber app on her phone and then typed in *correctional center*; the Park Row address popped up. She selected it. "The feds do things a little different."

"Then how do you get her out?"

Sam didn't want to tell Jess that she wasn't even sure she could secure Amy's release. "I don't have time to explain, but I'll update you, I promise. You should get to work so no one gets suspicious."

Jess hesitated. "Should I tell Larry what's going on?"

"I'd be blown away if he doesn't already know, but let's not get into the details with anybody until we know what's going on. I don't want to make things tough for you. Anyone asks you where I am, or what you know, just play dumb."

Jess eyed her. "Even to Larry?"

"Even him," Sam said, then realized something. "Shit . . ."

"What?"

"I forgot my croissant."

In the Uber, her phone rang again. This time, it was not an unfamiliar number. It was "DOUG WSJ."

Doug Pinnix was a reporter that Byers often had to hassle. Sam herself had once chased him off a story involving a brokerage firm that had bribed one of Cuomo's former aides, a guy named Tony Odom. Doug had hung out outside Tony's apartment every day for a week badgering him, and on Friday that week Sam (on orders from Larry to "take care of that Doug guy") had met him in the hallway. She'd gotten in his face and told him to fuck off unless he wanted trouble, letting him imagine for himself what trouble was. So Doug was not her biggest fan.

"Sorry, gimme one sec," Sam said to the driver, who was in the middle of telling her how he cured his glaucoma with Ayurveda. She picked up: "Yo."

"Sam, hiii," Doug said. He sounded way too cheerful for how early it was. "Doug Pinnix at the Wall Street Journal. You free to talk?"

"Not really."

"That's too bad. Because it looks like your ex-wife just got arrested?"

"No comment," Sam said flatly.

"And your PR firm is currently representing her hedge fund, correct? I find it a little weird you wouldn't have a comment."

"You can talk to—" Shit, no, she couldn't tell him to call Larry. She had no idea what was going on here, and Larry's loyalties lay with Atlantic first and foremost. "Doug, actually, can I call you back in two hours?"

"Well, I am on deadline," Doug said. The Uber rolled to a stop in traffic; Sam bounced her leg, claustrophobic and annoyed.

"What's the deadline?" she said.

"Five."

"Well, it's nine in the morning now, man," Sam said. "You'll make it. Bye-bye."

"Looking forward to hearing back. Talk to you later."

"Asshole," Sam said after she hung up, but she didn't mean it. She knew she was the asshole here.

On her phone, she pulled up Safari and started Googling the way Jess had done. Speaking of Jess, Sam already had several unread texts from her, as well as one from Bobbi who had apparently seen the arrest on one of the TVs at her gym, a couple from old Chicago friends who were veiling their morbid curiosity under polite concern, two from her mom, and one from Dani about weekend plans. She ignored them all.

It looked like Amy had been the only Atlantic employee arrested. That was fishy. If they had charged her for conspiracy, which Sam suspected they had, then at the very least Paul would have been arrested as well. She Googled for arrests of Zilpah employees instead, and way down on page one, there it was. From this morning:

Pharmaceutical executives indicted for fraudulent opioid trials https://www.justice.gov › Department of Justice › Office of Public Affairs › News Oct 11, 2017 - *On October 11, 2017, the District Court for the Northern District of Illinois unsealed a 40-count indictment charging four individuals connected with Zilpah Drugs, including former COO Tom Naftalis, in a $1 billion stock manipulation scheme.*

"Fucking Tom Naftalis!" Sam exclaimed.

"Ah?" her Uber driver said.

"Nothing, nothing, sorry."

MCC was a clusterfuck on that particular Friday. There must have been a big drug bust on the water that morning, or something similar. There was a line for the metal detectors, and once she got upstairs there were a couple dozen handcuffed guys waiting on benches for processing. They were guarded by some feds in their rubber-soled shoes and a couple of staties, one of whom was nursing a busted lip and a bloody hand. A few of the handcuffed made approving noises about her female presence and were quickly shushed by the cops.

When Sam finally got to the front desk C.O., he looked up at her with the exact same empty expression that Trevor of Starbucks had given Dani. "Business?"

"I'm an attorney," she said. "I'm here to see Amy Igarashi—"

"Did we know you're coming?"

"She's being interrogated right this second," Sam said. "She asked for a lawyer. Her—*her* lawyer. I'm it."

He sighed. "You got state ID and a bar card?"

Fuck. Fuck fuck fuck. "Yeah," she said, stalling for time as she pulled out her beat-up leather wallet and dug past a blood donor ID, Duane Reade card, MetroCard, Cigna card—there it was, finally, her bar card. She hadn't thrown it away after all. "Yeah, here," she said, handing it over along with her license.

The officer looked at it and frowned. "Miss Di—DiSee—"

"De-cheeky-oh," she enunciated.

"Alright." He took them both. "Thank you, counselor. You're gonna follow Marshal Ted," he said, gesturing over her shoulder. Sam spun around and saw a short, pug-faced federal marshal wave at her. "You're gonna put all your stuff in a locker. You need a quarter. You got a quarter?"

"Yeah."

"You're gonna wait a while. Then Ted's gonna take you to

see Ms. Igarashi. Okay? Okay." He looked back down at his computer monitor. Interaction over.

"Hang on," Sam said. "How long's a while? Because my client has the right to an attorney when she's being questioned, so I'm not sitting around here twiddling my thumbs, alright?"

He flicked his eyes up at her. "Miss, no one asked you to twiddle anything."

"I want to see her *now*." She got very New York as she said this. *I wanna seeuh naaaoh.*

He sighed. "Soon as we can process you into the system, alright?"

"Alright." Sam turned to Ted, who beckoned her politely, and she followed him.

Seven FBI agents had busted through Amy's hotel room door at 7:33 a.m., which she knew because she happened to be looking at the clock radio when it happened. They came in shouting "Hands in the air!" She thought she was being robbed before the first agent appeared at the end of the hall in the classic yellow-on-navy jacket, his hand on the butt of his holstered pistol.

A redheaded female agent had pushed her down onto the bed and handcuffed her while another showed her a pair of warrants. The redhead was rough with her, bending her arms at strange angles and digging her short nails into Amy's skin.

"Ma'am," the agent with the warrants said, "my name is Special Agent Wally Turedo. Do you understand why we're here today?"

"No," Amy snapped, blowing a lock of hair away from her face. "I really don't."

"We're here because a federal judge has signed a criminal complaint against you in a fraud and insider trading conspiracy. You are being charged with securities fraud under U.S. Code 18."

With the state she'd been in lately, this should have given her a heart attack. She already had enough cortisol running through her veins to stop a horse. Instead, Amy felt serene in a grief-stricken way. She wanted to cry, but refused to do so in front of seven feds.

She was Mirandized while they trashed the hotel room: garbage cans were upended and the trash examined, her laptop and cell phone were placed by gloved hands into plastic bags, the pockets of her coat were picked through for scraps of paper. She watched all of this in petrified indignation on the bed, afraid to move, the agent's fingernails digging into her forearms and her head at an awkward angle.

Amy didn't understand this over-the-top manhandling—like she was Al Capone and might whip a Beretta out of the waistband of her pajama pants—until she made it to the interrogation room. It was like the ones on TV but even smaller, terrifically claustrophobic, with two little metal chairs on either side of a table and two-way mirrors in front of and behind her. She refused to talk except for the most basic biographical information, but they kept prodding her, questioning her, even after she had asked for an attorney. And then Wally held up an iPad displaying a photo of a laptop that had been smashed into smithereens and said, "Do you know what this is?"

Amy didn't react; she just stared back at him. Her spine and jaw felt leaden.

"This is Tom Naftalis's laptop." Wally flicked to the next photo: an object so smashed she couldn't make visual sense of it. "And his BlackBerry. This is what he was doing when we were waiting for him to answer the door. Tried to flush the phone down the toilet while we were busting into the bathroom."

"Okay?" Amy said. "Can I speak to my attorney?"

"We're just taking down your basic information still, and then we'll let you call."

"I thought you were showing me pictures of laptops."

Wally laughed at this.

Amy did her best to channel Sam, trying to imagine what Sam would say, trying to remember the things about the law she'd learned from listening to her discuss cases and razz storylines on *Law and Order: Criminal Intent*. Recalled fragments danced through her head: *never incriminate yourself, be polite but shut up, demand an attorney, demand to see the warrant, volunteer nothing, you have the right to know what you're being charged with, the cops want to trick you.*

But this was easier said than done: Wally was being reasonable and kind to her, making her guard slip. Plus, a lot of the questions he had asked didn't feel incriminating: *What's your name? How old are you? Where do you live?*

Finally, they brought in a crappy old landline and let her make a call. There was never any doubt in her mind that Sam would be the person she called. Yeah, because she was a lawyer, and yeah, because of what they'd discussed the day before, and yeah, because Sam's was one of the few phone numbers she still had memorized, but it went beyond that. Sam was like a Boy Scout with a switchblade. If you knew her, and you were in trouble, or you wanted someone dealt with, she was the one you called. No one knew this better than her former wife.

After Amy hung up, she finally cried. It was embarrassing. Wally offered her a tissue, which was somehow worse. She felt like she had in fourth grade when an argument with her best friend led to a fistfight on the blacktop, which got her sent to the principal's office. The fight being all her fault made it so much worse. All she could do was cry, fat tears dripping onto her Minnie Mouse shorts. No one felt sorry for her, and her parents were so disappointed when the school called later that night. "We don't hurt our friends," her dad had said.

Her throat burned just thinking of this. Her dad had been sick with kidney disease for the last year; despite the tens of thousands of dollars she had poured into specialists, he remained frail and not quite himself. It was going to devastate him to see this on the news. His brainy, bold success of a daughter was disgraced and losing face.

The door opened some time later, and there was Sam: disheveled and pale, in her work clothes. Oh, no, it was Friday, she had work. Had she taken the day off for this?

It occurred to Amy again that Sam must not hate her after all. The idea was almost untenable. Sam? Waspish, exacting, Sicilian-tempered Sam, who when they were married would spurn a restaurant for years if they forgot the banana peppers on her sandwich once?

Afraid to say anything in front of Wally, Amy just stared up at her ex-wife, aware of how pitiful she must look in her jumpsuit.

"Hi," she said.

"Hi," Sam said.

Her eyes were blazing with that look she always got around cops: like she could spit nails. She'd confessed to Amy, years ago, that this was an act. She drank with prosecutors and cops at all the same bars; there were no hard feelings. But the feelings looked genuinely hard to Amy now.

Sam extended her hand to Wally, who shook it. "Sam DiCiccio. I'm Ms. Igarashi's representation."

"Special Agent Wally Turedo, FBI, nice to meet you. Ms. Igarashi told us she didn't have counsel in New York," he said.

Amy looked to Sam for an answer.

"Her employer doesn't retain counsel here," Sam said with care, then inclined her head in a tiny nod to Amy before turning to Wally. "I'm representing my client, and my client alone. I do not represent Atlantic Capital Management in any respect."

"Well, that one is between you and her," Wally said.

"Are the feds pursuing an investigation into anyone else at Atlantic?" Sam said. "I know you guys just raided Zilpah and made four arrests there."

Wally laughed. "Nice try, but I'm only authorized to talk to you about the charges against Amy."

"And those are?"

"Securities fraud, conspiracy to commit securities fraud, wire fraud, and conspiracy to commit wire fraud," Wally recited.

"Okay. Can I talk to my client in private?"

Wally looked at his watch, which was plain with a cheap band. Amy hated that she noticed things like that compulsively now. "Sure."

He stood, offering Sam his chair. She took it like a starving guy being offered a hot dog, collapsing into it and then staring with canine focus at Wally's retreating back until the door closed behind him.

"I didn't ask you to be my lawyer," Amy said in a low voice the second they were alone. "I don't want you to get caught up in this, okay?"

Sam leaned in close and whispered, "Well, that's too fucking bad. 'Cause you know what? Something isn't right here. Why's no one at Atlantic been charged but you, Ames? Huh? What's up with that?"

Amy, who had spent the last several hours working this same question into tatters in her own mind, had no answer. "Maybe the feds want me to flip on Paul," she said.

"But if you were here because of the conversation with Paul, you'd be charged with just conspiracy and obstruction, not insider trading. Actually, you wouldn't be charged with anything. That's not enough evidence to get even a grand jury to indict on. There has to be more."

"Right."

"As it is, on these charges, you're likely facing at least a year or two in federal prison."

Amy's stomach flipped hard, and bile crept up into her throat. "Oh," she said.

"Something's not right," Sam repeated. "You need to cut ties with Atlantic. When he comes back in here, we're gonna get rid of these charges, okay? You're gonna sell Paul down the river. Everything you know on the table, in exchange for leniency."

"Okay," Amy said. "Okay, okay, yeah. I mean . . ." She blew out a sigh, her heart dropping like a stone as she realized that, yet again, her life as she knew it was over.

"But don't say anything until I can figure out what's going on here," Sam said. "Don't respond to a single question unless I give you the okay. And I might interrupt you sometimes and guide your answer."

"That's fine."

"I just know you always hated when I interrupted you."

"As my wife, not my lawyer. As my lawyer, honestly, do whatever you have to do."

Sam grinned. "Okay."

She got up and went to the door, then stepped into the anteroom to converse quietly with the feds. Under the table, Amy nervously twisted her fingers. This went on for five or so minutes, although it could have been shorter or longer than that. This windowless, clockless room was pulling and stretching time like taffy. It sounded like Sam said *warrant* a couple of times.

Wally returned and took a seat, dropping a manila folder down and opening it. Sam got out a little notepad and a pen.

"Okay," Wally said. "Amy? Your attorney here wants to know if it would be possible to get your case dismissed, so she's asked us to go over some of the evidence we have against you, ahead of your arraignment. I have the affidavit here as well."

Amy nodded.

"These emails are what our charges today are based on," Wally said, and tapped the papers in front of him. Though upside down, they clearly were emails, printed in black and white on what was probably an old printer.

Sam said, "Can I take a look at those?" She sounded entirely calm, like she was asking to rent a beach umbrella.

"Why don't you let me put them in context first," Wally said with an officious little smile. Even though he'd arrested her, this was the first time Amy disliked him.

"Go for it," Sam said.

"Over the course of their investigation, the SEC and FBI combed through a year's worth of pertinent emails from both Zilpah and Atlantic executives," he said, and flicked his gaze between Amy and Sam's faces. They both remained nonplussed. "We found several deleted emails from May that corroborated a theory we'd been developing about the case. These emails are the cornerstone evidence of our charges."

"And what theory is that?" Sam said, giving nothing away.

Amy watched Sam, not Wally. Wally's face was irrelevant; he would think he had her dead to rights no matter what the truth was. Sam was the real weathervane for how bad things were.

However, Amy kind of did want to reach across the table and snatch up that folder that he was playing with. What emails, Wally? What happened to the nice guy from a minute ago?

"We believe that Paul Weller, who we interviewed several times over the course of our investigation—"

Is guilty! Is guilty! Is guilty!

"—was an unknowing go-between for Ms. Igarashi and Zilpah," Wally said. "We believe that as Mr. Weller was meeting with Zilpah executives, publicly and in person, Ms. Igarashi used these meetings as cover while she communicated with Tom Naftalis, who advised her when to sell Atlantic's shares of Zilpah in order to recoup the vast majority of their investment without arousing suspicion."

Amy's head swam. Was that a joke? Naftalis was Paul's guy. Was this the cops lying to her, like she knew they were allowed to do? Were they allowed to lie to a lawyer?

Sam still looked calm, astoundingly. Did she believe this shit?

"I didn't do that," Amy blurted out. "I never spoke to—"

Sam's hand came down on the back of hers like a dropped cake hitting the floor. "Ame?" she said. "I would again recommend you don't talk here."

"You had lunch with Mr. Naftalis," Wally said to Amy, who wanted to react but didn't.

"She doesn't have to answer that," Sam said.

"I don't care if she answers it. It's a fact of the case. And then, in May, they exchanged these emails."

Wally finally pushed the folder toward them. Amy bent over the table, her hair making a curtain around her face, and began to read as fast as she could.

From: Tom Naftalis [mailto:tnaftalis@ zilpahdrugs.com]
Sent: Wednesday, May 23, 2017 1:28 AM
To: amyigarashi@atlanticcapital.com
Subject: Update on timeline

Hi Amy,
I would amend stop limit order to stop loss order ASAP. You are not going to make back the 47.5m. 44m is more in line with what you can expect. We just tonight became aware of leaks from inside the firm. I would set your stop loss at 200 a share, which you would be lucky to make back.
Best,
Tommy

From: Amy Igarashi
Sent: Wednesday, May 23, 2017 12:30 AM
To: Tom Naftalis [mailto:tnaftalis@zilpahdrugs.com]
Subject: RE: Update on timeline

Tom,

When do you expect this will hit the press?

Thanks,

Amy

From: Tom Naftalis [mailto:tnaftalis@ zilpahdrugs.com]
Sent: Wednesday, May 23, 2017 1:35 AM
To: amyigarashi@atlanticcapital.com
Subject: RE: Update on timeline

We expect this will have become full public knowledge within a few weeks, likely via WSJ. But this info has circulated enough privately that it will undoubtedly trigger a sell-off as soon as the markets open tomorrow. We will become a toxic asset within the hour.

From: Amy Igarashi
Sent: Wednesday, May 23, 2017 12:36 AM
To: Tom Naftalis [mailto:tnaftalis@zilpahdrugs.com]
Subject: RE: Update on timeline

How much do you think we could get at open?

From: Tom Naftalis [mailto:tnaftalis@ zilpahdrugs.com]
Sent: Wednesday, May 23, 2017 1:38 AM
To: amyigarashi@atlanticcapital.com
Subject: RE: Update on timeline

I would not sell at open with the amount of
exposure you have. That would be a huge red
flag for the SEC. You will need to give it an
appropriate amount of time for the stock to
tank before you pull the trigger. I would wait
for it to hit 220 if not 200. (Today closed at 270)
Best,
Tom

From: Amy Igarashi
Sent: Wednesday, May 23, 2017 12:40 AM
To: Tom Naftalis [mailto:tnaftalis@zilpahdrugs.com]
Subject: RE: Update on timeline

Received. Thank you

Amy's heart began to palpitate as soon as she saw her address atop the second email, and it only got worse from there. Tommy? She didn't even like the guy. She would never in a million years call him *Tommy*.

Of course she had set the stop loss at 200, and of course she pulled the trigger for the sale at 220 the following morning. Paul had ordered her to dump the stock early that morning, before the markets opened, and those were the only logical numbers available at that point in time.

The exact actions Amy had been forced into by Paul were laid out almost implausibly clearly in these emails. She was almost angrier about how stupid they made her look than anything else. As if she would ever write these things down! Even a child knew the cops could retrieve deleted emails. And why was Tom Naftalis gleefully selling himself down the river in emails he had to know the feds would subpoena? That didn't make any sense.

May 23rd at twelve-thirty in the morning. Did she have an

alibi? Amy couldn't remember if she'd stayed late at work that night—she so often did.

She clung again to the idea that the feds had fabricated these to get her to confess something. She looked at Sam, who was also poring over the printouts, her mouth tight. She flipped past the emails to the affidavit, and took a long look at it.

After a moment, Sam looked up at Wally and said, "This interview is over."

"Okay," Wally said.

"Sam," Amy whispered. "I would never be this stupid—"

"Amy, stop." Under the olive tones of her skin, Sam's face had gone a bloodless gray. "Don't say a word. Stop it." To Wally, she said: "When is she going to be arraigned?"

"At one," Wally said. "DOJ wants to get it out of the way so we can transfer the case to Chicago."

"Right." Sam wrote frantically on her little pad. "Is she free to go before that?"

"No, we're going to transport her."

"Right over to SDNY?"

"Yep."

"Alright. I'll be there."

"Can I make any more calls before that?" Amy said to Wally in desperation. He looked impassively back at her with his boyish white face. "Can I call Atlantic's general counsel? Please. Something's extremely wrong here."

Wally didn't get the chance to answer before Sam said in a soft voice, "Ame? I wouldn't make that particular call."

"I'd listen to your lawyer," Wally told her.

"Give us a second," Sam said to him.

He complied. The door swung shut behind him again.

"Three things," Sam said to her, staring into her eyes with the doglike intent from before. "Do you have an alibi for that night?"

"Probably not," Amy said, her voice barely audible. "I don't go out anymore . . . I'd have to look at my calendar, my texts . . ."

Her brain worked frantically. "Um, my bank records? But I can send emails from my phone, so I don't know how helpful an alibi would be."

"We'll look into it anyway. I'm just covering my bases. Does anyone have access to your email account other than you?"

Amy shook her head.

"Not even Paul?" Sam said. "Could Paul send an email as you?"

"As me? Ah . . . I don't actually know."

"Does he have access to your login information on the company server?"

Amy held up four fingers. "You said three questions," she said weakly, and Sam laughed. "I don't know. I really don't."

"Okay. Last question. Can we discuss the idea of you taking a plea deal?"

This bowled Amy over. Already they had pivoted to sending her to jail. "Sam," she said. "I'm being framed, I swear to God. I swear. I tell you I'd never in my life be so stupid as to put that shit in writing."

"Doesn't matter," Sam said. "It matters what they can make a jury believe. The evidence against you, right now, is pretty stiff."

"Has this been your plan all along?" Amy said, only half-joking. "Let your bitch ex-wife get railroaded, then help throw her in jail before she can prove she's innocent?"

Sam could have been offended. Instead, she laughed again. "Amy, I am not gonna do anything unless you ask me to. And a plea bargain is how you avoid jail."

Amy's head swam. "Okay, then yeah, we can talk about it."

Sam nodded and got to her feet, collecting her notepad. "Alright. Good to know." She gave her finger guns like a goofball. "I gotta go, I gotta hit work before you head to court."

"Sam—listen, I'm going to hire a lawyer," Amy said, feeling guilty. "You have a full-time job. This is insane. You can't represent me."

Sam got a look on her face like she had walked into a glass door. Amy knew her well enough to know that she had probably already forgotten about the rest of her life and had thrown her mind into this case, wholly and without reservation. That was just how Sam was—she couldn't half-ass anything.

"Well," Sam said, sounding a little embarrassed, "look, you can get a new lawyer when you go back to Chicago, alright? You're gonna be tried there, so you get a lawyer there, and I'll take care of you for now."

"That's fine," Amy said. "That works."

"Read the affidavit," Sam told her. "Read those emails again. Rack your brain for anything you can think of that would help your case."

CHAPTER 6

THE U.S. DISTRICT COURT
FOR THE SOUTHERN DISTRICT OF NEW YORK

It was 10:11 a.m. and no longer raining by the time Sam raced out of the grim beige blight of the MCC.

Her phone, retrieved from the locker, had thirty more texts on it than it had an hour ago. She put it on Do Not Disturb as she blew down the front steps in a rush, startling a short guy with a briefcase when she nearly knocked him into a bush like a linebacker. She yelled "sorry" over her shoulder and then lit a cigarette, which she smoked as she waited for her Uber to arrive.

A thought was ringing in the back of her head that she should go to a meeting. She was acting crazed, and felt it, too. But she didn't want coke. In fact, she wanted coke less than she had at any point in the last several months. She was high right now without it. When this was all over, when she came down from this, that's when she would jones.

In the back of the Uber, she made small talk with the driver while finally looking at her texts. Shane had reached out; he was her only college friend who had *Heard about Amy. Hope everything is okay.* That was kind, and it made her miss him, but he was still a reporter at the Trib. Sam wasn't stupid. She was sure whatever she wrote back to him would likely become a line in a story about Amy's arrest.

Reporters swarming you was how you could tell the walls were closing in. Doug had texted her again, but he could wait until after court. Right now, she wasn't talking. *Omertà*, as her family said.

Jess was waiting in their office when Sam got there, and had been shrewd enough to pull the blinds down ahead of her arrival. Sam dropped her umbrella in the stand by the door, which she yanked shut before turning around.

"So," Sam said.

"What happened?" Jess said, all aflutter. "God, Amy can't go to prison. Not even white-collar prison. She's too pretty, and I don't know what the Asian gangs are like."

Sam shrugged her coat off and tossed it onto her chair. "You know what the other gangs are like?"

"No," Jess said. "I mean, kind of. I like to watch A&E. Did you run into Larry on your way in?"

"No," Sam muttered, pulling their blinds down slightly with her fingers so she could peek out. Trina and Alan were working in the office across from her, looking unconcerned. Sean was loitering in the common area, probably checking sports scores like he usually did around lunchtime. But the visitor couches were empty—no Don, no Dan. No sign of them either, no empty coffee cups on the tables. "Did he talk to you?"

"So-ort of," Jess said. Sam turned to her again. "In the morning meeting, he said our new goal is to play it like Amy's arrest is the end of the problems for Atlantic. Like, the bad apple is gone basically, and now they can get back to business, and their investors can relax."

"Right," Sam said. "Makes sense."

Jess gave her the big eyes. "Are they going to arrest anyone else? Do you know?"

Sam came over to her, squeezing behind Jess's desk with her.

"Can I use your computer a sec?" she said, her fingers already hovering over the keyboard.

Jess nodded.

It was possible, on this floor, to hear office conversations from out in the hallway as you were walking by. Sam didn't want to be heard. She opened a Word document, then wrote, *I dont think so. Looks like someone's framing her. Sent emails from her address that made it look like she was completely aware of the insider trading and even negotiated it.*

Jess knocked her hands away and typed, *WTFFFFFFFFFFFF?? ?*

I know. I'm still trying to get a handle on what's going on.

That's what Amy said happened? Jess wrote. *That she was being framed?*

Yeah

Do you believe her?

Sam hesitated for a fraction of a second. *Yeah. She would never do something like this.*

Are you representing her? Bc I think you probably can't.

I told her to get a chicago lawyer.

Okay, Jess said. *Good.*

"Right," Sam said aloud.

Jess glanced at her and typed, *why the secrecy? are you worried about Dan/don?*

Worried about everybody but yeah, we can't trust them. Are they around?

I saw them in Larry's office when I got in, and then they left. He's been on calls ever since.

Did he ask where I was?

Yeah. I didn't tell him.

Thanks, Sam wrote.

Poor Amy, Jess wrote.

Sam nodded. She stayed leaning over Jess's desk, lost in thought, until Jess nudged her.

"Sorry," she said with a laugh, "but I do actually have work to do . . . I'm working on a Blackstone Group release. I can send it to you, when I'm done? You can look it over?"

Sam could tell that Jess was trying to restore some normalcy to the day. She nodded, stood up, and kept nodding until she was back behind her own desk. She opened the TweetDeck account that monitored mentions of their clients, then sat there squeezing a stress ball and looking at her screen absently while she listened to Jess type.

Sam didn't know Paul very well. She mostly remembered him as the guy who was responsible for giving Amy raise after raise. The brutal firings and battlefield promotions just looked like business as usual in the finance world, instead of the huge red flag they actually had been.

There were moments where he hadn't come off great, though, like when the two of them went to Benihana with Paul and his wife. Paul had insisted that Amy teach him to use his chopsticks instead of Sam, who, between the two of them, was the one actually using them. And he should have promoted her to full senior VP before he ever promoted Don, Dan or Jeffrey. Amy had often wondered aloud to Sam if Paul was being racist and sexist when he hesitated about giving her more senior responsibilities at the fund, while insisting on her technical competency. He had settled a case of sexual harassment out of court years ago, which Amy and Sam both thought was a red flag. But did that disrespect lay the groundwork for him framing her, or was she just a convenient target?

Larry came and knocked on their door around noon, right when Sam was thinking about hitting the road to get to Amy's arraignment on time. He poked his head in the door and said, "Sam? Can I have a moment?"

Sam exchanged a look with Jess, then nodded and got up to follow him. This was strongly reminiscent of being called to the principal's office. She kept glancing over at him as he led her, but

Larry gave nothing away; his face was blank, besides that slight smile he always had.

The sun was back out. It was hazy in the clouds over the Hudson, sending a glare through the windows of Larry's office that bounced off his glasses and made it hard to meet his eyes. She grew more nervous.

"Sam," Larry said.

Sam, whose leg was bouncing rapidly, nodded. "Yeah."

"I think I can guess where you were this morning," he said.

"Guess away," she said.

Larry laughed. It didn't put her at ease. "Were you with your ex-wife?"

She didn't see the point in lying, so she nodded.

"Right," he said kindly. "I understand. Did you render any legal advice?"

Sam nodded again.

He smiled at her, but the glare on his eyes persisted, so it was more sinister than anything. "Okay. I get it. I do. But I'm guessing Jess has briefed you on the pivot we're making as far as our defense of Atlantic. We're going to have to hammer Amy very hard in the public eye if we're going to protect Atlantic's reputation. And we'll need your help with that."

She was growing clammy and queasy, sitting here. Like the urge to vomit, a realization began to rise in her: she couldn't do that.

"Maybe I need to sit this one out," Sam said. "Because I was actually, um—I actually need to go back across town and be there for her initial appearance. I'm her only counsel right now."

"Okay," Larry said, now sounding like he was talking to a four-year-old. "Sam? You can't do that. I can't have my employees working against the interests of my clients. I understand why you went this morning — we hadn't had a chance to talk yet. I tried to call you, but I know you probably can't have your phone on you in those facilities, so I understand. I can waive all that.

But you're going to need to come on board now. We have to circle the wagons."

"No," Sam said, her voice sounding wild in her own ears.

Larry leaned forward. The glare was gone from his glasses; now there was one on his face. "No?" he repeated.

"No, I can't. Larry, come on. Please. She didn't do it. They framed her, I swear to God."

Larry was silent for a moment, his lips tucked into his mouth. "Sam?" he said, and she thought he was about to tell her she was delusional to believe this, but he continued: "I don't give a shit what they did."

Sam was absolutely poleaxed. She sat there, speechless. Not this from Larry, her nice-guy boss, the office's Uncle Lar-Bear. She brought him bear claws. He called her champ.

"We have a duty to our client," Larry said. "I give my clients absolute loyalty. I expect absolute loyalty from my employees."

"I am loyal! I've always been loyal to you. I've done all kinds of shit for you! But this is my, like, actual, real life!"

"This isn't your life?" Larry challenges. "You spend forty, fifty hours a week here. Your best friend works here."

"This has nothing to do with Jess. Don't drag her into this."

"Fine, then think of the rest of your coworkers. You're part of a team."

"Larry," she cried. "Come on. Please. They're railroading her. You help people who get railroaded."

His face was stone. "I help people who pay me," he said.

"Are you fucking serious?" she exclaimed.

"Are you?"

Neither of them spoke for a long moment. Sam became afraid that she might cry.

"I have to go," she finally said. "I'm her lawyer, at least for now. I have to be there . . ."

"If you go," Larry said, "I'm sorry, but you're fired. You'd be in breach of contract."

Tears did prickle in her eyes, then, but she blinked them back.

"Okay," Sam said, and got up. "Okay. Then, uh, yeah. I quit."

"You quit," Larry repeated.

"Yeah."

"You want to think about that for a second?"

Sam was agonized, but couldn't. All she could think of was a line from her wedding ceremony: *Marriage is something that should not be entered into unadvisedly or lightly but reverently, discreetly, advisedly, soberly, and in the fear of God.* Years later, this felt less like wise advice and more like a dire warning that she was once again failing to heed. At least she was sober now.

"I have to do what I have to do," she said.

Larry looked unmoved by this, but he nodded back at her and said, "I'm sorry to see you go."

"That's it?"

"I don't know what else you want me to say."

"Maybe that you understand?"

"No, I can't, because I don't understand," Larry said. "And even if I did, I'm not your friend. I'm your boss. I've rewarded your loyalty with my own, and now you're withdrawing yours. You just terminated our relationship. I can't imagine what you think I'd have to say to you."

"Okay," Sam said, feeling trembly. "Then I guess this is the end of the road for us."

"Correct," Larry said.

"What do I do?"

"Pack your desk and leave," Larry said. "Send me an email with a formal resignation letter by EOD—from your personal email, so I have it on file. I'll let you know if I need anything else from you."

Sam nodded and let herself out.

The walk back down the hall was surreal. She passed Sean and Christiana's office and distantly registered that they were having an argument about the Yankees. She felt so far removed from everything normal, like baseball.

In her own office, she got her coat and her umbrella, then picked some things up off her desk. A tiny snow globe that Bobbi had bought for her in Miami. The cornicello from her dad. A Miraculous Medal from her grandma. She packed them all into a pocket on her monogrammed briefcase.

Jess, who had been finishing up a call with a client as she did this, finally hung up. "Sam, Sam! What are you doing?"

"Packing," Sam said numbly. "I just quit my job."

Jess sprang to her feet, knocking her trash can over. "What?"

Sam slung the strap over her shoulder before coming over to Jess to give her a hug.

Jess looked baffled but hugged her back, squeezing her tight. She smelled strongly of Clinique's Happy, which she got in sample form at the Cherry Hill Mall. "What do you mean, you quit?" she asked in a tiny voice.

"He asked me to choose between Atlantic and Amy," Sam said.

Jess sighed. "Oh, God. Okay, please just think about this, though? Think about what you're doing."

"I know what I'm doing. It's not right. I can't let her down. I already let her down, big-time."

"Sam . . ."

Sam patted her hard on the back. "Honestly, I was alright coming to work here, 'cause I felt like what had happened to me was unfair," she said. "But it wasn't. I had it coming. I have to accept that. And most of our clients probably had it coming, just like the people I used to defend. But Amy, she doesn't deserve this, alright? She needs all the help she can get. This is my chance to finally put things right, and do something right and good."

She pulled back and looked at Jess, who was now tearful, too. Sam reached up to wipe a tear away from her cheek.

"I'm gonna be okay," she insisted. "I got this far, alright? You helped me a ton with getting back on my feet. You were the best. I'm not ungrateful for that at all. But it's gonna be okay."

Jess sniffled. "I really liked working with you, though," she admitted, and Sam laughed and brought her back into her arms. "It was more fun with you here."

"Me?"

"Yeah, you. Who else?"

Sam squeezed her, feeling guiltier. "Hey, say bye to everyone for me?" she said. "Tell Alan I'm sorry he's gonna have to pick up the slack on this one."

Jess laughed. "I will."

Sam walked to SDNY. It wasn't even a mile away, she had the time, and it was nice now that the rain had swept through and gone away. The air was cool; downtown smelled like the docks. She also wanted to smoke and needed to freak out, and freaking out in Manhattan traffic was like freaking out in a coffin. She had to be out pounding the pavement with her own feet. Every step was the physical expression of her buzzing internal thought loop of, *What the fuck, what the fuck, what the fuck?*

As she passed people on the street, she studied their faces and wondered what they'd think of her. She wondered if she would sound like an idiot to them, or a mensch. That was just her *voir dire* muscle trying to exercise itself, though. It didn't matter what anyone thought; what was done was done.

Courthouse security ended up annoyed with her because of her failure to disclose the two-inch folding knife in her bag pre-x-ray, which held up the line. "Ma'am?" one guy kept saying as he held the knife in the air like it was a pipe bomb. "Ma'am, we have to keep this. You can pick it up when you leave. You understand, ma'am?"

"Yep, I got it," Sam said, slipping her loafers back on. The knife was another gift from her grandma, who thought every woman and girl should walk around armed. "What floor is Judge Janine Militano on?"

"Fourth floor," he said, handing her back her briefcase. "Room 421."

Sam thanked him and hurried down the grand marble halls toward the bank of elevators. She'd never been to SDNY before, and she found its grandeur off-putting when contrasted with the grubby greed or queasy desperation of most federal crimes, which felt to her like they should be prosecuted in a basement somewhere. Here, bronze doorframes and gold millwork caught your eye everywhere you looked.

About fifteen other people were waiting for elevators. Unfortunately, one of them was Doug Pinnix, standing about twenty feet away.

"Sam!" he crowed, waving her over.

"Shit," Sam muttered. She went over to talk to him anyway, though, because she had an idea. Now that she was free of Byers and could do whatever she wanted, it was time to start playing dirty the way she used to.

Two elevators came down, and the attorneys who were waiting looked up from their phones and packed into them. Even though this left Doug and Sam alone, she sheepdogged him into a secluded corner for extra privacy.

Doug held up an iPhone with the voice recorder app open. She batted it down. "We're not doing that. This is off the record."

"Okay," Doug said agreeably. "Can I take notes for my records?"

"Fine."

He folded the top of his notepad back and pressed pen to paper. "Are you here as your ex-wife's representation?"

Sam blew out a breath of air and said, "I'm representing her at this arraignment. You can print that part."

Doug's rheumy eyes danced in his face. "That's interesting,

because your firm has pivoted in the last hour to smearing her as being solely responsible for the alleged insider trading at Atlantic Capital."

"I no longer work at Byers Broadwell," Sam said, figuring she might as well get out ahead of it. "You can print that too."

Doug's eyes danced more frantically. He scribbled this down. "Really?"

"Yep."

"Did you leave because of your prior relationship with Amy?"

"No," Sam said—fast, so she didn't have to think about it.

"So what exactly is going on here?"

Sam leaned a hand on the marble wall beside her and leaned forward, into Doug's space a little. He smelled like bar soap. "I'm gonna give you a tip," she whispered. "Deep background. Look into Paul Weller. This case is, uh, hinky. I think you probably agree, or you wouldn't have bothered coming all the way down here on a story you could have written based on court docs."

"Fine," Doug said. "Yeah, I smell a rat. I don't know who the rat is, though, and I'm not just going to take your word for it."

"When is insider trading on this level ever the work of just one person?"

"Four executives at Zilpah Drugs have been charged," Doug pointed out.

"Yeah, but nobody else at Atlantic. You don't find that weird? Think about it for a second."

"When I called Byers for comment, Larry Ochsner told me that Amy was responsible for organizing the materials for the purchase of the Zilpah shares, as well as organizing the sale of the stock."

God damnit, Larry! "She was being instructed by Paul, her *boss*," Sam said. "He's the one with the pre-existing relationship with Zilpah. He's the one who's buddies with Tom Naftalis."

Doug scribbled more, then laughed and said, "So basically—yes, you are Amy's lawyer, but this is a frame-up, she's totally innocent, and you need me to do your investigative work for you?"

"Hey, dude, do whatever you want. I'm just saying, if you can dig around, you could break a great story."

"Look, this is all well and good," Doug said. "Thank you for the tip. But I have a story I'm on deadline for, and I'd like a quote about it, in exchange for me listening to your conspiracy theory."

"Alright, uh." Sam ran her hand through her hair and tried to make her brain settle down. "On the record, my client is obviously innocent."

"Obviously," Doug repeated with an impish look.

"It's a travesty of justice that she was charged with this crime, and the facts will come to light sooner or later . . ." Sam paused and waited for Doug to catch up with his note-taking. "We have a strong defense, and Amy's legal team will work to get this ludicrous case thrown out before it can do any further damage to her reputation."

Doug looked up. "Team?"

"Team," Sam repeated. It was good to have a legal team; it made you sound powerful. Plus, that way it would look less chintzy and flimflam when Amy went back to Chicago and turned up with a brand-new lawyer overnight. It would look like a strategy. She had learned some things from her time in PR. "I'll see you upstairs, Doug."

She clapped him on the shoulder and headed over to the elevators.

Amy knew it was going to take all her willpower to get through this without dry heaving.

At least Wally had done her the courtesy of letting her call her parents. "My dad is sick," she told him. "Please, I just want to tell them that everything's okay."

Her mom was the one who came to the phone and picked up the call from a strange number with a sweet-voiced "Hello?"

Amy got choked up. She didn't know how to have this conversation; her sister Ellie was the one who was at ease with their parents. Amy walled herself off and threw money at them to apologize for being gay. She knew they loved her, but she was always terrified they didn't like her.

Ellie was an easier person to like: affable, breezy, carefree. She'd married a sterling, boring guy and had a precious baby daughter their parents adored. Amy was their pride, and Ellie was their joy.

"Mom?" she said. She wanted to have this conversation in Japanese, but she didn't have much Japanese about the American justice system. "I've been arrested. I guess you guys probably already saw on TV."

Michiko sighed. "Yes, we did. Are you okay?"

"Yeah," Amy said, as hot tears gathered in her eyes. "I didn't do it, I swear. I'm so sorry you have to see this."

"Sweetheart, it's alright."

"It's a mistake. They arrested the wrong person."

"It's okay," her mom said, to soothe her. "Things happen."

"No, I swear, Mom, I didn't do this. I'm fighting it."

"Is Samantha helping you?" Michiko said. "This is her branch of law, yes? Corporate law?"

Up until Sam's fall from grace Amy's parents had always liked her. Sam was kind and friendly, and had stepped up to do things around the house for them when Amy's dad first started to physically falter. After they split up, though, her parents stopped talking about Sam, as if doing so now made them sad. This was the first time in a year Amy had heard one of them mention her.

"Yeah," Amy said. "She's helping me."

"That's good." In Japanese, her mother said: "I'm sure everything will be alright."

Amy closed her eyes, so she could pretend she wasn't in this terrible little room. The tears clung thickly to her eyelashes. "Yeah," she whispered. "How much are you going to tell Dad?"

"A little," Michiko said. "He's sick, and we don't want to upset him. I'll tell him this is a mix-up."

"That's what it is, and I'm going to get it sorted out. Please tell him not to worry. And Ellie, too."

"Ellie is out on the floor right now, no phone," Michiko said. "She's coming by after dinner. I'll talk to her then."

Childish desperation nested in Amy's chest. She wasn't sure what she wanted: for her mom to pardon her as if she were the president? They couldn't protect her. All she could do was protect them.

"Okay," she said.

"Okay," her mother echoed her, sounding uneasy about how to end the conversation. "Call us again when you know more, please. Or . . ." She hesitated. "Have Samantha call us if you can't."

"I will."

Amy hung up and was alone in the little room again.

It was only a couple of minutes later that Wally came back in and said, "Time to go." He led her out into the drab hallway where two federal marshals were waiting for her.

"Are you going to handcuff me?" Amy said to no one in particular. The prison jumpsuit was humiliating enough, though she appreciated not having to go to court in her pajamas.

"Yep," the shorter marshal said, and from behind his back he drew a shiny pair of handcuffs.

Amy turned around, crossing her wrists behind herself and looking down at the floor, her cheeks hot. Cold metal bit at her wrists. There was something claustrophobic about being handcuffed; it made her feel like an animal.

"Are you going to perp walk me again?" Amy said.

"No," the marshal handcuffing her said. He was too close—

she could feel his breath on her neck, which made her drop her shoulder in an effort to recoil. He held onto her harder. "We have a skywalk to the courthouse. We'll take you through there."

"You should feel special, Amy," Wally said. "Normally you'd have to spend the night here in Little Gitmo. If you get bonded out, you can sleep in your own bed tonight."

Amy didn't even bother responding to this.

The walk wasn't momentous in any way. It was just drab hallway after drab hallway, and then a staircase, and then another hallway, punctuated by the beep of badge readers. This monotony gave Amy time to think, but she didn't use it.

It was obvious when they had passed over the skywalk into the courthouse, because the door opened into a hall of white marble, its ceilings waffled with little works of intricate art. Amy got emotional again, looking around. Grand institutions were one of her favorite things about New York, and now she was here as an accused violator of them.

The courtroom they delivered Amy to was large and roomy, but dozens of other defendants were packed into the rows of wood benches, making it feel crowded. The judge was in the middle of hearing a case about Amazon-related mail fraud.

She didn't see Tom Naftalis anywhere. Maybe they were holding him overnight before he got his hearing. Wally had made it sound like her same-day court appearance was a rare privilege.

"You've got an attorney here today, correct?" the taller marshal asked her.

"Yeah, uh . . ." Amy saw Sam's sandy-haired head pop up, and Sam waved her over. "She's right there."

"Go ahead and have a seat next to her," he said. "Wait for your case to be called."

Luckily Sam was sitting at the end of a row and was willing to scoot over, so Amy could sit on the end. Her pride in being innocent made sitting next to federal criminals feel like an injustice in itself.

"How are you?" Sam whispered. She was chewing gum, which she always did when she wanted to smoke but couldn't.

"Well, I'm in handcuffs and I'm accused of insider trading."

Sam waved her hand like this was trivial. "Besides that."

"Oh, besides that, I'm fucking great."

Sam laughed quietly, then looked up toward the front of the courtroom. Her dark eyes were fixed with focus under their hooded lids. "I've been trying to get a feel for this judge," she muttered. "I think she's tough, but fair . . . she's Italian, so maybe I have that going for me."

"Do we need her to like us? I thought this was just me pleading."

Sam shook her head. "She'll decide your bond, too."

Amy fell quiet and turned her attention to the judge, who was a dark-haired, older woman in glasses, squinting as she listened to a defense attorney talk.

"You read the affidavit?" Sam whispered to her.

Amy nodded. Over fifteen rambling pages it had explicated, in cop-speak, the simple theory of the case which Wally had already presented to her. She had written the pitchbook for the investment and organized the purchase of the stock; then she had lunch with Tom, which went to establishing a relationship between them. She had emailed with Tom, then organized the sale of the stock. There was a narrative in there, thanks to the fake emails; without them it was just a list of tangentially related events.

"Yeah," she said. "I looked over it, like, five times."

"So you saw their case is pretty thin."

She nodded. "It's all resting on those emails."

"Exactly," Sam said. She was quiet for a moment, and then without looking at Amy, she volunteered: "I put together a list of Chicago lawyers for you. The best people I ever worked with, or argued against on civil cases. I actually called a few while I was out in the hallway, and two of them sounded interested."

"Thanks," Amy said.

"One thing that might be a problem, though, is uh—"

Sam was interrupted by the judge, who had been wrapping up her arraignment of the Amazon thief, calling out Amy's name.

Sam crossed herself, spit out her gum into an index card and tucked it into her suit pocket, then stood and motioned for Amy to do the same. They walked down the aisle, all eyes on them. Amy's dry heaves came on strong, and she tried to mask them as a cough.

When they took their place behind the table, Amy peered past Sam, over at the prosecutors. There were three of them: two men and a woman. The man farthest to the left looked at her funny, like it was unusual for a defendant to be peering.

Amy was operating according to the logic of business meetings, where it was key to get a baseline read on your adversary as soon as possible, so you could spot it if they began to falter later. She had always been good at anticipating the vagaries of strangers. It was her supposed allies, like her boss and her wife, who managed to get the drop on her.

"Good afternoon, Your Honor," the same man said. "Julio Salazar, Debra McDaniel, and Michael Wyche for the government."

"Thank you," the judge said, nodding, and then she looked at Sam.

Sam's posture firmed up, almost imperceptibly. "Samantha DiCiccio for Amy Igarashi," she said. "Your Honor, I'm a member of the Illinois state bar, so I am going to have to move for *pro hac vice* admission for the sake of today's proceedings."

Amy hadn't often seen Sam in action as a lawyer when they were married, and she kept being surprised by how much better Sam spoke when she was. Gone were the mushy, smashed-together vowels and entirely dropped consonants.

"Okay," the judge said, glancing at her clerk, a young blonde woman. "Has Ms. DiCiccio filed a certificate of good standing with this court?"

"No," the clerk said, with regret, as if this was her fault.

The judge looked over her glasses at Sam. "*Are* you in good standing?"

"Yes, Your Honor," Sam said, sounding a little less confident now. "I have a disciplinary history of one suspension, which expired last year. I have requested said certificate via priority mail, and the court can expect to receive it later today."

"Okay, that's fine," the judge said. "I'll admit you for the purposes of today's proceeding. I'm not worried about that, especially since this is ultimately Illinois' case. Am I right, though, that you are, uh, married to your client here?"

Everyone in the courtroom fell quiet at once, and Amy felt dozens of interested eyes on her back like tiny pinpricks. Even the prosecutors were eyeing them with lurid interest now.

"Our divorce was finalized earlier this year, Your Honor," Sam said. She was laying it on thick with the *Your Honor*s.

"Okay," the judge said again, smiling. "That's pretty strange of you, but I don't know of any ethical regulation prohibiting it, so I'll let it go." She looked at Amy. She had milky blue eyes that were incongruous with her dark hair and deeply tanned skin. "Ms. Igarashi, I'm Judge Janine Militano. The purpose of today's hearing is to inform you of the charges against you, explain to you what rights you have in defending yourself against these charges, and determine the conditions of your potential release."

Amy nodded. She was teetering awkwardly behind the table—she kept having the urge to lean against it the way Sam was doing, but this was hard to do in a natural way when your hands were cuffed behind you. It made her feel like a drinking bird toy.

"What was the date and time of the arrest?" Militano asked the prosecutors.

Salazar cleared his throat and said, "Your Honor, the accused was taken into FBI custody this morning at 7:30 a.m."

7:33, actually, Amy thought.

"Ms. Igarashi, I understand you've been Mirandized and probably have been so advised by your, ah, ex-wife, here, but I'll again remind you of your right to remain silent in these proceedings," Militano said.

Sam inclined her head a tiny bit with an accompanying jerky movement of her chest, like she was trying not to laugh at the ex-wife comment. That was the exact kind of thing Sam would find funny.

"Have you had a chance to review the affidavit describing your charges with Ms. DiCiccio?"

Amy didn't know what to do, considering she had just been reminded about her right to remain silent. "Yes," she said, because that seemed safe.

"Do you waive its public reading?"

"Yes," Amy said, answering faster this time—anything to get this over with. The handcuffs, plus the loud typing of the court reporter and the attentive stares from those behind her, had put her on the verge of a panic attack.

Militano nodded. "How do you plead?"

"Not guilty."

Amy surprised herself with the way she said this: it was a powerful clarion sound that echoed against the high ceilings of the courtroom. Everyone was quiet afterward, like she had surprised them too.

Sam nudged her and smiled like she was proud.

"As for bail," Militano said, lacing her fingers together and leaning closer to her microphone. "Does the government have a number for us?"

"We do, Your Honor," McDaniel said.

"On that note," Militano said, and she turned her milky eyes on Amy. "The prosecution, this morning, requested a freeze order of any of your assets that have been tainted by this case. Considering your assets are drawn almost entirely from your employment at Atlantic Capital Management, and that you had used some of your own money to invest in the fund's initial buy of Zilpah Drugs stock, then funneled what you got back from the sale into multiple Swiss bank accounts . . . I have approved a freezing of all liquid monetary assets besides your checking account with Chase Bank."

The implications of this took a beat or two to fully register, and once they had, chills began running down Amy's spine. She opened her mouth, which was dry, then closed it. She had forty thousand dollars in her checking account. It was enough to live on, but not enough to pay a hotshot Chicago lawyer— not even enough to pay a retainer.

"Your Honor," Sam quickly spluttered, "for the record, we consider this an unnecessary hardship. My client has no criminal history whatsoever. She's financially responsible for her aging parents. Further, her keeping of Swiss accounts is a matter of financial prudence, not deception."

"And yet!" Militano said, the microphone crackling as her voice rose. "We are talking about a suspect with dual citizenship to a country with historically unsuccessful extradition. I consider Ms. Igarashi a flight risk, charged with a crime with potentially extreme financial penalties. The government is entitled to take steps to avoid a frustration of future judgments."

"Your Honor," Sam said again, sounding like she was charging back up a hill she had just been knocked to the bottom of. "My client will need a certain amount of cash on hand to hire and retain counsel."

"Hire counsel?" Militano peered over her glasses at them. "I'm sorry, so what are you, counselor? Moral support?"

"I'm her temporary counsel," Sam said, faltering.

The prosecutors looked thrilled. Amy wished for a chunk of the ceiling to fall on all their heads at once.

"Well, you may have just gotten a promotion," the judge said, her voice dry. "You're free to pursue an injunction on this, but I'd like to hear a bail number from the government now."

"Your Honor, we propose a two hundred-thousand-dollar personal recognizance bond." This came from the final prosecutor, Michael Wyche. It was like they were grade school kids taking turns giving a presentation. "To be cosigned by one financially responsible person, with travel restricted to the continental US. Ms. Igarashi would need to surrender both of her passports and the one firearm registered in her name."

Amy dry heaved into her sleeve again. This time a little bile came up. She couldn't believe they thought she might run away to Japan, where she went maybe once a year for work. She hadn't even visited her family there since she was twenty-seven and her grandma, her last remaining grandparent, had died. She had gotten drunk with a bunch of her cousins and rode on the back of one of their mopeds over the Rainbow Bridge into Tokyo to go clubbing. She wouldn't flee to Japan any more than she would Australia.

"We propose that the accused be released on her own recognizance today, with that surrender and the cosigning of her bond to be completed within ten days," Wyche finished.

"Is that agreeable to the defense?" Militano said.

Sam, who looked as pale and unsteady as Amy felt, said, "Uh, uh, yes, Your Honor. That's agreeable."

"Fantastic," Militano said.

There began a back-and-forth about venue, discovery, and the date for a preliminary hearing in dense legal jargon that Amy couldn't follow and didn't bother trying to. She just watched Sam's face, trying to gauge her reactions. Sam agreed to waive time to the prosecution before her hearing, which seemed to mean exactly what it sounded like, and Militano adjourned with a little tap of the gavel.

The hot-breathed marshal shuffled over to Amy. She was in

such a fugue state that she initially recoiled from him before she realized he had a key in his hands and was uncuffing her.

"You're free to go," he said. "For now."

He handed her a clear plastic bag that had her pajamas, phone, and wallet in it.

She looked at it, then at him. "What about all my luggage?"

"That's in FBI custody," he said, with contempt. "Good luck getting it back. Feel free to turn the jumpsuit in at your convenience, though." He jerked his chin in the direction of Militano. "You go see the judge now."

It was setting her teeth on edge to be spoken to like this. Amy was feeling spikes and flares of rage that she hadn't felt in a long, long time.

She had been angry as a kid. So many things had made her angry, often to the point of tears. The world was so plainly steeped in unfairness that she couldn't stand it. Her parents had begged her to make life easier on herself, to focus on beating everyone with her success.

At some point it had become clear they were right, and she started to numb herself to her anger. When she was at Harvard and was daily surrounded by loathsome privilege, she worked twice as hard as the trust fund kids during the day and spent her nights dancing with cute butch girls at Boston's handful of gay clubs. She managed to get along working in finance—when she was half the time the only woman in the room and nearly always the only woman who wasn't white—by emotionally detaching herself from every badly behaved man she worked with. Brokers would have screaming matches in the bullpen, and she would watch idly from her office, feeling nothing. No reproach or disgust, just satisfaction that she had ascended beyond the limits of their talent and skill, so much so that she could literally look down on them from her second-floor office.

Sam was the last person Amy could remember being truly furious at, and that feeling hadn't hit her until Sam had already been away at rehab for two weeks. She was numb up until the point that, on a whim, she went into Sam's home office (they had each had their own) and took stock of everything in it. The Mets player bobbleheads and small plants, a framed photo of the two of them at a Christmas party. Amy looked around until she was weeping and then smashed a resin José Reyes on the floor. Sam had ruined their entire life together, and she didn't even have the decency to stick around and fight for Amy. She had taken zero responsibility, and then she had run home to New York so her best friend and her mommy could baby her.

Now that Amy was near her again, it was harder to think of things that way. It didn't help that Sam was being sweet and tender. Amy had expected her to be cold; that would have been much easier to handle, because then she could have been cold right back. Sam's openness was dredging up the tender feelings Amy had had to kill to survive.

Her rage had been woken up for Paul now, and Tom, and whoever else had conspired to ruin her otherwise spotless career. They had ruined her because she was careful, and responsible, because she didn't like to get happy hour drinks with the finance boys and entertain their hideous talk about women. She had always been markedly different from everyone else at Atlantic, but she had never had another option. She never imagined she was putting a target on her back.

Judge Militano slid a piece of paper across the bench for Amy to print, sign, and date. She did this without even reading it. Her eyes were too bleary and her brain too foggy.

Sam walked her out of the courtroom, guiding her along with a light hand on her shoulder. "Ames, I am so sorry," she said when they reached the door, which Amy was all too happy to open by herself. What an underrated privilege it was to open a door. "I had no idea that was coming, which is my bad. I didn't have the chance to meet with the prosecution beforehand, but I didn't think they'd pull any shit like that this early on—I mean, it's gonna be different prosecutors in Chicago—"

Out in the hallway, Amy turned to her and said, "Can I borrow some clothes from you? The FBI stole my luggage."

Sam looked taken aback by the non sequitur. "Yeah, course."

"Good." Amy was in problem-solving mode now, and she didn't want apologies. "So how do I get a good lawyer? Do you know anyone who could bill me on contingency?"

"Ah . . . that's for civil cases, where they're expecting a big settlement."

"I know," Amy said in frustration, "but, like—I can't be the first person in a white-collar criminal case who's had their shit frozen."

"You're not," Sam said, "but it's a tough situation. I could file an injunction, but the judge is right. All of your investments are suspect right now, especially any money you've tied up with Atlantic, and that accounts for everything but your cash on hand. Um. How much is that, by the way?"

"Forty grand. I have forty grand in checking. That's it."

Sam looked queasy. "That's not good."

"You know I can't ask you to represent me," Amy said, lowering her voice. Sam looked agonized again. "You have an entire life in New York, and your job. I can't even pay you . . . it's not fair in any way."

Sam's dark eyes darted down toward the marble floor, and she mumbled, "Don't have a job anymore actually."

"What?"

"I quit," Sam said. She reached in her pocket to retrieve the pack of Doublemint that she'd been working on earlier. "Before I came over here. Larry said I could either help you and get fired, or stay there and help them, y'know, sell you down the river for the sake of protecting Atlantic. I told him to go fuck himself, and I came down here."

Sam had a way of making Amy feel like she was tumbling off the face of the Earth.

"Sam!" she cried. "Why would you *do* that? Oh, my God."

Sam shrugged and chewed her gum.

"God," Amy said again, though she'd be lying if she said she wasn't honored by the gesture.

"Anyway, I'm here if you want me," Sam said.

This was too much. Amy took a seat on the wooden bench behind her, trying to pretend that the security guard fifteen feet away wasn't listening to all of this. She looked absently down at her legs and was reminded that she was still wearing the terrible jumpsuit. It itched like it was made of burlap.

"I can't ask that of you," Amy said.

"I want you to," Sam countered.

She came over and sat down beside Amy, gently bumping her knee with her own. Amy looked up at her, dragging in a deep breath.

"I really think I could win this," Sam said. She sounded painfully sincere. "Honestly, even if you had the two hundred grand to pay a shark, you'd be just another case to them. I actually care about seeing this through, y'know? I want to win this case so bad. I'm hungry. I'm furious about what they're doing to you here."

Amy knew she was right. She also knew Sam to be an excellent lawyer when she put her mind to it.

"I'm furious, too," she admitted.

"Good. You better be. 'Cause if we can't figure out how to get rid of these emails, we're fucked."

"Did you seriously quit your job?"

"Yeah." Sam grinned. "The whole thing was kind of funny, honestly. The big drama of it all . . . Larry was so pissed."

"Sam," Amy said again in a small voice. Overcome by dangerous affection for her, she reached up to tuck a stray piece of hair behind Sam's ear. "What am I gonna do with you?"

Sam just kept smiling. "Hey," she said, "uh, by the way, since when do you own a firearm?"

Amy laughed. "I bought a little gun when we split up," she said. "I got nervous being alone in that giant apartment."

"I'm impressed."

"Don't be. I only went to the gun range once, and I hated it."

"Too loud?" Sam said knowingly.

"Too loud, yeah."

Amy laced her hands together in her lap and watched as two attorneys walked by, chatting to each other. They were so unruffled as to almost look bored, in comparison with Sam's keyed-up, leg-bouncing, gum-chewing presence.

When they had vanished around the corner, Amy felt the same calm settle over her that she'd felt when she was arrested. "Okay," she said.

"Okay?" Sam repeated.

"You're hired."

"Oh shit!" Sam whooped quietly and unwrapped another piece of gum. "You're making the right choice, I promise. I can talk circles around any prosecutor from Chicago. They suck donkey dick."

There she was—the fearless, cocky jerk Amy had married. Amy stopped herself from smiling.

"I'm going to pay you," she said. "Whatever you would normally bill per hour. I'll pay as soon as I can. We can put it in writing."

"Don't worry about that," Sam said. "You can keep paying me in cigarettes for now."

Amy shook her head. "I'm not buying you any more cigarettes," she said. "They're bad for you."

Sam smiled at this for some reason.

CHAPTER 7

ELLIE AND DANI

Amy's sister Ellie was a part-time broker at the New York Stock Exchange, one of a dwindling number of blue-jacketed fast-talkers who did their trading with shouts and hand gestures. They were like an endangered species of bird.

It was funny to Amy that she and her sister had ended up in the same industry, though they came to it from typically opposite angles. Growing up, Ellie wasn't particularly interested in school or books, was popular and unflappable, and thrived on chaos. She worked after-school jobs at fast-paced Jewish delis, saving up enough money to then take several gap years where she traveled around the country, staying at working farms and ranches, and at one point sustaining a permanent scar through her eyebrow from a horse kicking her in the face. When she finally made her way back to New York, she met a broker at a bar who liked her personality so much that he got her a job on the floor. So, if anything, Amy had copied Ellie, although she was already a freshman studying finance at Northwestern when Ellie announced her new career.

It was nearly 4 p.m. by the time Amy had changed into jeans and a T-shirt of Sam's, gone over a game plan with her, then departed from her Tribeca apartment and walked down Church Street to Wall Street. She had always loved Wall Street, but today it felt alien, with its Grecian facades and streets the same color as the buildings. There was a cold front moving into the city, and a stiff wind was making all the American flags flap frantically.

On the floor, things were already quieting down. Trading ended at four, and the traders usually had all split by four fifteen. Amy was lingering at the mouth of a hallway that opened onto the floor when she spotted Ellie, waving good-bye to someone, her blue jacket slung over her shoulder.

"El," she called.

Ellie looked around for the sound; then her face split in a grin when she saw Amy. She hurried over to her in sneakered feet, collaring her in a big hug.

Amy sank her face into her sister's shoulder.

"What did you do to yourself, idiot?" Ellie said, pulling back to look at her.

"So you saw the news?"

"Saw the news?" She laughed. "Uh, yeah, and it's all anyone's talked to me about all day. C'mon, walk with me. I need to pick Meg up from daycare."

Amy followed her into the marble lobby, hobbling along in a too-small pair of Sam's old Vans. "Mom thought you didn't know."

"Wishful thinking on her part."

"Right, she wishes she didn't know."

"You're out then?" Ellie asked, casting a look of worry over her shoulder. "They're not going to hold you till the trial?"

"Yeah. Actually, it's a little complicated. Ellie, I need to ask you a huge favor."

Ellie whipped her security badge in a little circle before she slapped it against a badge reader, beeping them through a turnstile and letting Amy avoid the security checkpoint shakedown she'd endured on the way in. "Money, I'm guessing?" She looked back over her shoulder at Amy, with a look of uncharacteristic suspicion on her wide, friendly face. "Bail?"

The turnstile hit Amy painfully in the hips before releasing her. "Bond," she said. "I need you to cosign my bond."

"What's that involve?"

"It's just a contract that says you're on the hook for two hundred thousand dollars if I flee the country before my trial."

Ellie laughed. "That's a lot of money, girl."

"I know."

Ellie was good for it, she knew. She and her husband would probably have to sell their Lower East Side condo to do it, and go live in a cardboard box, but in the eyes of the United States government she was a person who could reasonably foot a $200,000 bill.

"Well, you better not go anywhere," Ellie said.

"I wasn't planning on it."

"It's not like that's a given anymore," Ellie said, her voice echoing in the lobby. "You used to get anxiety attacks when I shoplifted earrings in high school, and now I'm watching you get arrested on Bloomberg."

This caught them a weird look from a guy who was coming out of the revolving door. Amy ignored him and hurried to catch up with her sister, who was speeding along as usual. "Listen, can I stay with you guys tonight? I have a flight out to Chicago tomorrow."

"Sure," Ellie said, pushing the door open and letting them out into the brisk early evening. "You can keep Meg busy for me and Calvin while we cook a Blue Apron."

"Perfect."

They started down the steps. Amy looked at her sister, studying the curve of her cheek and the sharp jut of her nose, the way her dark hair blew around her face despite its ponytail. She was desperate to commit her to memory; her time spent locked up that morning had awoken in her a primal fear of being caged and isolated. They could take her away from her whole world if she didn't find a way out of this thing.

"Ellie?" she said, her voice high. "Just for the record, I didn't do it. I got caught up in some shit, and I think my boss is trying to pin something that he did on me."

Ellie stopped, then turned and looked back at her, squinting against the setting sun. "I figured," she said. "I couldn't imagine you insider trading."

Amy hesitated, then said: "Sam is helping me. I, um, hired her. She's going to be my lawyer."

Finally, a genuine and serious reaction. Ellie's eyebrows leapt and her mouth flattened.

"Your cokehead ex is your *lawyer?*" she said.

Amy became overly aware of Sam's presence on her body: the LBI T-shirt, the worn-out jeans and the scuffed shoes.

"Yeah," she said.

Ellie sighed so heavily that Amy felt it in her jaw—little bubbles of rock-hard tension locking down the muscles there.

"Once I explain, it'll make sense," she added.

"Oh, I'm sure," Ellie said. She bounced down the remaining steps, her ponytail swinging with the shake of her head. "I'm sure Sam talked her way right into that one, yeah."

They stopped at the curb, and Ellie threw her hand up for a cab.

"I know that's what it sounds like," Amy said, "but can you not? I don't have any other options, first of all, because she's the only good lawyer I can afford right now. They froze my investments. All I have is the money I have in checking. You know I don't keep much in there."

"Yeah, look at that. Being overly responsible finally bit you in the ass."

"Stop it," Amy said, her voice full of little-girl hurt.

Ellie finally looked at her again. "Sorry," she said. "I'm just worried. I hate this. Are you okay?"

Amy shrugged.

"Is this why we've barely heard from you lately?"

A cab pulled up alongside them, and Amy shrugged again. "Yeah, I guess. Work's been insane because of this, and I got distracted, yeah."

Ellie's dark eyes roamed her face, seeming to look for extra information that her words hadn't provided.

"Okay," she said, and opened the car door for her.

The last thing Sam had expected, after throwing herself on the sword of her virtue and being, in her opinion, very good and noble and true was to start catching shit from everybody about it.

First came an exhausting phone call with Jess. That call was full of the paternalistic overtures that loved ones of addicts always tumble into, even when the addict is sober. Sam couldn't tell if Jess thought Amy was an addiction unto herself—a mirage Sam would always be chasing, like that first high—or if she thought a return to Chicago represented a return to coke-soaked bacchanalia. She pushed, harder than a friend ought to push, threatened to sic Bobbi on her, then finally said: "I can't watch you fall apart again."

Sam was stunned. Out of everyone in her life, Jess had seemed the least disturbed by her fall from grace, if not downright Pollyannaish about it.

"I'm not," she said, fumbling with her words. "I'm not falling apart. Honestly, I think I need to do this. I'll be crawling out of my skin if I don't."

"But what happens if you lose?" Jess said. "What will you do if Amy goes to jail, and you helped put her there?"

"Thanks for the vote of confidence."

"It could happen. It really could. Not because you're not a

good lawyer, but because of what you're up against. And even, like—what if you win, and Amy doesn't want you back?"

Sam was quiet for a moment. "I'm not trying to get her back," she lied.

She was released from this call by Trent, who called for Jess to come watch *Pump Rules* with him, and then she sat in her little kitchen with her head buzzing like it used to when she needed a downer. The day had felt like a cocaine binge: hit after hit of adrenaline and dopamine, her blood pressure never dipping below 140/90.

After that, Dani came over. It was almost implausible to Sam that Dani should still exist after the events of today. She had been dragged so thoroughly into the past that it felt like parts of her life had been undone—her time at Byers, her meeting Dani on Tinder, her bar suspension.

But Dani still existed and wanted to come over, as they had discussed that morning a million years ago. She brought a big bottle of San Pellegrino that she had lifted from her Starbucks, because Sam was one of the ten people on earth who liked plain San Pellegrino.

They settled down on the couch to cuddle and watch *The Good Wife*, which Dani insisted on watching with her so she could pause it every five minutes and ask, "Is that what would actually happen?" Sam didn't mind this; it was flattering, and a good exercise for her legal mind, which was getting flabby from disuse.

Tonight, though, Dani paused the show after five minutes and asked, "So . . . is your ex-wife, like, in jail?"

Sam was so destabilized by Dani bringing up Amy that she could only respond in the most literal way possible. "No-ooo . . ."

"Okay, then, what's the deal?" Dani said. She punctuated this by setting the tiny Apple TV remote down on the coffee table with a hard clink. Now they were in it. Now it was a whole thing.

Sam stared helplessly at the remote. "What are you talking about?"

"One of my friends sent me an article that you were quoted in, and it said you're her lawyer. It also said you don't work at your job anymore? And it had a picture of you two walking out of a courthouse together."

She fired all these facts at Sam like she was shelling her. Sam, who still had an arm around Dani, sat up straighter and crossed her leg over her thigh, then stroked Dani's shoulder with her thumb to pacify her.

"All of that's true," she said. "I took her case, and I had to quit my job over it, yeah."

"Okay," Dani said. "Sorry, but that's a little weird. No offense."

"What part of it is weird?"

Dani got up then and went into the kitchen—which the couch was facing away from, so Sam had to sit there helplessly and listen to her bang around in the refrigerator while the nape of her neck tingled from apprehension. She was Tony Soprano at that diner in the finale, and Dani was the guy in the Members Only jacket.

"There's nothing going on," Sam called to her without turning around. "I'm doing it as a favor to her. I am, uh. I'm gonna have to go to Chicago, though, for the trial."

Dani came back out into the living room with her Nalgene in her hand. She took it with her everywhere and stuck it into any available fridge because she couldn't stand the taste of lukewarm water. It was a quirk that had endeared her to Sam on their first date. "You're moving," she said, "to Chicago?"

"Not moving," Sam said. "Just like an, ah, extended business trip."

Dani sighed. "Okay, I'm sorry, this is too weird for me."

"Why, babe? Why weird? You and me are casual. I'll go, I'll come back, I'll hit you up, we can start hanging out again.

No big deal."

"It's just weird!"

"But what's weird?"

Dani didn't sit, which was a bad sign. "You're weird," she said. "I feel like you shouldn't even be dating people."

"What? Why not?"

"Because! I definitely feel like you still have feelings for your ex-wife, and obviously you're not actually trying to get over her, and, like—I'm sorry, I just don't want to be involved with that."

"But you can fuck me and fuck three other people at the same time, and that's cool?" Sam challenged. "That isn't weird or anything?"

"I'm not in love with any of them," Dani said. "And I'm not married. I'm actually really anti-marriage."

"I'm not married either."

"You're divorced. It's so different. Are you in love with her?"

"No," Sam said.

Dani rolled her eyes hugely. "Please. Even if I was trying to believe you, I couldn't."

Sam reached up for her hands and took one, squeezing it. "She more than likely doesn't want me back, okay? So what does that have to do with you and me? I like you, and we have fun. I like hanging out. I don't want you to walk out of here pissed. Can we talk it out?"

"I like you too," Dani exclaimed. "Which is why this is weirding me out. Like, there's a reason I date people who don't want anything serious, and are chill just doing whatever, and everyone involved is fine with that. I don't want to date anyone who's full-ass in love with somebody."

"That isn't what's going on," Sam lied again.

Dani took her hand away and put both of them in the air. "I'm gonna go," she said. "I'm sorry. I just need some space."

"Dani . . ."

Dani grabbed her hoodie and pulled it on. Sam watched

with dismay as she yanked it down hard, covering her butt, and then tucked her sheet of chestnut hair into the hood so she could pull it over her head. That was an anti-intimacy gesture if she'd ever seen one.

"How much space?" Sam said, her hand still lying palm-up on her thigh as if Dani's hand had only been temporarily withdrawn.

"Sam, why don't you just, um . . ." She exhaled through her nose. "You just sort your shit out in Chicago, and if you come back, and everything's cool, give me a call. If it's not . . . don't bother."

"Dani," Sam said, laughing. "It doesn't have to be this serious. We can finish the episode at least, come on."

Dani shook her head, then offered a quiet "Bye" before heading to the apartment door. Sam called "Take care," after her, then realized this was such an old-person thing to say.

Silence descended on the apartment. Sam leaned back against the couch and looked at the TV, where Julianna Margulies's frozen face was aiming a look of disappointment over her left shoulder.

The following morning Bobbi texted Sam, *come hang with me and grandma in central park?*

Their grandmother loved to feed the Central Park ducks. She had done so with bread for years, until she learned from the evening news that bread was bad for them and switched to frozen peas.

Bobbi often went with her, because she was a newlywed and had quit her clerk job at Nordstrom, but didn't have a kid yet. Her days were very free. That's why Jess threatening to get Bobbi involved had been such a threat: Bobbi had the time. Bobbi also had the mouth and the attitude to ride Amy out of town on a rail. She was so loud, she made Sam look demure by comparison.

In fact, Sam often heard Bobbi before she saw her. On a day like that Thursday, when heavy pale clouds blanketed the city and a misty rain pattered a sea of black working schlubs' umbrellas, it was hard to pick out an individual voice in a New York crowd. Not Bobbi's.

Sam heard her as she crested the hill that overlooked the pond via 59th Street, then spotted her sitting on a bench near the water, telling Nuccia about how she'd almost been swindled by her mechanic. This was the common thread to all of Bobbi's stories, that someone was always trying to get one over on her.

"He tried to tell me I ran down my battery not using it," Bobbi was saying when Sam walked up beside them. "I run that car every day! Every day I start that car up, Grandma."

Nuccia shook her head. "People," she said with contempt, and threw some peas into the pond. Ducks raced each other to where they landed and plunged their heads in the murky water.

"Morning, everybody," Sam said.

They swiveled to look at her. "Samantha!" Nuccia said, patting the bench next to her. "Sit sit sit."

Sam took a damp seat next to her grandmother and hugged her with one arm. Behind Nuccia's back, she and Bobbi cheerfully gave each other the finger—their usual greeting. That had started as a joke when they were in high school, and they'd never quite grown out of it.

Sam gamely made small talk with them for a while before dropping the bomb to Bobbi: "I'm heading to Chicago to try Amy's case. I fly out this morning, and I'll be back and forth, but I'm probably gonna spend a few months there."

Her lease was month to month, so dumping the apartment was easy, and then Edgar could move in with his girl. Sam was guessing Amy would put her up somewhere, considering she was working for free. When she came back to New York, she could stay with her parents, or Jess. She was acutely aware of the fact that by insisting on this course of action, she was essentially making herself homeless, but she'd rather become homeless than hand Amy over to a public defender.

"Oh, no way," Bobbi said, gaping at her. "No way. You're helping her?"

"She needs a lawyer," Sam said.

Nuccia was staring out over the pond without moving at all, not a muscle, not even her pupils. Finally, she spoke: "Amy, *allora*? Your friend Amy?"

Sam nodded. Her grandmother always called Amy her friend. Even at their wedding, she had said, "Oh, Sam and her friend look so happy." Nuccia knew what was up, she wasn't stupid. She was taking absurd refuge in plausible deniability, a way to know the truth without admitting she did. If she knew, she'd have to condemn it, as it was condemned in the eyes of the church.

"I liked her," Nuccia said. "She's in trouble? Criminal trouble?"

"Yeah. She's innocent, though."

Nuccia laughed. "Sure. Innocent, guilty. Help her anyway. She's a nice girl."

Gratified, Sam reached out for her grandmother's hand. It felt so precious—colder than a living hand ought to be, like touching a statue in a museum, with its butterfly-thin skin turned calico from age spots. Sam squeezed it gently.

"I will," she said.

"Of course you will," Nuccia said. "You know why? Because you're stubborn, just like my son." She threw some more peas.

Sam had an invite to Ellie and Calvin's place for a pancake breakfast, courtesy of Amy, but she didn't go straight there from the park. First, she had to pawn the shit she had packed into a

Gucci bag that morning. All of it had to go, even the Gucci bag itself.

She stood there in front of a sweaty, redheaded guy in a tiny shop whose sign read E-Z PAWNBROKERS: WE BUY & LOAN DIAMOND, GOLD, WATCHES, and watched him pick through a pile of Rolexes, necklaces, bracelets and Gucci pinky rings (so much Gucci, Jesus Christ). Finally he looked up and said, "I can give you ten grand for all of this."

It had probably cost her upwards of thirty, all told.

"Fuck that," Sam said. "Fifteen."

"Nah. No way."

"No way ten! Fuck out of here with ten. You crazy? The bag alone was three. Each of those watches was at least a grand or two—"

"I gotta *move* the shit," the guy said, gesturing emphatically with his hands, his hairy forearms pumping.

"Man, if you can't sell a genuine Rolex in New York, then you're in the wrong business. They're in great condition, too."

The pawnbroker lifted a tennis bracelet up out of the bag with his pinky like it was a piece of spaghetti. "Where's this from? These real diamonds?"

"Yeah, they're real diamonds! It's from Kay."

"Gold plated or solid gold?"

"Solid gold, Jesus. That cost me, like, four, and it was on discount, too."

He got a loupe out and started examining the bracelet, bringing it up into the dingy light where it sparkled.

Sam stared at it with an ache in her gut. She was as used to pawning her belongings as any other addict, but before when she had pawned things, she had coke to look forward to. She'd had that thrumming under the skin that made everything in the world feel worth it. Now all she had was trepidation and armpit sweat.

She was getting down to the last of her nice things, too.

All she'd been able to keep this time was her favorite Rolex and her wedding rings, plus her clothes. With seventy grand worth of rehab on her credit cards, no job, and limited savings, those would be next to go.

"Alright," the pawnbroker finally said. "Off this bracelet, I'll give you thirteen five for all of it."

"Fine. Sold." That was more than enough to get her by in Chicago. Ten would have been, too, but it was the principle of the thing.

The broker wrote her a cashier's check so she didn't get mugged to death on her way out, and she fed it to a Wells Fargo ATM a block away, enjoying the whir of the check being eaten before a sexy number popped up on the screen. Even after the good life had almost destroyed her, something about large amounts of money still got Sam a little wet.

The walk to Ellie and Calvin's condo sobered her, though. For about ten minutes she loitered clammily outside the building, not wanting to call up. Then she realized she remembered the door code, buzzed herself up, and loitered in the hallway just as clammily. It took getting a weird look from their next-door neighbor for Sam to suck it up and lay a hard knock on their front door.

Ellie opened it a moment later, looking frazzled. She brushed her hands off on a batter-stained apron and reached up to pull Sam into a brief hug. "There you are."

"Hey, El."

"Hi Sam," Calvin called from the kitchen, which butted so snugly up against the front door that you were in it as soon as you stepped inside. Ellie took Sam's coat and hung it up on a rack, then joined her husband back at the stove. There was a pancake assembly line set up.

"Calvin! My man. How are you? How are things over at WeWork?"

Calvin flashed her a smile. "I stay busy. Can't complain."

Amy was sitting on a barstool at the island, idly flipping through a magazine and looking exhausted. Next to her in a highchair was four-year-old Meg, much larger than the last time Sam had seen her, but still tiny in the grand scheme of things.

When she spotted Sam, Meg reached up to her with chubby arms, beaming. "Sam-Sam!"

Sam scooped her up. "Megumi, my favorite ex-niece."

"Oh, Sam, don't," Amy said. She was protective of Meg.

"Aw, she doesn't understand," Sam said. "That's above her pay grade. Isn't it, Meg?"

"Ame?" Ellie called over her shoulder. "You want any more pancakes?"

Amy looked down at her plate, where one still lay unfinished in a sad puddle of syrup. She cleared her throat and said, "No, I'm alright."

"So, how have you been, Sam?" Calvin said. He half turned and flicked his eyes over her. "You haven't been practicing law, right?"

"Uh, no," Sam said. "I've been working as a legal consultant at a crisis communications firm."

"And she quit," Ellie said, her voice rising incredulously on "quit."

"To represent Amy, yeah," Sam said.

"I was actually surprised to hear that you're doing that," Ellie said. She flipped the pancake she was working on. "I thought you got disbarred."

Sam grinned, stung, then set Meg back down in her highchair. "Nope, just suspended."

"Right, I must have misremembered. I mean, you were charged with a felony, right?"

"Misdemeanor possession."

"Ri-ight," Ellie said, drawing the word out. "And you're sober now, of course."

"Ellie," Amy said in a knock-it-off tone.

"Yeah," Sam said. "Just got my year chip."

"A year," Ellie said to Calvin, raising her eyebrows. "And how long were you using?"

"Ellie!"

"A year," Sam admitted. "She has a right to ask, Amy."

"No, she doesn't, because she's treating me like a child who can't make my own decisions," Amy said.

Ellie whipped around and gestured with the spatula. "Have *you* asked her any of these questions?"

While the sisters bickered, Calvin mouthed *sorry* at Sam. Sam laughed to indicate it was fine.

"I don't need any extra stress right now," Amy said to Ellie, who sighed.

"None of this is personal, Sam," Ellie told her. "You know that."

"I do," Sam agreed.

Meg was clearly unhappy about the tension in the room, and started to fuss. Sam slipped her Rolex off her wrist and gave it to her to play with, then leaned over the island to examine the sheaf of papers lying there. They were copies of paperwork from SDNY that had been signed at the bottom by Ellie, and dated today.

> *Mortgagers herein have executed a bail bond in the U.S. District Court, Southern District of New York, in the amount of $200,000 to secure bail in the case of UNITED STATES OF AMERICA v. Amy Igarashi, 2:17-cr-00745.*

> *This mortgage becomes due to the Lender if Amy Igarashi, the accused in the matter of UNITED STATES OF AMERICA v. Amy Igarashi, 2:17-cr-00745, now pending in the United States District Court for the Southern District of New York, should be*

determined to have violated the terms and conditions of bail set for her release in the aforementioned matter in accordance with the law.

The real property is located in the Borough of Manhattan, State of New York, in Block 100 with street address 177 E 3rd St. This property shall serve as security for the satisfaction of the bail conditions.

Sam looked up at Amy. "So you guys decided to put this place up as collateral?"

"Yeah, Ellie insisted. Against my objections."

"It's fine!" Ellie exclaimed, using a spatula to drop a heap of pancakes onto a large plate adjacent to the papers. "Sam, here, have some pancakes."

Sam appreciated the olive branch. "Can I file these papers somewhere for you guys?" she said, collecting them up into a handful and rapping them on the island.

"You can just set them on the coffee table," Calvin said.

"I want them," Meg whined, reaching out.

Sam rifled through the papers to find a nonessential one and handed it over.

"No, all of them!"

Sam laughed. "Your baby likes to play with Rolexes and federal bail paperwork," she said to Ellie.

Ellie laughed. "She's a sophisticate."

"Yeah, baby Paul Manafort."

Sam patted Meg on the head and went into the living room, where the curtains were drawn against the gloomy day outside. There were clear signs of Amy having slept on the couch—a pair of rumpled blankets folded on a cushion, an iPhone cord dangling over the armrest, a pair of earrings on the coffee table beside a used makeup wipe.

When she came back toward the kitchen, she had the

awkward decision to make of whether she should sit beside Amy. After hesitating a moment, she did. She compromised by angling her body away from her ex-wife, like she was about to bolt out the door at a moment's notice.

Amy looked listless, pale and unslept. Her perfect hair, which normally swept in a shiny arc across her upper back, was scraped back into an unkempt bun.

"You doing alright?" Sam said in a soft voice.

Amy nodded.

Sam knew what had happened to Amy last night: she got the late-night spookies. Facing down a potential prison sentence was tough enough for a hardened criminal; for someone like Amy, someone innocent, it was almost existentially impossible. This was part of why bail existed. The average person never anticipates freaking out so hard that they flee the country, but it happens.

Amy started digging into her purse on the barstool beside her, wincing like she had a headache as Meg's cries for pancakes grew louder. "Here," she said, handing Sam a United Airlines ticket sleeve. "We're leaving at two today. Is that alright with you? Is that enough time to tie up any loose ends?"

Sam felt like her life was nothing but loose ends, but she nodded. "You should've let me buy my own ticket."

In the kitchen, Ellie and Calvin grew quiet.

"I'm not broke," Amy said. "And I used miles anyway, so . . ."

"You just have to be careful with your spending now."

"Did you hear that?" Amy said, lifting her head and jerking her chin at Ellie. "*Sam* is telling me to be careful with my spending."

"Hey," Sam cried, while everyone but Meg laughed at her. And then, when she realized she was being left out of something adult, Meg started laughing too.

Ellie handed Sam a plate of pancakes, and Sam made dutiful work of it, even though Bobbi and her grandma had already made her have pizzelles and coffee with them. When Ellie took Meg down the hall to wipe the syrup off her face, and Calvin went over to the living room to put on Yankees postseason coverage, Sam finally addressed Amy again.

"So I got a few calls back this morning," she said in a quiet voice.

Amy was staring at the island, bleary-eyed. She gave a tiny nod to show she was listening.

"Your workplace doesn't keep security video longer than two months unless there's an incident. And the city doesn't keep CCTV footage longer than ninety days. So we can't use security footage to prove you weren't at the office late that night."

"Yeah," Amy said, without looking at Sam. "I figured. I was Googling about that last night."

"What about your badge card?"

"No, I thought of that too. But I don't swipe out when I leave. I only swipe in on my way upstairs."

"You sure there's nothing that can go toward establishing an alibi? Anyone you saw that night?"

Amy cleared her throat and let out a sigh. "No. But I did figure out where I was, from looking back at my texts."

"Where were you? Home?"

"I was at a jazz club right across from my office till pretty late."

"Wait, for real?" Sam said, filled with hope.

"Not so fast," Amy said. "I only got one drink, and I paid with cash. I always pay with cash there, because it's one of those places that keeps your card all night."

The hope left her in a big whoosh.

"Right," Sam said. "You always were paranoid about that."

Amy lifted her head a little, looking up at the light fixture suspended above them, the glow of it reflected in her dark eyes. "It's easy for someone to skim you that way," she said, but the way she said it was so distant that it sounded like wisdom half remembered from a past life.

"You're a regular there. The bartenders wouldn't remember you?"

"Remember one regular being there on one night, all the way back in May, when I spent the whole night in the corner reading a book and only ordered one drink? Come on, Sam."

"Do you keep your receipts?"

"You know I don't. No sane person does."

"Well, it's been a while since we've talked, Ame, I dunno! Maybe you lost your mind."

Amy laughed. "It doesn't matter anyway, unless you can prove the emails were sent from my office."

"Yeah, I looked into that, and I don't think we can."

"Great."

Sam clapped her hands together. "Alright. If we can't prove a negative, we have to prove a positive. Affirmative defense."

"We have to nail Paul," Amy murmured.

"Exactly."

"You know who he retained as his private counsel on this?"

"Who?"

Amy finally turned to look at her, meeting her eyes. "Hughes, Roper, Keating and Keating."

Sam's blood ran cold, much the way it had when Larry had said the words *Atlantic Capital Management.* "You're kidding me."

"I'm not."

"Those pieces of shit. Are you serious?"

Amy nodded again.

"This almost feels personal," Sam said in helpless desperation, like if she pointed out the impropriety, someone would swoop in and fix it. "Like, what the fuck?"

"Welcome to my world," Amy said.

Sam wasn't sure if she should take it as significant or entirely meaningless that Amy had gotten them seats together on their flight to O'Hare. She could have just put them in the same row, or in separate rows entirely, but she had given herself the window seat and Sam the middle.

She managed not to bring it up for the entire flight, until they started their descent over a moody, rain-soaked Chicago. Amy had woken up from her nap and was paging through a magazine with her sleep mask pulled up over her forehead.

"How'd you sleep?" Sam said, as an icebreaker.

"Not great," Amy said, still sounding drowsy. "Did you nap?"

Sam hadn't, not with a brain that had been on fire for forty-eight hours straight. Plus, she'd been too busy watching half of *The Imitation Game* on her little TV and trying to puzzle out whether Amy's arm brushes were intentional or just nervous fidgeting.

"Nope," she said. "Hey . . ."

"Yeah?"

The guy in the aisle seat coughed a very wet, thick cough, and they made horrified faces at each other, which made Amy have to stifle a laugh.

"Nothing," Sam whispered. "Just wondering why you wanted to sit next to me."

Amy furrowed her brow at her. "What? We're together— traveling together, I mean. I felt like it would be weird not to."

"Yeah. I guess."

"Plus, you're a known quantity to fly with . . . I didn't want to end up next to somebody disgusting."

"Right," Sam said. She wondered what she'd been hoping for Amy to say.

There was the familiar ding of the intercom, and then:

"Ladies and gentlemen, this is your captain," a smooth voice oozed through the cabin speakers. "As we start our descent, pleeeeeease make sure your seatbacksandtraytables are in their fulluprightposition. Make sure your seatbelt is securely fastened and aaaaaaall carry-on luggage is stowed underneath the seat in front of you orrrr intheoverheadbins. Thankyouuuu."

Amy rapped her knuckles on the rain-spattered window, through which the skyscrapers of downtown Chicago were visible. "Pretty."

"Pretty," Sam echoed, but she was looking at Amy.

CHAPTER 8

CHICAGO, 2017

Sam and Amy made their way through the airport together without talking. Amy was a more experienced flier, thanks to her time spent zipping around to the capitals of the finance world—Hong Kong, London, Tokyo, Sydney, Singapore—and she looked like she was in a commercial for YSL perfume while Sam struggled with her luggage and kept dropping her water bottle.

Sam was pretty sure you could no longer smoke at a taxi stand, so after they'd been in line for a few minutes, she got out her Juul and started hitting it. Amy glanced over, but didn't otherwise react. No one else they were in line with even seemed to notice; it was a steamy, smelly day. Rain was still echoing off the shuttle train tracks overhead, interrupted from time to time by the sound of a train.

Sam blew out mint-flavored vapor. "So," she said. "We didn't talk about this, but I'm figuring I can just find an extended-stay near your place? I have cash. I just pawned a bunch of stuff."

Amy looked at her again, with confusion breaking through her obvious preoccupation. "Extended . . . what, like a motel?"

"Yeah."

"Sam, of course you're not getting a motel. Are you crazy?"

She said this passionately enough that the guy in front of them cleared his throat and gave a half-hearted turn in their direction, like he wanted to know what was going on, but not badly enough to involve his whole body.

Sam lowered the vape and looked at Amy. "What am I getting then?"

"You'll stay with me. I thought that was the plan."

Sam went very still like Amy was a deer or a horse who would run out into taxi traffic if spooked. After a moment, she said, "I didn't think you'd want me in your house."

"We need to confer, don't we?"

Sam laughed at her lawyerly use of *confer*. "Well, yeah."

"And strategize?" Amy wrung her hands. "So, I'll need you close by. I have a guest room, it has a bathroom, you'll have total privacy. I mean, technically it's my office, but it has a bed."

So this wasn't about Amy wanting her back, it was about Amy wanting her legal mind on call at all times. Still, though, there was something suspicious about the anxiety with which Amy was making this demand.

Sam decided not to read too much into it. "Where you living these days?"

"I'm renting a house in Forest Glen," Amy said. "It's tiny, it has a garden."

"Sounds nice."

"It is nice. And if you snort coke in it, I'll kill you."

The guy half turned again, this time with slightly more energy.

"I'm sober, Ames," Sam whispered.

Amy shot her a hard look. She looked very pretty when she did that. "Yeah, well."

"I didn't think you'd left the city. You're such a city girl."

"Forest Glen isn't leaving the city."

"Two years ago you'd have said it was."

"A lot's changed since then," Amy said, her voice curt.

"Guess so."

The line moved forward, and the nosy guy started packing his luggage into an idling cab. Sam hit her vape again. Emboldened by the nicotine head rush, she said, "I'm guessing you're not seeing anyone?"

Amy laughed. "Why, because I'm inviting my ex-wife to have a sleepover at my place?"

"Well, yeah."

"No, I'm not seeing anyone," she said, the curt tone gone, replaced by something almost playful.

Sam felt like she always did at the beginning of a Hail Mary play: full of delusional self-confidence, pointed like an arrow at the object of her desire, propelled forward by an unerring conviction that she would get whatever it was in the end. But this time she couldn't tell if the feeling was about Amy, or about winning Amy's case.

"Good," she said by accident.

Amy looked at her out of the corner of her eye, like any more contact would be dangerous.

"Good for you, I mean, that you're single," Sam clarified. "Explaining me might be hard."

"Explaining you's always been hard," Amy teased her.

Now that was flirting, absolutely. Sam knew Amy. She knew what Amy flirting sounded like.

The taxi in front of them pulled away, ferrying the nosy guy to his destination, and another one pulled up in its place. They busied themselves packing their luggage into the trunk, careful not to brush arms or elbows as they did.

Amy's house was cute. It was a low-slung one-story with an attic and big windows, and was nestled in a leafy part of Forest Glen, somewhat hidden by a collection of bushes and hydrangeas. It looked like the kind of place someone would go to be alone. More than that—to hide.

Amy took Sam's single piece of luggage from her when they got in the house, and carried it away to the guest bedroom. Sam tried to follow her, but Amy put a hand up and said, "Wait, I want to straighten up in there," which Sam took to mean that the duvet was askew or something. She didn't care, though, because that gave her the chance to snoop around the living room.

Amy had decorated with care, and Sam recognized a lot of the art and furniture from their penthouse. She had given all that stuff to her in the divorce. Amy had picked most of it out, anyway, and it would be such a huge pain in the ass to have things shipped out from Chicago just to rot in pricey storage because they were too big for her tiny Tribeca apartment. Sam's divorce attorney was perpetually frustrated with her (join the club) and kept begging her to take something, anything, even alimony, but Sam just didn't want to think about it anymore. She wanted it all to be over and done with. Every time she tried to focus on the finer financial details of what was, on a grand scale, Amy leaving her, she felt like her head was full of bees.

Sam didn't realize how much she had missed their things, though. Her breath hitched in her chest when she noticed a Tiffany lamp on an end table.

It was the lamp that Amy had got her for their first Christmas as a married couple. When Sam had unwrapped it, Amy sheepishly told her that she'd noticed how she was always posting photos she'd taken of Tiffany lamps in bars on her Instagram, so she figured she must think they were pretty.

Sam hadn't responded for a second, she was so surprised. It had never even occurred to her how much she liked Tiffany lamps, but holding an authentic one in her hands, her chest had ached with affection and gratitude.

It ached the same way now. Sam was surprised to see the

lamp in such an obvious spot, too, considering how much it must remind Amy of her.

She moved on and turned her attention to the rest of the room. It was lined with stuffed bookshelves, and their most massive leather couch had pride of place, facing a relatively small television that had Apple TV and a few other dongles hooked up to it. Sam picked up the remote and idly switched it on: CNBC popped up. Of course. Amy only watched two channels: ABC7 Chicago and CNBC.

Sam moved on, interested in the framed photos on the walls. There were four: Amy hugging Meg; Amy, Ellie and their parents posing with cherry blossom boughs in Shinjuku Gyoen; Amy laughing at a restaurant with her two best friends and college roommates, Caroline and Leah; and Amy at a World Series Cubs game with three of the couples they used to be friends with when they were married: Melissa and Tom Cramer, Lana and Mickey Weister, and Hayda and Danny Hatwal-Walker.

These friendships had been their initial passes into Chicago high society. Tom was the corrupt alderman to the 32nd Ward, which was populated almost entirely by white yuppies, and he and Melissa had sponsored them to become members at Skokie. Lana, who was née a Duchossois, had gotten them invited to the Children's Ball two years in a row.

Sam heard Amy's footsteps behind her, and then Amy clearing her throat. "Okay, it's ready in there," she said. "You can go freshen up if you want."

"Thanks," Sam said. She tapped a knuckle on the glass of the photo she'd been looking at. "You still in touch with these guys?"

Amy's eyes flicked to the photo, and her face dropped a little—more with resentment than sadness. "Oh," she said. "Uh, not really, to be honest. Obviously we went to the World Series together, but, you know, you and I had just . . . I think you had just left for rehab actually. So they were probably trying to be nice by inviting me."

138

"Right."

Sam could sort of remember watching the World Series in rehab on Long Island. She had been so shell-shocked from the turn her life had taken, and so zonked out from cocaine withdrawals, that it barely registered. When she got out and was finally starting to feel like a human being again, she kept being bowled over by the re-realization that the Cubs were World Series champions and Donald Trump was the president. She felt like Marty McFly.

Sam hadn't even voted—she was too dizzy from topiramate, which her rehab had put her on because of her withdrawal tremors. When the returns had started looking bad for Clinton, Amy called her from a watch party Tom was having, and left the phone on speaker. Sam had spent that night in bed, disoriented and shaking, listening to a bunch of Chicago Democrats scream "You're fucking kidding me!" at Wolf Blitzer on the TV.

"I kind of thought you got our couple friends in the divorce," Sam said to Amy, backing up to the couch and taking a very awkward seat on it. What does one do with one's hands while sitting on a couch? She crossed her legs and put both hands on one knee like an insane person. "Just 'cause, uh, I never heard from any of them at all after I went to rehab."

Amy took a seat just as awkwardly in an Eames armchair across from the couch. They had gotten that one for cheap ("cheap") from their vintage dealer, because the matching ottoman was missing. "I didn't hear from them for much longer after that," she said. "I think they felt that since I was no longer part of a couple, and because it was kind of an um, Chicago society scandal, that they were well within their rights to just sort of back slowly away from me. Plus, they all started trying to get pregnant this year, so that put me out in the cold, too."

"Oh," Sam said. "Assholes."

Amy smiled in agreement. "I still hear from Hayda, though."

Sam glanced around the room, trying to ward off a hot

prickling in her eyes. "God, I'm sorry," she said. "I really kind of blew up your life, didn't I?"

"Sam . . ."

"No, deadass. I thought I just blew up mine. I thought you'd be fine once I was gone."

Amy stared resolutely at the hardwood floors, like she was experiencing a similar prickling. "One thing you don't need to apologize for is our friends being crappy people," she said, her voice catching. "That's not on you." She laughed. "Probably it's on both of us, for picking them."

"I guess I just thought you were supposed to hang out with assholes when you started making the big money," Sam said, and Amy laughed again.

"Me too," she admitted.

Sam rubbed her hands on the leather of the couch. Outside, she could still hear rain, and the occasional sonic intrusion of a passing car. "They were never that great to us to begin with, anyway."

"No, they weren't," Amy said. "I always felt alienated. We should have hung out more with our gay friends."

"But what lesbians did we know who were pulling down eight hundred thousand a year? Who could have related to us?"

Amy shrugged. "No one."

They were quiet for a moment, with nothing to look at but each other.

"Do you want dinner?" Amy asked, popping up abruptly from her chair. "I was going to order out. I mean, order in. Like, DoorDash or something."

"Yeah, that's—"

"Pizza?"

Sam laughed. "Please no Chicago pizza. I've been back eating good pizza for too long. I can't do it."

"Thai?"

"Sure."

Amy went into the kitchen where Sam could still see her and opened her laptop where it was sitting on the island.

"You heard of apps, Grandma?" Sam teased.

"Shut up," Amy called back. "I hate logging into stuff on two different things. I never remember my passwords."

"Yeah, okay, Grandma."

Amy didn't have a comeback. She went quiet, and all Sam heard was keystrokes; she looked up and over at her curiously.

"You're kidding me," Amy said aloud.

Her voice was suddenly different. She picked up her glasses case from the island, opened it with a snap, then put them on and put her face close to the computer screen.

Sam got up and made her way to her, past the little dining nook (new table, but the same stiff Neiman Marcus chairs that Sam had never liked) and into the kitchen, where Amy was looking at her laptop like it was a snake.

"What?" Sam said, leaning her elbows on the marble island.

"They fired me," Amy said, sounding stunned. "I mean, I guess that's not a, a *surprise*, or anything, considering—it's not like I was going to—like, they did *frame* me, but—"

"Wait, back up. They fired you over email?"

"Yeah." Amy took her glasses back off like she was tired of seeing things, and dropped them with a clatter onto the island. "Is that legal? It is, right?"

Sam nodded. "Illinois is an at-will employment state."

"God. Son of a bitch. Paul didn't even do it himself. This is a boilerplate letter from HR. It says I violated the terms of my employment, and they want me to come pick up my stuff tomorrow, to turn over my badge and clean out my desk. How am I going to go over there?"

"Alright, hang on, breathe a little."

Amy exhaled a laugh. "I'm breathing."

"Is there anything from there that you need? Or anything that could be useful to the case?"

"I don't know. No, I guess. I have some stuff with sentimental value . . . I have a letter my dad wrote me when I got into Harvard. I keep it in my desk."

"How is your dad, by the way?" Sam said, careful to keep her voice even and free of pity.

"His condition's been stable," Amy said, her voice tight, and quickly changed the subject. "The email says the FBI already combed through my office, so I don't even know what's still in there. Is it worth it to go? I feel like I'm going to lose my shit if I have to look Paul in the face."

"Probably security'll escort you to your office and back, so I don't think you'll see anyone," Sam said. "If you want the letter, I'd go. The FBI wouldn't have taken that unless they were being absolutely sadistic. Plus, you do have to turn in your badge."

Sam reached out for the MacBook in front of Amy and tugged it away, turning the screen to herself. She tabbed out of Outlook and went back to the DoorDash page, where the page for a Thai restaurant was open.

"You still like that green curry?" Sam said to her.

Amy, who had been staring into middle distance, flicked her dark eyes up to meet Sam's. She nodded. "Yeah."

"Alright. I'll order that, and then I'm getting pad thai."

Amy nodded again. "Can I have some?"

"Sure."

Sam forgot where she was when she woke up around eight the next morning. She stared at the ceiling for a moment while her brain came back online, thinking. Chicago came back to her first—it was something in the air, especially after the rainfall, a musk that was immediately recognizable. She thought for a moment that the last year had been a bad dream, and her heart leapt, but then she remembered everything else, and it fell back down.

Amy was still asleep. Sam went down the hall and eased her bedroom door open a crack so she could check, and there she was, spread-eagle across the bed with her dark hair all over the place. She was snoring. She used to wear snore strips when they were married. Her room was immaculate, and barely had more personal touches than the guest room/office did. A large watercolor of a sailboat was the only thing hung on the walls. Sam got the feeling she didn't spend a lot of time in here.

"Ame?" she whispered.

Amy made a noise.

"I'm gonna go to the courthouse. I have to file for discovery and stuff."

"Oka-ay," Amy muttered into the pillow.

"I'm gonna take your car, if that's okay."

She yawned and finally looked up. "That's fine. I'm taking an Uber to Atlantic, since they're making me turn in my parking pass."

"You have a phone?"

"I had an old iPhone in a drawer. I reactivated it last night."

"Okay."

"You'll have to put gas in the Beemer," Amy added. "I haven't driven it in weeks. I was using Atlantic's car service a lot."

Sam nodded. She wanted to say something else, but she couldn't think of anything. "Good luck," she added lamely.

Amy laughed a grim laugh. Actually, more accurately, she said, "Ha-ha-ha" like it was words.

"Yeah, well, you know what I mean. Don't stab Paul if you can help it."

"Ha! Yeah."

This was concerning. Sam was afraid that reality was setting in for Amy now that she was home and that the shimmer of depression, which had been evident yesterday morning during pancakes, was growing into something real. That wasn't good for their case. She needed Amy to be passionately angry, not beaten-down and resigned. She needed the Amy who had said *not guilty* with such force that she made a whole courtroom full of criminals feel awkward.

Sam still wasn't sure where they were, as far as emotional intimacy. They'd had some nice moments last night, but she didn't think Amy would take too kindly to being comforted right now, not by Sam, who had run off at the lowest point of their marriage. That wound was clearly still fresh. So, perversely, the only way to react here was to err on the side of caution and abandon her again.

"I'll, ah, text you," Sam said, before making her exit.

The termination email came from HR, but Paul's assistant Donna had been the one to email Amy and let her know that she was expected at Atlantic's offices in the Board of Trade building at noon on Sunday. That time and date had probably been chosen specifically to make sure the office was as deserted as possible. Amy wanted to think this was to benefit her, but in truth she knew it was for the sake of all her ex-coworkers, and Paul in particular. They were afraid of her losing her mind and causing a scene.

Maybe she would cause a scene. What was stopping her now? No, really, that was the question—what was stopping her from doing absolutely anything? Just the knowledge that there was a well-oiled PR machine already in place, one that had lurched into motion the second she was arrested. Already stories were coming out in *The New York Times* and the *WSJ* and the *Trib* about how Amy, evil scheming dragon lady, had almost caused the downfall of noble philanthropic Paul Weller with her greed. Even Sam's college friend Shane had written a piece that fell somewhat into that trap. Amy couldn't blame him; he was surely being fed the same story by any source he could get his hands on.

The machine was already chewing up her reputation, and if she made any sudden moves it would catch her fingers in its mechanisms and rip her arms off.

Her Uber driver didn't talk, which was fine. Amy took a Valium and listened to jazz in her headphones, trying to make the drive longer with the power of her mind, but they still got there entirely too fast. She took a deep breath and thanked the driver, then tripped in her heels on her way out of the car and toppled into a sedan they were double-parked alongside.

"You okay?" the driver called.

"Yes," Amy lied, and closed the car door before he could argue with her.

Everything about this situation was so foreign that when Amy walked up to the front desk security guy, Craig, whom she'd known for years and years, she had no idea what to say. She just looked at him in silence until he looked up from his computer.

"Hi, Amy," he said, smiling.

"Hi," Amy said, with a stab of grief at the thought of kind Craig thinking she was a criminal.

"Security'll be down in a second to escort you upstairs, okay?"

"Okay," she said.

"You can wait right here."

"Okay."

Amy stared down at her manicured hands where they lay on the marble counter of Craig's desk, and then, when the two security guards came to fetch her, she stared at the walkie-talkies hanging from their belts. They talked to each other about Halloween as they walked her to the elevators, what their kids were dressing up as, what their wives wanted them to do around the house. She wanted so much to have normal small talk, too, but there was an impenetrable barrier between her and them.

Amy had never realized she could miss small talk this much.

Anxiety swelled in her chest like a balloon as they got closer and closer to the twenty-fifth floor. Her hands got clammy, and the elevator seemed to shrink around her. The security guards' voices faded in her ears until their words were mushy nonsense.

A bell chimed and the door opened. They stepped out, then turned and looked at her expectantly. She had arrived at the lobby of Atlantic.

"Ma'am?" one of the guys said—the one on the right, who had a mustache. "This is it."

"I know," Amy said.

"Okay. Can I have your badge, please?"

She slipped her badge out of her pocket, but the lanyard snagged as it came out, and she dropped it on the floor.

"I'll get that," the mustached guard quickly said, and snatched it off the ground like it was a bomb. "Do you have any other company property on you, or in your possession?"

"No," Amy said. "The FBI has my work phone and laptop, and my executive assistant has the physical key to my office."

"Any hard copies of company documents at home?"

"No."

Mustache beckoned her along the same way he had downstairs. Amy began to follow them again. She had to walk an extremely familiar path through the lobby, past Haven the administrative assistant, who pretended not to see Amy, and across the atrium trading floor toward the stairs that led to a row of second-floor offices. There were five guys on the trading floor pulling a weekend shift, and they stared at her as she went by, but the offices looked empty otherwise. If anyone of importance was here today, they'd be on the twenty-sixth floor, where Paul's office and the boardroom and the video-conferencing facilities were.

The security guards let her go into her office by herself while they waited outside. This made her feel a little less like a criminal, even though all her walls were glass. She walked by the now-empty desk in the anteroom before her door, where her assistant Kelly used to sit, and wondered with a pang if they had fired her too. Amy hoped they had just reassigned her to the admin pool.

She hadn't heard from Kelly, which didn't surprise her. Most of her social circle seemed to be keeping their distance. When she had reactivated her old phone the night before, after Sam had gone to bed, concerned texts from only eight people came in.

Amy had lain awake after that, looking at the camera roll on her old phone. She had tossed it in a drawer in fall 2016, when the iPhone 7 came out. Right before Sam got arrested. There were so many photos on it of their life together, it took her breath away to scroll through them.

There were signs of trouble there that she could only see now, in hindsight. In a photo of Sam cooking dinner, under the harsh light of their old kitchen, you could see how her cheeks were hollowed out, how her eyes were sunken and rimmed with dark circles. Amy spent five minutes zooming into and out of that photo with two fingers, transfixed, wondering how she could have missed it.

She was content then; that was how. Amy was smiling in every photo of herself that she found, her own cheeks rounder than they were now, her eyes dancing. She was so much happier then than she could now even remember being. A year in purgatory had given her emotional amnesia.

As Amy stepped into her office, she could see the FBI had done their usual damage. They had tipped all her trash cans out to get the papers from them, and left behind used tissues on the floor. Gross.

Her computer and three of her four monitors were gone, but they had left the main one that she used to log in, its cords now dangling impotently over the edge of her cherry-mahogany desk. Amy beelined for that desk and opened its top drawer to find that the letter from her dad was still inside. She grabbed it and shoved it into her pocket.

No-Mustache had handed her the cliched cardboard box, so she put some things in it. She had a few desk knickknacks, and a ton of expensive hardbacks on her bookshelf like *Buffett: The Making of an American Capitalist*, and *One Up on Wall Street*, and *Security Analysis*, and *The Essays of Warren Buffett*.

The FBI apparently thought she might be hiding evidence of a crime behind all her Warren Buffett biographies because they had ransacked the shelves, knocking a lot of her books onto the floor. When Amy knelt to pick those up, she spotted something stuck to the underside of her desk: a Post-it.

She shuffled across the floor on her knees and peered at it. It was the Post-it that she had written her computer password on back when she had to update it in January.

The thing was, Amy had never stuck that there. She had kept it at the bottom of her monitor, and when it disappeared one day a few months later, she assumed that the cleaning staff had just gotten a little overzealous. But she would never stick something on the underside of her desk, like a teenager hiding gum. Someone else had done that. Maybe the same someone who would have needed her password to log into her computer and send those emails to Tom Naftalis.

Her brain worked fast. Figuring it was better than nothing if not as good as a pair of latex gloves, Amy ripped a page out of the back of *Security Analysis* and used it to pull the Post-it free, then wrapped it inside the paper carefully so she didn't smudge any prints. This went inside of her cardboard box.

When she stepped back outside her office, she was trying not to smile, but the security guys didn't seem to notice. They just started walking her back down the stairs in silence.

The three were almost back at the reception area when Paul walked out of an office door and directly into their paths.

Amy stopped short. She and Paul stared at each other.

"Amy," Paul said.

The security guys stopped too, turning to identify the source of the sound. They both looked paralyzed by Paul's presence. They had a job to do, which was to ferry Amy to her professional death with no stops, but Paul was very powerful.

"I don't have anything to say to you," Amy said, her heart pounding.

"Well, that's unfortunate," Paul said. "An explanation would be nice."

If he hadn't just said that to her, it would be hard to believe that he just said that to her. Amy lunged into his space, ignoring a "hey, hey" from Mustache. She was now so close she could smell his aftershave and oud cologne.

"I know exactly what you did," she whispered. Paul looked back at her with mild curiosity. "And you're not going to get away with this, I swear to God."

"Amy," Paul said, "I have no idea what you're talking about."

"You did this!"

"You seem confused. Are you feeling alright?"

"Tell me how you think you're going to shield yourself from this when you were the one who set everything up with Zilpah. That was your buy."

"You wrote the pitchbook, Amy."

"After you tipped me off! Why me, why did you frame me?"

"I have no idea what you're talking about," Paul said, sliding his hands into his pockets and glancing over at the security guys. "Can you two go ahead and escort her downstairs, please?"

"This isn't over," Amy said as one of them grabbed her by the arm.

Paul winked at her, which was absolutely infuriating.

"It's *not*," she cried, while Mustache and No-Mustache dragged her away toward the elevators.

"Sayonara, Amy," Paul called after her.

Amy whipped around, her spine stiff and her face hot, but

she only caught a brief glimpse of Paul's retreating back before she was pulled around the corner.

CHAPTER 9

WHO'S FRIEDA?

Sam went straight to the law library at U of C after she left the US District Court for the Northern District of Illinois. There she had filed for discovery, as well as filing a motion to suppress the email evidence. She also filed a motion to dismiss the conspiracy and wire fraud charges against Amy, because the crimes therein were basically covered by the insider trading charge. Both of these motions were going to get denied, but she didn't care. She just wanted to start burying the prosecution. She would have filed even more motions, except she remembered this judge from back in the day, and she knew he was not a fan of stunts like that.

Sam had never argued in front of The Hon. John Frederick Devoy, but she'd had colleagues who had. He was a big-time old Chicago Irish liberal, which worked somewhat in their favor, but he hated corporate corruption. So Sam was going to have to put Paul and Tom on trial in Amy's stead, and presenting an alternate defendant was not the easiest legal defense. She was going to be free to cross-examine Tom, who had already been named as a witness for the prosecution, but as far as hostile witnesses went, he topped the list.

The law library was not at all fun and made her wish she had some cocaine. The legal scholar part of her brain had shriveled like a raisin. Sam kept sneaking glances at the kids around her, all ten years younger, staring fanatically into their MacBooks like they were inventing cold fusion instead of studying for CrimPro.

Amy had texted her while she was still at the courthouse: *I have to tell you something and ask you something but I can't do it over the phone.* Sam wrote back, *ok do you want to meet up for dinner??* to which Amy said *Yes*, so that was promising, but Sam hadn't heard from her since. She spent hours glancing up from the mind-numbing text of *Securities Law: Insider Trading* to look at her dark iPhone screen, hoping that it had lit up when she wasn't looking.

Around six, she texted Amy, *what restaurant?* Amy didn't respond, so Sam headed out into the frigid Chicago wind, tapping at her phone with frigid hands: *yo. Amy. yo.* She found Amy's car, got into it, and sent another *yo* while she was shivering and waiting for the inside to heat up. Luckily, Amy always got the cold-weather package for her BMWs.

Finally Amy called as she was pulling onto Lake Shore Drive. "Hey," she said, sounding a little too friendly. "Sam?"

"Yeah," Sam said. "I'm in the car. We eating?"

"Yeah, um. Can you just—do you have a second to talk?"

"Not really, I'm driving. You at Umai by your old office?"

"I am, actually, but Sam—"

Sam spotted a cop car to her right out of the corner of her eye. "AmeIgottagobyeI'monmyway," she blurted, then winged the phone onto the passenger seat floor.

It was a busy time of day in the city, and Sam ended up spending ten minutes circling the block around Umai before a spot opened up directly in front of it. She spent those ten minutes mulling on Amy's case and, to a lesser extent, her weird trepidation about Sam joining her for dinner.

Umai was less crowded than expected, given the dense foot

traffic on the sidewalks outside. The hostess was good at her job, acting delighted to greet Sam like she had been waiting for her all day. She was attractive in an Amy-ish way, which Sam regretted noticing.

Amy was sitting in a booth toward the back of the restaurant with another woman who was about ten years older. They were deep in conversation, and their body language was intimate and familiar. Sam stopped short, staring at them. Amy looked up and stared back at her, looking caught.

"I have the last of your party here to join you," the hostess said, smiling, unaware.

"Thanks," Amy said, dropping her gaze and fixing it on the drink menu in front of her.

As the hostess walked away, Sam slid into the booth next to Amy, encumbered by her puffy winter jacket and thick scarf. There were already half-finished drinks on the table.

"She would've taken your coat," Amy said.

"I want to keep it," Sam said. "It's mine." She tipped her chin at the woman sitting across from them. "Who are you?"

The woman smiled. She had an infuriating smile, very knowing and intelligent, and of course she wore glasses and was sexy in a professorial way. "I'm Frieda Wagner."

"Oh, great, it's Frieda Wagner!" Sam said. "Sorry, I don't know who the fuck that is."

"Sam," Amy snapped.

"She's exactly how you described her," Frieda said to Amy.

Sam's blood rose in her face and chest. She shot a look at Amy.

Amy looked up from her drinks menu at Sam to say, in a careful tone, "Frieda and I dated for a while after the divorce."

Sam had already known this in her gut, so it actually calmed her to hear it admitted to. "Yeah? When did that start?"

"In February. We dated for five months."

This felt to Sam like having a kettlebell swung into the side of her head. "Five months," she repeated, her stomach curdling. "Okay. And who are you, exactly?" she said to Frieda. "What do you do?"

"I'm a psychiatrist," Frieda said.

"*Your* psychiatrist?" Sam said to Amy.

"Jesus, no," Amy said.

"What are you doing here, Frieda the psychiatrist?"

"I ran into Amy at Starbucks earlier," Frieda said. "And I invited her to get a drink, because she's going through a lot right now."

"I know she's going through a lot right now," Sam said through her teeth.

Frieda looked amused, which was just making Sam angrier. She wanted to ask her outside so they could smack each other around, but women in their world didn't do that, which was infuriating. Educated, classy women like Amy and Frieda looked at you like you were crazy if you expressed a desire to pound on somebody.

"Sam, we were finishing up talking," Amy said. "You can go sit at the bar, and then you and I can have dinner together."

"I don't want to go sit at the bar," Sam protested. "Why do I have to go sit at the bar?"

"Because you're acting like a child."

"I'm a child? Why can't you talk about whatever you were talking about in front of me? What was it?"

"She was just giving me some advice on taking care of myself during this whole thing," Amy said.

"What, I can't hear that?"

"No, I guess you can. I guess it doesn't matter."

"I should go," Frieda said, getting up. "Amy, we can talk some other time, when you're free."

"You know what," Sam said, "we're gonna be working pretty hard to keep her out of prison, so I wouldn't rain check if I were you."

"Sam, you don't speak for me," Amy said.

"All I'm saying is Frieda shouldn't feel like she should leave on my account. Frieda, sit. You want to order a drink?"

"I don't drink," Frieda said.

"Oh, good, me neither. You smoke? Let's go outside and smoke." Sam pulled out a pack of cigarettes. "Maybe we can get properly introduced."

Frieda looked at Sam for a long moment. She was all glasses and turtleneck and stern mouth, like a librarian from a cartoon. "It's interesting that you think I want to fight you."

"Who said we're gonna fight? I'm offering you a cigarette."

"You're offering to take me outside."

"Well, you can't smoke in a restaurant anymore," Sam told her. "News flash, Grandma."

Frieda's eyes twinkled while her mouth remained flat.

The emptiness of the restaurant was making their voices carry, and at this point several people at the bar were listening while pretending not to be. Their server was pretending to be busy filling the soy sauce at another table, probably waiting for a break in the action so she could ask if they wanted to get an appetizer or maybe leave the restaurant.

Amy grabbed Sam by the hand and squeezed it, hard. "Sam, go outside. Go smoke and calm down, let me finish my conversation in private. When you come back, we'll have dinner."

It was hard to argue with her when she sounded so sincere and desperate. Sam picked up her smokes, said "Fine," and headed out into the Chicago cold with them.

Waiting for Frieda to come out was torture. Sam sat at an outdoor table, smoking and watching people and cars go by, watching as the sun went down. It only took a few minutes for her anger to ebb, and once it did she felt like a real asshole. Not when it came to Frieda, though, because she had already decided Frieda was deficient of character: first for being a psychiatrist—Sam specifically hated psychiatrists—and second

155

for swooping in on Amy when Sam was so freshly out of her life. A forty-something doctor should know better, shouldn't they?

Smoke filled the air around Sam as she finished one cigarette and began another. A weak tickle was forming in the back of her throat, signaling phlegm that would need to be violently hacked up, but she ignored it. She loved filling her entire personal space bubble with the smell of self-destruction.

Finally, the bell at the top of the restaurant door jingled. Sam looked up to see Frieda putting her gloves on. They were classy gloves—the kind Amanda always wore, the kind Bobbi used to help rich ladies pick out at Nordstrom.

"We gonna fight?" Sam said in a hoarse voice, getting to her feet. She didn't really mean it, even though she was posted up like she did. She was trying to be funny.

"No," Frieda said. "I'm going to get a cab and go home."

"Not an Uber?"

"I'm not a fan of the union-busting business model," Frieda said, glancing at her. "The annihilation of the cabbing industry."

"Yeah, I guess. I just figure if it's gonna happen anyway, we might as well hurry it along so we can get to fixing it faster."

"Ah, an accelerationist."

"Nah, not an accelerationist. Just a realist. But I bet you're surprised I even know what that means."

"Not at all," Frieda said. She finished putting her gloves on and walked a few steps from the door, looking to the street as if scanning for cabs. "I know you're well educated."

"Yeah? What else do you know about me? 'Cause I don't know anything about you."

"What do you want to know?"

"I want to know if she loved you," Sam said, without a moment of hesitation. She needed to cough, but she held it back.

"No. I loved her, and she didn't love me."

"Oh," Sam said. Her cigarette, burning for this entire

conversation, was half ash by now. She flicked the ash onto the ground below. "Okay."

"She was completely hung up on you, actually," Frieda said. "That's why I'm surprised you were so aggressive toward me."

Sam barked a laugh. "Hung up? On me? She barely wants me around."

"Barely wants you around? You're living in her house, you're the one person standing between her and prison."

"I'd plead it down to time served on house arrest," Sam said. "She's a first-time offender."

"You're awfully literal," Frieda said, raising her voice over the sound of an ambulance roaring by them. Red lights flashed over her face, briefly revealing middle-aged tiredness. "And easily fixated, and a stimulant addict . . . I'm curious, have you ever been evaluated for ADHD?"

"Excuse me? Have I ever what?"

"Just asking."

"No, I haven't. Have you ever been evaluated for fucking Asperger's?"

"I have, actually."

"And?"

Frieda waved her arm in the air, flagging down a passing cab. "Turns out I'm just blunt. Do you actually think she barely wants you around?"

"I think she's tolerating me 'cause she needs my help, yeah," Sam said, tossing her cigarette butt into the ashtray stand beside her.

"Then you should ask her why we broke up," Frieda said, and walked away.

Sam stared after her, her vision fixed like a dog's, her heart speeding up. She watched as Frieda got into the waiting taxi, then disappeared down West Fullerton.

Amy was sitting with her head in her hands when Sam walked back to the table. The signed check lay in front of her with her debit card atop it. Sam slid into the booth across from her, apprehensive, watching her for movement.

"That's a side of you I always hated," Amy finally said after a moment. She lifted her head, and her eyes were angry. They glittered like black tourmaline.

"So, no dinner?" Sam said.

Amy scoffed at her.

"Come on. What do you want from me, Amy?"

"You humiliated me!"

"You humiliated *me*! Why didn't I get a warning, huh?"

"I tried to warn you," Amy said. "I wanted to explain it to you in person, but you wouldn't stop and listen to me—"

"I had to hang up, I was driving, there was a cop! What, I'm gonna somehow clairvoyantly guess you're having dinner with your ex-girlfriend who I didn't know existed?"

Amy was quiet.

"Why didn't you tell me about her?" Sam said.

"You didn't ask," Amy said, lowering her voice as a waitress passed by. "It's not your business, but you didn't ask."

"I did ask. I asked if you were seeing anyone."

"Well, and I'm not."

"But I took that to mean there hadn't been anybody."

"Oh, so I'm supposed to sit in my house crying over you year after year," Amy said, swelling with anger, glittering more ferociously, "while you walk around our hometown with some big-titted twenty-two-year-old?"

Sam looked at her, stunned. "Who told you about her?"

"Jess."

"Jess? When did Jess tell you about her?"

"I texted her! I asked if there was anything I should know about what you'd been up to, after you took my case, and she warned me you had a girlfriend and sent me her photo."

"Okay, well, she's twenty-six, first of all."

"Great, fantastic."

158

"And second, we broke up before I came out here."

Amy stared at her for a moment, then started waving her hand at nobody in particular. "Can someone please come pick up this check?"

Sam leaned forward, angry again. "It was just sex," she said. "Me and her, it was just sex and some company for both of us. We weren't even exclusive. You had this woman in love with you! You were with her a month after our divorce was final?"

A waitress came and scooped the check off the table, whispering hurried apologies for the delay.

"Oh, what, did you interrogate her on her way out?" Amy said. "That is so like you. You think you're Tony Soprano or something. You're being so controlling right now."

"*I'm* controlling? You're getting oppo on me from Jess, and *I'm* controlling? And I don't think anything. She asked me if I wanted to know."

"She shouldn't have done that," Amy said. "She doesn't know you like I do."

"Know what about me?" Sam said. Her heart was hammering in her chest, and her vision was tunneled onto Amy's face like they were in a boxing match.

"That you don't give up, you never give up."

"What am I supposed to be giving up on?"

Amy didn't answer. She looked grief-stricken.

"I have news for you, Ame," Sam said. "Look around yourself, look at what you're doing right now. You're crazy too. You're not giving up either. That's why we worked so well together: we're both winners. We have the killer instinct, we come to win. We don't come to roll over and die."

"The difference is, I don't have a choice in this," Amy said. "But you can walk away."

"No, I can't."

"You can. And maybe you should."

"Only if you ask me to," Sam said. "Are you asking me to?"

Amy gazed at her. "No," she said. "Sam, how could I? After everything you've already sacrificed? Come on."

"I don't care what I've sacrificed," Sam said. "I made that choice on my own, I didn't consult you, and I'm a grown adult. So if you want me gone, I'm gone. But I'll say again that I think I am the one person on Earth best suited to helping you win this case."

The waitress returned. "Thanks for dining with us tonight," she said, as cheerfully as she could manage. "Please come again."

On autopilot, they each mumbled polite good-byes. Sam felt numb as she got up and followed Amy out the door, handed over the keys to the Beemer, then pointed out where it was parked. Amy had a cardboard box in her arms that she'd stashed under the table at the restaurant, and Sam held the backseat door open for her as she slid it in.

As they drove home, Sam sat staring out the window, her lips buzzing from the sheer amount of nicotine she'd ingested.

"What did you want to tell me?" she said when Amy had pulled onto I-94. She didn't get a response right away, so she glanced over at her. "You said you had something to tell me."

Amy drove the same way she moved through the world—with effortless composure. She barely touched the steering wheel, only resting one or two fingers lightly against it. The yellow beams of three different streetlights passed over her face before she said in her *I'm-still-mad-at-you* voice: "I found the Post-it I had put my computer password on last winter. I thought it got thrown away, but someone had moved it and stuck it under my desk. I wrapped it in a piece of paper and I took it with me in my things." She jerked a thumb toward the backseat, at the box.

Sam lit up with excitement. "Oh, shit! Ame!"

"I was thinking we could get it privately tested for fingerprints. That's a thing, right?"

"Honestly, I wasn't even thinking like that, but this is huge. Paul was for sure in New York when the emails were sent, right?

So if the person who sent them did hack into your physical computer—"

"—we know a third person was involved. Yeah, I came to that too. Maybe I shouldn't have taken it," she fretted. "I broke the chain of custody. Maybe it could have been police evidence."

"Chain of custody was already broken. The feds tossed your office, right?"

"Yeah."

"So it'd be pretty hard to prove they weren't the ones who moved a Post-it. You'd have to have concrete proof it had been somewhere else first."

Amy was quiet for a moment, but Sam could tell her problem-solving brain was working at one hundred miles an hour and wouldn't rest until it hit a brick wall. "We could still get it analyzed privately though, right? Could it be admissible? I was doing some Googling, and I read that fingerprints can stay on paper for decades."

"It depends. I'd have to handle the argument really well. But there's a chance, sure. It's absolutely worth a shot."

"But even if there is a print, we'd have to have another print to compare it to, right? We'd have to know who touched it, then find a way to get prints from them . . ." Amy sounded demoralized. "I don't even know where to start. I have literally no way to find out who would have gone into my office on a random night seven months ago. It's not like Paul has a designated accomplice."

"Vice president of forged evidence and insider trading," Sam said, and Amy laughed. "I have a friend in Chicago I could track down. He used to be a cop. He's a PI now. He could probably help us out with print analysis if that comes up."

"A PI? Why haven't you already called him?"

"Because," Sam said uncomfortably, "he does freelance work for my old firm. That's how I know him. And they're, y'know . . ."

She sighed. "Retained by Paul."

"Right."

"That's a pretty big conflict of interest."

"Yeah."

Amy smacked the steering wheel. "Shit."

"Yeah. Look, I have some stuff in my back pocket. I'm trying to maneuver here. I'm just a little out of practice."

"Sam," Amy said, "not that I don't have faith in you as a lawyer, but we're kind of running out of time for you to get back in practice."

"I know," Sam said. "I'm, uh . . ." She made a split-second decision to not say to Amy *this would be so much easier if I could just go back to snorting blow.* "I'm at ninety percent. Don't worry."

Back at the house, Amy turned all the lights on like she was trying to drive away the despair that was creeping up on both of them, then went into the kitchen to make tea. Sam went into the living room to turn the TV on and saw there was a story on the local news about razors in Halloween candy. Was it really almost Halloween again? The last year of her life had lurched by in the blink of an eye.

"Hey Amy?" Sam called. "Just out of curiosity, uh . . . Frieda told me to ask you—"

In life, you get to experience a handful of truly surreal coincidences that are mostly good for recounting at parties. Sam racked up another one as she was standing there watching ABC7 and one of their reporters started pounding on the front door.

At first she thought it was the cops because who else bangs on a door like that? But then she heard someone yelling at a theater-actor decibel: "Amy Igarashi? This is Patrick Ellis with ABC7 Chicago, do you have a moment to talk?"

"Ame," Sam called, but Amy was already rounding the corner of the kitchen, looking pissed. "Ame, don't answer it. If you don't answer, they'll just leave and say you couldn't be reached for comment, no big deal."

Amy strode past her and yanked the door open as if she hadn't spoken. "You're trespassing," she said.

Sam slunk deeper into the house and sat down in an armchair so her shadow couldn't be spotted through the curtains. The light from a flash shining garishly in Amy's face meant she was definitely being filmed, but at the end of the day all an attorney could do was advise. Sometimes your client made bad decisions despite you.

"Sorry to bother you. I just have a few questions," Patrick said. "Is it true your ex-wife is representing you?"

"Where'd you get my address?" Amy demanded. "I'm unlisted, I have DeleteMe. How'd you find me?"

"Ma'am—"

"Get off my steps. No comment. That's all I have to say to you, good night."

She slammed the door and flipped both locks, then did the latch before coming over to sit on the couch kitty-corner from Sam, shaking with adrenaline. She crossed her legs, and Sam tried not to notice the way her pencil skirt slid up her thighs. "You know, I've never liked Patrick Ellis. I've always thought he was smarmy."

Sam laughed in spite of herself. "Amy . . ."

"I know exactly what that was, too. That was a warning shot from Paul. He must have leaked my address to them."

"You think?"

"I ran into him today at the office," Amy said. "I basically let him know I know he framed me. I threatened him."

Sam exhaled in frustration. "That's unlike you," she said.

"I know. I didn't mean to. It just came out."

"I know how angry you are, but you have to tighten up here. Don't talk to Paul, and don't talk to reporters, okay?"

"You know, I've been through this before," Amy said, fixing her with a look. "When you got arrested, the press hounded me as well as you. They called me at work all the time."

"I didn't know that," Sam said.

"I know. I never told you."

Sam had nothing to say to that.

"I don't even understand why me being charged is a story," Amy said. "Beyond the angle of you defending me, which I guess is kind of unique. I guess that plays. But it isn't like I stole money or anything. I just saved us from losing fifty million. Even if you think I did that maliciously, it's not very sexy when you compare it with what Zilpah did."

"This shit is all part of Larry's playbook," Sam said. "Controlled and continuous leaks to the press, to keep them hammering a target who isn't your client. This is gonna continue, and it'll only get worse when it goes to trial."

Amy nodded.

"I don't want to go to trial, though," Sam said. "And neither does the prosecution, 'cause their case is so thin. I want to either get this dismissed at your preliminary hearing, or take a plea. As far as I'm concerned, those are the two options."

"I don't want a plea."

"Amy, don't make that decision now."

"I don't want to plead guilty to this," Amy said, sounding fierce. "There has to be a way to win this thing. I can't just give up."

"It might be the only way I can keep you out of prison," Sam said. She didn't like to admit how dire the situation was, but she knew that was selfish of her. She wouldn't sugarcoat this if Amy were anyone else.

They fell quiet. In the kitchen, the kettle started screaming, and Amy got up to go take it off the burner. Sam followed behind, lingering at the edge of the kitchen like a little kid, unsure of herself.

Amy looked up as she was pouring hot water into two of the yunomi teacups that her mother had given them as a wedding present. "What's up?"

"Frieda told me to ask you why you guys broke up," Sam said.

Amy set the kettle down. "You still like your tea sweet, right?"

"Yeah."

Amy made a face at this, but pulled a box of Domino sugar from the cabinet above her head. "We broke up because she was convinced I was still in love with you."

Sam's heart fluttered and began to pound. Her face felt sickly hot. "Oh," she said, looking around at everything in the kitchen besides Amy. "Were you?"

Amy hovered a hand over the teacups, like she was testing the warmth of the water. She liked to use loose green tea, which meant no stirring. "At the time, all I remember being was angry."

Sam stayed quiet.

"Of course I love you," Amy said, still not looking at her. Sam's fluttering heart leapt in hope. "I'll love you for the rest of my life. But there's more than that to a relationship."

"I don't know if that's true. I think that's the most important thing."

"Sam," Amy said, like she was pleading with her. "Please, I can't do this right now."

Sam straightened up, lifting her chin. "You were jealous about Dani earlier," she said. "I could hear it. I know what you being jealous sounds like."

"Like you weren't jealous of Frieda? You threatened to beat her up!"

"So? I never said I didn't still love you. I never said I didn't want to be together." For half a second Sam considered pumping the brakes, but she didn't have it in her. She was not the brakes-pumping type. "You wanted the divorce, you forced it on me, you didn't even have the decency to have a final conversation with me about it."

Amy reeled on her, looking furious. "You didn't have the

decency to fight for me," she yelled. "I just wanted some time apart so I could process what had happened, and you ran away! You were the only person I've ever trusted to take care of me, and you ran away. I needed you, Sam!"

"I needed you! I needed my wife!"

"I needed *my* wife!"

They were both near tears, at that point. Sam's eyes were hot, and she could see Amy's were glimmering.

"We can't do this," Amy said. "We need to concentrate on my case, okay? I need to get my life back so I can pay you like you deserve, and give you yours back."

"Amy . . ."

"Go sit," Amy said. "I'll bring the tea out."

Sam returned to the armchair and let a few hot tears leak out; they fell from her face and stained her dark jeans. She kept her arms wrapped around herself in a hug. She wanted so desperately to wrap those same arms around Amy.

When Amy came back, she set the tea on the table and went to Sam. She put a hand on her shoulder and bent over her, her dark hair becoming a curtain that shielded them both. "Hey," she whispered in her sweet voice. "Do you have any idea how grateful I am to you for what you're doing?"

"Thanks."

"I'm sorry about Frieda. I didn't want to spring that on you."

"Sorry for being a dick about it."

Amy laughed and stroked her hair. Her touch was so gentle it made Sam's stomach hurt. "Let's strategize," she said, going over to take a seat on the couch. "Is there anything you want me to tell you about? Like how we do buys at Atlantic, or how Paul operates?"

Sam wrapped a hand around her teacup and took a sip. It still wasn't sweet enough for her liking. She picked up a legal pad and pen she had left on the table earlier. "I want to hear everything you know about Tom Naftalis," she said.

"Okay," Amy said. "Why him in particular?"

"He's in custody, so I can get to him if I need to. And if he knows he wasn't actually sending those emails to you, he might be our only shot."

"We can't say for sure how much he knows."

"What does your gut say?"

Amy didn't say anything for a moment. She looked in the vicinity of the coffee table but appeared to be seeing beyond it. "I think he must have known everything," she said. "Otherwise, how could Paul have covered for himself? I mean, what if Tom and I had talked? We would have figured out what happened."

"Right." Sam put the legal pad down on her lap. "Hey, Ame? Some of the things I might have to do as I try and get this case dismissed . . . they're not all that ethical."

"What does that mean?"

"I'm gonna be crossing some lines . . . bending some rules."

"Oh," Amy said, and exhaled.

"Is that okay with you?"

"Well, what do you mean by bending the rules?" Amy said. "Stuff that could get you disbarred? Because you already have one strike against you."

Sam hesitated, then said, "I might have to talk to people I'm not really supposed to be talking to, or find slick ways to finagle evidence that's not available to me through discovery. But I don't want you to worry, and I promise I'll be careful."

"As long as you're not hurting or intimidating anyone. Don't break any fingers."

Sam laughed. "No, nothing like that. Friendly conversations only."

"Do you need to cross lines to defend me?" Amy said.

"Yeah," Sam said. "We're up against a machine. I can't beat it myself without pulling out every stop. It's just that this situation is fundamentally fucking unfair, you know? We're at a disadvantage through no fault of our own, so I have to compensate."

Amy shot her a look. "Don't try to manipulate me with the concept of fairness."

Sam put her hands up and laughed. "Hey, if you want me to be a good girl, you just let me know. I'm your counsel, so you do actually have some input here."

"Well, I wouldn't ever ask you to be a good girl. I know you too well to even bother."

Sam felt a little thrill in her stomach in response to this.

"I just want you to keep your best interests in mind," Amy said. "I feel bad enough about you having to represent me, I don't want to see you getting suspended again. You have to think past this case, you know?"

Sam wanted to laugh. She had absolutely no ability to think past this case. "I can take care of myself," she assured her.

Amy was quiet for a while. Sam sipped her tea and watched her. She finally broke the silence with: "Paul said sayonara to me when I was on my way out."

Sam shook her head in disbelief. "Did you spit in his face?"

Amy laughed. "I wanted to."

"Fucking asshole. These fucking assholes. I want to beat his face in."

"Sam . . . that's what I'm saying . . . this is why I don't want to plead guilty, okay? I can't let these guys win." Amy looked at her. "Can you? Could you stand that?"

"To protect you, yeah," Sam said roughly. "I could let them win if it protected you, if it came to that."

"I don't know if I can."

"I hear you. I get it."

"No, you don't. You don't get it. My reputation being destroyed isn't just about me. It's about you. It's about my family."

"I know what me ruining my own reputation did to you."

"You said yourself just yesterday that you didn't know until I told you," Amy said. "Look, you don't have to defend yourself.

I'm not attacking you. We just think about things differently. I have different things at stake." She rubbed her forehead. "But I don't want you going further down the rabbit hole to defend me just because I won't plead guilty."

"Look, forget I said anything."

"Your situation is precarious enough as it is."

"If I win this case, I'm going to dine out on it for the rest of my life," Sam said. "If I win this case, we'll turn around and hit them with the craziest wrongful termination suit anyone has ever seen. Let's just think like winners, okay?"

Amy gave her a brief smile, and they fell quiet again. In the silence, Sam had the chance to remember something. She slid her hand into the pocket of her pants, digging around, then unearthed the cornicello keychain, which she handed to Amy.

Amy looked at it in her palm, her brow knitting. "What is this?"

"It's good luck."

"Is it?"

"Italian good luck anyway. It's protection, y'know, from bad vibes."

Amy laughed, then closed her hand around it. "Thanks, Sammy."

CHAPTER 10

URGENT CARE

Jess was not impressed by the update she got when she called Sam on Monday.

"That's not reassuring," she said, when Sam told her that they might have a fingerprint. "That's so far from reassuring. That makes it sound like you guys are Scooby Doo."

"Like we're *both* Scooby Doo?" Sam said in a quiet voice. She was skulking at a table in a diner on Wabash Avenue that she knew from experience her PI friend John Zborovan ate breakfast at almost every day. It was around 8 a.m., but she had been lying in wait for him for more than an hour. "I feel like only one person gets to be Scooby Doo."

"You know what I mean. Listen, have you been going to meetings?"

Meetings? For one crazy second, Sam thought she meant meetings with the judge and prosecution, and then she remembered she was a coke addict. "Ah, yeah," she lied. "I went to one over the weekend."

"No, you didn't. I asked Amy, and she said you were at the law library all weekend."

"Amy doesn't keep track of my every move. And can you

170

guys stop talking to each other about me?" The bell over the door to the diner jingled, and Sam leaned forward, craning her neck to see who it was. Not John. Shit. "It's creepy. I don't like it."

"You have to go to meetings, Sam."

"You sound exactly like my mom," Sam said. She'd had a very similar conversation with Mel the night before, except Mel told her she should be going to church, and so should Amy, to ask God for forgiveness, never mind that she wasn't Catholic. Then Sal got on the line to ask Sam if she needed some "walking around" money. She had said no, at least for now.

"What, is that supposed to be a bad thing? I like your mom!"

"Hey, are you at work right now?" Sam looked at her watch, but the time wasn't right. It said it was 5 p.m. "You'd be at work by now, right? Have you seen Larry? Does he seem nervous, or confident?"

"I'm not spying for you."

"Amy's ass is on the line here, and you won't spy on Larry for me? It's not even spying. Just go hang out in the break room and wait for him to walk by."

"I'm worried about you relapsing," Jess said in her most stern voice.

The bell jingled again, and Sam's head snapped up. It was John this time, wearing a knit cap and whistling. He made his way over to the counter and took a seat. She was invigorated by the sight of him. She was snorting lines of hope.

"Jess, I gotta go," Sam whispered. "I'm not relapsing. Bye. Thank you for worrying about me. Send me a Larry update. How are you? How's Trent?"

"I'm fine, and I'm not telling you anything about Larry unless you go to a meeting."

"I'll go to so many meetings, I swear. I'm at a meeting right now actually, I gotta go, no phones allowed, bye."

Jess was yelling at Sam about how annoying she was when Sam hung up. She crept up behind John, then dropped into the seat next to him.

A waitress came over to them. "Hi there, John. Can I get either of you anything?" she said. She was middle-aged with a *Da Bears*-level accent.

"Just coffee, thanks," John said, sneaking a subtle glance at Sam, who was leaning into his personal space.

"Just coffee for me, too," Sam said, and winked at the waitress, who smiled before walking away.

"Shit," John said, as soon as she was out of earshot. "Sam, I'm gonna pray to God this is a coincidence."

Sam clapped him on the back. "Nope."

"What do you want?"

"How are you, John? How's your mom?"

"None of your business. What are you doing here?"

"I wanted to say hi," Sam said. The waitress came over and dropped off their coffees, and she started pouring sugar and half-and-half into hers. "And ask you a few questions."

John sighed.

"You still working for HRKK?" Sam said, taking a sip of her coffee.

"Yes."

"You doing any work for Paul Weller? I know he's a client of theirs now."

John shot her a sidelong glance. "What's this about?"

Sam took an envelope containing a $500 bill bundle out of her coat pocket and set it on the wood counter between them.

John raised the flap on the envelope with one finger, exposing the money. "What are you doing?" he hissed, but Sam waited him out. She knew he was bribable; he'd been bribed before.

"Leaving a tip," Sam whispered.

"Bullshit. That's for me."

"You think? I dunno. I think it's just kinda lying there."

John waited about three seconds, then snatched the money and stuffed it into his own pocket. He began furiously stirring his coffee like it was at fault for what he'd just done. "I've been tailing someone for Paul, yeah."

Sam's heart leapt. "Who?" she said, peeking over at him.

John stared into his coffee mug. He was a nondescript older white guy, which served him well as a PI, though there was still something about him that said *cop*. "Guy who works at the hedge fund. I can't tell you his name."

"Jesus, John, I just dropped five hundred bucks and I can't get a name?"

John shook his head. "Paul's the real deal," he said in warning. "You don't want to fuck with him."

"Yeah, I know. He's framing my ex-wife. He's trying to send her to prison. What did you always used to say about baseball? The fix is in?"

John shot a look at her. "Wait, your ex-wife? She's this woman they arrested?"

"And she didn't do it is what I'm saying. Paul did all the insider trading."

"Huh. That'd explain some things."

"Like what?" Sam said, hitting him gently in the bicep with the back of her hand. "Come on. What'd he retain HRKK for?"

"He said he's worried about civil action from investors, I guess on the basis of recklessness with their funds," John said.

Sam suspected this was bullshit that Paul had fed the firm as a cover for whatever work he was asking them to do for him. He had to be worried about the case against Amy falling apart.

"And what I'm doing, toward that, is tailing one guy."

"Who, though? Which guy?"

"I can't tell you, Sam. You understand the situation. I give you a name, and what? You subpoena him? You go to his house and smack him around? This is Chicago. I'm no idiot."

"Lower your voice," Sam warned him. "Is that all you're doing for them then? A tail?"

"Yeah, that's all. They have me on him most days now."

"What are you looking for him to do?"

John shrugged. "They wanna keep him close, that's all. They want to know if he meets with a journalist, meets with an investor, meets with the feds . . ."

"Meets with them about what?"

"No idea. I just got instructions to follow the guy around and call the firm whenever I see him talking to somebody, plus take photos. I'm making good money on this, the retainer's huge."

Not enough money to refuse a bribe, though. That was the problem with everybody these days: it was never enough. Sam had been like that, before she found out money couldn't protect her from herself.

"Can you tell me anything else about him?" Sam said, desperate. She was sure the tail had to be Paul's third Musketeer, the Post-it snatcher.

He hesitated. "Just that he's senior-level."

"Everybody at this place is senior-level! Jesus."

"I already said too much, Sammy." He got up, downing a lot of his coffee in one go. "I'm leaving. You chased me out of my breakfast joint, you happy?"

"Tip the waitress for real, please," Sam said. "Be a gentleman. I'll get your coffee, but help me with the tip."

John dutifully slid out a twenty and tucked it under his coffee saucer.

"One more thing," Sam said. "Can you tell me where's best to go get some evidence tested for fingerprints?"

John was silent for a long moment, then got his wallet out and removed a soft, beaten-up business card that he handed to her. *AAA Biometric Services, Inc.*, the faded lettering said. "Ask for Shelley when you go. She's an old friend of mine."

"John, you are my favorite person."

"I'm a fucking idiot is what I am," John muttered, walking away.

"Join the club," Sam yelled after him.

Sam did have a meeting that afternoon—a chambers meeting, not a 12-step. It was supposed to be a chance for the defense to sit down with the judge and the prosecution and talk honestly about the case, and maybe about a plea deal, but Sam was going to try to throw Paul under the bus instead. It was her chance to plant doubts in Judge Devoy's head before the preliminary hearing in two weeks, when Chicago prosecutors would have to sell to a Chicago judge the same case that New York prosecutors had already successfully sold to a New York judge, before the government could convene a grand jury. That was good, because Sam would get the chance to cross-examine this time. She was better on the cross than she was at any other part of being a lawyer.

When Sam pulled into the courthouse parking lot in Amy's Beemer and stepped out, she was feeling confident. And then she pulled the door shut behind her, locking the keys in the car along with her case binders, her bar card, and her ID.

As soon as Sam realized what had happened, her heart plummeted through her ass. She hurried around the car in a panicked circle, rattling every door handle, peering in the windows like that would help somehow. "Shit! No, no no. No. Fucking shit, you're kidding me. You have got to be kidding me." She checked her watch: it was 11:47, and her meeting was at noon. Missing this meeting would totally discredit her in the eyes of the judge, and she was already pretty discredited as it stood.

Sam walked away from the car, full of adrenaline. Acting on impulse alone, she picked up a brick she found on the ground, then walked back over to Amy's car. She hesitated for exactly one second to look around for witnesses and cross herself before she smashed it through the passenger side window.

She shut her eyes as she did it, but she could hear the glass smash. Sam opened one eye carefully and peeked at what she'd done. Perfect: there was a binder-sized hole in the center.

As she was grabbing her stuff, she heard someone walk up behind her. Sam whipped around and saw a female security guard standing there, looking aghast.

Sam yanked the binders through the shattered window hole and held them up. "It's my car, it's my car, I swear to God I'm just taking my binders out. Sorry, I locked myself out—"

"Relax, hon, I know," the guard said. "I saw you get out when you parked. Just making sure everything's alright."

Sam sighed in relief.

The guard pointed at her hand. "You're bleeding."

She was right. There was blood streaming down Sam's palm and over her wrist, staining the cuff of her dress shirt. She had cut herself without realizing.

"It's the evil eye," she said, staring at her hand. "Holy shit."

"Excuse me?"

"I'm an attorney, I have a meeting upstairs in ten minutes," Sam said to her, motioning in the direction of the monolith that was the courthouse building. "You got a rag I could wrap my hand in? Please? A clean one?"

The woman sighed. "Come here," she said, beckoning Sam. "I got you."

Sam only ended up being about a minute late, although arriving a minute late with your hand wrapped up in a bunch of blood-soaked gauze called attention to every second of that minute. "Good afternoon, everybody," she said to the shocked-looking Judge Devoy and two representatives of the United States. She hurried deeper into Devoy's ornate chambers and shifted her blood-smeared binders under her arm so she could reach across his desk and shake his hand with her uninjured left. "I'm Sam DiCiccio for the defense. So sorry for my tardiness, Your Honor, I had an accident in the parking lot."

"Do you need medical attention, Ms. DiCiccio?" Devoy said, looking unimpressed in a way that made Sam immediately nervous. The male prosecutor looked like he didn't know if it was okay to laugh or not.

"No, Your Honor."

"Alright, then we'll proceed."

Sam settled into the only empty leather armchair.

"Ms. DiCiccio, I'm AUSA Megan Williams. We spoke on the phone Friday," the other prosecutor said. "This is my co-counsel, AUSA Brian McQuown."

"Nice to meet you guys," Sam said, again offering each of them her uninjured hand to shake. They were cut from the usual cloth of federal prosecutors: ill-fitting suits, no-nonsense haircuts.

"Okay," Devoy said. He was no-nonsense himself, with a hard Irish face that looked as if it had been carved from wood. "I wanted to meet with the three of you ahead of our first hearing, since the posture of this case is somewhat unusual. We've already had a change of venue, and the prosecution is offering me limited evidence and only seven witnesses? I don't think I have to remind any of you that these are serious charges."

Sam was relieved to hear him say this. Megan and Brian looked uncomfortable.

"And we need to talk schedule because this timeline is feeling somewhat rushed," Devoy added. "The defense waived time for the prelim, but that only amounted to ten extra days, all told?"

"Your Honor," Megan began, "as you know, we plan to call Tom Naftalis as a witness, and his team is currently working out a plea deal with DOJ that is contingent on his testimony against Ms. Igarashi."

"Okay," Devoy said. "And why was a resident of Cook County arrested and arraigned in New York in the first place? Does Justice get a kick out of wasting taxpayer dollars?"

Megan and Brian looked at each other.

"Ms. Igarashi happened to be in New York at the time the FBI made the Zilpah arrests," Brian said. "We wanted to execute all arrests and search warrants simultaneously, in order to, to, uh—to avoid potential destruction of evidence."

"To avoid potential destruction of evidence," Devoy repeated, squinting at Brian with his wooden face. He tapped his big desk. "And yet you only brought me four pieces of evidence, AUSA McQuown."

Sam couldn't help but grin.

"I don't know what the hell you're smiling about, Ms. DiCiccio," Devoy said, turning his rheumy dark eyes on her. The grin immediately faded. "You are in way over your head here."

Sam sobered. "Yes I am, Your Honor."

"You don't have a firm behind you, first of all, so I know you're already buried in paperwork. You're defending your ex-wife, second of all, which I suppose is not a conflict of interest, but it is one of the weirder instances of representation I've ever seen. And if she's anything like *my* ex-wife, I don't understand why you would be sticking your neck out on a securities fraud case that's being pursued with this much prosecutorial zeal."

"I object to that characterization," Brian said immediately.

"Overruled," Devoy told him.

"It was a rhetorical objection, Your Honor."

"I know. I was making fun of you." He turned back to Sam. "What is the defense you're planning to mount before this court?"

Sam cleared her throat. "I'm going to be arguing on the basis that my client didn't send the emails that the prosecution is hanging their entire case on. She's prepared to testify under oath that she didn't communicate in any way with Tom Naftalis on the night in question."

"Fascinating stuff," Devoy said, like she was recapping an episode of *Columbo* for him. "And you have an alibi you plan to call as a witness? Any evidence to submit to the court?"

"I'm building my case," Sam said. "And I'm waiting on discovery."

Devoy looked at the AUSAs. "Well?"

"Ms. DiCiccio will have discovery by the end of the week, Your Honor," Megan said. "She already has our witness list."

"And what a long, long witness list it is," Devoy said with great sarcasm. "Three lay witnesses, two experts, and two character witnesses."

The three lay witnesses were Tom Naftalis, Don the cokehead, and the broker who had actually executed the sale of the shares. Sam still wasn't sure how Paul had dodged a subpoena, considering his level of involvement, but Amy kept reminding her that he had a friend at DOJ. No one knew how high up, but the consensus at Atlantic was: high.

"Other witnesses are being investigated," Brian said.

"Good. Ms. DiCiccio, obviously your motion for discovery is being honored, but I'm aware you have also filed several motions in the spirit of the strategy you just outlined to us."

"I have, Your Honor."

"I'll tell you right now that your motion to dismiss the charge for conspiracy has been denied," Devoy said, with a stern look. "A compelling procedural argument was not made. You may amend your argument and file the motion again if you would like to torture me."

Sam nodded that, yes, she would like to torture him.

"Same thing for the motion to suppress, but I invite you to please refile that once I've heard preliminary arguments. I need to actually hear the prosecution argue for the email evidence before I rule on whether or not it can be excluded. Just to make sure I'm not wasting my time, though, did we want to discuss a plea?"

"At this time, my client has no plans to plead guilty," Sam said. She felt a stabbing pain in her hand and disguised a wince. "We can return to that conversation at a later date."

Megan and Brian looked like two little kids who were losing at Skee-Ball.

Devoy looked at his watch. "Okay. Is there anything else that any party wishes to raise? I have a lunch at The Berghoff in twenty minutes."

"Isn't The Berghoff right next door?" Megan said.

"Yes, but it takes forever to get seated this time of day."

Megan and Brian looked at Sam, who looked back at them.

"No issue, Your Honor," Sam said.

Amy was waiting by the Beemer when Sam made her way back through the parking lot. She had been a few blocks away at the library, so she could sit in peace and probe her brain for facts that would aid her testimony before coming to meet Sam at the courthouse so they could get lunch. However, Sam's hand was now dripping blood down her pant leg, so lunch probably wasn't a good idea. Not even if it was as close as The Berghoff.

"Sam!" Amy cried, when she caught sight of her. "What the fuck happened to my window?"

"I threw a brick through it," Sam yelled back, closing the distance between them in a hurry.

"*What?*"

"I locked the keys inside—my binders were in there, and my ID, and stuff. I couldn't miss this meeting, Ame, I'm sorry, I'll pay for it—"

Amy's own hand went to her mouth. "What happened to your hand?"

"You have an accent right now," Sam said, feeling a little giggly. "You never sound so New York."

"Sam, this isn't funny. What happened? You're covered in blood!"

"Uh." Sam slowed down as she reached Amy, and held out her shaky right hand, which was entombed in blood-stiff gauze. "I cut it on the window."

Amy looked at it in horror, then reached her own hand out. "Give me my keys, I'm taking you to the ER."

"No, please, not the fucking ER. They'll charge me a million dollars, and I'm back on COBRA," Sam said, handing them over. "Let's go to urgent care—they do stitches at urgent care. Plus we won't have to wait as long."

"Yeah, but if you bleed out at urgent care, they'll just call an ambulance anyway."

"I won't bleed out." Sam patted her with her good hand and opened the door to the backseat, since the passenger front seat was covered in shards of glass. Then she lay down with her hand elevated in the air.

Amy shot her a look of worry before shutting the door behind her. She ran around to the driver's side and pulled the door open, hopping inside. "You promise?"

"I promise."

Kendra, the receptionist at the urgent care on Michigan Avenue, didn't share Amy's opinion that Sam was experiencing a medical emergency. She immediately pissed Amy off by handing every single form to Sam, despite the fact that Sam's dominant hand was nonfunctional.

"And can we please get the name and number and address of your emergency contact," Kendra droned while typing something into her computer. She handed Sam yet another paper, which Amy yanked out of her hand before Sam could accept it.

"Can we see a doctor now?" Amy said. "She needs stitches. Do you honestly need an emergency contact? I'm right here. I'm her emergency contact."

"Ma'am," Kendra said patiently.

"This is an emergency!"

"Ma'am, we get people in here who have been shot, okay?"

"Do you make *them* fill out fifty forms?"

"Amy," Sam said, laughing softly. "It's okay, I promise."

Kendra turned back to them. "Fine, you can head back now and finish the forms while you wait," she said. "Jody? Jody!" She beckoned to someone. "Nurse Jody will take you back, alright?"

Sam wobbled as she rose to her feet, and Amy grabbed her by the arm. "Careful," she said, then walked behind Sam as she followed Jody, watching her in case she stumbled.

It felt to Amy as if all the worry and love she'd felt for Sam in the past twelve months, which she had repressed to protect her own heart, were now resurfacing in her like the blood that was soaking through Sam's bandages.

Amy sat in a stiff little armchair with her coat piled on her lap, watching as Jody took Sam's vitals, then unwound the gauze to examine and clean her hand. He was gentle, and distracted Sam with jokes, making her laugh while he touched a gloved finger to the jagged edge where her skin had torn apart.

"You'll probably need stitches," Jody said. "But not too many. Doctor Yasemin will be in in a minute to take care of that."

He left them alone. Sam looked at Amy, seeming not to want to look at her own hand.

"I feel bad," she said. "Making you rush me over here."

"You feel bad?" Amy said. "Sam, I feel terrible. You're taking this case so seriously."

"I mean, you could go to prison."

"Please don't feel like you ever need to smash a car window in with a brick on my account."

Sam shrugged.

Amy looked down at the clipboard and started filling in whatever Sam had left blank. "What address should I put down for you?"

"Yours," Sam murmured. "Or my parents'."

Amy, feeling acutely aware of how reckless she was being with her heart, said, "I'll put your parents'."

She kept filling out the papers until the doctor arrived, then set them down so she could watch. Dr. Yasemin stretched Sam's forearm across a small table with a light affixed to it, and started cleaning out the wound. She used tweezers to pluck out tiny, twinkling shards of glass.

Sam was looking at Amy again, averting her eyes from her hand. Amy was transfixed by the wound, though. She felt a responsibility to it.

"Ame," Sam whispered. "Hey. I think we have a chance with Devoy."

"Don't think about that right now. Are you in pain?"

"A little," Sam said, but Amy could tell she was lying.

"I'm about to inject lidocaine," Dr. Yasemin said. "I'll prescribe some pain medication, too."

"It's fine. I'll take Tylenol," Sam hurried to say. "I'm an addict."

"Okay, I understand."

Amy felt another pang of guilt. "I think you can have opioids. You were never an opioid addict."

The doctor finished cleaning Sam's hand and went over to a cabinet, pulling out equipment that was encased in sterile plastic sleeves. Sam watched this with a wary look, her shoulders hunching protectively over her wiry frame. She wasn't a big fan of needles.

"I can't do downers, Ame," she said, without taking her eyes off the doctor. "If I do downers I'll want to come back up. It's just a bad idea."

"Okay. You'd know best."

"You know, your ex thinks I have ADD," Sam said. Her gaze flicked over to Amy, and she smiled at her. "She thinks I was self-medicating or something."

"Yeah, she floated that theory to me while we were dating. It made a certain amount of sense."

Sam wrinkled her nose. "I don't like that you talked about me to her."

"Please, honestly, don't be offended. Obviously I talked about you to her, since we'd literally just gotten divorced. Would you rather hear that I didn't talk about you at all?"

"No," Sam admitted. "But I don't want to hear your girlfriend was f—freaking hypothesizing about me."

"Frieda just found you interesting, not in a bad way."

"And, what, you think she's right about the ADD?"

"I don't know, I'm not a psychiatrist."

"Psychiatrists are full of shit," Sam said, flapping her uninjured hand. "Everything's a diagnosis. Nobody can ever just live their life."

"Sam, you're a homeless, unemployed recovering drug addict, and you just threw a brick through my car window."

Sam looked offended, then cracked up laughing. "I guess you have a point with that."

Amy started laughing, too. They were still laughing when Dr. Yasemin came back, laying her suturing supplies on the little table, and touched a gloved finger to Sam's palm. "Can you feel that?"

"No," Sam said.

"Excellent."

The doctor picked up what looked like a small pair of scissors, then held them in one hand as she used forceps to peel back Sam's skin. Sam looked queasy and started mouthing something to herself—probably a Hail Mary. Pray for us now and at the hour of our hand lacerations.

They left with a marked-up bottle of extra-strength Tylenol that the urgent care added to Sam's bill, and Amy drove them over to

Tony's Auto Glass Repair in Englewood. She knew the titular Tony—he was the brother of a BMO Harris banker she was friends with, one of the few people who had reached out to her after she got arrested—and he was always telling her to come to his shop if she needed a window replaced.

Tony was so entertained by the story of Sam's stupidity that he gave them half off the repair costs. Amy hugged him for this. It was weird for her to be in a good mood right now, considering what a disaster everything was, but it was easier to see the humor in life when she didn't feel so alone. In the Uber on the way back to her place, she remembered how alone she'd be if she had to go to prison, then shook the thought off like a fly.

Sam had told her a few times now that a guilty plea was the only way she could guarantee Amy no prison time. She kept saying it out of the blue, like she was trying to catch Amy by surprise to make her point stick. She didn't have to do that. Amy knew she was right—she just didn't see how she could live with herself if she did plead guilty. It was like squaring a circle.

Amy looked across the backseat at Sam, who was looking out the window, cradling her hand in her lap. The battered streets of Englewood passed by out the window: empty parking lots, empty sidewalks, beautiful old houses with their windows boarded up.

She unbuckled her seatbelt and moved across the seat to Sam, picking up her hand to examine it. Amy's neck prickled as she felt Sam's gaze shift to land on her. Even without meeting Sam's eyes, she could tell it was a loving look, and full of heat.

Amy's own eyes flicked to the front seat in a moment of gay worry. Their Uber driver was an older woman, and small, so even if she was a violent homophobe, all she could do to hurt them was drive the car into Lake Michigan.

Amy ran a thumb over where she knew the dissolvable stitches were, hidden beneath a bandage. "It's feeling okay?"

"I'm fine, Ame," Sam said.

185

"I know you don't like needles."

"Who does like needles?"

Amy laughed. "Nobody. Doctors?"

"Yeah, that's why they're all sickos."

"Your doctor seemed nice."

"She was a secret sicko."

Amy finally met Sam's eyes, which softened as she did so. She reached up to stroke Sam's hair back from her face.

"You shouldn't be doing all of this crazy stuff for me," Amy said, her voice huskier than she wanted it to be. "Quitting your job, all of it . . ."

"Look. I was dead before this case, you know? The Sam you knew, she was dead. I was just sleepwalking through life."

"Were you asleep or were you dead?"

"Stop," Sam said, laughing. "I—you know what I mean. I'd rather have two months of this than twenty years of the way I was living before. I need a fight, you know? But I'm fine. I'm gonna be fine."

Amy felt like a deer at the edge of a highway, but she leaned closer to Sam anyway, into her space. Sam closed the distance, and their lips brushed. Heat shot up Amy's spine toward her head, which felt very light on her neck all of a sudden.

"Amy," Sam murmured, breaking the kiss to nuzzle her and wrap a hand around the back of her head. Amy tingled wherever Sam touched her. "What's going on?"

"I don't know," Amy said. "I'm sorry, that was stupid."

"No, no, baby . . ."

Hearing Sam call her baby physically hurt, like a sucker punch to the stomach. "No, it was. I didn't mean—just forget it, please."

She moved away, back into the middle seat, pulling out of Sam's grasp.

Sam had a complicated look on her face. "Can we talk at least?" she said.

186

"I don't know what there is to talk about," Amy said.

"You kidding me? Everything."

Amy didn't respond. Her cheeks were burning. Silence descended over the car and stuffed it like cotton, pressing at the windows, swaddling them. Their Uber driver glanced in the rearview mirror once, but said nothing.

CHAPTER 11

US SINNERS

The two of them spent the rest of that week in an uneasy ceasefire. Neither of them brought up anything uncomfortable, like the kiss, or the divorce, or plea bargaining. Sam worked on the mountain of legal paperwork that had been set before her, read her old textbooks, pored over the discovery she was receiving, and kept her hand wound clean. Amy worked on fleshing out her timeline of events and calling her old coworkers to pump them for information individually. Almost no one was talking, or even taking her calls, and the handful who were willing to talk didn't actually know anything, although they wished her well. Jeffrey was one of the few who talked, and the only one who asked her how she was. Amy remarked to Sam that Jeffrey sounded worried about her, then added, "But he always sounds worried about everything."

Amy liked to sit out on her little backyard patio as she made these calls, bundled up in a Patagonia fleece, her dark hair flowing over her shoulders. Sam would watch her through the little windows above the sink when she went into the kitchen to wash her hands or grab a paper towel. Amy always seemed so at ease on the phone.

Happy memories of their marriage were returning to Sam's coke- and depression-ravaged brain in a steady trickle, and one of those memories was the battle it always took to get Amy out the door to make their dinner reservations after she had been sucked into a phone call with an investor. Amy was punctual, but she loved winning more than she loved being on time to things.

"Fred," she once exclaimed into the phone as a giggling Sam tried to drag her off the couch toward the door. "You know I believe in this investment. Do you believe in me? Let me—I'm sorry, one sec, my partner is trying to get my attention." Then she put her phone to her chest, trying not to crack up, and playfully kicked Sam, who was groaning about her low blood sugar.

They did briefly forget the tension on Wednesday, when Shelley from AAA Biometric Services called to let them know that she was able to pull an almost complete fingerprint from the Post-it note, and it didn't match the print of Amy's that she had provided when they went to drop it off. They hugged and yelled and danced around the kitchen, leaving Shelley on speakerphone on the island.

By Friday, Sam needed to get out of the house for something besides a jog around the block or a walk to the bodega for cigarettes. She decided Jess probably had a point, and found an AA meeting at the Cook County Admin Building at two o'clock. The state's attorney was in that building, so she'd been there a million times, and she knew a good coffee shop down the street where she could cool her heels beforehand, away from the tension that was filling Amy's house like carbon monoxide.

There was one problem with this plan: she had gone to this coffee shop all the time when she worked at HRKK, and so had everyone else at HRKK. Sam hadn't even gotten in the door— in fact, was still on the sidewalk—when she bumped into Jack Piper.

She and Jack had started at the firm around the same time, shared an office for years, and were both sixth year associates

189

when she got fired. Sam expected to remain friends with him after that, but soon he began leaving her texts to him on *Read*, and then her few remaining allies at the firm let her know that Jack, who envied her partner-track promotion to counsel, had muscled in on her clients and her position the second she left. He was one of the few people Sam never wanted to run into.

He smiled when he recognized her. "Sam!"

"Jack," Sam said. "Hey, man. How's it going?"

"Good, good." He was holding a cardboard tray of coffees—probably picking up orders for the name partners, ass-kisser that he was. "You?"

"I'm great," Sam lied.

"I'm glad to hear it. We were all pretty worried about you for a while."

"Were you?" Sam said, squinting up at him through the noon sun.

"Yeah, I mean . . ." Jack smiled indulgently at her, the way you would smile at a misbehaved child with cancer. "You were really going through some stuff."

Sam smiled back. "Jack, you were doing as much cocaine as I did, maybe more. And I bet you still are."

Jack laughed. "Sam . . ."

"What?"

"Do you always have to be so combative?"

"I do," Sam said. The two of them stepped aside to make room for a group of suits passing by them, moving under the coffee shop's awning. They were in the legal district, and everywhere you looked there were people in suits walking fast, talking into their Apple headphones.

"Okay," Jack said, smiling more, but the smile was angry now. "Okay, then I feel like I can say this to you, since you don't want to be polite. Everybody at Hughes Roper thinks you're fucking crazy, okay? There's no way you win that case. You don't have a prayer. And I don't understand why you would trash what's left of your career for this."

"It's funny, Jack, but it actually feels pretty good to defend someone who's innocent."

"You think she's *innocent*?" Jack exclaimed.

"I know she's innocent."

"Since when do we think our clients are innocent? Since when do we care?"

"Since I stopped only caring about money," Sam told him.

Jack looked at her in horror like she was a dead squid or a fatberg—some appalling creature that had no business being on a Chicago sidewalk. He was a redhead who went pink in the face a lot, and he was doing that right now.

"You might end up there someday too," Sam said. "You might find something you care about more than being this person. You might realize there are people that deserve our help more than Paul Weller and companies that dump coal ash in the river, you prick. And yeah, I can tell you're still a cokehead, I can see it in your face. So be careful."

"Is that a threat?" Jack demanded.

"It's a warning," Sam said, squinting harder, her eyes starting to water from the blazing sun behind his head. "I didn't think it could happen to me till it happened to me."

Jack shook his head. "You've legitimately lost your mind," he said. "I can't believe I've been defending you to people."

"Yeah? Defending me to who, Jack? My clients you poached?"

That was when he walked away from her. "Get some help, crazy dyke," he yelled over his shoulder.

Dull rage thudded somewhere behind her sinuses. "Fuck you," Sam yelled back, redundantly giving him the finger.

She was about to turn on her heel and go get some coffee, but she felt a prognostic prickle on the back of her neck as she watched him approach a black Audi A8 that was street parked about thirty feet away. When Jack opened the passenger seat, she saw a familiar face: Don. Don from Atlantic Capital.

Jack handed Don the tray of coffee, and he accepted it, saying something in reply that made Jack laugh. As Jack was heading around the car toward the driver's side door, Sam bolted into the coffee shop, her hands sweaty.

She was pretty sure the person who had hacked Amy's email for Paul was the same person who HRKK was keeping on a tight leash for him. It made perfect sense: that was the one person who she knew for sure could bring down Paul's house of cards. Even if Tom Naftalis was in on the frame job, which he presumably was, he likely wasn't an eyewitness to the emails being faked. And Paul, being a bigger fish for the SEC than Amy, would look to prosecutors like an appealing target for Tom to make shit up about. Tom, in Paul's eyes, had been neutralized.

But if the weak link was Don? He was also on the witness list for the prosecution. That meant that coming clean would mean admitting not only to wire fraud, criminal impersonation and insider trading, but to perjury, too.

Even if she could get to him somehow, how the fuck could you convince someone to do that? Sam felt like she was buried under a rockfall and only became more buried each time she tried to move.

"Ma'am?" the barista said. Sam looked up at her. She had gotten into line without even thinking about it, and the whole time she was lost in thought, the line had been inching forward.

"Cappuccino?" she said.

The barista nodded. The way her ponytail swung under her black cap made Sam think of Dani.

All of this came back to a question that had been tickling her brain for days: why had Tom protected Paul in the first place? What did he stand to gain from that? Amy didn't have the answer—Sam had asked her several times now. She kept saying, "Loyalty? All I can think is loyalty. They've been friends for decades."

That wasn't it, though. If there was one thing Sam understood intuitively, it was the mind of a white-collar criminal.

"You know how the boys' club works, Ame," Sam had said to her. "It's not about loyalty. It's about coverage. When stuff like this happens, it's everybody for himself."

"I know," Amy had replied, clearly frustrated. "I know. But I can't get in Tom's head, I barely know him."

Sam drank her cappuccino in a daze as she headed over to her meeting. The Cook County Administration Building looked like a big ugly wafer. It was very '90s in color, that kind of yellowed, desaturated beige that Sam associated with her childhood. Walking inside made her feel like she was going to her middle school principal's office, where she had got sent a lot when she was in her class clown phase. The principal, Mr. Powers, had found her obnoxious at first, but eventually warmed up to her after listening to her plead her case on a near-weekly basis.

Sam's brain was frantically working the case even as she glided down the drab hallway to room 108, where the meeting was. She got another cup of coffee out of habit and said hellos to a few people, her shoulders squared and voice flat so nobody tried to make conversation. It wasn't out of rudeness; she just didn't want them to interrupt her ruminating. As they all filed into the room and settled into the semicircle of chairs, she texted Amy, *What do you know about Don? Besides that he's a cokehead lol*

The meeting went like meetings always did, which is to say it felt like church. There were readings from the holy texts and the passing of the collection plate, which Sam didn't put any money into, because she had stuffed her remaining cash into the coffee shop tip jar due to a pang of Dani-related guilt.

When they did introductions, everyone there turned out to be an alcoholic, except one older guy with a strong Chicago accent who introduced himself as a Demerol addict. He pronounced it "Demmeroooole." Then he added, "I used to drink, too." When the introduction got to Sam, she dragged in a breath and said,

"Hi my name is Sam I'm a cocaine addict," without pausing between words.

"Hi, Sam," they chorused back at her. Some of them looked curious. Addicts who went in for cocaine exclusively were an oddity, like calico cats.

Sure enough, the meeting leader Debra prodded her: "Would you like to share, Sam?"

Sam shook her head and stared down at her hands in her lap, rubbing a thumb hard over one of her palms. "I'm good."

"Okay. If you don't mind me asking, how long have you been sober?"

"One year."

There was scattered clapping; she smiled awkwardly. The introductions moved on, and she lost herself in thought again.

Sam left the meeting feeling like she had been dutiful but had also somehow shirked a duty. The twelve steps had never felt quite so useless to her as they did right now. It was one thing in rehab, when she was a raw nerve, to emotionally fall apart in a meeting and treat it like a therapy session. Now she couldn't get back to that mindset of community with other addicts. The electrified third rail of her arrogance separated them: she could not be like these people, so she had never really been like these people, and it almost felt like her sobriety was contingent on believing that.

She was pulling onto Amy's leafy street when Bobbi called her. Sam grabbed for the phone, and as she did, she spotted two reporters on Amy's lawn. She quickly dogged the wheel to the right and street parked the Beemer, then picked up. "What's up?" she said.

"Sam," Bobbi said. It sounded like she was crying. Sam's heart jerked. "Are you driving or anything? Are you in the middle of something?"

"No, what's wrong?"

"Grandma died."

Sam felt slapped. Her face and chest got hot, and a buzzing developed in her ears. "No," she said reflexively. "No fucking way, we just saw her."

"I know. She was sick, apparently . . . we just talked to her doctor."

"Sick?"

"She had cancer. She didn't tell anyone, and she didn't want treatment." Bobbi's voice caught. "I found her."

"Oh, shit, Bobbi, no. Jesus Christ. I'm so sorry." Sam hated hearing this. She was only ten months older than Bobbi, and they had always been protective of each other—more like sisters than cousins. They had hid in the girls' bathroom together on the morning of 9/11, staying calm by smoking cigarettes they'd stolen from Bobbi's mom and praying. They spent their teenage summers going to Rockaway Beach so Bobbi could flirt with lifeguards while Sam tanned.

"It's okay. She was in bed," Bobbi said. "It just looked like she was asleep."

Tears pricked Sam's eyes. Nuccia was old, but she never seemed like the kind of old that led to dying. She was tough in an Old World way, tough like grapevines.

She wasn't sure what year she was born in, and her parents had died when she was a teenager, so she couldn't ask. On her birthdays, instead of buying number candles for her cakes, they piped on a ton of flowers with frosting. Nuccia loved flowers.

Sam leaned over the steering wheel, rubbing a thumb into her temple. "Is my dad okay?" She knew what it was for an Italian guy to lose his mom.

"He's been better. He went to bed actually. I'm over at your parents' right now, 'cause mine are still in Florida. I'm sitting here with Aunt Mel. I sent Chrissy to the deli for cold cuts." Chrissy was Bobbi's sister.

"Hi sweetheart," Mel called in the background.

"Hi Mom," Sam said. Her throat tightened up as she said it,

and a lump developed. "You okay?"

"I'm fine. I'm so sorry, Sammy. I know you girls loved your grandma. I loved her too."

Sam nodded. A tear leaked down her cheek. "Well, uh. We know anything about the funeral or anything?"

"Not yet," Bobbi said. "You'll come back for it, right?"

"Yeah, are you kidding? Just tell me what day so I can get my flight."

"Yeah, yeah! I'll text you. I'm still in the middle of calling everybody. I gotta call Sticky next."

Sam laughed and sniffled. "He's gonna take this hard."

"I know, I know. Alright, let me go, here. Love you."

"Love you."

Sam got out of the car, feeling shaky. She was having a very childish reaction to the news, the same one she remembered having when each of Mel's parents died, and when her childhood dog Pepper got hit by a car. That *no no no* reaction. *No, I reject this, I don't want it to happen, so make it unhappen. I didn't sign off on this shit.*

She walked down the sidewalk in a daze, her hair ruffled by a breeze that was blowing through the treetops that arced over the street. They were still mostly green, but blazing yellow and orange in some parts.

The waiting reporters sped over to her as she approached the house. There were only two of them, but they clearly recognized her.

"Ms. DiCiccio?" the one who reached her first said. He was a handsome young guy in a checkered dress shirt; he held a voice recorder up as he spoke. "Hi, my name is Tyrone Peoples. Can I speak with you for a moment?"

Sam shook her head. "You guys can't be on the lawn," she said to them, without any passion. "This is a private residence."

The old guy rolled his eyes like he'd heard it all before.

"Okay," Tyrone said, "that's cool, but can we talk?"

Sam's fuzzy brain zeroed in on his press badge. It said *Chicago Tribune* in that familiar blue font. "You work at the *Trib*?"

"I do, I'm a business reporter."

"You know Shane Alvarado?"

He nodded.

"You tell him to give me a call," Sam said. "I'll talk to him. I'm not gonna talk to anybody I don't know."

"Ma'am—"

She was already cutting across the grass to get past them, heading toward the house. She wasn't even sure what she was going to say to Shane, or how he could help her, but the fact of the matter was that she needed more investigative types on her side. Sam wasn't an investigator; Sam was a pit bull. You did not send a pit bull to do the job of a retriever.

Amy was huddled on her couch in an afghan doing a crossword when the front door opened. She looked up at Sam, who was deeply disheveled, and said, "Did you run into the reporters? I tried to give you a call to warn you just now, but I think you were on the other line. Why did you text me about Don, by the way? I don't actually know if he's a cokehead, but he does have a huge gambling problem. His wife left him over it. Is that anything?"

Sam kicked the front door shut as she hung her coat up on the rack, then folded her arms across her chest. "Amy?"

Amy put the newspaper down. "What's wrong?"

"My grandma died."

"*What?*"

"Bobbi just called me. That's who I was on the phone with."

"Wait, just now? You just found out?"

Sam nodded. She was now crying silently and taking her shoes off at the same time. Amy felt a stab of affection toward her for the fact that even in this moment she was remembering to take her shoes off.

"Oh, Sam, I'm so sorry . . ." Amy went over to her and wrapped the afghan around her shoulders, then tucked the ends together like a cape, which made Sam laugh through her tears.

"People die," Sam said, and sniffed. "It's what happens."

"That doesn't make it less hard. You guys were close."

"I just feel bad crying to you about this when—" Sam broke off. "Y'know. When your dad's sick."

Amy tensed. "He's not going to die," she said.

Sam tucked her lips into her mouth, which hurt Amy, because that was what she did when she didn't want to tell the truth.

"I'm going to make you some tea," she said, petting Sam's hair like she would have done when they were married. "Go sit down."

Sam clung to her. "You don't have to do that."

"It's fine, I'll make a cup for both of us . . ." Amy wrapped her arms around Sam, holding her close. She reached up to stroke the back of her head, running a thumb over the triangle of hair at the nape of her neck under the spot where her hair disappeared into a messy bun.

Sam buried her face in Amy's neck, making Amy's spine tingle. She was about an inch taller, which Amy had always thought was the perfect amount. Ideal for kissing.

Amy's heart was pounding as she pressed a tiny kiss to Sam's jaw.

Sam immediately moved her head to kiss Amy on the mouth—close-lipped, tentative, but there was no mistaking the intention, which gave her a thrill in her stomach. Amy kissed back, parting her lips. Sam made a soft noise.

Amy drew back an inch. "I'm sorry," she said.

"No, no, Amy." Sam cleared her throat, exhaling a warm breath against Amy's neck. "Don't be."

"No, this is terrible timing, I feel like an asshole. I only meant to give you a hug."

Sam took Amy's face in her hands. "I don't need a fucking hug," she said, smiling at her.

Amy laughed.

"I'm serious. If you want me . . ."

They kissed again, deeper this time. It felt as if the entire past year was gone in a snap, just like that, like their bodies had never been apart. Amy felt dizzy, and she could tell Sam did too; they were clinging to each other and leaning hard on the wall behind them. Her gut was pulsing with heat.

"I want you, but I want to be careful," Amy murmured, nuzzling her throat.

"I don't."

"You're grieving, you're shocked."

Sam pressed their foreheads together, and Amy kissed her again, then drew back. "And you could go to jail. Don't you want to feel good right now? I do."

Amy nodded. She did. She was so tired of doing all the right things and getting nothing but misery and anxiety out of it. She wanted to do something stupid that felt good. She wanted to touch Sam.

They kissed again, unable to stop themselves. Then she took Sam by the hand and led her down the hall to her bedroom.

CHAPTER 12

THE NINTH STEP

Nuccia's funeral was set for Sunday, so Sam got a flight for Saturday morning. Amy did, too.

Sam told her ten times she didn't have to come to the funeral, but Amy kept insisting, so she finally dropped it. Things between them felt delicate. It wasn't too awkward that they had slept together or anything—they were adults, they both understood it had been a weak moment—but now it was unclear where they stood.

Sam knew where she wanted to stand; that was the problem. She lay in Amy's sheets afterward, smoking a cigarette in bed (with Amy's permission) and listening to her shower, and her whole body ached from how much she wanted her back. It felt like she had the flu.

It was very nice of Amy to want to come to the funeral. Sam knew this. It was too nice actually. She had been training herself so hard to not react to Amy reaching out to her, and she had failed three times now—with the fight, the kiss, and then sex. She had to get a grip before she got her heart broken all over again.

That was the mental state Sam was in when she accidentally

picked another fight while they were getting settled into their Airbnb in Queens. Her parents had offered for her to come sleep on their couch, but Sam knew they didn't have any room to spare. Relatives would be pouring in all day Saturday, expecting hospitality from Sal, his sister Andrea, and his brother Luke. They even had two of Nuccia's cousins coming from Italy.

The Airbnb was a little two-bedroom on Austin Street, over the subway line from where her parents lived. The two-bedroom part was important. Sometimes Airbnb listings lied to you about there being a couch to crash on, and she couldn't risk adding to the ambiguity about their situation.

Sam had just gotten off the phone with her dad, who had sounded awful and said little, and was standing in the kitchen watching Amy lay out black clothes on the living room floor.

"You don't want to wear a dress, right?" Amy called to her. "Because you could borrow one of mine if you want. If not, I'd go with the turtleneck and slacks."

Sam snorted appreciatively at her use of the word *slacks*.

"But if you wear a turtleneck, I won't wear this dress," Amy said, tapping her finger on said dress. "It has a high neck, and I feel like it's weird to match at a funeral."

Amy's phone vibrated on the kitchen counter, where it was charging. It was a text in her group chat with Leah and Caroline. Caroline had said, *Amy, we just wanted to ping you again. Is everything okay? Can we do anything to help you out?*

Sam wondered idly if she was dodging them. "Ame," she said, "can we talk?"

Amy bounced nimbly to her feet and came into the kitchen. She moved around Sam to fetch a glass from the cabinet and pour herself some water from the Brita filter by the sink. "What's up?" she said, her tone restrained.

"Um," Sam said. "Pretty obviously my family is going to notice you're with me tomorrow, and they're gonna ask questions. And I just want to make sure we're on the same page with, like . . . stuff."

Amy smiled at her. "Stuff."

"Yeah."

"What stuff?"

"I need you to stop jerking me around," Sam said.

Amy's smile faded. "You think I'm jerking you around?"

"I'm not saying I didn't want yesterday to happen—obviously I did. But it shouldn't've happened."

"What makes you say that?"

"Because you don't want to be with me, I can tell. You told me—back in January, you told me you'd lost all trust in me forever, and then you divorced me without a word. And then you didn't speak to me for eight months. Is that the behavior of a person who has any interest in making it work with somebody?"

Amy brought her hand to her face and pinched the bridge of her nose. "Sam, we didn't have a marriage, at that point. We were living separate lives and barely speaking. You had run away to New York, and you weren't coming back. You abdicated all of your responsibility in our relationship. Getting divorced was a formality! It was mostly necessary for financial reasons!"

"You divorced me for *financial reasons*?" Sam exclaimed. "Do you hear yourself?"

"Well, is anything I said untrue?"

"We were barely speaking because you wouldn't speak to me! I was in New York because you didn't want to live together!"

"I only wanted a little bit of space. I needed some time alone. I was so angry at you, Sam, you humiliated me!"

"We should've been together through that shit," Sam said. Her chest was aching like she was having a heart attack, and the ugly kitchen felt incredibly small. "You should've been with me, I should've been with you."

"You were afraid," Amy accused. "You were so scared of facing me, because for once you were unlucky, you couldn't talk your way out of things, you fucked up and got caught, and you fell apart. Do you have any idea how angry that makes me to even think about, with the situation I'm in right now?"

"You should've called the feds the second Paul told you to sell those shares," Sam said, staring her down. "And you know it. And if you had, maybe we wouldn't be where we are right now."

"Do you think I don't think about that every day?" Amy said. Her face was bright red, and her voice was ragged. "But it's not like it would've mattered. He had already framed me. This is how it always happens, right? I just wake up one day to find a knife in my back."

"Oh, I'm the same as Paul? 'Cause I got sick, and I fucked up, and I needed my wife? That's the same as framing you for a fucking federal crime? Really, Amy?"

"No, you're not, but, God, Sam, you broke my heart! I haven't been myself all year. I've been walking around like a zombie!"

"So not only am I the same as Paul, but it's also my fault that you didn't tell the feds that there was a possibility your boss had committed a crime?"

"No, no. I meant I was in denial. I've been on autopilot, just getting through the day, that's all I meant by that."

"That's no excuse."

"I know that!" Amy cried. "But it's the only one I have! Do you think all of this doesn't completely torment me? Do you think I don't hate myself for how blind I was in both of these situations? I thought I could trust Paul to do the right thing. I thought I could trust you to tell me the truth. I was wrong. I was an idiot. I was avoidant. I've always been avoidant, and you both used that against me."

"Well, it's a shitty thing to be! If you had decided you were okay with insider trading, fine, take that stance, but you refused to take a stance! You wanted to stay in denial!"

"Because I'm *not* okay with insider trading," Amy snapped. "But I'm not the whistleblowing type either, so yes, I stayed in fucking denial! I had no other choice! Do you understand that everything I do is for my family? I support my parents. I take care of my friends financially when they need it. I covered Caroline's hospital bills last year. Do you have any idea how ruinous it is to be a whistleblower? You can never work in your industry again. You get humiliated in the press. They would have smeared *you* if I had come forward! They would have dredged up your arrest and put us both through all of that all over again! And for what? For something I had nothing to do with?"

Sam was shaking with hurt and anger, and she didn't have any control over her mouth or temper, which was never good. "You know what, I need you to stop pitying me," she said. "You fucked me out of pity, and you clearly just came to this funeral out of pity and a sense of obligation, 'cause I'm helping you out and we used to be married. But I don't need that. I really don't."

"You asshole," Amy cried. "You think I don't care about you and your family? I *was* your family!"

"You said it yourself, Amy, you act out of obligation. You act on autopilot. So maybe I need to back the fuck off and stop inflicting myself on you." Sam backed out of the kitchen and headed for the entryway, fumbling for her jacket and making sure her phone and wallet were in the pocket. "I need some air."

"Sam." Amy came after her and grabbed her arm. "Samantha. I do not pity you!"

Sam shrugged out of her grip and didn't look at her. "Amy, I just need some air. Please."

Amy let out a sound that was half-laugh and half-disbelief. She sounded tearful. "Fine, okay. Whatever."

Tears were leaking down Sam's face too as she stepped into the hall, which smelled like cooked fish. In the elevator, she slumped forward and batted them quickly off her cheeks with her hand.

Cocaine would have made her feel better.

Cocaine always made her feel better. Sam felt like it smoothed the wrinkles in her brain, the way water smooths a stone. When your brain was smooth, there were no ridges and valleys for the bad, racing thoughts to hide in. You felt like you could do anything.

Alcohol made her dumb but maudlin. Alcohol killed the thoughts but kept the feelings, while cocaine kept neither. Cocaine was like lidocaine, and alcohol was like Tylenol.

But if she was going to do something stupid, it was much safer to drink. Yes, she was an addict and excessively tempted by mind-altering substances, but Sam had never been an alcoholic. The only reason she drank when she was doing coke was to soothe her nervous system so she could sleep after.

Sam wandered the streets for a while before ending up at a tiny and colorful Cuban restaurant. The walls were bright yellow, and about a million people were there on a Saturday afternoon for some reason. She huddled at the corner of the bar so she could lean on the wall and watch the door. Three drinks in, she realized that people were coming in wet, and she could hear rain on the roof.

God was crying for Nuccia obviously. Sam lifted her glass to no one and then crossed herself ironically. If Nuccia were here, she would say "Feh!" and throw a slipper at Sam for being a smart-ass. Her vision was starting to blur, and her head was getting hot and heavy.

Five drinks in, an old, tanned guy with a big white mustache walked over to her and set a glass of water down. "You're cut off," he said, giving her a sharp look. "I don't like drunks in here, okay? This is a family restaurant."

"There's a *bar* in your family restaurant," Sam said. She was making a valiant effort to sound sober and considered herself successful. "And I'm not a drunk."

"You just drank five drinks in an hour. You're alone. You're a drunk."

"That's rude," Sam slurred at him. "That's slanderous. I'm a lawyer."

"Sober up," he said. "You want some chips? You can have chips for free. You should eat something."

Chips for free. That was so nice of him. Sam put her head down in her arms on the bar out of shame and sadness. The guy gave her an awkward pat on the arm and walked away, leaving the glass of water.

Sam got her phone out in her lap and started trying to text Jackie, despite the fact that she could barely see. She almost texted Jack Piper by accident, which made her giggle. Jack! Help! Oh, wait, Jack had called her a crazy dyke. What a bummer. They had been such good friends at the firm, or maybe not. Your good friends usually didn't scream *crazy dyke* at you in the street, or steal all your clients.

Tired of trying to text, Sam called Jackie instead, lifting the phone to her ear.

"Hello?" Jackie demanded.

"Jackie," Sam slurred. "I'm drunk. I drank."

"Oh, shit. Alright. Where are you? I'm picking you up. You do coke?"

"No, I just drank."

"You get ahold of any coke?"

"No! I haven't even tried. I'm at a bar in Queens."

"Drop a pin."

"I'm, um, I can't. My fingers don't work. Do Find My Friends."

"Oh, my God, you're such a pain in my ass," Jackie said. "Hold on . . . Okay, I got it. You're out in Forest Hills? Fine, I'll be there in thirty."

"You're the best. I love you."

"No, you don't. Stay put until I get there, and do not go find drugs."

"I don't want drugs," Sam said into her arms. "I want to be

a normal person."

"I can't understand a word you're saying. Let me go, I gotta drive."

"Bye."

Sam drank the glass of water. The free chips appeared, and she ate some of those. She hadn't eaten since the morning of the day before. Oops. She looked at her phone some more to busy herself. Amy had texted: *are you okay?* Sam sent her the thumbs up emoji. She didn't want Amy to worry. She wasn't angry at her; she was just afraid of her.

She scrolled through Twitter. The Astros were playing the Yankees that night, and everyone was tweeting about Justin Verlander. Her brain oozed over the tweets without actually parsing them for information.

Someone patted her hard on the back. Sam thought maybe it was the owner, back to kick her out, but it was Jackie. She had a leather jacket on and looked worried. Sam pulled her into a hug and swayed back and forth with her.

"You're a mess," Jackie said.

"I always look like that."

"It's worse right now. C'mon. Let's get away from the alcohol. I got you a coffee."

Jackie herded her off of her barstool and toward the door. The faces of people in the restaurant and the yellow walls smeared together in Sam's vision as she stumbled along.

Jackie had street parked her big Jeep. Once Sam was settled in the passenger side, she handed her a giant Dunkin' iced coffee that was the color of tan paint and tasted like it.

"Thanks," Sam said. "You didn't have to do this."

"I'm your sponsor."

"You didn't have to drive all the way out here in the rain. I'm fine."

"Oh, macho macho macho," Jackie said. "Shut up."

Sam laughed and hiccupped.

"What happened?" Jackie said.

Sam was glad they were in the car, so they could look out the front windshield at the rainy street instead of making eye contact with each other. Jackie had probably done that on purpose. She knew Sam pretty well by now. "I got in a fight with Amy."

"Your ex?" Jackie sounded confused, and Sam realized that a lot had happened since their last conversation. So she filled her in, which was taxing for her drunk brain.

"Okay, I get it," Jackie said, once Sam had described the fight. "You're afraid of getting hurt by her again, and you're pushing her away, even as you're pulling her toward you."

"Don't make me sound irrational," Sam protested. "It's totally irrational. I mean rational. I'm being rational."

Jackie was quiet for a while. "You know what I think about you?" she said. "My grand unified theory of who you are as a person?"

"Macho macho macho," Sam mimicked her, but she sounded more like Kermit the Frog than Jackie. Jackie laughed.

"No," she said. "I think you're an adrenaline addict. You like it when your heart is beating fast and you don't have to think too hard about stuff. Right?"

"I guess."

"Think about it. Everything you've been doing this past week, week and a half . . . you don't want to think, or feel, or deal with stuff. That's why you've never liked meetings. That shit is so boring to you. You want to fuck and fight and snort coke and yell."

Sam thought about this as hard as she could, being as drunk as she was. "Amy's ex thinks I have ADD."

Jackie flapped her hand. "I don't know about all that. I think you just need to learn to be alone with your thoughts."

"My thoughts are bad," Sam murmured. "I don't think I like me very much."

"I know you don't."

"Woof."

"Like that's special among addicts? Please. You're normal."

Sam finished the coffee and stuck the empty, ice-filled cup in a cup holder.

"Can I be candid with you?" Jackie said, looking over at her.

"You're always candid with me."

Jackie ignored this. "I never felt like you were that committed to the program. Which is fine. You don't have to be a zealot about it, as long as you're committed to sober life. But you weren't really, because you weren't committed to life. You stopped living when you lost Amy and your job. You're a low-bottom addict, you know this. You hit the trifecta—charged with a crime, lost your job, lost your spouse. If you'd had kids, you would've lost custody."

Even as drunk as Sam was, that thought sent a chill up her spine.

"But the thing about a low bottom is it sets you up to build a meaningful new life from scratch. A lot of people do that when they get successfully sober like you did. They reevaluate their priorities and take a hard look at themselves, and they end up happier than before." Jackie cleared her throat. "I know you, Sam. I know how much you were going through the motions at that job you had, and with that girlfriend of yours. You didn't figure out how to live in a more moral and selfless way. You didn't make new friends. You were just treading water. That isn't what someone does when they're grateful they got their life back from an addiction that could have killed them."

Sam took in a shuddering breath. "Um," she said. "I was just waiting . . ."

"Waiting for what? For life to go back to being a bunch of highs? For it to go back to being nothing but winning and money and snorting blow? You couldn't sustain that, and you didn't. You have to learn to live a regular, boring life, like everybody else."

"I was waiting to feel better," Sam insisted.

"You'd be waiting forever, because your idea of feeling good is being high."

Sam bent over, her head in her hands. She stayed like that, swaying a little. "I shouldn't have slept with Amy."

"No, you shouldn't have."

"But I want to fix things with us."

"You don't fix things with sex. You have to rebuild the trust between you. Things like that take time and work, and they're boring. And in the end, maybe it can't be fixed. You have to just take that chance."

Sam started to cry again. "I should've been here . . . When my grandma died, I shouldn't've been in Chicago, I should've been here."

"Yeah? What were you gonna do?" Jackie said. "Stop her from dying?"

Sam cried some more in a messy, childish way. She hated hearing herself and wanted it to stop, but Jackie rubbed her back like it was okay.

"You have to live your life, Sam," she said in a gentle voice.

When Sam got back to the Airbnb, Amy was gone. She had left a note on the wicker coffee table that said *I went for a walk.* Sam made coffee in the Keurig so she could sober up more, then took a seat on the wicker couch and watched TV for a while, flipping back and forth between ESPN and *This Is 40.*

Finally the front door opened. Sam muted the TV and looked up at Amy, who was closing a big black umbrella. She had packed an umbrella for a two-day trip? That was so Amy.

"Hi," Sam said. Her head was still swimming, but she felt sobered.

Amy hung her umbrella on a hook by the door and came into the living room. She didn't sit; she stood with her arms crossed. "Hi."

Sam nodded at the TV. "You think the Yankees have it in the bag tonight?"

"I don't care. I hate the Yankees."

"Oh, I know, me too," Sam said. "Overdogs."

Amy laughed, then sat down on a wicker chair. The amount of wicker in this apartment was appalling. "So where did you go?"

Sam took a moment before she said, "I went to a bar and I drank."

Amy's face dropped, and she looked down at her hands. Her jaw and mouth got tense. "You drank?"

"And then I called my sponsor, and she came to get me, and we talked. Look, I'm sorry I walked out, and I'm sorry I slipped up. It won't happen again."

"Was it because we fought?"

"No. Not at all. Everything just kind of got on top of me. And when this is all over, I told Jackie, I'm gonna go to therapy. Like, for real." Sam rubbed her thumb against the ring on her index finger. "I don't think the program is helping anymore. At least not enough to get me through any kind of tough time."

To her surprise, Amy nodded and said, "That makes sense. You've been working your ass off on my case, I know. I hear you going to bed at two and three in the morning."

"I've had your help," Sam demurred.

"I can only help so much, though. I'm not a lawyer or a paralegal. I'm a stockbroker."

"When we get back, we'll do a full court press," Sam said. "I'll try to track Don down." She had filled Amy in on her Don Post-it guy theory during their flight to New York. "And we have the fingerprint. So that's something."

"Right."

"We'll keep doing witness prep for you," Sam said. "I know you don't want to testify at the prelim, but I think you should. We need that testimony on the record."

Amy nodded. "I'm just worried about fucking things up. I've read that defendants make bad witnesses."

"Not my defendants," Sam said. "And I wanted to say something else. Um. This is kind of hard. I wanted to ask you not to come to the funeral tomorrow."

Amy did a double take. "What? Why not?"

"I'm sorry. I know you came all the way out here and our tickets weren't cheap—"

"Sam, who cares? I used miles! Why don't you want me there? I want to give your family my condolences—it's the polite thing to do."

"I was thinking you could go visit your family instead," Sam said. "You should see your parents. I think they're probably worried about you."

"Why don't you want me to come?" Amy repeated, her tone flat. Her eyes were glittering again.

Sam looked down and rubbed her hands over her jeans. "I think we're acting a little too married, and it's confusing me. It'd confuse everybody else, too, if I brought you. They'd ask me all these questions and think we're back together, and you know a lot of them are homophobes, and I can't deal with that, not when I just want to say good-bye to my grandma and be there for my dad."

"Sam . . ."

"It's for the best, Amy, it is. I'm sorry. I'll make sure everyone knows you wanted to come, that you're not being rude. I know that's important to you."

"I wanted to be there for you," Amy said.

"Out of obligation."

"No, not just that."

Sam inhaled a shaky breath. "Ame, it's not a good idea I don't think. I got caught up in things after—after we slept together. I let myself think things had changed. But nothing really changed."

Amy's face fell more. "In my head, I always thought we'd still be there for each other through stuff like this," she said. "Is that stupid?"

"You divorced me," Sam said. Her chest was all hot and tight. It felt like her heart was pressed in a waffle maker.

"I know," Amy said. "I just . . . I don't know what I thought. I guess I never stopped thinking of you as a person in my life."

"Is that why you came to me for help, when you realized Paul was guilty?"

Amy nodded.

"It's just vestigial," Sam said.

"I guess."

The waffle maker feeling became more of a hydraulic press feeling. It was hard for Sam to breathe like this.

"You should go visit your dad," Sam said. "Tomorrow. Go see him, please, do it for me."

"Okay," Amy said in a husky voice.

Sam stood up, swaying a little. She wasn't completely sober yet. "I need some air," she said. "I actually mean that this time. I'll be outside in the courtyard."

"Sam . . ."

"I promise I'm fine," she said, hurrying toward the door and grabbing the umbrella that Amy had left.

There was an old guy in the courtyard trying to get his little white dog to poop. Sam sat on a bench, watching them from under the umbrella. The old guy's hand shook as he reached down to pick up his dog's poop, and the sight of this would have made her cry if she hadn't been distracted by her phone vibrating in her pocket.

She looked at the screen. Shane Alvarado. Well well well.

Sam picked up. "Hi there," she said.

"Hi," Shane said. "You stalking me?"

Sam laughed, delighted by the easy humor in his voice. He sounded exactly like he had in college. "Stalking you? No."

"Trying to get ahold of me, then?"

"Sure, trying to get ahold of you, if you're interested in a story."

"And the story is that Amy is being framed?"

"Yeah, exactly."

"A week ago, I get a call from my friend Doug at the *Wall Street Journal*," Shane said. "He says, hey, I saw you wrote a story on the Amy Igarashi arrest, and I wanted to let you know I had a weird conversation with this crazy lawyer I know. Somehow I just *knew* that was you, even before he said your name. And then he said he figured I must know you 'cause we're connected on LinkedIn and I only have twenty connections."

"Twenty? That's weak." Sam had three thousand.

"Definitely not the point, but anyway. Doug said you told him a crackpot story about Amy being innocent and framed by Paul Weller, and that even if there was no truth to it, it was still an interesting angle that you're defending Amy as her ex-wife and you're peddling conspiracy theories about her innocence. Like, good local Chicago color, but not a story he would pursue. So I filed it away as string. Then I get Tyrone coming back here yesterday from his stakeout, saying you wanted me to call you."

"So what gives? You call back a day late?"

"I was on deadline yesterday." She could tell he was smoking, and it made her want to smoke. She dug her cigarettes out of her pocket without even consciously thinking about it, and lit one. "But I am intrigued."

Sam took a drag. "So how can you help me?"

"How can you help *me*?"

"Unlimited access to me as a source, on the record, exclusively. I won't talk to anybody else."

"What about Amy?"

"Once we either beat this charge or plead guilty, you can talk to her all you want."

"She doesn't have an NDA?"

"She signed one on employment, yeah, but it was about trade secrets and internal ops. No non-disparagement clause."

"Hmm. Does that have anything to do with the big sexual harassment lawsuit that Paul settled with an Atlantic trader back in 2009?"

"Bingo. They took non-disparagement out of their contracts after that. And that takes us back to how you can help me."

"Explain what you think happened," Shane says. "Walk me through how you think she was framed."

"Off the record?"

"Of course."

Sam told him the whole story. He was a good listener—only interrupting to make sure he had the details right, and saying "Hmm" in the right places.

"Real asshole, this Paul guy," Shane said when she had finished.

"Yeah."

"You are the most profoundly pussy-whipped person I've ever known, by the way."

"You can go fuck yourself," Sam said.

He laughed. "Alright, well, I'll see what I can find out. I have a friend in the police department, but I don't know how much help he'd be with this. It sounds like you know what happened, but you don't know how to prove what happened."

"That's pretty much where we're at."

"Not ideal," Shane said. She heard him exhale smoke. "Yeah. Well, let's stay in touch. The *Sun-Times* keeps scooping me lately, so I need a good exclusive."

"Okay," Sam said. It wasn't much, but it was something. "Shane?"

"Yeah."

"Can I apologize to you?"

"For what?"

"It's just part of the twelve steps. I want to make amends."

"Amends?" Shane said. "You didn't do anything to me when you were on coke. You ditched all of us way before that."

Sam smoked some more. "I want to make amends for ditching you."

"Oh, Sam, whatever. It's not like I'm still best friends with everyone I hung out with in college. We're in our thirties now."

"I just think the way I did it sucked."

"Yeah, it did, but it's way in the past."

"I'm apologizing anyway."

Shane was quiet for a moment. "I appreciate that," he said.

"And honestly, our snob friends ended up being assholes," Sam said. "They ditched me and Amy when I started going off the rails. So I got what I had coming."

"Sounds like it."

"I miss you guys sometimes," Sam said. "I miss you and Amanda mostly. And your text was nice. I'm sorry I didn't hit you back."

"It wasn't all that nice," Shane said. "I was fishing for a quote."

"I figured. It was still nice to hear from you. I thought you all thought I was an asshole and sat around talking trash about me."

"Nah, we don't sit around *tawkin' traaash* about you," Shane said, in a broad and inaccurate imitation of her accent. "Maybe a little bit, when you started hanging out with everyone we hated . . . going to Sunday brunch with the corrupt mayor of Little Poland, Tom Cramer. I understood why you switched up on us. I was just surprised you could be that much of a hypocrite."

"I am too," Sam said, ashing her cigarette and then rubbing her head. The alcohol was turning into a dull ache in her temples. "Anyway, I'm sorry, is what I'm trying to say."

"And apology accepted is what I'm telling you. We're cool."

CHAPTER 13

KEN AND SAL

Sam got ready slowly the next morning. She was only a little hungover, but the day was already stretching ahead of her interminably.

The night before, when she felt sober enough, she had gone over to her parents' house. They had a ton of people over, as Sam expected, and most of the women were crowded into their tiny kitchen. Her dad met her at the door and gave her a mute, tight hug. He hadn't shaved, which was jarring. He always shaved.

Sam put on the turtleneck and pants Amy had picked out for her, then looked at herself in the bathroom mirror. Amy was right—they went well together because they were the same shade of black. She wore a gold cross necklace, even though no one would be able to see it, and slipped on some low heels. Her mom couldn't get on her case about the pants as much if she wore heels.

In the kitchen, Amy was making coffee.

"I'm going," Sam said, tightening her watch on her wrist. "I'll see you tonight?"

Amy nodded.

"Say hi to your parents for me?"

"You too," Amy said, staring at the Keurig and not looking at Sam. "Give them my condolences."

"I will, I promise."

Sam walked to Nansen Street where her aunt Andrea lived. Nuccia had been living there for the last year, ever since she had a bad fall. Andrea's was where they were setting up for the wake, which would precede a big dinner at Portofino's. The same boxes got ticked at every funeral. Sam would do this someday for Sal, and then her kids would do this for her, if she ever had any.

The rain had left it cool in New York, and Queens was still swaddled in thick clouds. The air reeked of dead leaves and mildew. In the absence of the comforting tobacco smell of a cigarette, Sam dragged in a lungful of the gross air before she knocked on Andrea's door.

Bobbi got the door and brought her in for a hug. She had fresh tears on her face, but her mascara hadn't run, which was a mystery to Sam. "Hi Sam."

"Hey," Sam said, squeezing her. "I like your dress."

"Really? Thanks, it's from Target. I forgot I didn't have any black dresses. I always throw things out after I wear them to a funeral."

In the living room, Sam saw her dad with his arm around his brother, his face pale and taut as Luke talked, moving his arms like he was telling a story. Her mom, aunts, other uncle and cousins were packed into the small space, with the younger guys sitting on the arms of couches or standing.

That was it: all of Nuccia's immediate family. Her husband had died when Sal was thirteen, and her siblings all went before she did, too. They had lost their matriarch. They looked like a grieving herd of elephants.

"Hi sweetie," Mel said.

Sam waved generally at everyone. They all waved back, some looking more friendly than others. Marissa, who had never liked her (homophobe) didn't even smile. "Shit, everybody's

218

here. Am I late?"

Luke laughed. "Only late to listen to me embarrassing your dad."

"He's telling the Camaro story," Sal said with regret. "Sammy, let me take you upstairs. I wanted to show you something."

Sam waited as Sal extricated himself, then followed him up the creaky staircase. He led her to the back bedroom which had been added in an expansion, and jutted out weirdly into the back yard. Nuccia had slept here. The walls were covered in paintings of Jesus and framed photos of her grandchildren graduating from college.

Sal went over to a desk where some opened, age-yellowed envelopes appeared to have shed jewelry and handwritten papers. "She left a letter for you."

"For me?" Sam said. She took her hands out of her pants pockets so she could accept a piece of paper from her dad.

"That isn't it, though. That was part of her wishes for her service," Sal said, and sniffed.

Sam unfolded the paper. It featured a crudely drawn casket, which made her laugh, and four smiling stick figures, one at each corner. They were labeled ANTHONY, EDUARDO, SAMANTHA, and JOSEPH. Joseph was Sticky's government name.

"She wanted me to be a pallbearer?" Sam said, touched. "I thought that was for the guys."

Sal nodded and started weeping afresh. Sam hugged him, kissing him on the cheek.

"I'm sorry," he sobbed.

"Don't be sorry. You loved Grandma."

Sal pulled back and wiped at his eyes. "I gotta get back downstairs. Here's the letter ..." He handed her another piece of paper and a small box. "Thanks for coming home, kid."

"Dad, Jesus, of course."

"Don't say Jesus like that. Not in here." Sal's eyes darted

around like his mother's ghost was about to smack him upside his head. Then he squeezed her arm and left the room. Sam could hear the stairs creaking as he went down them, then a swell of conversational noise.

She shut the door for privacy, then sat on the edge of the bed, which was covered in a quilt Nuccia had made. She set the box beside her while she read.

Dear Samantha,

Please forgive me if I do many mistakes in this letter. I have never mastered writing English in my life and it is because I hate it.

I wanted to write you a letter because I want you to know you are a good girl. I love all my grandchildren, but you are the only one who ever surprise me. You surprise me always. Today you come to tell me and tell Bobbi you are going to go to court for Amy. I could have blown away on the wind. So funny you are.

I will be gone soon and you will not get this until after. So now that I am gone I want you to know that everything will be okay for you. I know a girl like you, when I am growing up in Italy. She wore pants and cussed and spit. Everybody think she was crazy and they never messed around with her. I bet she had a great life.

You are like a good Italian boy. You are angry and proud and crazy. My favorite grandson. Does that make sense in English?

Ti voglio molto bene.

- Grandma

Toward the end of the letter Sam was crying so much she had to put it down. When she picked it up to finish, she started smiling through her tears, which made her laugh, which made her cry more.

When she finally regained her composure, she picked up the little box and opened it. A small piece of paper was curled around a handsome gold watch. It read, *Samantha, this was your grandfather's. It was too small for him always. Does it fit you?*

Sam took off the watch she was wearing and wiped her wet cheeks before slipping the new one around her wrist. It felt fragile in its old age, and didn't seem to be ticking, but it fit perfectly.

When Amy got to her parents' apartment on 172nd, she rested her forehead against their front door. She could hear them talking inside, and it was comforting. It reminded her of waking up early on the weekends when she was younger, and listening to them talk in the kitchen down the hall.

It wasn't that she didn't want to see them; she just didn't want to upset them. Her sister was so much better at smoothing the edges of things. If Ellie had gotten framed for insider trading, she would be able to swan into their parents' home, laughing and making small talk, and her good cheer would make them forget anything troubling was going on. Not Amy, who had knife elbows and a zombie face and a sad, sad mouth. Each time she caught her own reflection in the windows of the subway on her way over, she had thought, "Who is that sad, thin woman?"

The good smells from inside the apartment were leaking into the hallway. Michiko was a *kōdō* practitioner and ran an aromatherapy store out of a tiny shopfront down the street. Even when she was cooking, their apartment smelled like lavender and licorice.

The lavender was what drew Amy to finally knock. She wanted to be surrounded by the smell of lavender.

Michiko came to the door, immaculately dressed as always. She looked Amy over for a moment, then cupped her face in her hands and gave her a loving smile. "Sweetheart."

"Hi Mom."

Michiko took her into the kitchen and handed her a cup of tea, then herded her into the living room, where her dad was in his chair watching *Frasier*. Amy sat motionless on the couch holding her tea as her mom draped a blanket around her shoulders, the way Amy had done for Sam the other day.

"Amy," Ken said to her. "You look cold."

"She is cold, I can tell."

"I'm not that cold," Amy protested.

"You're too used to Chicago," Michiko said. "Where's your coat?"

Amy looked down at the peacoat she had on. "I'm wearing it."

Ken laughed at something that was happening on *Frasier*.

"I have to go down to the store to take care of some things," Michiko said, stroking Amy's hair. "I'm sorry to run out when you just got here . . . Would you like to come with me?"

Her mom had a staff of three, but she was still always running down to the shop to make sure everything was running smoothly without her. It was their primary source of income now that her dad could no longer work. Amy gave them as much money as their pride would let them accept from her, but she knew all of it went to their medical bills.

"No, that's okay," Amy said. "I can hang out with Dad."

"We will *hang out*," Ken intoned humorously. "Don't worry."

Ken looked about as bad as he had the last time Amy saw him, which caused a lump to rise in her throat. He was thin and his breathing was labored. His record player sat in the corner like always, and his five favorite jazz records were stacked on the floor beside his chair.

When Michiko had gone, Amy moved closer to her dad, sitting at the end of the couch. Ken reached out to take her hand and gave it a weak squeeze.

"How are you feeling?" she said.

"Fantastic," Ken lied.

They were quiet for a while.

"Dad?" Amy said. "I didn't do what they charged me with. You know that, right?"

Ken muted the TV and kept her hand in his, but he didn't

look at her. "We don't have to talk about this," he said.

Amy's eyes burned with tears yet again. She blinked them back. "I want to explain what happened."

"You don't have to. You say you were framed, I trust you. No big deal."

"It is, though. I embarrassed you and Mom."

"No, no no."

"You were so proud of me."

"I'm always proud of you." He looked at her, smiling. "Your sister told me you don't want to plead guilty."

"I can't," Amy said. "I couldn't do that to you."

His dark eyes searched her face. "Do what?"

"I can't plead guilty and say I did something that I didn't do, that someone framed me for, and let him get away with it—let everyone think *I'm* the criminal."

"Why not?" Ken said.

"Dad," Amy cried. "Are you serious?"

"Yes. What are the facts? You plead guilty, or you face prison? Why is it better to go to prison over something you didn't do than to pretend you did it?"

Ken said all this with such uncharacteristic intensity that he had to stop and wheeze for a moment. Amy handed him his glass of water and waited until he took a sip.

"I might *not* go to prison," she said. "We might be able to win the case."

"Does Sam think you can win?"

Amy dropped her gaze to the floor. "She wants me to take a deal just in case, if we can't get it dismissed."

Ken squeezed her hand. "Listen to her. Attorneys know best."

"I can't believe you'd be okay with this," Amy said. "It would destroy my professional reputation. I don't know if I'd ever even work again."

"You'd find work. Consulting. There's always work for

someone of your caliber."

"But people would know what happened! Your friends would know, Mom's clients would know. Ellie and Calvin's friends and coworkers would know."

Ken smiled at her again. "Amy," he said, his voice gentle. "Would you go to prison to prove a point? Your family needs you. We want you here. We don't want you suffering in prison. It's no place for you." He put his other hand over the top of hers, to make a hand sandwich.

She got the implication. It would be cruel to put her father through his youngest daughter's imprisonment, as sick as he was, and it might make him sicker. The worst-case scenario was the potential tragedy of him dying while she was inside.

Despite the fact that Amy agreed with all this, she still couldn't square the circle. "How can I let them win? How do I just roll over? I didn't *do* it."

"Very easy. You just do it, then it's over. You lose the battle, you win the war."

Amy's eyes got hot with tears again. She drank some of her tea to try and ward them off, not wanting to upset him further. "If it comes down to it, I might have to," she said. "I just needed to know it wouldn't hurt you and Mom."

"Yes. It's okay. Don't worry about us, just worry about you."

Amy felt limp with relief. She didn't even know the burden she was carrying until she set it down. She bowed to her dad, to say many things—mostly thank you—and he kissed her on the top of her head like he used to do when she was a little girl. She laughed, but stayed still for a long moment before lifting her head back up, out of respect. He smiled at her.

Underneath the relief, something was rising back up in her: that insistent little voice that kept saying, *this isn't fair.*

"Dad, listen," Amy said in a soft voice. "It's my name, is the thing. If I plead guilty, I can't ever clear my name."

"Prison is something you cannot play chicken with. If you

can play it safe, do that."

"I know. I know that. I just have this, like, unbearable shame about this whole thing. And it's something I didn't even do."

"You know, we've never been ashamed of you," Ken said. "All your life you've been thinking everyone is ashamed of you." He tapped the pad of his index finger against her forehead, his touch feather-light. "That's all in there. No one is ashamed of you. Worried about you, yes. Ashamed, no."

He punctuated this by turning *Frasier* back on. Amy, wiping tears from the corners of her eyes, took this to mean he had said all he wanted to say on the subject.

Mel was unimpressed by Amy's absence, and brought it up no less than seven times before Sam snapped during the drive to the funeral home, "I asked her not to come, Mom, okay? She really wanted to come. We had a fight about it. She sent her condolences and everything."

"Okay," Mel said, putting her hands up. She turned her head and looked out the window as leafy streets rolled by.

Sal cleared his throat. "That was nice of her."

"Yes it was!" Sam said passionately.

"Relax, Samantha," he added.

Sam felt ten years old again in all kinds of ways.

The funeral home was a squat little building on the commercial strip of Forest Hills, between a hardware store and a laundromat. Sal street parked and got out of the car, running his hands through his hair. Mel wrapped an arm around him as they made their way across the sidewalk.

Sam followed behind them, her hands in her pockets again. She paused in the parlor room while her parents disappeared down the hall toward the viewing room; she always had to steel herself before she saw a body in a casket.

"Sam," a familiar voice said from behind her.

Sam wheeled around. Jess and Trent were standing there, holding hands, dressed in funeral attire. Trent even had on a suit. She had never seen him in one before; it was funny to see his stacked baseball player body rebelling against the confines of wool.

"Aw, guys," she said, pulling Jess into a hug. "You didn't have to come . . ."

"Of course I did," Jess said. She sounded downright offended. "You asked me to, and I like your grandma."

"I know, but not everyone would show up to a funeral."

"Not everyone is me."

"I know," Sam said, pulling back to smile at her. "I know."

She hugged Trent, too, which seemed to surprise him. "Thank you for coming, man. That's sweet of you."

"Hey, no problem," Trent said. "Jess said you're like family."

"We are," Sam said. "She's the little sister I never wanted." Jess gaped at her in offense, and Sam brought her in for another hug. "Excuse me, the little sister I never even thought to ask for, 'cause I never thought I'd get this lucky. Better?"

"Much better."

The two of them waited in the parlor while Sam went down the hall for the family-only viewing. Marissa and Chrissy, who hadn't even been that close to Nuccia, wept at the sight of her. Sam and Bobbi hung toward the back of the room with their arms around each other, waiting for the crowd to shift.

"They completely fucked up her lipstick," Bobbi whispered in Sam's ear. "She'd be so pissed."

Sam laughed under her breath. "Wrong color?"

"Wrong color, way above the lip line, everything. We should sue."

The service at the funeral parlor was Catholic in an anesthetizing way. The priest had a microphone malfunction halfway through and had to duck out, leaving the now-closed casket at the front of the sad, carpeted room as the only thing for the mourners to turn their gaze at.

This quickly became too uncomfortable to bear in silence. Once everyone around them had started talking at a low murmur, Sam leaned over to Jess on her left and whispered a recap of the last few days.

"God," Jess whispered once she was done. "How's Amy doing?"

"She's okay, I think. She's coping. How are you? How's work been? Awkward?"

On Sam's right, Mel nudged her.

"Sorry." Sam pointed at her phone in her lap and mouthed *text me* to Jess.

Jess nodded. Her French-tipped nails flew over her phone keyboard. *work has been honestly pretty normal, except Larry knows you and i still talk so it's awkward bc he's been hiding everything about our Atlantic strategy from me*

Lol do i finally get to hear about Larry, since i went to a meeting?, Sam wrote back.

ummm you BARELY went to a meeting and then you immediately relapsed soooo . . .

I did go to a meeting though!

fine. yeah that's basically all that's been going on, he's shutting me out

I'm sorry jess. I never wanted to fuck up your job for you

you didn't, Jess replied. *i wouldn't have helped them hurt amy anyway. i think what they're doing sucks and i honestly look at larry differently now. i've been applying to jobs, i have an interview with the wing on wednesday*

Sam lifted her head. "Seriously?"

"The Amy thing isn't the only reason," Jess whispered. "I keep thinking lately about what kind of things I want to do in the world. Like what energy I want to put out in my lifetime. It would be cool to do something I actually believe in."

"I hear you."

When it was time to carry the casket to the hearse so it could take Nuccia up to Our Lady of Mercy for Mass and burial, Sam squeezed through thick crowds of Italians toward the parlor where Tony, Sticky and Ed were waiting.

"Hey," they all called when they saw her.

"Hey," Sam said back.

Without another word, the four of them piled into a hug.

"Pallbearers," Ed chanted like they were in a football huddle, making everyone else laugh. "Pallbearers . . . pallbearers . . ."

A dour little guy appeared, wheeling the casket toward them. His polo had a *Leitch and Sons Funeral Home* logo on the breast. "This casket isn't too heavy," he said. "You shouldn't have much trouble. But you need to be careful maneuvering into the church. I'll get my dad so he can explain how to handle it on the stairs."

He disappeared back around the corner and into the chattering, bustling crowd of mourners in the hallway. Most of them were clutching Kleenexes and prayer cards. Sam caught the eye of her second cousin Tina and winked at her; Tina laughed.

Sticky slapped his hand onto the side of the casket, letting out a loud sniff. "One more trip around Forest Hills, Grandma."

Sam put her hand on top of his. Tony and Ed followed suit.

Amy hung out with her parents into the early evening, until Ellie came by with Calvin and Meg. She decided to get going then, so she could meet Sam at the wake. She wanted to give her former father-in-law her condolences, and she wanted to tell Sam about the plea deal.

When she said good-bye, her dad squeezed her hand again and said, "We'll see you soon?"

"Very soon," Amy said. "I'll be back on Halloween to go trick-or-treating with Meg."

Ken's eyes twinkled, but Michiko and Ellie shared a sidelong glance like they didn't know whether to believe her. Amy ignored this and kissed Meg good-bye.

She was halfway down the hall when Ellie appeared in their parents' front door and said, "Let me walk you out, Ame."

"Sure," Amy said, surprised, and waited for her to catch up.

In the elevator, Ellie looked her over. "So what do you think the odds are you won't go to jail? Pretty good?"

Amy shrugged. "Sam says she thinks she could plead me out of any jail time."

"Have you gotten an offer yet?"

"Sam talked to the prosecution, but she wouldn't tell me specifically what they're thinking. She says any offer on the table right now would have tougher terms because my hearing hasn't happened yet, and she doesn't want me to get nervous."

"Oh," Ellie said. "That's not what I was hoping to hear."

"Me neither," Amy said, and they both laughed.

"If you do have to go," Ellie said, "for whatever reason, I just wanted to, like . . ."

The elevator settled onto the ground floor and the doors creaked open. When they got out, Amy moved a few steps out ahead of her sister, so she could turn and search Ellie's cheerful face for clues as to what she was feeling.

But Ellie stopped in her tracks and looked at the ground as she spoke. "I just want you to know, I'll take care of Mom and Dad. Financially, and everything else. I don't want you to worry about that."

"I wasn't," Amy lied.

Ellie wrung her hands, which was a gesture Amy recognized as one of her own. "God, this is so weird. If one of us was going to go to jail, I always thought it would be me."

"Seriously?"

"Yes! Are you kidding? I'm, like, the fuck-up."

This was so confusing that Amy had to put her hands in the

air as if to steady herself. "I'm sorry, how are you the fuck-up? You're so clearly their favorite."

"Oh, please!" Ellie exclaimed. "That's you! You're the good girl. You've always done everything right. You're the one Dad is so proud of."

"But you're the one they love to be around. You're the one that makes them happy."

"Amy . . . come on. Do you know what we talk about half the time when I come visit? You. You, and your great career, and how smart you are. They keep saying they hope Meg is smart like you. Which makes me feel great, by the way."

Amy was pleased and stunned and confused all at once. "But I'm a lesbian," she said, sounding dumb even to herself.

"Yeah, exactly. Do you know how they would've reacted if that was me? They would think I was acting out for attention or something. With you, they were shocked, but they got over it like that." Ellie snapped her fingers. "They started saying it wasn't any of their business. You can do no wrong, to them."

"Being gay isn't *wrong*—it's just what I am."

"You know what I mean. You can't hurt them."

"This is so weird to hear," Amy said. "I swear you're their favorite. You're the charming one—you make everything lighthearted and easy."

"You think you aren't like that, too?"

"With clients, yeah, but it's an act I put on. I'm not actually like that. For you, it's who you are."

"No, it's who I have to be to make up for everything else. People trust you, and stuff. Mom and Dad think I'm a flake."

Amy struggled for words. "Why have I never heard any of this before?"

"I don't know," Ellie said, looking glum.

Amy felt like the older sister then. She brought Ellie in for a hug. "If everything turns out okay," she said, "I'm going to move back to New York, alright?"

"You serious?"

"Dead serious, I promise. I want to be around more."

What was left for her in Chicago, anyway? A company that had destroyed her life? Memories of Sam, and friends who had ditched her? They could keep it.

The wake was at Sam's parents' house, where Amy had spent several Thanksgivings. She rang the doorbell and waited, hugging her arms to herself. Her parents were right, it was chilly out.

Sal answered the door, looking tipsy. "Oh," he said. "Hi, Amy."

"Hi," Amy said, extending her hand to him. "I'm sorry for your loss. And I'm sorry I missed the funeral, I'm sure Sam explained, but—"

Sal batted her hand away and hugged her. Amy patted him, surprised by the force of the gesture.

When he drew back, his eyes were bright with tears. "Thanks. You here to see Sammy?"

Amy nodded. He welcomed her inside and shut the door on the cold, then held up a finger before disappearing back into the house, which was loud with conversation and laughter.

Sam popped her head out of the doorway that Sal had disappeared through, then made her way toward Amy, disheveled and smiling. The black turtleneck kept her appearance pulled together, but her sandy hair was messy; it looked like she had been raking her hand through it a lot. Her slacks had come unironed somehow. "Hi," she said, when she got to the door. "You came."

"I don't have to stay," Amy said.

"No, please stay. All the assholes went home, so no one's going to bother us."

This wasn't terribly convincing. Amy knew Sam's family didn't have much goodwill toward her. She changed the subject with, "How was the funeral?"

"It was good." Sam nodded, then put her hands in her pockets like she did when she wanted to soothe herself. "It was what she would've wanted."

"Good, I'm glad."

"Sticky fucked up his reading," she said with a crooked grin. "He had Psalm 23, and he skipped a line. He said 'the Lord makes me lie down in quiet waters.'"

Amy laughed. "Did anyone notice?"

"Oh, everybody noticed."

"Poor Sticky."

"Honestly, Grandma would have laughed. So . . . I don't think you came all the way out here just to ask me how the funeral was, right?"

"No. No. I, uh, I want you to know it's okay if I ultimately have to take a plea deal."

The smile slid off Sam's face. "What? Why now?"

"I talked to my dad, and he said it's okay with him and my mom if I have to plead guilty, so that weight is off me."

"Ame, I can win this for you, I swear to God. I'm still in the fight. I know I've been telling you to consider the option, but it's not 'cause I don't think we can win."

"I know, I know. But if it starts to look that way . . ."

Sam seemed to struggle for something to say. A burst of laughter echoed in the house behind her.

"It's just, what do we even have right now?" Amy whispered. "An orphaned fingerprint? A hunch about Don? Your college friend is maybe going to talk to a police source, who's going to do . . . what? We have no idea."

"We have your testimony."

"Which is useless against Tom's, considering the electronic evidence."

"Amy, please," Sam begged. "I thought you thought I could win this."

"I don't know if anyone can win this. I think they've fucked me, and I think it's entirely possible that I just have to accept that. I think one of us needs to be realistic about this."

"Please, Amy, please don't give up yet, okay? I need you. I can't do this without your help, you know that. But I *can* do this."

"I'm not giving up," Amy said. "I'm not in any way giving up. It's killing me to even say this stuff. I just want you to know that if at any point, this starts to look hopeless, you can tell me. I don't want to be so delusional that I end up spending years of my life in prison."

Sam stared at her. "Is this about us or your case?"

"What? The case!"

But in a flash, Amy saw things from Sam's perspective: Sam couldn't possibly understand the profundity of what Amy's dad had told her—and in her view, Amy had been alternately angry and reticent ever since they slept together, so what else could have changed her mind?

Amy's throat got tight. She had the strange impulse to protect Sam from her.

"Can I get you a glass of wine, or a plate of food, or something?" Sam said, after a beat of silence. "You want to come in for real?"

Amy hesitated. "No, that's okay," she said. "I just wanted to let you know. I'm going to head out." She wanted to go back to the Airbnb, put on some loud jazz, and turn her brain off.

Sam looked like a scolded golden retriever. "Okay."

"Can I have a cigarette?" she said on a whim.

Sam looked surprised. Her hand started to go to her pants pocket, then stopped. "No."

"No?" Amy teased her.

"No cigarettes for you."

Amy wanted to kiss Sam again, looking at her now. She

could tell Sam wanted to kiss her, too; it was the way her mouth and eyes had softened.

"I'm gonna go," she repeated, reaching behind herself for the doorknob. That was the right thing to do. She was mixed up about what she wanted, and being framed made her feel as though she and Sam were two rats trapped in a Skinner box together, pulling desperately at levers. Those weren't the conditions you started dating your ex-wife under.

"Okay," Sam said again.

Amy slipped out the front door and fled down the cement steps like Cinderella, her peacoat fluttering behind her.

CHAPTER 14

DON QUIXOTE

"I'm here to pick up discovery," Sam said through a hole in the glass.

"Bar card," the clerk said to her without looking up from her computer.

Sam fed her bar card through the hole. It sailed onto the desk below, and the clerk picked it up. "You can have a seat, ma'am," she said, inclining her head toward the row of leather seats behind Sam. "It'll take us a minute to collect everything."

Sam went and sat down, then squinted at the magazine rack that sat underneath a TV tuned to *Hot Bench*. The US District Court for the Northern District of Illinois, Eastern Division, did not have good magazines. They had no *People*, just *Men's Health* and some *In Touch*es from 2015. Sam didn't like *In Touch* because they made up so many of their stories. It seemed kind of pointless to print a magazine wherein nearly everything was made up.

She was getting engrossed in a *Hot Bench* episode about a dognapping when she heard a voice that sounded familiar—enough so that it made the back of her neck prickle.

Sam turned in her seat and saw three men conferring in the

doorway that led to the AUSA offices. One guy, presumably an AUSA himself based on his cheap suit, was talking in a low voice to two other guys: Paul Weller, and an attorney for HRKK who had been a first-year when Sam was a fifth-year. She couldn't even remember his name now.

Paul was chuckling with the AUSA. Jesus Christ, that wasn't good. Sam remembered his laugh from the dinner she and Amy had had with him. It was rich and oily with charisma, the type of laugh that made you feel obligated to laugh along with him.

"Alright, you guys have a good one," the AUSA said. "Thanks for coming in for this depo. I'm pretty sure we won't have to call you back in, but who knows? It's a weird case."

"No problem," Paul said. "I'm happy to get out of the office on a Tuesday."

They all laughed again. Sam whipped back around before Paul and the attorney could turn in her direction, and she lifted the magazine to hide her face as they passed her on their way to the door.

She couldn't stay still for long, though. As soon as Paul disappeared into the hallway, she found herself filling with anger until it rocketed her out of her seat and out the door.

Sam found him waiting in the bank of elevators, talking quietly with the guy from HRKK. She waited for Paul to look up at her, then stopped in her tracks, staring him down.

Paul nudged his lawyer. "You can meet me downstairs, Cory."

Cory looked at Sam without seeming to recognize her, which was insulting. What was the point of having your reputation incinerated if even your former coworkers forgot about you afterward?

Sam jerked her head toward the elevators. "Bye, Cory."

Cory put his hands up like he didn't want to be involved and hit a button for the lobby elevator. It came immediately, leaving Paul and Sam alone in the gleaming vestibule. She stared at him. He looked thinner than she remembered, but not in a sickly way—more like he had taken up CrossFit. Other than that, he was still a nondescript, well-dressed white guy in his late fifties. His one distinct feature was his pale blue eyes, so light they gleamed in his head like marbles.

"You need something?" Paul said to her. "It's Sam, right?"

"Yeah," Sam said. "Why are you here? I thought you weren't on the witness list."

"Looks like you're working with outdated information," Paul said.

"So I guess your friend at Justice could only shield you for so long, huh?"

Paul didn't react to this.

"What were you giving a depo on?" Sam said.

"I don't think that's something I should discuss with you."

"I'm gonna find out anyway. I'm the defense on this case. I'm probably gonna get a copy of it in the discovery I'm waiting on."

Paul shrugged. "I gave them a description of our interactions with Zilpah."

"Bullshit. If you told the truth in there, you'd be in handcuffs."

Paul put his hands up the same way Cory had, and laughed. "O-o-kay. So Amy has you wrapped up in this conspiracy theory where I'm responsible for her criminal behavior?"

"Stop fucking around, Paul," Sam said. Her heart was fluttering in her throat like she had swallowed a hummingbird, but her voice sounded calm. "How long do you think you can keep this up? Even if she goes to jail, I'll appeal. I'll find exculpatory evidence sooner or later."

Paul turned and actually looked at her, not through her the way he had before. "I've been hearing from your former coworkers that they expect you to take a guilty plea any day now," he said. "You can't appeal a plea. Once it's in, that's it."

Sam squeezed her hands into fists. "They don't know shit about my strategy, so I wouldn't be listening to them if I were you."

"Really? Because they said when you worked there, you pleaded out, settled, or had dismissed almost every case you worked on. Jack Piper tells me you almost never went to court if you could help it."

"I don't have to go to court on this either," Sam said. "I'll get this dismissed at her hearing, easily."

"Okay," Paul said. "And when is that hearing?"

Sam fell silent. It was tomorrow. She and Amy had spent the whole week so far studying obscure legal precedents, doing witness prep, poring over the discovery they already had and waiting to hear from Shane—but a smoking gun had yet to materialize.

The prosecution had made an offer to her: a sentencing recommendation of up to thirty months, and a $200,000 fine. Sam told them to go back to the drawing board on that one, even though it would probably turn into a six-month suspended sentence and $50k after the hearing. She couldn't afford to fuck around with Amy's life.

Paul smiled at her. "Sam, I understand. What do you have to lose? But you are going to lose. I know you're buried in paperwork, and that you have no case. I see what's obvious, which is that Amy is manipulating you based on your past relationship."

His voice was gentle, but not in a condescending way. He was able to affect a tone like he really did understand, he could see things from your perspective, so wouldn't you like to see things from his?

"I just want to hear you admit it," Sam said. "I'm not wearing a wire or anything. I just want to hear it."

"I have no idea what you think you want me to admit to," Paul said.

"The same thing we've been talking about this entire time."

"I'm talking about the reckless criminal behavior of my trusted employee, which could have brought my fund down single-handedly. What crackpot story she told you, I don't know."

"Do you think this is gonna work on me? You think there's any part of me that doesn't believe Amy? You think I don't know exactly what you are, and exactly what you did? You destroyed her life to save your own ass. You better get ready to be arrested, and you better get ready to run Amy her fucking money, too, because the second I get this case dismissed I'm gonna sue you for wrongful dismissal and lost wages. I'm gonna sue Atlantic into the fucking ground. You're gonna wish you ate that fifty mil, 'cause I'm into your ass for a hundred mil. You're *done!*"

Paul's mask of polite disinterest slipped. His eyes fixed on hers, husky-like; then he flicked them down with contempt at her hands. "What, are you going to punch me?"

Sam looked at her closed fists before releasing them. "No, I'm not stupid enough."

Paul reached out and hit the button for the lobby elevator, then started pulling on a pair of leather gloves. He didn't look up from his hands as he said to her, "You're playing a dangerous game."

Sam waited with a thrill in her gut, wondering if he was about to admit to something.

"You think I'm some small-time gangster like Tony Odom? You think you can threaten me with defamation, retaliation? I could make your life very hard. I don't think you're aware how hard."

"Why would an innocent man bother?"

Paul straightened up and laughed at her. "Why would anyone bother? I'm the face of my fund. You think I can afford to have you running around Chicago, lying about me? Yeah, I know what you've been up to. Your friend Larry does, too, and he's mobilizing the press right now. You think it's been bad? It's about to ramp up . . . I give Amy a week before she can't stand it anymore. You of all people must know how much she hates being humiliated."

The elevator dinged, and Sam stepped in front of the doors,

staring Paul down.

"Why would an innocent man bother," she repeated.

"Get out of my way. Go back to Paramus."

"*Paramus*? I'm from Queens, dickhead. What is HRKK doing for you, huh? Who's the guy you have them tailing—is he the one who sent those emails? Is it Don? Is he having second thoughts? Is he trying to go to the press or the feds? Are you trying to shut him up?"

Paul reached an arm out and swept her out of his way like she was tissues on a table. The elevator doors opened.

"You wouldn't be threatening me if you weren't scared," Sam taunted him. "If you were innocent, what the fuck would you have to be scared about?"

He stepped inside, then met her eyes. "You really think it matters if I'm innocent or not?"

Sam lunged after him, furious, but the elevator doors were already closing. They almost closed on her face as he stood there, smirking. She slapped the shiny gold metal and let out a roar of frustration that hurt her throat. "Shithead! Fucker!"

She bolted back into the clerk's office and over to the desk, feeling rattled. The clerk looked up. "Oh, good, I was wondering where you went. I have your files right here." She patted a cardboard box on the desk.

"Is Paul Weller's deposition in there?" Sam said. "The one he just gave?"

The clerk looked confused, and shook her head. "If he just gave it, it won't be in there. The scopist is probably still working on it. This is everything new they had for you as of nine this morning."

"Okay. Thanks."

Sam took the box and hurried out, through hallways and down staircases, into wind so cold it hurt, across the courtyard of the Dirksen Federal Building and under the shadow of the giant blood-red sculpture in the center of it. She dropped the box into the backseat of the street-parked Beemer, locked it back up, then walked another half mile to the riverfront, wiping her nose with her jacket sleeve when the frigid air made it run.

She called Amy as she stood beside the river, staring at the glassy surface of the water. Maybe if she jumped in, everyone would take pity on her. "Promising young lawyer driven to suicidal insanity by corporate conspiracy." No, they'd probably all assume she was on drugs.

Amy picked up. "Hey, what's up?"

"I just ran into Paul."

"You're joking."

"No, I'm not. He was at the courthouse, giving a deposition for the prosecution. Ran into him is the wrong word, honestly, I kind of chased him down."

Amy listened to the entire story in silence until Sam got to the stuff about Larry, then said, "So he's counting on me taking a plea deal? He's been counting on that this entire time, so I can't appeal?"

"Yeah," Sam said. "That was the impression I got."

Amy nodded grimly. "You know, he's using everything he knows about me against me. He knows my dad is sick. He knew I would come around to wanting to avoid prison because of that, especially if the alternative is to keep getting humiliated in the press and have my assets stay frozen indefinitely."

"Amy, I know how you feel, but you have to keep your eyes on the prize. I talked a big game to him, but you know as well as I do we're on the edge here."

"What are you saying?"

"I'm saying even if pleading guilty is what he wants you to do, that doesn't mean it's not the right thing to do for *you*."

"What if I plead, and the next day we get evidence that exonerates me?"

Sam rubbed her palm over her face. It was so cold out that the joints in her hands had stiffened. "You were just saying to me

Sunday you're okay to take a plea."

"And you were just telling me not to give up. See, this is what Paul does to people: he gets in their head and rattles them. I can hear it in your voice that he rattled you."

Sam looked up and forced herself to stare where the sun was sparkling off the skyscrapers, until her eyes hurt so much she had to close them. "Yeah. You're probably right. Hey, Ame, I know the timing is bad . . ." She paused as a guy walking his poodle went by. "I know this probably isn't what you wanna talk about right now, but what about us? What are you thinking about us?"

There was silence on the other end of the line. Sam stood there, her sweaty hand gripping the rail, her heart thumping in her throat.

"I don't know," Amy finally said. "I don't know what to think about us."

"Then how do you feel?"

"That's not—I can't base what I objectively think off of how I feel."

"I'm not asking you to do that, I'm just asking you straight-up how you feel." Sam felt like she was pulling teeth. "Just tell me, please."

"It's hard, Sam. I think you want to go back to how things were before, and that's impossible."

Sam shook her head even though Amy couldn't see her. "No," she said. The cold air stung her throat. "I don't want to. I know I can't go back, I get that now. I have to move forward. But I want to move forward with you. I want more than just us being able to be friends, or us hooking up, or even leaving the door open for something down the road. I want you back, straight up. I know I've kind of been dancing around that, but, y'know, there it is."

"Do you think I didn't know that?" Amy said, not unkindly.

"I dunno," Sam said, embarrassed. "So what do *you* want?"

"I want to be able to trust you."

"You can!"

"I mean in the context of a relationship, Sam."

"But you can, you can trust me! You're trusting me right now!"

"I'm trusting you to be my lawyer, and my friend," Amy said. "That's so different. It's one thing if my lawyer breaks her sobriety, but it's a totally different thing if the person I'm with does."

"I had a few drinks. Like you've never had a few drinks?"

"I'm not sober. I'm not a substance abuser! Look, I'm—" Sam tried to interrupt, but Amy kept going. "Let me talk. I'm not being judgmental or anything. It's not my place to be upset, so I'm not."

"That's not how that works, Ame! You're upset if you're upset. You're allowed to be mad that I drank."

"Fine—fine! I am a little mad! I thought you had turned things around. I thought you had learned how to deal with bad feelings instead of just reacting to them."

"At least I do react," Sam snapped.

"What is that supposed to mean?"

"I mean you're a lot angrier than you pretend to be."

"I know I am," Amy said, her voice even. "I just got this from Frieda the other week."

Sam swallowed a hurt scoff at the mention of Frieda.

"I've never been allowed to act angry," Amy continued. "Finance is a white guy's game. I've always had to be the most calm, competent person in the room."

"But Paul used that against you. Paul used that to fuck you over. And the things you feel are still in there, eating you from the inside out!"

"Do you think I don't know this? Does it change anything about the way things are?"

"I'm saying maybe finance isn't the best place for you."

"Probably not, but it's what I love to do."

"That's how I feel about the law, and look where it got me," Sam said. "So is the rush we get from this shit actually worth it? I don't think so. Because I lost you, and now you're afraid to come back. How is that worth it?"

"Sam, I care about you, that's why I'm afraid. If I didn't care, I wouldn't care. You could do whatever you wanted and it wouldn't affect me. But you were the one person—you were the person I felt like I could set everything down with. You made me feel safe."

Sam's throat hurt.

"Losing that killed me. Watching you get dragged through the mud and go through rehab killed me. I can barely watch you go through the wringer for me with this case, but I know it would hurt you more if I tried to keep you away. I understand that you want to protect me. And, obviously, I would prefer to not go to prison."

Sam laughed, and Amy laughed too.

"I don't just want to protect you," Sam murmured. "I *need* to."

"I know," Amy said. "I do. I love that about you. It's been so hard for me to not fall right back in love with you."

"Ames, Jesus Christ, if you love me and I love you, we can make it work! I get it, I failed you. I let you down big-time. But I'm ready to make it up to you. I'll do whatever you need me to do. I told you I'm gonna go to therapy, as many times a week as I have to, and I'm gonna get a new job—I can go be a bond lawyer or whatever—"

Ring ring ring.

Sam took the phone away from her ear and saw that characteristically Byzantine iPhone call waiting screen. Her heart leapt into her mouth when she noticed the top of the screen said *Shane Alvarado.* "Amy, I gotta go."

"You what?"

"We'll talk later, sorry, I have another line, I gotta—"

She hit *End* and *Accept*, then heaved the phone back to her ear, crouching into a squat and leaning against the railing. "Hello?" Sirens blared from the street as Shane started talking. She stuck a finger in her other ear to drown them out.

"—something for you," Shane said. "I emailed it to you. I figured you probably don't have Signal."

"Sorry, wait, I missed the first part?"

"Oh, yeah, sure. Let me back up and walk you through the whole thing. So a couple days ago I asked my friend with Chicago PD if he could run a check for any incident reports involving the twenty-fifth and sixth floors of Board of Trade in the past year. He didn't get back to me, so I figured that was my answer. But I was just about to head out for the day, and I got a call from him. He said there was one incident—they had a call for a prowler from someone in the building across the street who saw weird activity through the window around 1 a.m. Guess what day?"

"If you say May 23rd, I'm going to lose my shit."

He laughed. "May 23rd."

Sam's heart was going even faster now than it had been while talking to Amy. She sat down with her butt on the concrete.

"Apparently, they normally would have alerted building security, but a cop who was walking that block decided to go check it out. He went upstairs and found a guy lurking around, but it turns out the guy worked there. He showed the cop his work badge, the cop cleared the report, and it didn't end up in the police blotter or anything. I don't even think I could have gotten it with a FOIA, 'cause it wasn't a full report. It's just notes the cop took that he logged for dispatch."

"And?"

"And he took down the prowler's information. Full name and address."

Sam took the phone away from her ear again, hit speaker, and opened her email inbox. She laughed when she saw the subject line EYES ONLY, then tapped it with her thumb.

As she scrolled through the email and read the name *Jeffrey Wallace*, her breath left her lungs. Even though her legs were still weak, she jumped to her feet, exclaiming, "No way." This was like cocaine times a million.

"Okay, so you know him?" Shane said. "You think that's your guy?"

"I'm about to find out. Thanks, Shane."

"My pleasure."

Sam got back in Amy's car and started driving toward the West Loop address Shane had sent her. She could have called the police, but she had so little proof of any wrongdoing on his part—they would never take him into custody in time for tomorrow's hearing. Plus, she wanted to clap eyes on him now. From what Amy had said, Jeffrey was a paranoid, anxious guy who had always been in over his head at the fund thanks to the Peter principle. He was a walking flight risk.

Sam parked in a garage across the street from the apartment building. It had free spots, but she had to drive five floors down to find them, then take a gloomy and slow elevator ride back up to the surface of the earth. When she stepped back outside, blinking, she realized the sun was going down. Only fifteen hours remained until the hearing.

She gave her name to the building concierge as Stephanie Winslow. Stephanie was an attorney who had worked at HRKK at the same time Sam had, and hopefully still did. An excruciating minute went by as the concierge called upstairs and then stood there going, "Yes. Okay. Yes, sir. Thank you." Sam restrained the urge to drum her fingers on the marble surface of his desk.

The concierge clicked his landline back into its hook. "You can go upstairs," he said. "He's in apartment 515."

Sam flashed a smile to hide her astonishment that this had worked. "Thanks, man."

She walked away fast—not fast enough to arouse suspicion,

but fast enough that no one would have time to change their mind about letting her upstairs—got in the elevator, and pressed 5. When the shiny doors had shut, she used her reflection in them to check her hair. A little messy. Sam smoothed it down with sweaty palms.

515 was all the way at the end of the hall. It was the corner apartment, likely the one with the most windows and the best view. Sam stood in front of the door for a moment, dragged in a deep breath, then knocked hard.

Nothing. She knocked again, and a moment later, the door opened. Jeffrey stood in front of her: gray-faced, unshaven and unslept, looking scared out of his mind.

CHAPTER 15

ALL THE KING'S MEN

Jeffrey's eyes got huge when he saw Sam, and he tried to close the door in her face, but Sam's time as an enforcer for Larry had taught her to anticipate that. She had wedged the sole of her boot in the doorway before his hand even moved.

Sam watched as the door bounced off her foot. "Nervous about something?"

"Please, seriously, I can explain," Jeffrey said.

Sam muscled her way into his apartment and let the door shut behind her. His place was gaudy, with a lot of plants, big art, and gold accents. Most *nouveau riche* guys favored a sleek, modern look, but Jeffrey had a heavier touch. A wallet and passport were lying on a small table next to his coatrack.

"Okay," she said. "Explain."

"Well." He hesitated, reaching up to rub at the back of his neck. "Why exactly are you here?"

"I'm here 'cause I know everything," Sam said, striding past him and into his big, ugly living room. She had a seat on a massive leather sectional. "I have the *whos*—what I need are the *whys* and the *hows*. And I have a feeling you want to get all this off your chest, because I know you're the guy Paul is keeping on a tight leash, and if he's afraid of you going to the press or the feds, he must have a reason to be. He's not stupid."

Jeffrey shuffled toward her looking pained, like he had kidney stones. Despite being a free man, he was already dressed like he was on house arrest—white T-shirt, gray sweatpants, gym socks with holes—and his face had a corpse-like pallor. All the lights in the apartment were on, but the curtains on his many windows were pulled shut, so only a dim glow from the sunset was creeping in. "Yeah," he said, looking at her from the corners of his eyes like she was a cop. "I, uh, I've made some threats."

"To Paul?"

"Yeah."

"That's pretty dumb of you."

Jeffrey kept looking at her funny. "Take your shirt off," he said.

Sam, electrified by female fear, looked around her immediate area for a weapon. "Excuse me?"

"I mean in case you have a wire. I won't say anything unless I'm sure you don't have a wire."

Shit, a wire would have been a good idea. Sam tossed her jacket off, then unbuttoned her shirt, exposing her sports bra. She held the two sides of her shirt apart like she was selling him watches.

"All the way off, please."

"Jesus, Jeffrey." Sam tossed everything on the floor, then for good measure she pulled her jeans down, kicked them to the side, and showed him her bare legs and boy shorts. "Happy?"

He held his hand out. "No. I want your phone, too."

Sam sighed, but she bent to dig her phone out of her jacket pocket, then handed it to him. He gave it a blank look while she put her clothes back on. It was obvious he had no idea what he was doing.

"I'd put it in the other room," Sam said. "If you're worried about me recording you."

Her plan was to say whatever she had to say to get him feeling safe enough to open up, then worry about getting evidence later.

"Right," Jeffrey said, clapping his hands together and snapping his fingers. "Good, uh, good thought. You want some water? I have sparkling and still."

"Still is fine. You need to start talking, dude. Now."

Jeffrey went into the kitchen; her view of him was blocked by a giant and ultramodern fireplace that didn't go with the Cheesecake Factory decor. Sam leaned back as far as she could so she could keep an eye on his curly-haired head bobbing around.

He set her phone down on the kitchen island and came back with a glass of water for her. No ice, how European of him. He sat down in a chair across from her and looked at her.

"Why did you send those emails, Jeffrey?" Sam said.

Jeffrey did something gross then: he started crying.

"Jesus," she said, watching him. He obviously didn't cry very often. He was honking like a goose and kept trying to wipe his tears away with his bare hands. Sam yanked a few tissues from the Kleenex box on his coffee table and tossed them at him. "Here."

"I don't know what the fuck I did," Jeffrey wept. "I'm so fucked. I've stayed home sick from work all week, I can't stop Googling to try to figure out what they'd charge me with—"

"Preparing false evidence," Sam said. "Wire fraud, criminal conspiracy, insider trading."

"Stop, fuck, stop." Jeffrey got himself under control and started drinking Sam's water. "Should I go to the feds?" he said, and sniffed. "Should I flip?"

Sam thought of the conversation she'd had with Amy in that hotel bathroom, which couldn't have been more than two weeks ago, but felt like it had happened before the dawn of recorded time. "The feds could protect you," she said. "I could take what you know to them, and potentially get you an immunity deal . . . depending."

"Depending on what?"

"Well, I don't know the whole story," she said. "So start talking."

Jeffrey leaned back in his chair, lacing his hands over his head. He was every inch the overgrown frat boy. He sniffed again, then said, "What do you know?"

Sam had to play this right. If he didn't think she knew enough, he might clam up, but if she said something that was wrong, he might do the same. "I know that you took orders from Paul Weller to break into Amy's office and send emails to Tom Naftalis as her, agreeing with him to short the stock at a certain amount, and framing her for insider trading."

She shut up without saying how she knew any of this, and watched his face. It didn't change much.

"We didn't short the stock," he said. "That's a different thing."

"Okay, fucking whatever, I don't speak your stockbroker language. Sell it before it tanked I guess is what I mean."

"Yeah," Jeffrey said. "That's more accurate."

"Why?" Sam said, leaning forward in her seat. "Why would you help him frame Amy? That's what I don't get."

Jeffrey squirmed, looking down at his hands. Tears shone on his eyelashes.

"I can tell you want to tell me. You want to get this off your chest, Jeffrey."

He nodded.

"So tell me," Sam urged him.

"I had to do it," he mumbled.

"You had to do what?"

"I had to cooperate with Paul. You don't get it."

"Help me get it then!"

Jeffrey put his face in his hands. He had the energy of

251

Oobleck, or iron filings held together by a magnet—a mess that could fall apart in an instant if the pressure being exerted on him changed. Sam wanted to dig her fingers into him like he was a bruised apple.

"I went to New York with Paul at the end of April," he said, the words sounding rehearsed. "We went to dinner with Tom Naftalis. We were already invested in Zilpah, were looking forward to the drug being approved by the FDA in the summer. That was what Tom had told Paul."

"Right. I know all this." Amy had theorized through the timeline with Sam in-depth, cross-referencing her memories with texts and emails. They had built out a whole calendar of criminal activity.

Jeffrey hiccupped. "I had the hotel room next to Paul," he said. "Tom came to see him, and I could hear them talking in the hallway. Then I could hear them talking in Paul's room. Yelling, mostly. Like, a half hour later Paul knocks on my door and comes in to talk to me."

"And?"

"He told me . . ." Jeffrey went quiet. "This is kind of embarrassing."

Sam waited.

"He told me that it was all bullshit," he said. "He told me that Tom had arranged for the results from the drug trials to be manipulated. He said that now that I knew, I was in this with him, and I had to help him work out a way to dump the stock quickly before we lost our investment."

"And you didn't go to the police?"

"I know I should have."

"Yeah, you should have."

"Listen, I never felt right about it," Jeffrey said. "I thought about going to the feds a hundred times, I swear to God. But once you're a whistleblower, that's it. That's the end of your career. I'm only thirty-one."

Sam couldn't help asking him, "Why are you thirty-one and a senior vice president at a major hedge fund?"

For the first time since she muscled into his apartment, Sam saw Jeffrey bristle. "I'm good at my job," he said.

"Yeah? Amy never thought much of you."

"Well, that's shitty because I always liked Amy."

"Really? You liked her enough to frame her for insider trading?"

"I got trapped," Jeffrey said. He talked like someone who was about to vomit but pushing through it. "Paul—okay, Paul promoted me because of what I did. What I agreed to do. I'm good at my job, but that was why."

"Jesus Christ."

"After I took the promotion, I knew I couldn't go to the cops. That's conspiracy, right? Like, *quid pro quo*? But I didn't know what else to do."

Sam ground her teeth instead of telling him he was a coward. "What exactly did you do for Paul? Take me through it step by step."

"We planned it with Tom," Jeffrey said. "We knew we had to do the actual dirty work in person. We told him we would regroup and fly out to New York again once we had decided what to do. Tom was already under suspicion inside Zilpah, because people were figuring out there was something wrong with the trials, that they didn't have a lot of the paperwork that the FDA was asking them for, because Tom had worked with one of the scientists to fudge the numbers. I guess he was sure they would get away with it, and then it fell apart, and he started freaking out. He was looking for an escape route."

"Which was?"

"Paul," Jeffrey said.

"What do you mean by that?"

"Hold on. I'm getting there. So, Tom knew Paul didn't want to lose the fifty mil, that that would probably make the fund insolvent. We could have taken the financial hit, but the problem was that all our other investors would have lost their trust in us and pulled their money out."

"Like a bank run."

"Exactly." Jeffrey seemed calmer now that he was in his element. "So Tom told Paul, I will help you do whatever you need to do to recover the money, but we're running out of time. This could happen any day now, so you need to figure out a way to sell without looking like you were tipped off. And the market had taken a hit since we bought the stock. It's been volatile this year, so we were about twenty points down, and it didn't make sense to sell unless we knew it was about to crater. We knew the SEC would come after us."

"So Paul decided to plant evidence to point them toward Amy once they did. He made sure he would save the fund and get off scot-free."

"Yeah."

"And you helped him do it."

"Paul came up with the idea," Jeffrey said. "He told me what he would need me to do, and then we flew out to New York to explain it to Tom in person. I flew back that night. I waited till everyone was gone, then I went into Amy's office, logged into her computer—"

"How'd you get her password?"

"She had it on a Post-it. Paul had noticed that—it's part of the reason he picked her. He knew we could get into her computer."

"Christ," Sam said. She would never have thought that Amy's geriatric computer habits could bite her in the ass this badly.

"I logged in, and I gave Paul the signal—I called him and hung up after a few rings. He was with Tom, and he gave Tom the go-ahead to send Amy the email. We emailed back and forth, then I deleted the emails and got out. A cop stopped me in the lobby because someone across the street called in a prowler, and I talked my way out of it. I showed him my badge." He laughed; the sound gave Sam a chill. "He apologized to me, actually. He was like, 'Sorry for bothering you, sir.'"

"And then what?"

"Once everything was taken care of, Paul flew back on a red-eye. He met with Amy in her office the next morning and told her to make the sale. The numbers in the email, that was already stuff we'd agreed upon — they were all numbers you could probably find in Amy's cost-benefit analysis. Amy's a smart trader."

Sam didn't like to hear him complimenting Amy. "What I don't get is, why would Tom agree to incriminate himself even further?" she said. "Why would he agree to put insider trading in writing?"

"Because Paul told him he had him covered, that he'd lean on his friend at DOJ and help Tom cut a good deal, then take care of him afterwards," Jeffrey said.

Sam nodded. "Okay. So that was the in. That's why he involved Paul."

"Exactly. Paul told Tom he'd make sure he had a job once he got out of prison, and he'd be rewarded for taking the L. And they go way back, Tom and Paul. They grew up together, they went to school together, they went to Harvard together. Same neighborhood, same nannies. It's like a code with those guys. The extra time Tom would have to serve for insider trading wouldn't matter, because serving that time would guarantee he had something waiting for him when he came out."

"Jesus Christ. It's exactly like the Mafia."

"Right. So, yeah, that's why Tom agreed to frame Amy. He was willing to throw himself to the dogs to protect Paul, 'cause he thought Paul had his back."

"But did he?" Sam said.

"I mean, no, it doesn't look like it. Paul totally switched up, and he's acting like he had nothing to do with any of this. I tried to bring it up to him, I asked him if he had visited Tom in jail, and he looked at me like I lost my fucking mind and told me to never say Tom's name to him again. I don't know if he ever actually leaned on his friend at DOJ, or, if he did, how much power that friend has. So I think, like, Tom incriminated himself way more than he had to, and now he's getting nothing out of it."

"You think Tom could be turned?" Sam's heart sped up. She had Tom on the stand tomorrow.

Jeffrey shrugged. "I don't know. If there was something in it for him."

"What if he realizes all this, and he gives the feds what he knows about Paul?" Sam said. "He'd incriminate both of you. It's better for you if you go to the feds yourself, Jeffrey. You don't want them banging down your door with a subpoena. If it goes down that way, then they have all the power. If you turn yourself in, you keep some power. You get to cut a deal."

Jeffrey squirmed a little in his seat. "But me cutting a deal helps you," he said. "What if you're only telling me that so I turn myself in and get Amy off?"

"I mean, after what you did to her, getting Amy off is the right thing to do."

"Okay, and?"

"It's never too late to start doing the right thing," Sam said. She got a shot of adrenaline as she said that, like her body was trying to let her know that she had meant it.

"I don't care, honestly," Jeffrey said. "I'm sorry for how this sounds, but I really just don't want to go to prison."

"An immunity deal could ensure that."

"But you can't even guarantee that you could get me one, can you?"

"I can't guarantee anyone anything, Jeffrey. I can't guarantee the sun will come up tomorrow." Sam would have just lied to him and said she could, but you could get in major trouble for lying to a client, and Jeffrey was an enemy combatant and proven stool pigeon.

Jeffrey sniffed. "People would know, though, right? They would find out that I was the one who flipped. Like in *Wolf of Wall Street.*"

"Oh, my God, dude. This is real life."

"But that was based on a true story."

"Jeffrey," Sam exclaimed, leaning forward. "You have a decision to make here. Either you come forward and make a deal, or you wait to get caught."

"It's not a guarantee that I'll get caught," he said.

"You just told me everything!"

"But I didn't give you any proof. And you didn't exactly give me good news."

Sam laughed in disbelief. "Good news? Do you even understand what you've done?"

"A decent lawyer would be able to get me off if I made a deal," Jeffrey insisted.

"No lawyer on the planet can guarantee you complete immunity from prosecution!"

"I'm not turning myself in unless I have that, so."

"Oh, yeah? What are you gonna do then? Sit here in your apartment with the blinds shut and go crazy, waiting to get arrested?" She was being charitable by saying "go crazy"—she was pretty sure Jeffrey had already gone crazy.

"What do they do to you if you come in to make a deal?" Jeffrey said. "Do they arrest you?"

"I mean, it depends. If you're confessing to a crime, yeah, you're probably going to be detained for questioning for a while. If you agreed to testify against Tom and Paul, they might put you in protective custody. No matter what, you wouldn't be allowed to leave the state."

Jeffrey stared at the floor, his leg still bouncing. He looked gray-faced and nauseated. "'Scuse me," he said, getting up. "I have to go to the bathroom."

He walked away into the hall. Sam lost sight of him, which made her nervous, but she assumed he was probably going to go throw up. People often throw up in these situations.

"Hey," she called, "I can come with you to DOJ and sit with you the entire time. It isn't as scary as it sounds. I'll make sure they treat you right, I'll keep you from saying anything that would damage you too much. I know how to handle this. Yeah, it's not a guarantee, but the odds are good . . . Jeffrey? Yo. Jeffrey!"

She fell quiet and heard a soft click: the front door shutting.

"Son of a BITCH," Sam yelled, jumping up from the couch and bashing her shin on the coffee table. She swore as she hobbled into the kitchen to retrieve her phone, then into the front hall, clutching at her leg.

She noticed immediately that the wallet and passport that were on the front table were gone. Fuck, fuck fuck. She should have tackled him and held him down and called 911 or something. She should have found a way to record him. Now he could be in the wind within the hour.

Sam wasn't giving up without a fight. She limped down the hall to the elevator and punched the button over and over until it returned. Downstairs, she raced into the lobby like a madman and demanded of the concierge, "Did Jeffrey Wallace just leave through here?"

The concierge looked up at her with wide eyes. "Uh, yes ma'am," he said, looking confused.

Sam hurried past him. Once out on the street, she scanned the rush hour traffic crawling down the street in front of her, then spotted a lanky, boyish goon disappearing into a taxi half a block up.

"JEFFREY," she screamed, pushing past passerby and breaking into a run. In New York, they wouldn't even have reacted, but in Chicago this earned her a few looks. "You shit!"

She was too late, though. Up ahead a light turned green, and the grinding traffic began to move. Sam kept running, keeping an eye on his taxi and squinting through the twilight to read the number on it, but it was a lost cause. Jeffrey had slipped away.

She slowed to a stop, nursing her sore shin. From behind her, she heard a completely unexpected voice saying her name.

Sam turned and saw Amy.

"Yo!" she said, breathing hard.

Amy's brow was knit, and she had her phone in her hand. "Why are you screaming 'Jeffrey, you shit' and running down the sidewalk?"

"Why are you *here*?" Sam countered, even though she was glad to see her.

"I did Find My Friends on you, I was worried after you hung up and never called me back. And then I thought it was weird that you were at Jeffrey's apartment building, and you weren't answering my texts, so I came down here."

Sam took her by the shoulders and pulled her closer to the street, beside some newspaper boxes, so they were out of the way and earshot of pedestrians. "Jeffrey is Post-it guy."

Amy's eyes got huge. "No."

"I know. He confessed everything, then he ran away from me and jumped in a taxi."

"*What*? Going where?"

"I have no idea. I didn't mean to ignore your texts, sorry. He took my phone off me so I couldn't record him. And he grabbed his wallet and his passport on his way out."

"He's probably on his way to O'Hare," Amy said. "We should go." She turned in Sam's grip and started looking around wildly as if for a taxi. Her face had lit up with hope.

"Ame, Ame, you think we're gonna find him at O'Hare if that's even where he went? It's the busiest airport in America, he could be anywhere, and we have no idea where he's going."

"Doesn't matter! We'll find him and stop him."

"What, like a citizen's arrest?"

"We'll have the cops stop him."

"On what evidence?"

Amy sagged in her arms. "So you have nothing?"

"No, not nothing. I know exactly what happened, and I have info to go after Tom on the cross tomorrow. Let's go get your car," Sam said, squeezing her arm. "I need to go home and look at my notes."

Amy drove them home; she felt Sam was too jittery to drive the Beemer. This was fine with Sam, who wanted to tell Amy everything that had just happened. She was pensive as she drove, staring hard out the windshield and drumming her hands on the steering wheel a lot.

"I can't believe these guys," she finally said.

"I know. It's nuts."

Amy shook her head. "I thought Jeffrey liked me."

"He genuinely did actually," Sam said. "He said so."

"Wow, okay. I mean, with friends like these."

Sam laughed.

"You know, I spent so long trying to prove myself," Amy said. "I wanted to be one of them so badly, or to prove I was better than them. To find out that they're this . . ."

"Corrupt?"

"Stupid! That they're this stupid. I knew they were corrupt, but I almost can't even believe how stupid they are."

Sam laughed. "Ame," she said, "if Paul had come to you like he came to Jeffrey, you would have gone to the feds, right?"

"What, back in May? Yes! Immediately." Amy was quiet for a moment. "There was never any way out of this, you know? All this scheme did was prolong the inevitable. There was no way to protect the fund from insolvency—we were sunk the second we invested in Zilpah. These guys love to pretend that playing by the rules is a sucker move, but then they end up in situations like this. I mean, even if Jeffrey gets away, what kind of an existence is that? Who wants to spend the rest of their life looking over their shoulder? They don't think long-term."

Sam nodded. "I understand them," she said. "It's like being an addict. You don't think past the next hit. I wasn't thinking past the next case, the next paycheck, whatever. Then all that went away—the prestige, the money—and I didn't even miss it that much. Not the way I missed you."

Amy didn't take her eyes off the road, but she stretched her right hand out to Sam. Sam took it and held it for the rest of the drive.

As soon as they got in, Sam dropped the box of discovery onto Amy's coffee table and started pawing through it, pulling out manila folder after manila folder. Amy went into the kitchen to make coffee. When she came back, Sam looked up at her, crestfallen.

"They drowned me," she said. "We're never going to get through all this before tomorrow."

Amy set two mugs of coffee on the table. "Hey, we only need one smoking gun, right? We know everything—now we just need to pin some evidence to what we know."

"Yeah, but what evidence would that be? What would nail Jeffrey?" Sam called after Amy as she went back into the kitchen to grab some almond milk.

"The fingerprint," Amy said, hurrying back. "If it's his. It has to be, right? Shelley said they thought it came from a male in his thirties."

"That kind of fingerprint science isn't always the most scientific."

"But an exact match would be pretty much bulletproof."

Sam splashed some almond milk into her coffee and took a sip. "For our purposes, yeah. Where do we get a comparison print for Jeffrey, though? I guess I could have lifted some of his mail or something, but that would never be admissible."

Amy stared at the array of manila folders for a moment before something burst into her mind. As soon as it did, she couldn't believe it hadn't occurred to her sooner. She clapped her hands together, then pointed at Sam. "Jeffrey had a DUI."

"A DUI?"

"Yes. A DUI he got in Chicago in 2011."

She watched as the significance of this rolled slowly over a clearly exhausted Sam. "Wait, Cook County has his fingerprints?"

"Yes!"

"I can subpoena for them!"

"Yes!"

"Ame!"

"I know!"

Sam was still for a second, then got up and shrugged her jacket back on. "Okay, I'm gonna run down to the station and see if Shane's friend is there. I want to get a paper copy of the notes that cop filed, with the cop as a witness, and I want to get Jeffrey's fingerprints. I'll have to wait till the morning to file a subpoena, but I can have the cops make sure they have all that ready for me ahead of time."

"When does the court open?" Amy said.

"Eight thirty."

"My hearing's at ten. Is that enough time to get that stuff into evidence?"

"Just enough," Sam said. "You should sleep, Ame. I'll be up all night, but you should look fresh in the morning."

"There's no way I'm going to be able to sleep. Just give me something to do."

Sam smiled at her.

"What?"

"Nothing. I guess all you can do is keep going through discovery, looking for that smoking gun."

"I'll find it," Amy said, with all the confidence in the world.

Sam smiled wider. "I know you will," she said. "Um, listen ..."

Amy, worried this was going to be relationship talk, said, "We don't have a lot of time."

"No, I know. I just want you to be aware that, uh, the prosecution may not take kindly to me going for Tom's throat tomorrow. My cross-examination is going to be part of the official record, which means it's going to impact the Zilpah case, too."

"Right, makes sense. What does that mean?"

Sam exhaled. "It means, as far as any plea deal they're currently considering offering you after your hearing . . . the terms of that deal could potentially get worse, if I push too hard."

"What, like, punitively?"

"Yeah." Sam eyed her. "Do you still want to do this? Knowing that, do you still want to step on the gas, here?"

Amy thought about it hard for about ten seconds, then nodded and said, "Yes."

"Yeah?"

"Yeah. I'm done playing it safe. If we're doing this, we're doing this— we're not half-assing it. If there's a risk they'll punish me for that, it's one I'll have to take." The worst part of pleading would be the admission of guilt, anyway. Amy wasn't too worried about anything else the government wanted to throw on top of that.

"Alright, understood," Sam said with a nod. She scooped Amy's car keys out of the bowl by the front door, and then she was on her way.

Amy sat down on the couch where Sam had been and bent over the folders, flipping them open and peeking inside. Most of the discovery was documents in endless amounts, page after page of Tom Naftalis's emails and Atlantic's financial statements from FY2017Q1, until she found a folder with something different in it: photographs of her old office.

Amy slowed down and started poring over each of them.

The photos showed her office both before the feds tore it apart, and after. The after photos were of her computer and her binders full of notes in FBI bins, her hard drive stored separately in a vacuum-sealed evidence bag, the framed copies of her Northwestern and Harvard diplomas sitting in a plastic tub.

She got through to the end of the stack and started again from the beginning, paying even closer attention this time, and then she spotted it: one of the before photos was angled low enough that you could catch a glimpse of the underside of her desk, including a patch of bright yellow.

Amy's heart sped up. She went into the kitchen and rummaged through her junk drawer to find a magnifying glass, then returned to the photo and peered through it.

There it was—the Post-it. You couldn't see enough to read the characters, but the black lettering was clearly the same, and at the top leftmost corner there was a telltale splotch of dark red from where an uncapped marker had bled onto the stack inside her drawer.

Amy texted Sam, her fingers flying over her phone keyboard. *I found an fbi photo that shows the Post-it under my desk from before they tore my office apart,* she said. *So that proves we didnt plant it right????*

YES, Sam texted back almost immediately. *That gives us a chain of custody*

Are you at the police station?

I am yeah im waiting for shane's friend to get back. He's out on a call. Amy you should get some sleep now

Amy looked up at her wall clock. It was 1 a.m. somehow.

Okay, she texted back. Fatigue crushed her as soon as she did, and she lay back on the couch, giving herself a moment to regroup before she got up to wash her face and brush her teeth.

—w— —w— —w—

Amy was still on the couch when Sam shook her awake the next morning.

"You gotta get ready," Sam said, looking at her watch. Amy groaned and pushed her hands away. "I let you sleep as long as I could, but—"

"What time is it?"

"Seven forty-five."

"I'm up!" Amy said, jumping to her feet. She was a quick riser. Sam was the groggy one who hit snooze a hundred times each morning. This used to drive Amy crazy, though now she was thinking back on it with fondness. "I'm up, I'm up. What should I wear? What look are we going for?"

"Puritanical," Sam said immediately, like she had been preparing for this question. "But not, like, weird. You know what I mean? Conservative but not orthodox?"

"Got it," Amy said, thinking of a suit that Michiko had picked out for her when they went to Saks Fifth Avenue together the day after Christmas. It was light gray, almost white, and the pleated skirt went past Amy's knees. She had bought it to please her mom and had never worn it once, had left it hanging in its garment bag this entire time, so it would have the added benefit of looking fresh and crisp.

Amy got ready at lightning speed, putting on mostly nude makeup with a sheer pink lip gloss that made her look a few years younger, then smearing mascara on her eyelid by accident, of course, because you only do that when you're running late and in a hurry. She fixed this, pulled her hair into a Gibson tuck, then laughed at herself in the mirror. She looked like her very proper Buddhist grandmother did in every photo of her from the 1940s.

She went to her shoe organizer and selected a pair of peachy nude Louboutin pumps that elevated the look from sad pilgrim to stylish, virginal widow, then looked up as she was slipping them on and jumped upon seeing Sam lurking in the doorway.

"Sorry," Sam said. She was wearing a plain black suit with black heels, but the dress shirt underneath was a shimmering heather-colored fabric, like she was trying to match with Amy discreetly. "You look beautiful."

Amy swallowed over a lump in her throat. "So do you."

"Uh, doubtful." She was grinning as she said this. "Not like you. I think I look like I feel, and I feel like I'm about to barf."

"Don't barf," Amy said. She was a little emetophobic.

"I won't."

Amy went over to her and started to fix her hair without even thinking about it. Sam had pulled it back, but stray pieces had already worked their way out and were framing her face. She clucked her tongue as she noticed an inexplicable smudge on Sam's cheekbone, and she licked her thumb to wipe it away. "Sweetheart," she muttered, without thinking. It was a smudge of cigarette ash; Sam smelled like she had been smoking all night.

Sam kissed her, somehow both taking her by surprise and not taking her by surprise at all. Amy leaned into the kiss, wrapping her hands around Sam's slender waist. The lump in her throat exploded into butterflies that headed south, then further south.

Sam was the one to break the kiss. "We gotta go," she said, and wiped her mouth. "You got lipstick on me."

"It's a tinted balm."

"You got tinted balm on me."

Amy kissed her on the nose, and Sam swore in protest.

"You'll live," Amy said, laughing. "Let's go."

"Hey," Sam said, hanging onto her arm. "I like seeing you laugh. That night you called me over to your hotel, I felt like I could barely make you laugh . . . you sounded like you hadn't laughed in forever."

"I probably hadn't," Amy said. She patted Sam's lapels so they laid flat.

"Look, I just want to say," Sam said. "No matter how it goes today, I'm going to see this thing through till the end. Even if we get slaughtered out there, I'm still on your team, okay?"

"I know. Thank you. Let's go."

She led Sam out of her bedroom by the hand, down the hall and into the living room, where she made sure that the photo she had found the night before was tucked safely inside a folder. It was a beautiful day, with the sun pouring in every window of the house. Amy noticed that her heart was beating rapidly in her chest. She had taken half of a Xanax in the bathroom, but it hadn't had time to kick in yet.

"Ready?" Sam said.

"Yep."

Sam held Amy's keys out. "You wanna drive?"

Amy inhaled, then extended out her palm under the keys. Sam dropped them into it. "Yep. Thanks."

CHAPTER 16

THE U.S. DISTRICT COURT
FOR THE NORTHERN DISTRICT OF ILLINOIS

They arrived at the courthouse too fast. It reminded Sam of her night of dreamless sleep before the SATs, when she had gone to bed with a rock of dread in her stomach and then, in the blink of an eye, her alarm was going off the next morning.

She didn't even do that well on the SATs, all things considered, but she still got into Chicago. Maybe today would be like that. Lose the battle, win the war.

Amy was breathing shallowly as she parked the Beemer, enough so that Sam said, "You want to take a minute before we go in?"

They had arrived ahead of schedule—there had been no traffic. It was like everyone in Chicago had sensed that something big was going down today.

Amy shook her head. "No, I'm okay."

"Okay," Sam said. She kind of wanted to take a moment before they went in, herself. Her palms were slick with cold sweat.

She followed close behind Amy as they walked through the parking lot and up the pearly marble of the courthouse steps, through the automatic doors and through the metal detectors. The building was just opening up for the morning, and attorneys were all around them like a school of fish. As they went through security, Amy made polite small talk with the security guards. The sound of her talking, and the sound of her Louboutins clicking on the marble floor, were both reassuring to Sam.

In the clerk's office, *Hot Bench* was on again, and there were a few attorneys sitting around, either looking at their phones or staring into space as they waited. Amy took a seat while Sam went up to the glass partition and said, "I have subpoenas for a witness, and for production of documents, that I need filed with Chicago P.D.'s District 11, ASAP. I was already over there last night, they're aware these are on their way, I spoke to Captain Jones, and I spoke to Officer Will Courtney—"

"Hang on, hon," the clerk said, putting a finger up. "Okay. You want to send these over there *right* now?"

"Yes. Please. I have court at ten."

"What case?"

"I'm defense counsel in the United States versus Amy Igarashi. Her preliminary hearing is this morning, I'm trying to get this into evidence before then."

"Okay. One second." The clerk turned to her computer and started typing loudly with her acrylics. "Why didn't you submit this to us earlier?"

"I didn't know the evidence existed."

"So you want to file a subpoena duces tecum and a witness subpoena, and District 11 has established to you that they're happy to comply and have an officer deliver this evidence to the hearing taking place in one hour, then testify?"

"Correct."

"Okay. We'll do our best."

With that, everything was now out of Sam's hands. The only thing she could do was do her best in court. This realization made nausea start to churn her stomach.

Sam thanked the clerk and returned to Amy. "So, done deal. By the way, I might barf soon, for real."

Amy put down her *Redbook* and looked up in concern.

"I've barfed before court before," Sam said bracingly. "You want to go outside? I might smoke."

"Is smoking going to help? You look pale."

"Objection," Sam said, teasing her. "Argumentative."

"You look objectively pale. I have eyes."

"There are fluorescent lights in here and you're prejudiced by being worried about me. Overruled."

Amy stood, laughing. "Oh, so you're the judge, too?"

"Yep."

When they stepped outside, it was clear that Sam was far from the only attorney who needed a morning smoke. The hunched figures of attorneys dotted the courtyard, all huddled against the chilly wind coming off Lake Michigan, trying to keep their cigarettes lit. Sam used Amy's torso as a windbreak while she lit hers.

"Tell me again what our strategy on the stand is," Sam said, taking a drag. The wind gusted again, this time so bitterly that Sam's cigarette went out and fell out of her mouth due to her lips going numb. "Son of a bitch. Shit."

Amy, who seemed unbothered by the cold, inhaled. "I have to smile," she said. "At both the judge and the prosecutors. But don't smile at *you* too much, because we don't want to seem overly collegial."

"Correct." Sam picked up her cigarette, but didn't relight it.

"I need to come across as intelligent and poised and in control, but when I'm questioned on my alleged illegal activities, I need to seem puzzled and innocent. I need to sit up straight with my hands in my lap the entire time."

"Correct."

"I need to control my expressions, and not tense up or show anger. I need to play it very loose and take it one question at a time. I need to wait a beat before I answer each question, because I don't want to step on your objections."

"It's just like presenting a pitch," Sam said. "You're building a case. You're good at building a case."

"We're creating a new narrative that casts a reasonable doubt on their narrative."

"Right." Sam imagined cross-examining Tom Naftalis, and her stomach gurgled some more, rejecting the stale Uncrustable that she had dug out of the back of Amy's freezer to have for breakfast that morning. "I'm going to go throw up," she declared.

Amy winced. "You want me to come with you?"

"No, stay here, keep getting fresh air. It's good for your brain."

"Is that why you're smoking?"

Sam was so defeated by this that she just made a huffing sound and left, to Amy's clear amusement. On her way back into the courthouse, she spotted the security guard who had helped her when she cut her hand open, standing against the wall between a closed door that said "Jury Lounge" and a fire extinguisher.

"Hey," Sam greeted her.

The woman looked back at her and blinked. Of course, she probably saw thousands of people a week.

"I hurt my hand, the other day?" Sam added, lifting her palm. "You gave me gauze. I just wanted to say thank you again."

"Oh!" the woman said. Her nametag said Frances. "Oh, no problem, honey. You doing alright now?"

"I am. I got stitched up."

"Good, good. You back here for court?"

"Yeah, I have a hearing."

"Good luck," Frances said, winking.

This heartened Sam as she went into the bathroom and threw up in a businesslike manner. The act of doing so additionally heartened her because it reminded her that she was only human. You could not feel superhuman while throwing up. This somewhat relieved her of the insane expectations she had developed for herself over the last twenty-four hours.

There were other women in the bathroom, but Sam, being a recovering addict, wasn't worried about vomiting in their earshot. She had done much more embarrassing things in front of much larger numbers of people. After she flushed the toilet, she pressed her forehead to the cool metal of the toilet paper dispenser.

Jackie said she had to live her life, but it was more than that: she had to learn to fail and live with it. If she failed Amy today, she would have to live with it. If Amy was forced to take a plea deal and be marked for the rest of her life as a felon, they would both have to live with that, and Amy would be the one to decide once and for all if she wanted to take Sam back. It was Amy's choice, not Sam's. Sam would just have to keep on living either way.

Or she would have to jump into the Chicago River with a cinderblock tied to her feet, but who wanted to do that? Not her anymore.

Up until the failure, though—the failure which now seemed inevitable to Sam as she knelt on the floor of a gleaming federal bathroom—she would try her very best. She wasn't going to flinch in anticipation. She was going to run straight into the spinning blades of the jet engine that was the Department of Justice.

"I'm a good lawyer," she said out loud to herself.

The minutes passed sickeningly as Sam and Amy waited in the hallway, chewing Altoids and trying not to sweat through their clothes. Ten minutes before the hearing, the doors opened, and the pertinent people from the previous case on the docket filed out of Devoy's courtroom. The bailiff glanced at Sam and said, "The United States versus Igarashi?"

"Yes," Sam said, as her heart sped up.

"Come on in," he said, indicating the courtroom with his head. "You're early."

Sam squeezed her eyes shut and said, very fast and under her breath: "Hail Mary full of grace the Lord is with thee, blessed art thou amongst women and blessed is the fruit of thy womb Jesus, HolyMarymotherofGod pray for us sinners now and at the hour of our death, amen."

Then she crossed herself and kissed her own hand. Her grandfather's watch felt heavy on her wrist.

"You ready for this?" Amy said.

"I think so. Are you?"

"Yeah," Amy said. A gleaming smile slashed across her face. "This might sound weird, but I'm actually starting to look forward to it."

"Doesn't sound weird at all."

"How do you plan to get Tom to talk?"

"I'm gonna do what I do best," Sam said. "I'm gonna piss him off."

Amy's smile got bigger.

An elevator across the hall from them chimed, then opened. Out strode Doug Pinnix, Shane, and the two DOJ lawyers.

"Sam!" Doug called jovially. "You have a minute to talk?"

"No, I have no minutes," Sam called back.

Amy, clearly fed up with journalists, turned on her heel and strode into the courtroom. Sam hung back for a moment to say hi to Shane. The DOJ attorneys squeezed by her, giving her tight-lipped smiles as they did.

"I was expecting Tyrone," Sam said to Shane as he swaggered up, chewing gum. "Isn't he on this story?"

"I went ahead and took this hearing off his hands," Shane said. "I had a feeling it might be explosive."

"Hmm," Sam said.

Doug looked between them, his eyes alight. "Has she been talking to you off the record?" he said to Shane.

Shane snapped his gum and said nothing.

"You just get a good seat for the show, Doug," Sam said, then slipped into the courtroom.

Amy was already seated at the defense counsel table, her hands folded in her lap, staring at the empty judge's bench. Across the aisle, Megan and Brian were talking quietly and organizing their files.

Sam joined Amy, dropping into the plush black desk chair beside her and making the wheels squeak.

"What do we do now?" Amy whispered.

"Pretend to be discussing something important," Sam whispered back. She set one of her binders on the table between them and opened it, pointing to a random line of her motion to dismiss the email evidence. "This is important because it's, uh, important."

Amy nodded. "That sounds important."

"It is."

"Who was that other guy in the hallway who knew you?"

"Shane's friend Doug, from the *Wall Street Journal*. I'm guessing Shane told him he might want to be here today."

"In case Paul goes down?"

"Exactly."

"Good," Amy whispered. "I want him humiliated in every paper in the country."

"I don't know if this is gonna make it into every paper in the country."

"Okay, then I want him humiliated in the *Journal, Bloomberg, Barron's* and *Forbes.*"

"It's a plan."

People were still filing into the gallery, but Sam didn't turn around to look because that was nervous rookie shit. She sat with her back ramrod straight, staring down at her notes without reading them, wiping her sweaty palms on her thighs every few seconds.

A moment later the courtroom doors closed, and the chambers door on the right-hand side of the bench opened. The bailiff at the front of the room snapped to attention. "All rise," he bellowed.

Sam was on her feet before the thought to stand had even fully entered her brain.

"The United States District Court for the Northern District of Illinois is now in session, the Honorable Judge Devoy presiding."

"Good morning," Devoy boomed as he took his seat. He was very tall, and cut an intimidating figure on the bench—his big Mount Rushmore head looming above the sea of black that was his robe and chair. "You may be seated. Are we all ready? All witnesses present and accounted for, no one needs to be rounded up?"

"Yes, Your Honor," Megan said.

"Excellent. I'm sure all counsel is familiar with my clerk, Elizabeth Lloyd . . ." He motioned to a woman on his far left, the same one Sam had just talked to.

Sam caught her eye and mouthed, *Subpoena?*

Elizabeth shrugged and shook her head.

" . . . our pretrial services officer, Ashanti Gregory . . ."

"Yeah, I know her, she keeps calling me to make sure I haven't fled to Japan," Amy murmured.

" . . . and court reporter Jennifer Wilhelm. Present counsel, introduce yourselves into the record, please, starting with the United States," Devoy said, and cleared his throat.

Megan and Brian both stood. "Megan Williams, Northern District of Illinois, AUSA."

"Brian McQuown, Northern District of Illinois, AUSA."

Sam stood, too; she felt all eyes move to her. "Sam DiCiccio,

Your Honor," she said. "For the defense."

Devoy smiled. "Ex-wife to the accused."

"Correct."

"Are there any statements that need to be made before we proceed with the evidence in this case?" Devoy said, glancing between the tables.

Sam had a sudden, glorious flash of inspiration. She knew exactly who she could call to the stand in lieu of Officer Will Courtney.

"Your Honor," she said, "I filed a subpoena first thing this morning to produce a witness and new evidence from the Cook County police department, based on information I received last night. Unfortunately, I'm not sure how quickly the officer will be able to get down here with that evidence, which is in the form of a fingerprint comparison. But I do have other evidence with me that I was going to introduce, in the form of a police document, which the officer in question is actually the author of."

"It sounds like you'll have to wait and see if this goes to trial, and introduce both pieces then," Devoy said. "You're well aware that this hearing is a venue for the prosecution to present their case."

"I am aware of that, but I believe I can impeach their key witness today, which would poke a massive hole in the plaintiff's case," Sam said. "And this evidence is a cornerstone of that impeachment."

"How bold."

"Yes, Your Honor. The thing is, there is another party present in the courtroom who is familiar with the police document, and can testify as to its authenticity."

"Alright," Devoy said. "Who is that?"

"*Chicago Tribune* reporter Shane Alvarado," Sam said, and pointed behind herself, in what she hoped was Shane's general direction.

There was a ripple of murmuring in the gallery.

"Objection," Megan said. "This is a preliminary hearing. The defense cannot call a brand-new witness."

"Overruled," Devoy said. "I'll allow it for the sake of entering this piece of evidence."

"Your Honor—"

"AUSA Williams, I wouldn't press this particular issue," Devoy said. "I'll be candid. The lack of evidence in this case is a serious problem for the United States."

Amy grabbed Sam by the forearm and squeezed; Sam bumped shoulders with her and tried not to smile too much.

"Objection as to foundation," Brian countered. "Defense is asking the court to accept that a reporter is acceptable testimony on the veracity of a police document?"

"Good question," Devoy said. "Ms. DiCiccio?"

"Your Honor, obviously the officer himself is the best source of testimony on this evidence, and I am happy to have him testify at this hearing if he is able to make it here in time," Sam said, her heart beating faster with every word. "But Mr. Alvarado, in his capacity as a journalist, can testify as to its authenticity because he was shown this evidence personally by Cook County police officers just yesterday afternoon, in response to a formal document request."

"And Mr. Alvarado is in this courtroom?" Devoy said, looking around as if expecting Shane to pop out at random.

"Yes, Judge."

"Okay. Overruled. Mr. Alvarado may testify as a lay witness, and the court will give appropriate weight to his testimony."

"You didn't do witness prep with him," Amy said under her breath.

"It's cool," Sam whispered back. "I'm improvising. Stay loose, co-counsel."

Amy stifled a laugh, issuing a puff of air from her nose.

"Mr. Alvarado," Devoy said. "Please rise and approach the stand to be sworn in."

Shane got up, scowling, and walked down the aisle to Sam, who led him over to the witness stand.

"I can't cover this fucking story now," he hissed to her. "I'm in the story."

"Sorry," Sam whispered back. "That's what you get for scooping Tyrone, though. Maybe you should get him down here."

"No whispering," Devoy boomed at them.

"My apologies, Your Honor," Sam said, as Shane discreetly gave her the finger and then took the stand. She walked over to Brian and Megan, adding, "I'm now showing the document to opposing counsel."

Megan grabbed the paper like it owed her money and pored over it. After a long moment, she said, "No objection."

The bailiff swore Shane in while Shane stood there glaring daggers at Sam, then took a seat.

"Can you state your full name for the record?" Sam said.

"Shane Alvarado."

"Thank you, Mr. Alvarado. What is your occupation?"

"I'm a reporter," he said, shaking the press pass around his neck to emphasize this.

"With what paper?"

"The *Chicago Tribune*?" Shane said, shaking the press pass harder.

"And how long have you been in that role?"

"Eleven years."

"Are you familiar with an incident at the offices of the hedge fund, Atlantic Capital Management, that occurred in the early hours of May 23rd this year?"

"I am," Shane said.

"Objection," Megan called. "Foundation?"

Sam turned to her. "I'm getting there."

"Overruled," Devoy said. He had his chin in his hand, and looked like he was enjoying this.

Sam turned back to Shane. "Are you also familiar with the crime that Amy Igarashi stands accused of committing in the early hours of May 23rd of this year?"

"Yes," Shane said.

"Have you written about her arrest for the *Tribune*?"

"I've written two stories on it, yep."

"So in your capacity as a journalist, you'd say that you've been collecting evidence and documents that relate to this case?"

"I guess you could say that."

Sam went back to her table and opened her binder, pulling out a photocopy of the cop's notes. Amy stared at her with an expression like she was watching a train bear down on a clown car. Sam winked at her, then took the paper back to Shane.

"Mr. Alvarado," she said, handing it to him. "Is this document, marked Exhibit C for identification, familiar to you?"

Shane gave it a cursory glance. "Yes."

"Can you please explain to the court what this document is?" Sam said, pushing it into his hands.

Shane took it, with annoyance evident on his boyish face. "This is—these *are*—notes made by Cook County police officer Will Courtney on the morning of May 23rd. Or a copy of them."

"May 23rd of this year," Sam said loudly, turning to the court reporter.

"Of this year, yeah."

"Objection, foundation," Megan said. "How does he know that?"

"Mr. Alvarado," Sam said to Shane, "how do you know these notes were made by Officer Courtney on that date?"

"Because he showed them to me yesterday and said exactly what I just told you."

"Overruled," Devoy said.

"Can you read them into the record?" Sam prodded.

Shane let out a sigh. "2 a.m. this morning, received alert from dispatch regarding a possible prowler on the twenty-fifth floor of the Board of Trade building. Entered the offices of a hedge fund located on that floor and found three occupants—two cleaning staff and one employee of the hedge fund, one Jeffrey Wallace, who produced identification. No suspects located and no arrests made. Appears to be a false alarm. Report has been closed."

"Thank you, Mr. Alvarado. So, we could reasonably assume from this document that Jeffrey Wallace was at the offices of Atlantic Capital Management between the hours of 1 and 2 a.m. on May 23rd?"

"Oh, objection," Megan said crossly. "Leading."

"Sustained," Devoy said.

"Withdrawn. Nothing further." Sam turned back to Devoy. "Your Honor, at this time the defense moves that the document marked Exhibit C be admitted into evidence."

Devoy put his hand out, and Sam put the paper into it. He studied it for a moment, scowling with concentration.

"Alright," he said. "This, uh, piece of paper with writing on it is now in evidence. Wish it was a formal police report, but oh well."

"Me too, Your Honor," Sam said.

"Don't get cute with me," Devoy said, and pointed a finger at her. "Take your seat so the prosecution can start calling witnesses, we don't have all day. Mr. Alvarado, thank you for your time, you may step down."

"Thanks," Shane said, scrambling out of the witness box. "I have to go call Tyrone," he hissed at Sam as he hurried past her.

"Thanks, Shane," Sam called after him genially, then took a seat beside Amy. "They're about to call you. You ready?"

"Very," Amy said. Her eyes were glittering again.

Megan stood. "The United States calls defendant Amy Igarashi to the stand," she said.

Devoy nodded. "Ms. Igarashi, approach the stand to be sworn in."

Amy rose with elegant grace and walked up to the stand,

her skirt swishing, the click of her Louboutins muffled by the dark courtroom carpet. She had raised her right hand before the bailiff even opened his mouth to say, "Please raise—okay. Do you swear to tell the truth, the whole truth, and nothing but the truth?"

"I do," Amy said.

"Please be seated."

Amy took a seat, her hands coming together in her lap. Sam stared at her, her quick heartbeat speeding up further, making her empty stomach churn. Megan approached the stand, and Amy stared at her, her dark eyes like a hawk's.

"Good morning, Ms. Igarashi," Megan said. "We haven't met before, have we?"

"No, we haven't."

"You were employed with Atlantic Capital Management up until recently, correct?"

"Until a few days ago, yes," Amy said.

"How long were you employed with them?"

"Ten years total."

"And what positions have you held there?"

"I started as a trader," Amy said. "Then I moved into risk management and analysis."

"Did you execute trades as a trader?"

"Yes."

"How many?"

Amy shrugged. "Thousands."

"As a trader, did you make stock investments with Atlantic's assets under management?"

"Yes, all the time."

"And as an analyst," Megan said, turning on her heel and walking back to her desk, "did you often advise on specific trades that were then executed by the traders?"

"Yes."

Megan took a piece of paper from her binder and brought it

to Sam. "I'm showing opposing counsel Plaintiff's Exhibit B, an email sent by Amy Igarashi at 7 a.m. on May 23rd, instructing trader Mac Watson to sell Atlantic's holdings of Zilpah Drugs at a stop-loss of 200 dollars per share."

Sam scanned her eyes wildly over the email, but there were no objections available to her. "Uh, okay," she said, like a dipshit.

Megan brought the paper over to Amy. "Do you remember sending this email, Ms. Igarashi?"

"Not vividly," Amy said. "I send a lot of emails."

"Okay. But you do concur that you sent this email?"

"Yes."

"Do you remember where you were from 1 to 2 a.m. on May 23rd of this year?"

"I don't specifically recall where I was," Amy said, "but texts I found on my phone from that night indicate to me that I was at a jazz bar near my former workplace."

"And why were those texts not admitted into evidence?" Megan said.

Devoy looked at Sam, who stood.

"They were inconclusive, Your Honor," Sam said. "The defendant texted a friend, in reply to a question about what she was doing that night, 'My usual.' Ms. Igarashi knows herself what the significance of that response was, but it doesn't go to objectively establishing her location to the court."

"Understood," Devoy said. "Go on, AUSA Williams."

Megan turned back to Amy. "Do you have the Outlook email application on your cell phone, Ms. Igarashi?"

"Yes," Amy said, flicking her eyes to Sam for a second, then looking away again.

"Did you have it on your phone on May 23rd, 2017?"

"Yes, I did."

"And you were logged into the email address of Amy Igarashi, no spaces, at Atlantic Capital dot com, through that app?"

Amy was quiet for a second. "Yes."

"That was your work email address?"

"Yes."

"So if you wanted to, you would be able to send emails from that address remotely, correct? You wouldn't have to be in your office, at your desktop?"

"Objection, compound question," Sam said, jumping back up. It was a weak objection, but she had to throw something out in front of this line of questioning.

"Overruled," Devoy said. "It's the same question, just needlessly repeated."

Megan pursed her lips at this.

"Yes," Amy said. "I was able to send emails remotely."

Megan went back to her table again. Brian passed her a few pieces of paper, and she walked over to Sam with them. "For the record, I'm showing opposing counsel Plaintiff's Exhibit A, an email sent by Amy Igarashi at around 1:30 a.m. on May 23rd, taking instruction from Tom Naftalis on when to sell Atlantic's shares of Zilpah."

"Objection," Sam said, standing again. Her ass had barely had time to touch the chair. Court was exhausting. "Facts not in evidence. The plaintiffs cannot prove this email was sent by Amy, only that it originated from her email address, and they are perfectly aware that I plan to argue that point today."

"Let's not start referring to the defendant by her first name, shall we, counsel?" Devoy said.

Sam's face flushed with prickly heat, and she nodded.

"Your Honor, Ms. Igarashi just told us this is her email address," Megan said.

"Okay, well, you're still going to have to prove to me that she actually sent the emails," Devoy said. "So, sustained."

Megan inhaled, then brought the emails over to Amy. "Did you send these emails?"

Amy gave them a perfunctory glance. "No," she said.

"But you've seen them before?"

"The first time I ever saw them was when I was shown them by the FBI," Amy said, looking totally unruffled. "By Agent Turedo, who's sitting in the back, there." She pointed into the gallery.

"Okay," Megan said. "You acknowledge, though, that these emails originated from your email address?"

"They did."

"But you maintain that you didn't send them."

"I do," Amy said.

Devoy glanced between Amy and Megan, his brow furrowed. "Alright, I think we can move on here . . ."

"Ms. Igarashi," Megan said, "do you know the penalty for perjury in Illinois? It's a class three felony, punishable by up to five years in prison."

"Objection," Sam said, jumping up again. "Asked and answered."

Devoy put his hand up. "Yeah, sustained, Ms. Williams."

Megan nodded. "Ms. Igarashi, what does this email say? Can you read this line here out loud for the court?" She pointed to the paper.

Amy's eyes went to where her finger indicated. "'I would set your stop loss at 200 a share, which you would be lucky to make back,'" she read aloud.

"And that's from an email sent by Tom Naftalis to your email address, as established?"

"Yes."

"And you were responsible for crafting the pitch deck for investors, before Atlantic made their fifty-million-dollar investment in Zilpah Drugs?"

"Yes," Amy said, still calm. "I wrote the bulk of it."

"Do you know Tom Naftalis?" Megan said.

"A little," Amy said.

"Did you have lunch with him in March of this year?"

Amy nodded. "I did."

"What did you discuss at that lunch?"

"Zilpah's future," Amy said. "And the results of the drug trials that were ongoing at the time."

"Thank you, Ms. Igarashi," Megan said, and strode away. "Nothing further."

Devoy watched her go, then said, "Ms. DiCiccio, would you like to cross-examine?"

"Yes, Your Honor," Sam said, springing back to her feet and approaching Amy. Her heart was still pounding in her chest, *ka-thug ka-thug ka-thug*, but she felt steady, driven on by an insane energy. "A—Ms. Igarashi, how well do you know Tom Naftalis?"

"Not well at all," Amy said.

"And how often did you discuss the Zilpah buy with him, prior to May 23rd?"

"Once," Amy said. "Our lunch in March. That was the only time we communicated directly."

"And how did that lunch come about?"

"My boss, Paul Weller, told me that Zilpah was looking for a cash injection as they sought a share of the opioid market, and that he wanted me to sit down with Tom so he could pitch the company to me. That meeting formed the basis of the pitch deck I ultimately wrote for our investors."

Amy was doing great. She was innately believable and almost plaintive. With her dark hair pinned back and framing her face in an oval, plus her gauzy white clothes, she looked like an angel. Devoy was watching her with interest and concern.

Sam put her hands on the witness stand. "Did Tom Naftalis at *any* point confess to you that Zilpah Drugs was faking the results of a drug trial in an attempt to manipulate their stock prices?" she said, in her most theatrical attorney voice, making it sound as if this were a ludicrous question to even ask.

"No, never," Amy said.

"Did you send those emails that AUSA Williams showed you?"

"I did not."

"I understand Mr. Naftalis is here today as a witness," Sam said. "Can you even point him out in the gallery?"

"Objection," Brian said, standing.

Devoy peered at him. "And what are we objecting to? Theatrics?"

Brian stared back, blank-faced, his mouth open. "Uh, withdrawn, Your Honor."

"Can you?" Sam urged Amy. She knew from studying photos from news stories about the case that Tom had grown a beard and let his hair get shaggy, and it would be genuinely hard for Amy to pick him out of a crowd. Her lack of recognition lent credibility to their defense.

"Uh," Amy said. "I . . ." She squinted, then pointed. "Is he in the back row? On the right?"

"Yes, that's him," Sam said, following Amy's finger with her eyes. There in the gallery sat Tom Naftalis himself, handcuffed and staring at them with dislike. "Tell me, Ms. Igarashi, after Atlantic sold its stake in Zilpah, did you see Mr. Naftalis again?"

"I did," Amy said, wringing her hands in her lap. Seeing Tom must have spiked her nerves. Shit. Sam tried to smile reassuringly at her, and clasped her hands together, trying to model the appropriate witness posture. Amy picked up on this and clasped her own. "I got dinner with him in June, along with Paul Weller. Paul and Tom are very good friends."

"Would you describe them as lifelong friends?"

"I always assumed they were. I can't say for sure."

Sam's mind blanked for a second, and in her desperation to cling to the present moment the blankness opened into a yawning gulf of terror. She could feel everyone staring at her as she clawed through her brain for the next plank of her cross. "Ms. Igarashi," she said to stall for time, wondering if it would look weak if she went to consult her notes.

"Yes?" Amy said.

Up until now, Amy's tone had been professionally impartial,

warm but devoid of emotion. But inside of that *yes* was something familiar: hundreds of mornings when she had nudged Sam awake, saying, "Honey?" It was loving, and tender, and private. Amy was making sure she was okay.

A dam broke in Sam's brain; her thoughts came rushing back in. She shot another smile at Amy, and Amy smiled back with her eyes, her lips barely twitching.

"Ms. Igarashi," she said again. "Who told you, on the morning of May 23rd, that a stop-loss order needed to be set for Atlantic's Zilpah shares?"

"Paul Weller," Amy said. "He came by my office before the market opened."

"And were you surprised to hear him say that?"

"Yes, I was. In fact, I argued with him about it."

"That's strange," Sam said. "Because those emails would indicate the stop-loss order was something you had already worked out the night before, with Tom Naftalis."

"They would," Amy agreed.

"But Paul was the one who insisted the shares be sold that day?"

"Yes, he did."

"Did he give you an explanation?"

"No," Amy said.

"And the dinner you mentioned," Sam said, striding a few steps away from Amy and then turning back around. "What happened at it? Did Paul and Tom discuss anything?"

"Objection," Megan said. "Hearsay."

"Overruled," Devoy said. "We have Mr. Naftalis right here. He can testify as to this dinner."

Amy peeked at Devoy out of the corner of her eye, then said to Sam, "Yes, I remember specifically that Paul, who was inebriated, clapped Tom on the shoulder and said, 'My boy saved our asses.'"

"And how did Tom respond?" Sam said, moving up close to

the witness stand again, like they were slow dancing with each other.

"Tom shushed him," Amy said.

There was murmuring in the gallery. Sam turned to see that Brian and Megan were conferring quietly, their heads bowed low. Doug was writing frantically in his notebook.

"Ms. Igarashi, who is Jeffrey Wallace?"

"Jeffrey Wallace is a senior vice president at Atlantic," Amy said.

"Is he close with Mr. Weller as well?"

"Yes, they work closely together."

"Was he involved with the Zilpah buy?"

"In his capacity as a senior vice president, he was often involved with large buys, including Zilpah."

Sam nodded. "And what has his demeanor been recently?"

"He's been extremely nervous," Amy said. "He's been making a lot of paranoid comments."

"Objection," Megan said. "Your Honor, hearsay."

"Sustained," Devoy said, but he was stroking his chin.

"Withdrawn," Sam said. She returned to her table and gathered up evidence: the results from AAA Biometric Services, the photo of the Post-it, and the Ziploc bag containing the Post-it.

"Ms. Igarashi," she said, first bringing Amy the Post-it and showing it to her. "What is this?"

Amy glanced it over. "That's a Post-it note with my old password to the Atlantic server."

"Got it. And when did you create that password?"

"January of this year."

"When did it expire?"

"June sometime," Amy said.

"And where did you put this Post-it note when you created that password?"

"On my desktop monitor," Amy said. "In my office."

"So," Sam said, glancing at Devoy. "Anyone who had access to your office could have used this password to log into your computer?"

"Hang on," Devoy said. "Doesn't she have a username? I have a username on my computer. I have to type in both."

Sam turned back to Amy. "Did you have a username?"

"Yes," Amy said. "But it's the same as my email address."

"So anyone who had access to your office, and had emailed with you previously, would have been able to log into your computer in May of this year?"

Amy nodded. "Correct."

"And in doing so, they could have sent an email as you?"

"Yes. My programs like MetaStock are two-factor locked, but Outlook isn't."

"Would your coworkers, including Mr. Wallace, have access to your office after hours?"

"Yes," Amy said. "Jeffrey had executive-level access thanks to his badge. I had a key to my office, but I never locked it because you have to badge into the executive suite anyway."

Sam held up the FBI photo. "What is this a photo of?"

"That is an FBI photo that shows my office on the day they raided it," Amy said. "You can see the Post-it is stuck underneath my desk, where I never placed it. I kept it on my monitor."

"And when did you get it back?"

"When Atlantic gave me supervised access to my office to pick up my things, I found it underneath my desk and took it with me."

Sam held up the fingerprints, then turned to show them to Devoy, who peered at them. "What am I holding now, Ms. Igarashi?"

"You are holding a fingerprint analysis of a fingerprint found on the Post-it note," Amy said.

"And is every fingerprint on it yours?"

"No."

"Are the remaining fingerprints mine?"

"No," Amy said. "Not according to AAA Biometric Services, who took both of our fingerprints and compared them with the print on that Post-it."

"That's weird," Sam said, turning to the gallery, even though there was no jury to appeal to. "This Post-it, which has *your password to your computer on it*, has been handled by someone else?"

"I think we get it, Your Honor," Megan said, sounding annoyed.

Sam turned back to Amy. "Please feel free to answer the question, Ms. Igarashi, that was posed before you were interrupted by the prosecution."

"Ms. DiCiccio," Devoy said, "this is not a circus. Please take that to heart."

Sam grinned at him.

"Yes, it seems that the Post-it has been handled by someone else," Amy said.

"Nothing further. Thank you."

"You're welcome," Amy said. The glitter in her eyes had become a twinkle.

"The witness is excused," Devoy said.

Sam reached her hand out to help Amy down from the witness stand, not caring how it looked, since what she really wanted to do was pull Amy to her and kiss her with tongue.

Amy let her hand linger in Sam's a second longer than was appropriate, and stroked her thumb down the center of Sam's palm as she let her go. This sent shivers all the way down Sam's spine. She followed Amy back to their table.

Megan stood, clearing her throat. "The United States calls Tom Naftalis to the stand," she said.

This time, Sam couldn't resist the urge to look back into the gallery. Two marshals stood with Tom, taking him by the arms, and guided him up the aisle with his cuffed hands out in front of him. Tom's bearded face was puffy and pasty, his hair lank.

Sam watched him go by, and Tom glanced at her. His expression didn't change.

Amy didn't look at him. She kept her eyes straight ahead, her hands laced together and resting on the table in front of her.

"Do you swear to tell the truth, the whole truth, and nothing but the truth?" the bailiff asked Tom.

"Yes," Tom said. His voice was quieter than Sam had expected it to be.

"Please be seated."

Devoy sat back in his chair with his hands laced behind his head, eyeing Megan as she crossed the carpet back up to the witness stand.

"Mr. Naftalis," she said. "Please introduce yourself to the court."

"My name is Tom Naftalis," he said.

"And where were you employed for the last six years, Mr. Naftalis?"

"I was the chief operating officer at Zilpah Drugs."

"And why are you in the custody of the US government?" Megan said, turning back to the gallery.

"In my time as COO, I orchestrated a stock manipulation scheme," Tom recited, sounding almost bored. "I manipulated the drug trials of our newest product so that we were able to make false claims about its efficacy to the FDA."

"And what happened as a result?"

"The FDA became suspicious and alerted the SEC. The SEC opened an investigation, in conjunction with the FBI and DOJ. I became aware of this and warned several investors who I had convinced to buy significant shares of Zilpah."

"And one of those investors was Amy Igarashi?" Megan said. "Operating under the auspices of Atlantic Capital Management?"

"Yes," Tom said.

"You spoke to her personally?"

"Yes, multiple times."

Next to Sam, Amy inhaled and straightened up in her seat. Sam put a hand on her shoulder.

"Don't worry," she whispered.

"Including a lunch in March of this year, when you discussed Atlantic's investment in Zilpah?"

"Yes," Tom said.

"And you have no reason to believe that anyone but Amy herself was the author of the emails you exchanged with her email account on May 23?" Megan said.

"None," Tom said.

"Is your testimony today identical to the answers you gave when questioned by the FBI after your arrest two weeks ago?"

"Yes, it is."

"And who from the FBI questioned you? Is that person here today?"

"Yes."

"Can you point him out for the court?" Megan said.

Tom had a glazed look in his eyes as he indicated Wally in the gallery with his pointer finger. "Agent Wally Turedo."

"Excellent. Thank you, Mr. Naftalis. Nothing further."

As Megan headed back to her desk, the courtroom doors opened. Half of those seated turned around; Sam was one of them.

There stood Will Courtney, wearing his police uniform, holding a manila folder in his hand. Sam's heart leapt.

"Your Honor," Sam said, scrambling out of her seat. "I need to, uh—before I cross Mr. Naftalis, I need to introduce new evidence that's just arrived."

Devoy looked at her, then at Will, who was striding up the aisle of his courtroom. "Is this the evidence you were talking about when we began?"

"Yes, it is." Sam turned to greet Will and shake his hand before leading him to the bench.

The clerk looked up at both of them. Her eyebrows, which were supremely arched and possibly microbladed, made her look like she was incredulous about everyone who crossed her sightline. Most people would have found this quality intimidating, but Sam was Italian and nuts, so she didn't care.

"Ms. DiCiccio," Devoy said, sighing. "I just want to remind you that this is a preliminary hearing."

"Judge, I can either get you this evidence today so you can have everything you need to dismiss this case with prejudice, or you can spend months on it only to find out the prosecution never had merit," Sam said. "Dealer's choice."

"I'm not even going to dignify that with a response. Who is this?"

"This is Will Courtney from Cook County Police."

"Hi, Judge," Will said. "We've met before, I believe. I've testified in front of you."

"I'll take your word for it," Devoy said. "What are you here for?"

"Your Honor, I was the officer who responded to the call for a prowler at Atlantic on May the 23rd," Will said. "And I'm dropping off our response to a subpoena for a print comparison we did for Ms. Di—uh—"

"DiCiccio," Sam said.

"Right, sorry." Will laid the clear evidence bag he was holding on the bench in front of Devoy. "So, basically, we took a look at the print she had that private firm pull off of the Post-it, and at her request we compared it with prints on file for Jeffrey Wallace, who we arrested for DUI back in twenty-eleven. And, uh, they did match."

Devoy stared at the bag. "Uh-huh," he said. "Okay. So, what do you want to do with Mr. Courtney, Ms. DiCiccio?"

"I'd like to question him out of order," Sam said. "Please. Before I begin my cross on Mr. Naftalis. This evidence is vital to my impeachment of him."

Devoy's stare moved from the bag to Will's face. "Do you have time for that?"

"Uh, yessir," Will said.

"Mr. Naftalis, please step down," Devoy said to Tom. "We will resume your testimony momentarily, once this evidence is introduced."

Tom looked at Sam, instead of the judge. His face was still an unreadable rictus, but he seemed a bit shaken.

Will climbed up, swore the oath, and sat down. His radio let out a burst of police chatter, and he quickly turned it off. "Sorry."

"You're forgiven," Devoy said drily.

Sam repeated what she had just gone through with Devoy for the entire court, with additional color and pizzazz this time. Will was a good witness. Cops often were, if they were on your side, because they knew what the judge wanted to hear. Sam had a gut feeling that Will had come away from his interaction with Jeffrey with a dislike of him that would make it satisfying to see his ass thrown in jail, and she milked that to her advantage. When she took a moment to glance behind her at the prosecution, Megan's jaw was bulging like she was grinding her teeth.

"As a police officer," she said, "would you consider this Post-it solid evidence, despite the lack of a chain of custody?"

"I think the fingerprint evidence itself is pretty rock solid," Will said. "I mean, I can confirm, as far as my expertise allows me, that this piece of paper was touched by Jeffrey Wallace, at the very least. And he was present at the location of the offices of Atlantic Capital on the night that I responded there."

"Thank you, Officer Courtney. Nothing further."

"Does the prosecution wish to cross-examine this witness?" Devoy said.

Sam turned and looked at Megan. She inhaled, then said, "No, Your Honor."

Amy caught Sam's eye, beaming. Sam did a tiny fist pump for her benefit, then turned back to the judge.

"Your Honor, at this time the defense moves that the documents marked Exhibit E, F and G be admitted into evidence," Sam said.

"Motion granted, if there are no objections," Devoy said.

Sam looked at Megan again. She shook her head.

Sam turned back to Devoy. "I'd also like to move to dismiss," she said, knowing it was a Hail Mary. "It's clear that the United States cannot even remotely prove beyond a reasonable doubt that Ms. Igarashi was the one who sent those emails that their entire case against her hinges on."

"Motion denied," Devoy said. His wooden face looked tired, like this was way too much to contend with at ten in the morning. "This is the definition of circumstantial, and for the fortieth time, Ms. DiCiccio, this is a preliminary hearing. We go by a different standard here. You've practiced civil law, haven't you? Right now, the United States has a preponderance of the evidence. They do not need to go beyond a reasonable doubt. Please, go ahead with your cross-examination of Mr. Naftalis, because we do have limited time today. Mr. Courtney—thanks for coming down here. At this time, you are excused."

Shit.

Will nodded. Sam whispered *thanks* to him as he climbed down and walked away.

"Mr. Naftalis, please return to the stand," the clerk called.

Tom stood from the gallery, still handcuffed, and shuffled forward, led by one of the marshals. There was something so pitiful about him that Sam felt a human pang in her gut.

"You're still sworn in," the clerk told Tom, who nodded.

Sam approached the stand, coming within Tom's personal space bubble so he knew she had no fear of him. He smelled like cheap deodorant. Even being a big-dick COO couldn't get you the good stuff inside Little Gitmo.

"Mr. Naftalis," she said.

Tom looked up at her, his gaze fixed.

Sam felt a sudden wave of fatigue and faltered. No, no, she had to focus. The goal line was in sight; she just had to get there. Weak, demoralized Tom was the linebacker standing in her way.

When she looked back into his eyes, she felt another pang. He was a real person.

Sam scrapped the first question she had planned to ask. "Mr. Naftalis," she started again. "How long have you and Paul Weller been friends?"

Tom started to speak and had to clear his throat. "Forty-five years," he said shortly.

"When did you meet him?"

"I was sixteen."

This was like pulling teeth. "Where did you meet him?"

"At school."

"Which school?"

"The Collegiate School in Manhattan."

"And you went to college together as well?"

"Yes."

"Where?"

"We attended Harvard together," Tom said, like each syllable was costing him money.

"Would you describe him as a good friend?"

"Yes."

"Where's this going?" Devoy said.

"Um," Sam said. She wasn't entirely sure; she just wanted to keep tugging at the thread of Paul until this whole thing unraveled. "I'm, uh. Mr. Naftalis, would you—? Uh . . . sorry, withdrawn. One moment, please."

She wiped her clammy palms on her pants as she went back to her table and pretended to search through her notes. She didn't look up to check, but she got the distinct impression that everyone in the gallery was staring at her.

"Sam," Amy whispered. "What the fuck?"

"He's not going to say it," Sam whispered back, leaning

down. "Unless I make him furious about Paul. I know Paul is trying to throw Tom under the bus, but I don't have Paul on the stand, I have Tom. What's—what's Paul's deal, Amy? You would know—you know him. Would Tom resent him for anything?"

Amy shook her head, looking bamboozled.

"Ms. DiCiccio," Devoy boomed.

"He's a narcissist," Amy said quickly. "That's—that's all I have. He doesn't really care about anyone, I guess. Tom doesn't seem like—I get the feeling he actually cares about people. He kept mentioning his wife at dinner, and I think he cares about Paul. Also, Paul is worth way, way more money than Tom. I told you, Paul is absurdly wealthy."

"Thank you," Sam whispered, and returned to the stand. "I apologize, Judge. I just needed to refresh my memory on a piece of DOJ's evidence."

Devoy looked at his watch, then back at Sam, glaring from under his bushy eyebrows. He was probably already thinking about lunch.

"Mr. Naftalis," she said, "what reason do you have to believe that Amy Igarashi sent you those emails on the morning of May 23rd?"

"I have no reason to believe that she didn't," Tom said. "They came from her account. She ordered the trade the next day, as we discussed."

"Right, but in light of the evidence, you realize that it's entirely possible that she herself did not send those emails?"

"That seems like a far-fetched scenario," Tom said, lowering his gaze as he said it.

"Well, here are the facts," Sam said. "You told Agent Turedo during your FBI questioning that you had every expectation that the SEC would investigate the massive stock sell-off that occurred the morning that Zilpah's price hit rock bottom?"

Tom hesitated, but this was incontrovertibly on the record. "Yes."

"So one would assume," Sam said, taking a step back so she could pace back and forth in front of him, "that if you were willing to commit insider trading just to save Atlantic fifty million dollars, that, being aware the SEC would then investigate them, you would take precautions to prevent whoever you were insider trading with from being caught red-handed?"

She knew this question was word salad as soon as it left her mouth, and tried not to visibly wince.

"Objection," Megan called. "Argumentative?"

"Overruled," Devoy said. "Answer the question, witness."

"I don't understand what the question is asking," Tom said.

"Let me rephrase. It seems like if Amy—Ms. Igarashi— were the one you were colluding on a crime with, she would be the one you met with in person, correct? But you only met her in person once before the sell-off," Sam said.

"I believe we only met in person once, yes," Tom said.

"And you decided to correspond with her from your work email address to her work email address, flagrantly committing a crime in writing, when you knew the SEC and FBI would find that evidence?"

"I didn't know," Tom said. "I deleted the emails."

"You thought the FBI couldn't retrieve deleted emails?" Sam said, raising an eyebrow at him.

"Yes," Tom said. He was obviously lying through his teeth, but there was nothing she could do about that.

"Okay," Sam said. "Mr. Naftalis, what was your net worth before Zilpah stock became worthless?"

Devoy made a "where is this going" face in her peripheral vision.

"I was worth around twenty-five million," Tom said.

"Do you know how much Paul Weller is worth?"

"No," Tom said.

"Can you make an estimate?" Sam pressed him.

Tom hesitated again. He looked uncomfortable every time

she mentioned Paul. "I would imagine that he's worth close to a billion dollars."

"Has that wealth disparity ever been a source of tension between you?"

"Objection," Megan called again. "Relevance."

"Sustained," Devoy said.

Sam got close to Tom again, so close she could see exactly where on his forehead his hair was thinning. It was mostly at the temples. "Mr. Naftalis," she said, "did Paul Weller ever request that you overtly implicate yourself in an incident of insider trading, in order to frame Amy Igarashi?"

"No," Tom said.

"Mr. Naftalis," Sam said, imitating Megan's chirpy voice, "are you aware of the penalty for perjury in Illinois? It's a class three felony."

"I am aware."

Sam's heart was pounding, but she charged ahead. "So if I were to, ahead of this case going to trial, track down Jeffrey Wallace, and if he were to tell me that he was instructed by Paul Weller to break into Amy's office and send you those emails—"

"Objection! Argumentative!"

"Sustained," Devoy said.

"—and if he were to flip, because he wants to flip, he told me so himself, Tom—if he flips on Paul, and the DOJ loses Amy, and they don't need you anymore, where does your deal go? Poof, bye-bye!"

"Ms. DiCiccio!" Devoy bellowed at her. "I will sanction you and hold you in contempt if you violate another ruling and continue badgering this witness. Rephrase your question with facts in evidence!"

Tom was absolutely bug-eyed, though, so Sam barreled ahead.

"Has Paul Weller had one word of communication with you since you've been in prison?" Sam said. "His friend of forty-five years, who risked prison to save his firm from financial ruin?"

Tom faltered.

"Counsel, stop editorializing," Devoy said, but he turned to Tom and added, "Answer the question."

"No," Tom said. "No, I haven't spoken to him."

"Are you aware that Jeffrey Wallace is being tailed and kept under constant watch by the law firm that Mr. Weller has retained to advise him on this case?"

"I am not aware."

"Objection," Brian cried. "Your Honor—foundation?"

Devoy put his palm down on the bench. "Ms. DiCiccio," he said, his voice terrifying, "you need to get this cross under control, or leave my courtroom."

Sam barely even heard him—she could feel Tom ready to break apart like a robin's egg in her hand. "Do you feel like you were abandoned by Paul Weller?" she said. "Did he go back on his deal with you? Did he throw you to the wolves because you screwed up when you falsified those trials, and you put his fund and his massive fortune in danger? Does he resent you enough to send you to prison?"

Tom made a wordless noise.

"You don't have to answer that," Devoy told him.

But Tom wasn't listening. He stood up, his eyes even buggier, and said, "Is what she's saying true?" to someone behind Sam.

Sam wheeled and saw Megan looking up with a stricken expression. "I—Mr. Naftalis, you're being cross-examined," she said.

"Is what she's saying true?" Tom yelled. "If they bring in Jeffrey, is my deal fucked? *Are you fucking me?*"

"Sit down, sir," the bailiff boomed from the corner. "Or the marshals will escort you out."

"Is my deal fucked?" Tom screamed to no one. "She knows everything! What the fuck!"

"Mr. Naftalis, you have to sit down and answer the questions,"

Megan begged him. "Please stop speaking extemporaneously."

The bailiff strode over and began forcing Tom back into his seat, a sight so absurd as to be almost comical. Devoy looked repulsed by Tom, like he had turned into a giant cockroach while on the stand.

Sam's eyes were pounding hotly in their sockets. She was filled with so much adrenaline that reality felt mushy and dreamlike. "Did Paul Weller collude with you to frame Amy Igarashi?" she said to Tom.

Tom shook his head, his face going even paler. For a moment it seemed like he wouldn't answer, and then he said, "Paul was in on it, and Jeffrey was in on it."

Sam felt like she had been hit by a bolt of lightning. She blinked, her vision going dark at the edges. "You gave Paul Weller insider information that he used to inform a trade of Atlantic Capital Management's stake in Zilpah?" she said, looking across the room at the court reporter to make sure she was still typing. She was. She was typing with fury, actually, and her fluffy asymmetrical hair was bouncing.

Sam looked back at Tom, who had turned his gaze from her. He was looking out across the court, at the door, and there was a longing on his face.

"Yes," he said. His voice was dull and flat.

There were audible gasps from the gallery.

"Your Honor," Sam said, walking a few steps over to the bench, shaking like she was coked out of her mind. "I would like to remove—like to renoove—I would like to renew my motion that the case against Ms. Igarashi be dismissed."

Devoy nodded. "Please go sit down," he said. "I need a moment, and then I'm going to rule on that."

Sam's heart leapt. "But the prosecution has more witnesses."

"Just go sit down."

"Okay," Sam said, and walked away on jelly legs. Out in front of her, marshals were escorting Tom out of the courtroom;

in the gallery, Shane and Doug were filling notebooks.

Amy reached an arm up for her as she wobbled into her seat, steadying her. "Sam. Sam, oh my God. What just happened?"

"I don't know," Sam said in a daze, stretching her aching legs out underneath the desk.

"Did we *win*?"

"Maybe," Sam said, regretting that she hadn't taken that golden opportunity to force Tom to say, explicitly, that Amy was completely innocent of the charges against her. Maybe he didn't even know. Maybe he didn't care.

"He said fuck like five times! In federal court!"

"He did," Sam agreed, watching as Devoy left the bench and went into his chambers.

Two minutes passed, which felt like an hour, with time sliding thickly over them all like a big slug. Everyone in the gallery was whispering to each other, and so were Megan and Brian. Megan was flipping papers around like she was expecting to find in her notes some obscure case law that could make her witness verbally shitting his pants unhappen to her.

Sam and Amy were quiet, though. They were holding hands under the table. Sam didn't even feel insecure about the fact that her palm was soaked with sweat.

Devoy returned, and the whispering quieted down until you could have heard a mouse skittering on the floor. He took his seat and steepled his fingers.

"I am shocked at the behavior I've seen today in this courtroom," he said. "The lack of professionalism from the defense, the complete lack of preparation and due diligence from the prosecution, appalling behavior from a witness . . . This is federal court. This is not a circus."

Sam felt like she was back in third grade and being yelled at. She lowered her gaze without meaning to.

"I've ruled on a lot of cases that have sickened me to my core," Devoy said. "I've seen the worst of human behavior. But this . . . the behavior in this case, the amoral and venal behavior that we scratched the surface of today . . . It's just disappointing. I worry so much about where our country is going."

No one knew how to react to that.

"Anyway," Devoy said, clearing his throat and shuffling his papers, "I am granting the defendant's motion to dismiss. I believe the prosecution has made grave errors in their construction of this case, and these cannot be put down to procedure and technical error alone. I think the United States rushed to indict an innocent person, or at least one innocent of the specific charges they have levied against her. Because of that, I am dismissing the charges against Ms. Igarashi with prejudice. This case cannot be brought again, and it is dismissed from my docket." He thumped the gavel. "Good riddance."

All the air rushed out of Sam's lungs in a noise with a *whuff*. Amy grabbed her, pulling her into a hug, hugging her and shaking. It took Sam a second to realize that Amy was shaking because she was crying.

"Ame, Ame," Sam whispered, stroking her hair. "It's okay. It's over. We won."

Megan and Brian came over to say congratulations while Sam and Amy were still locked in their damp embrace. Sam awkwardly shook their hands behind Amy's back and tried to pretend like it was normal to have your client's face buried in your shoulder.

"That was, uh . . ." Brian said, then trailed off. "I've never seen anything like that in federal court before. Wow."

"We underestimated you," Megan said, with an admiring look.

"In your defense, I think it's more that you overestimated your case," Sam said, going back to stroking Amy's hair.

They laughed.

"That's fair," Megan said. "Either way, congratulations."

"Thanks. You guys gonna go after Paul now?"

Megan and Brian exchanged a glance.

"I don't think we have a choice after today," Megan said.

Sam smiled. "Hey, good arguing against you, good to meet you guys."

Behind them, the bailiff heaved open the big courtroom doors. Everyone was slow to get up and start filing out, like they were theater patrons leaving an emotionally draining movie. Sam kept an arm around Amy as they headed toward the exit, even though Amy seemed fine and now livelier than Sam, who was turning back into jelly after briefly solidifying.

Out in the hall, Shane grabbed them and yanked them both into a hug. "This isn't very unbiased of me," he said, "but that was the craziest shit I've ever seen, and I'm so happy for you guys."

"Thanks, Shane," Amy said, laughing and wiping tears from the corners of her eyes with her pinky.

Sam thumped him on the back. "Where's Tyrone?"

"Stuck in traffic. I'm gonna give him all my notes. God, I wish I could write this story."

"Sorry," Sam said. "You might have saved our asses, though, if the cop hadn't shown up."

"Yeah, but at what cost?" Shane said, spreading his arms. "You owe me a story, Samantha."

"You want a story? How about an exclusive interview with me and Amy, with no questions off-limits?"

"That's a start."

Sam got pulled away by Doug, who wanted a sound bite, and by the time she was done with that, Shane and Amy had taken a seat on one of the courtroom benches and were deep in conversation. She stood frozen for a moment, a rock in the creek-like movement of the busy hallway, then remembered—Jess.

She found the nearest door to the courtyard and pushed it open, heading out into the frigid air, calling Jess as she did. She didn't expect her to pick up since Jess loved texting and hated phone calls, but after a few rings, she did.

"Hello?" she said.

"Jess," Sam said, her voice cracking. "It's over. We won. Amy's free."

"Oh my God!" Jess cried. "That's incredible, Sam. Are you serious?"

"Dead serious," Sam said. She was still walking, heading toward Jackson Boulevard, and when she got to it, she turned so she could see the Chicago River. It gleamed from a few streets away, a sparkling ribbon. Tears began to stream down Sam's face as she looked at it. "Tom Naftalis broke down on the stand. I, um, I got him to break down, I guess. He freaked because he thought his deal was going to get blown up if—well, it's kind of complicated. I'll send you the *Tribune* article about it when it's up. But she's free, Amy's free."

"That's the best thing I've heard all week. God, I was so worried! Congratulations, that's amazing, tell Amy I said congratulations, too. Are you guys coming back to New York now?"

The question hit Sam like a blow. Everything she and Amy had been ignoring for weeks was now going to have to be addressed and discussed. There was no more "once this is all over"—it was over.

"Oh," Sam said. "Uh, I have no idea."

Jess didn't seem to notice the change in her tone. "Okay, well, if you do, we need to go out to dinner to celebrate! You guys, and me and Trent. Okay?"

"Yeah, that sounds great. Hey, I gotta go, but I'll FaceTime you later, okay? Love you."

"Love you too, Sam. Congrats!"

Sam hung up and started walking north with no idea where she was going.

It took Amy and Shane a minute or two to realize that Sam had disappeared from the courthouse hallway. They checked the bathrooms and the lobby, then retrieved their belongings from the coin-operated lockers and went to check the courtyard in case she had gone for a smoke. Another five minutes had elapsed before Amy remembered that Find My Friends existed. She pulled it up, and there was Sam: a few streets away at St. Peter's Catholic Church.

"Maybe she went to a meeting?" Amy wondered aloud. "They don't let you have phones on in those."

"She found a meeting in five minutes?"

"It was just a theory."

Shane shrugged. "Either way, you found her, right? She didn't jump in the river or anything?"

Amy laughed. "I don't think so."

"Alright, well, I gotta get back to work. Congratulations, alright?" Shane said, bringing her in for another hug. "Hey, do something good with your freedom, alright? You got a second chance. Not a lot of people can say that."

"I know," Amy said. "Believe me, I know."

They said their good-byes, and Amy started heading in the direction of the church, huddling against the biting wind. She kept checking her phone every few moments out of worry, making sure the gray dot indicating Sam's location hadn't moved.

The door to the church opened easily, and as Amy stepped inside, she saw it was almost completely empty. It was gorgeous inside, filled with white marble art deco sculptures that glowed golden in the lights coming from above and pouring in through the windows.

Amy smiled hello at a guy who was mopping the floor in the entryway, then moved deeper into the church, looking for Sam. It wasn't hard to find her. The pews were deserted, except for one blonde head in the front row.

Her long skirt billowed around her as she strode toward Sam, even more worried now for reasons she couldn't articulate, but her anxiety vanished in an instant when she reached her. Sam was sitting there, bathed in golden light, bent in prayer. Her eyes were shut, and tears were streaming down her face.

Amy sat down beside her and reached up to stroke her hair. Sam opened her eyes.

"Ame," she sniffed, wiping her face with her sleeve. "How'd you find me . . ."

"I tracked your phone," Amy whispered. "Sorry, I didn't mean to interrupt you."

"No, it's okay. I actually was wishing you were here, 'cause it's like, so beautiful, and peaceful, but I felt like getting on my phone would fuck up what I was feeling, so I started praying instead."

Amy said nothing, just nodded.

"Listen," Sam said, and drew a shuddering breath. She reached over and placed a hand on Amy's knee. "I realized, um… I just wanted to say… I'm at peace with the fact that you might not want to go back to our relationship."

"Wait, wait—"

"No, let me get through this. I understand why you wouldn't. We just fought so hard for your freedom. I don't want you to be tied down to something if it's not what you want. I would never want to do that to you."

"Sam," Amy said, pained.

"Just—look, please don't feel like you have any obligation because I won this case for you. I did that 'cause I love you, and I'll always love you, but it's okay if you don't love me anymore. I don't want to live without you, but I think I've finally realized that I can." Sam shook her head. "It's always something, right? If I don't kill that mindset here and now, y'know, even if we got back together, there would always be some new thing for me to chase after. Wherever you go, there you are. So you don't have to worry about me. You have my blessing to move on with your life and do whatever makes you happy. Or if you want to take some time to think about it, even. I know I haven't necessarily earned your trust back—"

"Sam," Amy said again. "Look at me."

Sam looked at her, her dark eyes bright from crying.

"Come here," Amy said, and kissed her.

It was a long, tender kiss. Amy felt the cross and the saints towering over them like they were another person in the room.

When they finally separated, Amy's lips were buzzing. She touched them with her fingers.

"I love you," she told Sam. "You dumbass . . . I was looking for you so I could tell you that."

Sam looked breathless. "Same," she said. "I mean, I love you too." They both laughed. "I never stopped, though."

"I didn't stop either," Amy said. "I told you that. I was just afraid to trust you again, that's all."

"I know."

Amy inhaled, then admitted, "I wasn't fair to you, when we were married. We weren't fair to each other. What we had built didn't actually work."

Sam studied her, looking wary.

"We were both relying on each other to be superhuman," Amy said. "When things broke down for you, I couldn't handle it, because you were supposed to be the one holding me together. But then when things broke down for me . . ."

Her eyes grew hot, and she swiped at them, looking up at the saints.

"You could be there for me," she said, her voice hoarse. "Because you knew how it felt."

Sam stroked Amy's hair, then tucked a piece of it behind her ear. "It's okay," she said. "And you don't have to, ah . . . Don't feel like you have to make anything up to me."

"No, no, I don't," Amy said. "This isn't out of obligation. It isn't even just because I love you, I want you to know that. I could walk away right now, but I'm not. I'm choosing you."

"Okay," Sam said, her voice soft.

"I'm choosing this. I want this, I want to try again. But it has to be different this time . . . both of us have to be different."

"We already are, I think," Sam said.

"Yeah. I think we are, too."

"Will you come back to New York?"

Amy nodded. "I was already planning to. I want to be close to my family."

"And you'll give us a second chance, clean slate?"

"If you'll give me one."

Sam laughed a sweet, rich laugh. "Ame . . . no question."

"You know, no one else would have done for me what you did," Amy said, with a lump in her throat. "No one."

"Well, I wouldn't have done it for anyone besides you," Sam said. "I won't lie to you—this whole thing was a real pain in the ass."

It was Amy's turn to laugh. They kissed again.

CHAPTER 17

NEW YORK, 2019

"I can't see," Sam yelled as she staggered down the hallway of Amy's parents' apartment building, her arms wrapped around the straw pot of a kadomatsu, bamboo shoots blocking her vision. "Everyone watch out, I can't see."

"I got you," Calvin's voice said from behind her, placing his hands on her shoulders.

"Thanks, Calvin."

"You guys know they make small ones, right?" Ellie's voice said, and then Sam heard the jingle of a key in a lock.

"I want your parents to have a very auspicious New Year," Sam said, her voice muffled by bamboo.

"Our Christmas tree this year is scraping the ceiling," Amy said, sounding amused. "I'm worried about Sam's depth perception in her old age."

"Okay, when I was a kid, that was a flex. And I'm going to lift that ceiling when we renovate, anyway. That drop ceiling isn't original, there's no way. Not in a Victorian."

"I'd like to see that," Calvin said, sounding excited. "I love original ceilings."

"Me too!" Sam exclaimed.

"You shouldn't have gotten them started, Amy," Ellie said. She was still struggling with the door. "Mom!" Sam heard loud knocking. "You have the chain latched!"

Sam shifted the kadomatsu in her grasp so she could see a little. There was commotion from inside the apartment, and then Michiko's face appeared in the gap. "You're early," she said, and shut the door so she could undo the chain. "It's only ten."

"Baa-baa!" Meg cried, pulling her hand out of Calvin's and running to the closed door, looking pitifully at it.

Michiko opened the door a moment later and scooped Meg up. "Happy New Year!"

"Happy New Year," they all chorused.

"Happy 2019," Sam added, for the sake of accuracy.

"Mom, we brought you a kadomatsu," Amy said, pointing at Sam. "If you guys have room for it."

"Oh, my goodness," Michiko said, taking it in with wide eyes. "Well, maybe by the window? It won't fit by the front door. We have a miniature on the key rack, but this is so nice. So big. Thank you, girls."

Calvin started guiding Sam into the apartment and over to the window, where she finally set the large plant down in grateful relief, shaking out her numb hands.

Ken was in his chair as usual, looking no worse or better than the last time Sam had seen him. He was very thin and had a yellow pallor to his face, but he was beaming at all of them. Sam waited for everyone else to greet him before she leaned in for a hug—a gentler one than she would usually give. No rough pats for Ken.

"Happy New Year," she said.

"*Akemashite omedetou*, Samantha."

Sam went over and sat beside Amy on the couch, and they watched Michiko hand Meg to Ken. He started bouncing her on his knee, making her laugh. Looking satisfied that the baby was occupied, Michiko started distributing cups of tea.

"Mom," Amy said, taking the tea with her right hand, while her left lay interlaced with Sam's on her lap. Her new wedding band, embedded with conflict-free diamonds this time, sparkled on her finger. Sam liked looking at it. "You and Dad have to come see our new place now that we closed escrow."

"Oh," Michiko sighed, handing a cup of tea to Calvin.

"Queens is so far," Ken said.

"We'll pick you up. We have a car now."

The car was a 2018 Subaru, which they kept telling people they bought for safety reasons, not to fulfill the lesbian stereotype, though in truth they got it because Amy had been suckered by that touching commercial of the parents sending their daughter off to college in a Forester.

"I don't like cars," Michiko said. "I like to walk. I need fresh air."

"Well, you can't walk to Queens," Amy said.

"Yes I can."

"It's sixteen miles, Mom," Ellie said.

"I can walk sixteen miles," Michiko said, sounding offended that they would even question this. She sat down next to Ken.

"I'm ripping out the tile in all the bathrooms," Sam said, like this was an appealing feature for visitors.

"Yeah, she's been working on that since we moved in," Amy said. "Did ten hours on it the first day and nothing since."

"Hey, it's hard! I've been working a lot."

Amy smiled and twisted her left earring on its post. "I know."

"How is work going, by the way?" Calvin said to Sam.

"It's good," Sam said. "Switching practice areas is kind of weird. It's like, on top of learning new things, forgetting a lot of stuff you already knew. But I like my clients a lot."

"Do you see them in the house?" Michiko said, sipping her tea.

"I have an office in the shed," Sam said. "It's cool, I have a lot of, uh, lamps."

"But on your property? I don't like that," Michiko said. "Aren't they indigent?"

"No, no, they pay me," Sam assured her. "Well, most of the time. The rest of the time I get paid by nonprofits. But I get paid either way."

"Mom, come on," Amy said. "She's an immigration lawyer. We're all immigrants, right? They're people like us."

Michiko shrugged. "People are people."

"What does that mean?"

"I wouldn't invite strange ones in my house. What about when the baby comes?"

Amy laughed. "The baby is not immediately imminent," she said, touching her hand to her barely rounded stomach.

"I'll definitely have office space by then," Sam assured Michiko, who nodded in appreciation. "Money is just a little tight."

"She won't let me touch my savings for anything," Amy added.

"Not until we squeeze this wrongful termination settlement out of Paul," Sam said. "Anyway, my clients are all very nice people. I like working in the shed, actually. My commute is great. I just walk into the backyard."

Ellie laughed. "Amy, I am wondering, though, what you're going to do? I mean, you're going to stop working, right?"

"I can cut back my hours, and work from home," Amy said. "I do want to do something different, though. I'm not enjoying consulting as much as I thought."

Everyone was finishing their tea. Michiko got up in graceful silence and went into the kitchen to start refilling the kettle.

"Consulting is great," Calvin said. "You barely do anything, and you make a ton of money."

"That's what I'm not enjoying," Amy said. "It's like pulling a slot machine. I don't feel challenged, or like I'm doing anything meaningful. I've actually been thinking about maybe going to work for the city's inspector general office. They need auditors and investigators."

"Yeah, Amy wants to investigate stuff, now," Sam said. "That's my fault. I got her hooked."

"Not *stuff*. Just, you know, financial wrongdoing."

"You could become a private eye," Calvin suggested.

"Don't they usually catch adulterers?"

"Columbo," Ken said, and nodded at Meg. "I love Columbo."

"There you go, Amy," Ellie said. "Become Columbo."

"You could go work for the SEC," Sam said.

Amy laughed. "I could. They owe me."

Michiko returned with a plate of *mochi* balanced on her palm, and set it on the coffee table. "No more talking about work," she said to them. "I don't want to talk about my work, so you don't talk about yours."

"Are we going to the Brooklyn shrine, Mom?" Ellie said, taking a *mochi*.

"No, your dad is too tired. I have a *kamidana*." Michiko pointed to a tiny wooden shrine that was sitting on a shelf behind them. Sam and Amy both twisted 180 degrees to look at it.

"Where do you get all your tiny stuff, Mom?" Amy said.

"The internet."

"Of course."

"Go wash your hands, now. You're touching everything with your street hands."

Sam, eager to continue being the perfect daughter-in-law, vaulted off the couch and helped Amy to her feet, then sped to the bathroom.

"You can relax, sweetie," Amy said once she had shut the door behind them, leaning against the tiny, painted-over window that overlooked an alley. "No one's mad at you. Every time we see my parents, you act like you think they're mad at you."

"You do the same thing with my parents," Sam pointed out,

scrubbing her hands raw so she didn't chase away the prosperity spirits with grime from the Uber ride over.

"Your parents actually are a little mad at me, though."

"No, they're not. They're just Italian."

Amy laughed and started fixing her hair in the mirror. "How do I look?"

"Beautiful," Sam said without even needing to look up at her, though she did anyway. She stepped aside to let Amy go, and dried her hands on the hand towels, which were embroidered with kittens. "So do we pray for prosperity?"

"Yeah, fortune, prosperity, peace, good things in the New Year."

"I honestly don't have anything to pray for," Sam said, still looking at Amy, smiling. "I have everything I want."

"Pray for a healthy baby, and a good ceiling under the drop ceiling," Amy said, smiling back.

"Alright, done."

Amy shut the faucet off and dried her hands by flicking them at Sam, making Sam cry out in offense and wheel around. Amy giggled and wrapped her arms around Sam's waist from behind, squeezing her, smiling at their reflections in the mirror.

"Happy New Year," she whispered in Sam's ear.

ACKNOWLEDGMENTS

Thank you to everyone at Bywater Books who believed in this novel and contributed their talents to its publication.

Thank you to the friends who read this book before it was published, and cheered me on: Ksenia, Chelsea, Ana, Nicki, Audrey, Holli, Alex, Madeleine and Carina. Thank you especially to those who offered notes and advice, and in doing so made this a better piece of fiction.

ABOUT THE AUTHOR

DIANA DIGANGI was born and raised in the suburbs outside Washington, DC. She holds both bachelor's and master's degrees in journalism from Virginia Commonwealth University, where she started her career in television news, then returned to the DC area to pursue work as an investigative journalist. She now covers the federal government full-time while writing fiction in her spare time. In the tiny sliver of her day that she spends not writing, she likes to bike the trails in DC and Arlington, grill out with friends, play video games, and help her parents take care of the family whippets.

At Bywater Books, we're committed to bringing the best of contemporary literature to an expanding community of readers. Our editorial team is dedicated to finding and developing outstanding writers who create books you won't want to put down.

For more information about Bywater Books, our authors, and our titles, please visit our website.

www.bywaterbooks.com

CPSIA information can be obtained
at www.ICGtesting.com
Printed in the USA
JSHW040037181022
31788JS00002B/2